D1457523

MALITU BOOK TWO

NO SAFE HAVEN

JAMES LLOYD DULIN

G & D PUBLISHING

Copyright © 2023 by G & D Publishing

Advanced readers paperback edition 2023

Cover Illustration by Martin Mottet
Typography by Michael Dulin
Map by Gustavo Schmitt
Copy Edit by Victoria Gross
Proofread by Dominic McDermott

ISBN: 979-8-9871736-2-6 (paperback)
ISBN: 979-8-9871736-3-3 (Hardcover)
ASIN: B0CFTBVQH9 (ebook)

www.jamesldulin.com

CONTENT AND TRIGGER WARNINGS
As a note of caution, this story contains depictions of graphic violence, violence towards children including torture, racism, ableism, colonialism, war, child soldiers, genocide, death of loved ones, kidnapping, drug addiction, slavery, survivor's guilt, grief, trauma, and religious manipulation.

Some Authors may switch it up from book to book,
but all my books will be dedicated to my sons Sonny and Dominic,
and my best friend, wife, and partner, Aneicka.

ENNEA

THE STORY UNTIL NOW

A BRIEFT HISTORY OF ENNEA AND MALITU BOOK ONE

THE ORIGINS OF THE SONG

When Shunanlah prayed beneath the falling sun and the rising moons on the autumnal equinox, she changed the course of Ennean history. The Mother, the land and the creator, blessed Shunanlah with the ability to hear through the barrier between The Waking and The Mist, the physical and the spiritual planes. Gifted with the wisdom and the powers of The Shadow, one of the seven Great Spirits, Shunanlah defended her people from raiders.

In the turns to come, many knelt beneath Sokan, Kana, and Toka, the sun and the moons, as summer became autumn. The worthy were gifted the ability to hear into The Mist as well, hearing other Great Spirits and learning to wield their powers.

As time passed, some Ennean children started discovering that they had been born with the ability to hear the Great Spirits, earning the gifted ones the moniker of children of Ennea. However, not all children of Ennea sought to wield their gifts for the benefit of others.

Orphaned by the violence of wayward children of Ennea, a young girl prayed to The Mother for a way to stop such powerful people from hurting others. The Mother realized her mistake and marked the orphan's

spirit with The Balance, the last of the seven Great Spirits. Hearing The
Balance, the orphan gained the ability to steal the gifts of other children
of Ennea, and bring equity to the battlefields. Instead, she and The
Balance wielded their gift to gain power for themselves, or so the story
goes.

Prayers for power continued, but The Mother stopped answering. She
was unable to recall The Balance. The children of Ennea would have to
fight the spirit, whom they began to call The Thief, with the gifts she had
already given them.

Time progressed and language, as it does, progressed as well. The
fragments of The Mist that children of Ennea heard became known as
The Song, and the children of Ennea became known as dancers or spirit-
marked. And those who wielded their gifts to the detriment of others
earned the title Malitu.

The Forming of The Nations

Resources, time, and a desire for more of each brought people
together. Those looking for protection and those seeking more power
joined, forming the tribes that would become nations. As the nations
consumed more and more territory, they assimilated smaller tribes until
they could no longer expand their borders without war.

The nature of some became the folly of all, as the armies of Tomak,
Renéqua, Sonacoa, and Astile warred over contested territories. As one
conflict ended, another began until the number of active violent conflicts
soon outnumbered the nations.

This period of violence continued for nearly one hundred turns,
before a small network of nomads brought the leaders of each nation
together. As refugees from each of the four nations, the nomads had the
ability to speak to the nations on behalf of all people. They facilitated the
end of open conflict in a meeting now known as the Conclave of Spirits.

Though to say that the violence ended because of one meeting would be to dismiss the sacrifices of all the nomads who laid the ground for such a meeting over many long turns.

A fifth nation rose from the ashes of the Hundred-Turn War—Jani, a nation of nomads dedicated to serving Ennea and her people.

Although the fighting ended, old wounds did not heal so quickly. Forest dancers from Astile, marked with gifts of The Seed, used The Song to grow a forest of stormwood trees, known for their durability, around their border. The forest was rumored to be so dense that no one could traverse through it without the benefit of a forest dancer.

Other nations created their own barriers or used the natural barriers of the land to isolate after the war, but none so much as Astile. As time passed and their impenetrable border remained, the forest and Astile became known as the Lost Forest and the Lost Nation, respectively.

THE INVASION

Over two hundred turns after the Great War, or the Hundred-Turn War, ships arrived on the southern shores of Ennea. These pale new travelers were welcomed with care. However, it didn't take long before they revealed their true intentions. The Gousht Empire brought an armada of warships over the waters, laying siege to Sonacoa, the southern nation.

After calls for aid, Tomak and Renéqua joined the war against the Gousht. The combined armies of the three nations, with their knowledge of the land and the dancers amongst their ranks, nearly beat the Gousht's army back to the shore. No matter their advantage of numbers, the Gousht couldn't overcome The Song or the dancers who wielded it.

In the waning conflict, visions led Gousht priests to a cave at the southern tip of the Tilani Mountain Range. Within the cave, they found crystals with the ability to steal the power of dancers and use that power for their own gain.

Though the Gousht claimed their god led their priests to the cave—
and most Enneans did not know to refute these claims—they were in
truth led to the crystals by The Balance. After centuries of her name
being twisted and her descendants being abused by the people of Ennea,
The Balance decided to speak to Gousht priests and lead them to a tool
that could balance out the power of Ennea's dancers.

With their new weapon, The Gousht turned the tides of battle.
When the capital of Sonacoa, the Stone City, finally fell, the rest of Ennea
fell soon after. Only the Lost Nation remained safe, within its border of
stormwoods.

The Gousht burned smaller villages to the ground, stole the spirits of
every dancer they found, enslaved dissidents, and gained control of the
few cities remaining across Ennea. As the turns passed, they built schools
in occupied cities and compounds called mission schools to indoctrinate
the next generation of Enneans. They couldn't continue to send soldiers
to Ennea forever, not when their god commanded they continue to
expand his empire.

THE KAYLO'S EARLY TURNS

As soon as the Invasion War began, Kaylo's parents moved to Nomar,
where no one knew them and they could hide amongst the larger
population. If any of the rumors about missing dancers were true, no one
could know Kaylo was a forest dancer.

Life became a quieter version of what it had been, and Kaylo learned
to survive by blending into the crowd. The Gousht priest and soldiers
who occupied the village didn't bother people who obeyed their
directives, for the most part. Of course, sometimes they had to find ways
to fill the hours.

Kaylo's life revolved around his family, his best friend Shay, and their teacher, Munnie, an earth dancer who hid in the forest surrounding Nomar. Routine blended one day into the next until he and Shay had a run in with Rena, a Tomakan girl of a similar age whose parents served the Gousht. Enneans had a term for those serving the enemy—blood banners.

In the course of a single day, not long after his sixteenth birthday, Shay sacrificed herself to save Kaylo, he discovered his connection to The Balance as he killed the soldier who killed Shay, and a Gousht priest led soldiers to Kaylo's house with Rena as their guide. Having always put Kaylo first in everything and having no intentions of letting him die, his parents sent him out the back as they took up household items as weapons.

Angry, guilt-ridden, and grieving, Kaylo wandered the forest until he happened upon two Jani scouts, Jonac and Torrel. Regardless of how Torrel protested, Jonac welcomed Kaylo into the Fallen Rock Clan, a community of nomads.

Life with the Jani offered Kaylo the safety and security he needed, but he always had to keep himself distant. Hatred for The Balance or The Thief, as she was often known, ran deep through most communities in Ennea. The Fallen Rock Clan was no exception.

Kaylo lived with his guilty secret for two seasons, as it weighed him down. He began to mistwalk at night, visiting The Balance in the spirit realm. He assured himself he was only dreaming, but he couldn't bear the weight of his transgressions. After watching one family die, he couldn't continue exposing a new one to the dangers of a spirit thief, a malitu.

While helping Jonac and Torrel scout for a new location for the nomadic clan's encampment, Kaylo ran away. Only, he didn't get far before he came upon two soldiers assaulting a Sonacoan water dancer named Liara. The battle conjured up memories of how Shay died, and Kaylo intervened.

Liara survived the battle, but only after being severely injured. Kaylo needed Jonac's help to save Liara's life, and he took off into the forest after Jonac with Liara over his shoulder.

Nothing remained the same after the scouting party returned to the Jani encampment with a half-dead water dancer. Torrel's mistrust of Kaylo boiled over, and he attacked Kaylo, leading towards a falling out between Jonac and Torrel. When the Jani council of elders replaced Jonac as a scout, he took up an old habit of smoking susu root, a highly addictive drug that left him irritable and detached.

Despite running away to save his new family from the spirit he carried with him, Kaylo ended up tearing apart several relationships.

Several span passed as Kaylo nursed Liara back to health, and the two bonded. She knew what he was, a spirit thief, and she didn't recoil or treat him like a malitu. They became close. Then, in a moment of vulnerability, Liara asked Kaylo to help her. She had been on her way to rescue her sister when the soldiers attacked her.

Eventually, Kaylo agreed to help Liara, no matter how foolhardy it was to break into a Gousht mission school to free her sister.

They ran from the Jani encampment in the faded days of Autumn, but this time Kaylo was running towards something rather than away from everything.

After breaking into the mission school, a compound where the Gousht attempted to indoctrinate Ennean children to be members of the Gousht Empire, Kaylo and Liara hid amongst the captive children. Their deception allowed them to find her sister, Tomi, and an old friend of Kaylo's, Wal, but it put them in danger. Liara faced abusive punishment for defending her sister and standing up to a vindictive instructor, forcing Kaylo to work on a hasty escape plan.

Against all odds, they escaped with Tomi, Wal, and two other imprisoned youths, Adêan and Sionia. Kaylo led the group back to the Fallen Rock Clan, determined to tell Jonac the truth about what he was, but he never got the chance.

The Priest, the commander of the mission school, led a regiment of soldiers in a raid of the Jani encampment. He had used Kaylo to find the

Jani.

Battle erupted in the Jani tent city. Soldiers with stolen spirits clashed with Jani dancers. Bodies littered the encampment, and Kaylo lost himself to bloodlust. He captured stolen spirits, one after another, more than he ever allowed himself to take. Despite the pain, he used the spirits to cut down several soldiers, revealing himself as a spirit thief to Jonac and the other nomads.

In the final throes of the battle, The Priest revealed The Balance had gifted the Gousht with the crystals they used to win the war and colonize Ennea. Then he called on more spirits than Kaylo could steal and set one of the last remaining tents ablaze. Beneath the tent, Nomi, Soca, and Junera—the woman who embraced him as a son, and her two daughters who saw him as a brother—burned to death.

The sight flared Kaylo's rage, and he reached into his connection to The Seed, calling forth a near-impenetrable wall of stormwood trees. With the remaining Gousht on one side of the wall and the remaining Jani on the other side, Kaylo passed out.

He came to, badly burned and injured. Jonac and the few still-living nomads helped care for his wounds as they traveled, but as soon as he was well enough, they exiled him. After the pain he had caused them, especially Jonac, he didn't fight it.

Liara, Tomi, Wal, Adéan, and Sionia all followed Kaylo as he left the Jani. Somewhere out there, a group of rebels called the Missing fought back against the Empire. They may have only been a rumor, but Kaylo was going to need help if he meant to take revenge against the man he came to know as The Priest.

CURRENT DAY ENNEA

Kaylo, now thirty-four, had been hiding in the forest for a dozen turns when a Tomakan girl, Tayen, ran through the forest followed by two soldiers. Against every hard lesson life had laid at his feet, he intervened, leaving him with two dead soldiers and an orphan girl who needed him.

When Tayen woke up after being saved, she found herself living in a world without her family. The soldiers had killed her mother, father, and sister, and, for some twisted joke of the spirits, she remained alive.

Dreams of her family's death plagued her, her mother's eyes followed her while she was awake, and her sister's stupid whistle kept reminding her that her family had gone to The Mist. It didn't make sense why she would still be alive. She had to make use of her time and avenge her family. Blood owes blood, as the saying went.

When she found out the man who had saved her life was the storied warrior, the Hero of Anilace, Ennea's Thief, she demanded that he train her. Eventually, Kaylo made a deal to train her to wield her connection to her spirit ancestor, The Shadow, if she listened to his story.

They found a routine—chores and training through the day, and Kaylo's story at night. However, the Gousht didn't forget the soldiers who never returned. A small unit searched for their missing comrades, finding Kaylo and Tayen in the process.

Kaylo and Tayen survived the encounter, but lost much in doing so. Tayen took her first life, and Kaylo had to leave his home of twelve turns. One soldier escaped, and if the Gousht sent five when two soldiers went missing, Kaylo and Tayen couldn't wait around to find out how many more they would send now.

Gambling on the Gousht hesitancy to travel near the border of the Lost Nation since the war to reclaim Ennea erupted, Kaylo and Tayen headed north. With Gousht trackers on their heels, they found the freecity of Dasoon. The rundown ruin of a city hosted a community of people hiding from the war led by Hakan, a charismatic figurehead, and Nix, the commander of the city guard.

As the moons passed, Kaylo and Tayen found their rhythm in the freecity. Their new home offered them a place to outlast the winter, if nothing else.

After over a season together, Tayen had never seen Kaylo call The Seed. So, she built up the courage to ask him if he could still hear The Song, and he finally admitted he hadn't heard The Seed's call in several turns.

In the middle of their conversation, Nix came banging on their door to warn them that the Lost Army had come to conscript people into their war efforts. No matter how they ran or fought, the warriors of the Lost Nation subdued Kaylo and Tayen.

In a last-ditch attempt to escape, Kaylo stole a weapon from a warrior and waited for the others to call on the spirits imprisoned in the crystals they were wearing. However, his old friend, Wal, was amongst them. Now a commander in the Lost Army, Wal stopped his warriors from calling on their crystals.

Wal bound Kaylo and Tayen, then Nix as well, for her objections. Snow fell as they began the long journey to the Lost Nation, Astile.

CHAPTER ONE
CURRENT DAY ENNEA

If the archer loosed her arrow, the bolt would tear through Tayen's flesh and find the softest parts of her—mix and mingle her bile and blood.

A singular point to the left of Tayen's spine burned as if the arrowhead had already pierced her flesh. Of course, she could never predict where the arrow would hit. But after two days of the purple-clad warrior training her sights on Tayen, her imagination had picked a spot as likely as any other.

Her life belonged to the discipline of a stranger.

Yet again, she had lost control over her place in this world. Her body screamed at her to run, or fight, to do something other than submit. Instead, she marched north, bound to the rest of the sorry sods the Lost Nation had stolen from Dasoon.

The whistle Tayen's sister had carved for her brushed against the skin under her shirt. This small length of wood tied around her neck with twine was all that remained of her family.

She had to persist.

Gashes and cuts marred the tanned leather vests the warriors wore over their purple robes, like proof they had survived the raging war. Whereas Tayen's threadbare robes wouldn't even protect her from the snow-dusted north.

If only Kaylo had allowed her to fight, they might have had a chance to escape. Instead, the rope binding her to the others rubbed back and forth over her wrists, scraping away another layer of skin.

Every step brought her closer to the unpassable forest of towering stormwood trees—their majesty tempered only by their foreboding. The dark wood took over the horizon, accented by the light layer of snow dusting the empty branches. After today, any hope of escape would fade, like a dream in the morning light.

It's real, she thought as she stood in the shadow of the forest that had become a myth.

If the stories could be trusted, the forest grew so dense that anyone who entered without the spirit of The Seed to guide them would be trapped amongst the trees forever. It sounded like a daemontale, but looking on the immensity of it, she couldn't help but believe.

Two warriors strode towards the tree line. A shimmering green light broke through the gaps between their fingers as they each stopped and pressed an empty hand to a tree. The wood cracked. Black bark lightened and brittle branches broke, falling to the surrounding ground. Limbs above turned to dust and debris, then the trunks collapsed inward. Two crumbling columns fell and the ash of what had been unbreakable giants swept up into the air, erasing the warriors from view.

As the cloud settled, the warriors remained, but the trees had vanished. The living giants had done nothing to deserve their fate.

"Is that really the only way through?" Tayen asked.

"Forget the stories. There's nothing mysterious about the Lost Forest," Kaylo said. "The Lost Nation built a maze of stormwoods with no path through to the other side. Plenty of entrances, but no exits."

"Couldn't the Empire just burn the forest to the ground?"

"They've tried," Wal said from atop an immense horse covered in leather armor.

How did the boy from Kaylo's story become a smug bastard in command of a Lost Army regiment? Tayen wondered.

Wal looked like he could have been an uncle, which only made him more despicable. Most of the Lost Nation warriors were northerners, with golden-brown skin and closely cropped curly black hair. But Wal's skin bore the same shade of cedar brown as Tayen and Kaylo, his tight gray braids mapping his head in an intricate pattern before falling over his shoulders. If not for the series of small shapes tattooed in rows over each cheek, he could have been kin.

Every time she glared at him, she filtered all her hatred into a look. But in case he was completely oblivious, she regularly told him she hated him to clear up any confusion.

"Stormwood doesn't burn easy. Even if they burned down one tree, the fire wouldn't spread like a typical forest fire," Kaylo said.

"By the time they burned three or four trees, we had taken position and rained arrows on their garrisons," Wal said. "It was before my time in Astile, but the stories still bring a certain joy to my heart."

The jackass could call the land beyond the forest Astile or the Lost Nation. It didn't matter. Either way, the forest would trap her in a land that wasn't hers.

She waited for Wal to meet her eyes. "I hate you."

He smiled and drove his horse to lead the procession into the Lost Forest.

"You shouldn't antagonize him," Kaylo said.

"You're right. I should thank him and the archer with an arrow aimed at my back for their hospitality," Tayen said. "What would I ever do without you to guide me?"

"The arrows are to keep me in line. They won't do anything to you. They want us alive."

"Comforting."

"Can you two stop bickering? I'm trying to enjoy my death march in peace," Nix said from over Tayen's shoulder.

Nix never should have tried to defend Tayen and Kaylo. For her trouble, the lost bastards bound her wrists and threw her in line with the rest of the conscripts.

Only The Mother knew how many times the Lost Nation had
rounded up conscripts from Dasoon before Tayen and Kaylo came along.
And Nix had never interfered once. The protection and supplies the
Lost Nation provided Dasoon kept it standing. Yet, for some reason, Nix
intervened on their behalf.

It made no sense. In two moons, Nix had never shown a hint of care
for either of them.

Another set of trees collapsed into nothing as the small opening in
the forest wall slowly became a cavernous tunnel. The light from Sokan,
the sun and Ennea's First Daughter, died under the thick canopy of
stormwood trees. The warriors wielding stolen fragments of The Seed
disappeared into the darkness, the sound of ash collapsing to the forest
floor calling back.

If only Kaylo could call The Seed, they could escape into the chaos
of the forest, but of course, he could no longer hear The Song. Another
omission he had kept from her. The prick stowed away an endless supply
of secrets, revealing them long after they would have been useful.

In theory, he could steal the fragments of The Seed trapped within
the warriors' crystals, but if anyone noticed, Tayen would be littered with
arrows. She would fall to the ground looking like a bloody porcupine.

The remaining warriors struck up torches, and the light stretched into
the darkness. A large, antagonistic lost bastard grabbed the rope binding
the captives together and yanked them forward to begin the long march
through the narrow corridor.

As the forest enveloped them, the shadows snuffed out any lingering
hopes.

Something moved at the edge of the light, high in the trees. A
warrior peered down from a wooden platform wrapped around the tree,
tapping his bow on the platform's edge like an invitation to test his skill.
The rhythmic clicking echoed in Tayen's head.

If the floorboards broke beneath him, the archer would tumble to the ground and break open like a melon. The thought of it warmed her ever so slightly.

"The Lost Nation doesn't take risks. Even if the Gousht tried to push through with spirit crystals, their presence would be known," Kaylo said.

Tayen nodded absently. *There is no escape,* she thought.

As she turned back towards the entrance, a warrior went to work regrowing the trees that had been felled. *No escape at all.*

When the last trees crumbled away, the light of the falling day rushed into the forest. Kaylo blinked away the sunspots in his vision, and the first glimpse of the Lost Nation came into focus. White snow clashed against the dying green grass. The land rippled with rolling hills as far as he could see. Sokan lowered, and the sky became a dark blue ocean, as wind blew a soft cold through the evening air.

In the days before common tongue, Astile meant serene. The name fit. No wonder the rest of Ennea felt like they had lost something when the nation cut itself off from the rest of the continent.

Large clay-brick buildings interrupted the picturesque scene—outposts for the border guard. The gray-wash facades dulled the landscape. No doubt the outposts spread out over every stretch of the tree line.

There is a reason their borders have held against the Gousht for over twenty-five turns, Kaylo thought.

The warriors went about their business, building fires and setting another pot of gruel to cook over the flames. They erected tents for Wal and his coterie. The rest—warriors and captives alike—would sleep in the grass and dirt and snow another night, hoping the fires would burn hot enough to keep the winter at bay.

At least the warriors had blankets without holes.

Kaylo sat with the other conscripts. His feet had grown used to the long days of travel, but his wrists stung from the constant drag of the rope. The same thick red circle burned the skin of each stolen body, like a marker of ownership.

Warring had a way of changing people. Before the Gousht, this had never been the way of Enneans.

Tayen sulked, sitting as far away from him as their wardens would permit.

Since he met her, she had taken a life, been hunted by the Gousht, and been conscripted by the Lost Army. He should have never gotten involved. Tayen was a smart girl with enough guile and glib to carry her through life on her own.

Beside her sat the former captain of the Dasoon city guard, a slow rhythm moving through the rise and fall of her shoulders. A sour luck followed those who came across Kaylo's path.

On the other side of the firepit, the warriors milled about. The big dull one—though that hardly narrowed down the group—sat smiling and picking his nails with Kaylo's knife, the knife his father had given him.

The warrior's northern complexion looked even brighter in the firelight. Young, sharp jawline, warrior's physique—he would have been pleasant to look at had he not been such a jackass. Only two small rows of tattoos marked his left cheek, fewer than most in the regiment. The prick found every opportunity to antagonize Kaylo ever since he had broken one of the warrior's ribs back in Dasoon during their capture.

The knife ran through the grime under the warrior's dirty nails. He had no way of knowing the knife's significance. And yet, each swipe added to the disrespect.

A scraping sound stuck in Kaylo's ear. The warrior sat too far away for it to be the knife, but nonetheless, the scraping persisted.

Better to ignore it.

Tired and settled as they may have been, each of the thirty-two warriors carried well-kept blades. Knowing he was a spirit dancer, none of them would be foolish enough to reach for a crystal without training an arrow on Tayen first. Fighting wouldn't help anyone.

Kaylo dug his nails into the meat of his palm to ignore the scraping.

Then the bastard lifted the knife to pick his teeth.

"How's the rib feel?" Kaylo smiled wide as he could.

"Shut it, conscript." The warrior's hand fell to the injury on his right side. "In a fair fight, I'd break you like a chicken bone."

"You mean one in which I'm not tied up, unarmed, and on my knees?" A quiet claimed the camp, and Kaylo had everyone's attention. "You're right, I took advantage. Would you like to blindfold me as well?"

The young warrior jumped up, stalking over to where Kaylo sat, white-knuckling the knife. It was too easy. Kaylo waited for him to get closer, brushing off his compatriots.

Big, mean, and quick-tempered, Kaylo thought. *Fun combination.*

"Don't do it, Kaylo," Nix said. "Kill yourself if you want, but leave me out of it."

Kaylo stood up despite the warning and matched the warrior's glare, though he had to look up to do so. An impartial observer would likely guess the younger man had the advantage. He had a knife in one hand, and Kaylo barely stood past his shoulder. However, most observers don't look down.

The warrior stood flat-footed, while Kaylo bounced slightly on the balls of his feet. His bad knee was stiff, as always, but he didn't feel any pain. He waited for the bigger man to move first.

"What is going on here?" Wal called from the opening of his tent.

The warrior turned towards his commander.

That will do.

Kaylo jabbed his forearm into the larger man's throat before kneeing him in the stomach. When the warrior buckled in half, Kaylo brought the force of his locked fists down on his opponent's back.

Over two dozen swords scraped against their leather scabbards like a collection of whispers, as the young warrior collapsed to the ground.

Kaylo stepped away, smiling, with his bound hands high above his head.

Despite their youth, the warriors in Wal's regiment were well-trained—for the most part. They wouldn't kill him unless ordered to or if he presented an immediate threat. At least, that was the gamble Kaylo had taken.

"Why can't things ever be easy with you?" Wal said, the exasperation thick in his voice, as he walked towards the commotion with a large Tomakan woman on his flank.

Kaylo held up one finger before bending slowly to pick up the knife. Several warriors shifted anxiously, but he turned the knife in his hands so the blade filled his palm. "Would you mind holding onto my father's knife?"

Wal looked at him curiously, then down at the groaning warrior.

"For an old friend?" Kaylo said.

"Old friend indeed." Wal smiled. "You still have this old blade?"

With a simple motion from their commander, every warrior in his regiment sheathed their weapons. "I'll take care of this. You have my word," he said as he took Kaylo's knife.

"As for you," Wal said, rounding on the downed warrior. "Unarmed? Hands bound?"

Wal toyed with Kaylo's knife as he bent down to the level of the young northman, whose head hung like a scolded child. "This regiment isn't for the weak. Maybe the front lines will help you prove your mettle."

The young warrior lifted his head, his eyes begging for reprieve while he remained silent. All his unearned confidence vanished as Wal gestured for two warriors to escort the young man away.

Ever the performer, Wal opened his arms wide, turning to his audience. "Rest. The morning brings us another journey."

Kaylo's old friend cast him one last glance before strolling back to his tent with his guard in tow.

"Was that necessary?" Nix asked in a hushed tone.

For a moment, it had been the most necessary thing in the world. The turns had whittled away at his pride until only a sliver remained, in many ways, embodied by his father's knife. However, protecting one's pride could quickly sour to self-indulgence.

He did not answer Nix. Instead, he closed his eyes to lie on the patch of frozen earth beneath him.

———————

Myanack, the capital city of Astile, sprawled out from a single mountain jetting up out of the flat earth. The mountain had no place in a land of rolling hills and grassy plains. It must have taken a dozen dancers a hundred turns or a hundred dancers a dozen turns to mold the earth into a city such as this.

Kaylo simply stared. The structures surrounding the mountain paled in comparison to the magnitude of the mountain hallow. The sheer scale alone humbled other structures manifested through the power of the spirits, no matter how ornate or unique.

A trail spiraled from the base to the peak, with tunnels burrowed into the mountain along the way. *How many people could live in a hollowed-out mountain?* Kaylo thought. *Several hundred? A few thousand? Ten thousand?*

"Beautiful, isn't it?" Wal asked with an earnestness that struck Kaylo as peculiar.

"It would be under different circumstances." Kaylo motioned to his bound wrists.

"You do know how to spoil a moment, old friend." Wal turned to his unit and shouted out his orders. "You four, see to the horses. The rest of you, take the new recruits to their training barracks. Take care with these two ladies. I am rather fond of them."

Tayen spit at Wal's boots, flashing him a rude hand gesture. Wal winked at her with a smile as a warrior restrained her.

"Be careful, Tayen. Do what they tell you. I will fix this," Kaylo said.

"Haven't you done enough?" Her eyes were sharp, and her mouth flattened into a straight line.

"Kids—The Mother's blessing, am I right?" Wal smiled at his own quip as he cut Kaylo's bindings from the rest of the conscripted. "This way."

As the warriors took the line of newly enlisted conscripts to the barracks at the base of the mountain, Wal guided Kaylo up the spiral mountain path. "I suppose I don't have to remind you that if you do anything rash, Tayen will suffer the consequences?"

"Subtlety was never your strength. If you're going to threaten me, do it. If not, why don't you show me to my cell?"

Wal smiled his characteristic, full-toothed grin while he continued along the path in silence.

The higher they climbed, the clearer the view of the countryside became. Farmland outside the city stretched for days in every direction— some plots dormant for the winter, others fielding barley and other sturdy cold-weather crops.

These bastards could have fed the entire continent.

Wind blew in over the ocean cliffs to the west. High walls and steep drop-offs shielded the nation from the rest of the world. Give the Gousht a hundred turns and they would still be on the outside looking in. Kaylo had little chance of escaping.

"Welcome to the Citadel," Wal announced before stepping into the mountain hallow.

As Kaylo stepped into the entrance, a shiver ran through him, shaking the last of the winter wind from his skin. Oil lamps, hung every twenty paces or so, lit the hallway. As dim and gray as the outside of the mountain was, the inside felt warm and welcoming. Vibrant tapestries hung along the walls, light flickering over the bright colors.

It brought Kaylo back to the days training in his first kana's hallow. Munnie made her underground home a sanctuary. He forced himself to look straight down the tunnel. The comfort of those old memories had spoiled with age.

They passed several doors before they arrived at their destination, where Wal opened a stormwood door, gesturing Kaylo into his cell.

It was by far the nicest prison he had ever seen. A plush purple rug covered most of the flattened stone floor. The table was set for guests, freshly cut winter honeysuckle in a vase. A bed of braided hay covered with a quilt lay waiting for him in the corner.

After almost four days of walking, the bed seemed to serenade him.

Two decorative sconces held unlit oil lamps on opposite walls. Kaylo ran a finger over the smooth stormwood. The filigree was ornate. Practiced hands matched each detail between the two sconces. Only a master crafter could carve such hard, dense wood with this level of precision.

"You always had a thing for whittling," Wal said from the doorway.

"Calling this whittling is like calling Sokan a bright light. This is art."

"I'm glad you like it, old friend."

"Come off it, Wal. What am I doing here?"

"This is one of our guest quarters, and you are a welcome guest." Wal leaned against the wall and sighed heavily. "We don't have to be enemies, Kaylo."

"Then let me go."

"I think you know I can't do that. Ennea's at war, and we have to win her back, no matter what it takes. You're going to help us do that. After all, we have a responsibility to the people."

"Your king isn't my king, Wal."

"Oh, don't be shortsighted. Astile is the only hope Ennea has left. You once spoke of freeing the people, and this is the way to do that. Ennea needs to be united under a strong leader. We both know what happens when leaders fail."

"And what will happen to those who refuse to be led?"

Wal dropped his smile as he met Kaylo's eyes. His face settled, the tattoos on his cheeks underscoring his soft brown eyes. "Get some rest, Kaylo."

When the door closed, Kaylo walked over to the bed. Small slits in the stone allowed daylight through, while venting the smoke from the brazier that heated the room. He sat on the braided hay, and Sokan's light crossed the room as he considered his circumstances.

CHAPTER TWO

CURRENT DAY ENNEA

The army crammed almost a hundred children between the clay-brick walls of the barracks, some as young as ten, none past their swearing day. Until they offered their pledge to Ennea during the spring equinox on their seventeenth turn, no one had the right to call them anything but children.

One fading candle offered its light to the room. Slight movements rippled through the sea of bodies, and Tayen lay somewhere in the middle, packed between two strangers. Unfamiliar or not, their bodies were warm.

Eventually, she succumbed to her exhaustion. The children on either side of her kept her from tossing about as her nightmare played out in her head like countless nights before. Her family lying atop one another, covered in flames, her mother's dull green eyes screaming. The dust of their charred flesh mixed with the smoke in the air.

Tayen's eyes snapped open as she ran away from the soldiers who killed her family. She sat up and wiped the sweat from her forehead with her sleeve. The skinny northboy to her left stirred and groaned, but he didn't wake. Someone wept in the corner beyond the candlelight.

So many stolen children.

She reached for the whistle tucked underneath her shirt, the rough holes weathered after several moons of fiddling. This solitary possession tied her to the life she had lost.

Light flickered over the children surrounding her. The Lost Nation had snatched them from every corner of the continent. Their complexions ranged from the brilliant black of a thief's night to the golden sand of the eastern shore. A Sonacoan girl moaned in her sleep. A Tomakan boy leaned against the wall, rocking back and forth.

These are supposed to be warriors? she thought.

The Song hummed beneath the collection of small noises in the barracks, its subtle melody comforting her as her fingers danced along. Shadows shifted against the light cast from the candle ever so slightly. Kaylo had been right about one thing: secrets could be powerful tools.

Wal had escorted Kaylo into the mountain, and Tayen hadn't seen him since. The purple-robed goons had separated Nix and the other adults from Dasoon into another clay-brick building. If the army thought Tayen's age made her any less dangerous, they were wrong.

Blood owed blood, and her family deserved their vengeance. She had wasted too much time playing family with Kaylo. No more. Anyone who blocked her path would add their blood as offering.

Tayen lay back down, sleeping a dreamless sleep.

With the morning light, guards escorted the children to the far side of the mountain. Solid ground shifted into a field of sand beneath Tayen's feet. The Lost Nation had made obvious use of their stone dancers.

The children surrounding Tayen carried a certain uniformity about them. Despite their differences, they all wore some version of passed-down robes, sweat and blood stains coloring the natural light brown fabric. But, more than their clothing, they all bore the weight of their circumstances in their slumped shoulders and tired eyes.

Guards marched them into one of over a dozen muddy brown tents spread over the massive field. A fire blazed away within, doing its best to stave off the winter.

The children who knew the routine formed into rows, and Tayen followed suit.

Sand shifted under her feet as she waited for direction, making her adjust her stance. The only other time she had set foot on sand had been with her father. He had wanted her and her sister to see the ocean. It had taken days of walking before they reached the honey-colored beaches on the eastern coast.

With the beach tickling her bare feet and her father's hand enveloping hers, the water had seemed infinite.

A red patch of raked sand stole Tayen away from her memory, and she set her jaw. Whatever came for her, she would not give them the satisfaction of her fear.

The odd collection of recruits looked even less like soldiers as they stood in rows under the morning light. Two young warriors ordered the newest recruits to the front. Tayen complied, though 'recruit' seemed like an odd word for children stolen from their homes.

Near the end of the front row, Tayen stood between Daak, the Sonacoan boy from Dasoon, and a petite girl she had never seen before. Her stature would have marked her around Tayen's age—fifteen after the last moon—but her facial features were sharper, older. The girl's deep umber skin and closely cropped black curls marked her as a child of multiple nations. She carried herself with a looseness that didn't match the setting.

Something about her drew Tayen.

"Good morning, recruits." A warrior paced in front of them. Tattoos marked both of his cheeks—a series of lines and shapes with some meaning, but Tayen was damned if she could decipher the code. His purple robe draped over his wide shoulders, latched at the waist by a black leather belt.

Every warrior in the Lost Army wore the same uniform, but this man wore it differently. The fabric moved with his body without a single wrinkle or crease, as if the robe hadn't been touched since the tailor sewed the final stitch into the hem. The color gleamed. He stood like a flag placed over a conquered battlefield.

"For those of you who are new, my name is Commander Sola, and it is my honor to train you to serve in King Shonar's army. You may think that because you are children, I will take it easy on you. Some of you have doubts. Some of you don't want to be here. Well, the enemy won't take it easy on you. They don't care about your doubts or what you want, and neither do I. Ennea needs you, and you will serve her."

As he paced, his light brown eyes scanned over the new recruits, weighing them. His flat expression gave nothing away.

Despite the gray patches along his temples, his black curls marked him as a northerner, even if he was a shade darker than most of his kin. The slight differences broke the fiction so many Enneans believed by default. The shifts in their skin tones and curl patterns didn't care about borders. Their bodies were gifts from their ancestors, and their ancestors existed long before the lines on a map.

"Whoever you were yesterday doesn't matter. Today, you are a recruit. Today, your training begins. I will turn you into warriors worthy of wearing the King's colors." He stopped pacing and spoke to the front two rows. "First, I need to know what kind of stone The Mother gave me to shape. Every new recruit will fight today, and I will test your skills."

"Sola, I don ave any skills," the woman next to Tayen said. "I've never eld a sword before." Her words were soft and solid simultaneously, a polite declaration with a hint of a Renēquan accent.

Sola's face didn't twitch.

In a flash, he unsheathed his sword and slammed the flat of his blade into the girl's arm, forcing her crashing into Tayen. Instinctively, Tayen slipped her foot back, anchoring their weight in the sand.

At least Kaylo's training was good for something, she thought as she helped the girl find her feet.

"Recruits don't make excuses. They don't speak out of turn. They don't have the time. Recruits say 'Yes, Commander' and 'No, Commander.' Because recruits who don't pass their trials become servants in the mountain—without honor, without prospects. Understood?"

The girl met the Commander's glare. "Yes, Commander," she said in a stiff, staccato cadence.

The recruits traded small glances, some of them undoubtedly wondering what would be so bad about serving in the mountain. But the servant waiting over Sola's shoulder became a clear enough answer. The holes in her robes showed her pale and ashy skin beneath as she fidgeted and stared at her feet. Her weight concentrated on her right side, as if she needed to compensate for an injury.

Whatever burdens weighed the servant girl down may have been a threat to the other children, but another threat awaited Tayen in the Commander's words. If she became a servant, she would never be able to collect the blood she owed.

A soft scraping sound followed Sola as he dragged the tip of his sword through the sand—one step in front of the other until the line in the sand became a circle. Then he leveled his blade at the first two recruits in line, and they stepped into place, facing each other. The dirty servant girl limped forward to give each of them a wooden sword. Her gaze remained on the ground as she saw to her task before scurrying away.

Both the recruits looked at their weapons with uncertainty, as if they had been handed a riddle. But when the Commander called for the match to begin, they had to abandon their apprehension.

As soon as the first recruit moved, he tripped over his boots, the moment catching the other recruit too off-guard to take advantage. They moved like they didn't know how to walk properly.

Was I ever this shit with a blade? Tayen thought.

One of the recruits swung haphazardly, clubbing the other across the face, and that was it. The boy collapsed with blood dripping from a cut along his cheek.

When he didn't move, Sola ordered two of the recruits from the back row to take the injured boy to the infirmary, then pointed to the next recruit.

The winner remained in the circle, no more confident for having won.

And so it went. One by one, children in the first row entered and then exited the circle—some bruised, others limping, all glad to have survived. Of the fifteen recruits who had fought, none won a second bout.

As Sola moved his way down the line, the recruits waited in shrunken silence, apart from Daak, who bounced excitedly on the balls of his feet.

In the circle, a young northboy scrambled over the sand with amazing speed. His opponent—a Tomakan girl from Dasoon—lunged and flailed after the northerner, but continually missed. Each time she swung the wooden blade, her attacks lost speed—not that they moved all that quickly to begin with.

She swung her practice sword, and the northboy sidestepped the attack, swiping his blade across her midsection. She crumpled to her hands and knees, gasping for air.

This whole exercise was pointless cruelty.

Before the Tomakan girl straightened up to leave the circle, Daak strode forward and grinned at his opponent. The northerner did not grin back. He stood a full head shorter than Daak and at least a few turns younger. His speed had won him his first match, but he wielded a blade as poorly as the rest of them, and now, he was gulping down air.

Speed meant little without endurance.

"Yaktan," Sola shouted to start the match.

Daak rushed forward and swung his blade with his shoulder—powerful, but slow and unwieldy. The swords may have been wood, but had any of his swings connected with the northboy's head, it could have killed him. Whether or not Daak had considered this, it didn't seem to bother him either way.

Luckily, the northboy had caught enough of his breath. He shuffled over the sand, dodging Daak's clumsy attacks, until he found himself on the edge of the circle. He blocked one heavy strike after another. The wooden swords thunked like an axe chopping into an ironoak.

Each time the northboy attempted to maneuver away from the circle's edge, Daak volleyed another attack. Daak raised his wooden blade high and slammed it into his opponent's guard, pushing the northboy out of the circle and onto his ass.

That should have been the end of the match, but Daak continued his pursuit. The northboy rolled to dodge the first blow, but the second caught him in the ribs. He screeched in pain, and Daak reeled back for another strike.

Sola caught the wooden blade mid-swing. "Enough," he said, with a strange look on his face—somewhere between approval and wariness.

"I appreciate the vigor, but the match stops once an opponent is forced out of the circle," the Commander announced. "For those of you thinking about running from the circle, you will find my punishment harsher than your opponent's. Next!"

Tayen found her place opposite Daak, accepting her sword from the servant girl. She thanked the servant, but the servant shuffled away without a glance.

Daak eyed her as if she had said something foul about his mother.

The smooth hilt of the wooden sword brushed over her calluses as she swung it through the air. It moved easier than the branches she and Kaylo had used to train with. Light. Flexible. Ashburn maybe.

"Yaktan!" Sola shouted.

Daak dashed the four strides that stood between them, while Tayen waited. His wooden sword bounced with a lack of control as his arms swung in time with his gait.

Tayen heard Kaylo's voice. "Protect your blade. Protect your hold." She smiled.

Before Daak had time to draw back his sword, Tayen struck his wrist with the flat of her blade.

It was quick, barely more than a tap, but it worked. Daak dropped his weapon to the sand to clutch his wrist.

Maybe it had been a little more than a tap.

She leveled her blade to his throat.

His eyes went searching from her to his sword lying in the sand, as if the truth of what had happened mystified him. Nostrils flaring, his gaping mouth became a toothy snarl, which was all the warning he offered.

As he pounced at her, his scream twisted in her ears.

The air rushed from her lungs as she crashed onto the hard sand, her head slamming back, causing her to bite her tongue. Blood coated her mouth, tasting like bad well water.

Daak hovered over her as she lay on the ground. If he had been any kind of fighter, he could have used the seconds before her shock wore off. Instead, he glared down at her as if he had won.

The boy's bones popped as she drove her fist through his jaw like a knife through roast boar. Then her world went silent.

She rolled the boy over, perched atop him, and punched him again. His cheek bone cut her knuckles, but she kept swinging. The force of each blow crept up her muscles. Someone grabbed for her, but she pulled loose and struck the boy again.

By the time Sola and his assistants pulled her off of Daak, blood trailed from a gash in his lip, his right eye had started swelling, and his nose turned unnaturally in two places.

Two of the recruits from the back row dragged him away from the circle. Sola was saying something to her, but only The Song and her anger existed. Daak's boots traced tracks in the sand as the recruits dragged him away.

Is he dead? she wondered, but couldn't bring herself to care if he was. Then her face exploded in pain.

Her head snapped to the side when Sola struck her. The meek servant girl met Tayen's eyes. Fear. *She's afraid...of me?*

All the recruits stared at her with the same expression. Her hands hurt. They were slick with blood. She pulled a jagged pebble from her knuckle and held it up. *A tooth?* There shouldn't have been a tooth in her knuckle. She let it fall into the sand.

Her vision shuttered, then she met Sola's eyes. He looked at her like he was waiting for her to say something, but what? Had he asked her a question? She couldn't read the expression on his face. He wasn't angry. He definitely wasn't afraid. Was that pride?

"Recruit, do you need to see a healer?"

Why would she need to see a healer? Nothing made sense. "No." Her voice sounded odd to her, like someone else spoke in her place. Sola's expression shifted slightly and then she corrected herself. "No, Commander."

"I've seen what I need to today. Rejoin the ranks."

Tayen walked back, still not fully settled into her skin.

The petite girl next to her whispered, "Thank Ta Mother," and walked to her position in the circle with the next recruit.

They fought and Tayen watched, but it didn't matter. Her chest felt lighter than it had since she had found her family murdered. The air filled her lungs like a cool breeze running through her. Her lips curled slightly and her eyes watered, but she did not cry.

As she looked at her bloody hands, she felt powerful.

The fire started in Nix's lungs and spread from there. Each breath fueled the pain. *Too many turns wrangling simpletons in Dasoon,* she thought as she dusted her hands with sand to clear the sweat from her palms.

None of these farmers and runaways knew how to wield a blade, even a wooden one. They would have had more luck with an axe or a pitchfork.

The unit commander, Yansar, nodded another recruit forward to face Nix with no attempt to hide her smile. One after another, Nix hacked her way through the new recruits. This exercise had begun as a way to weigh the stock. Now, the Commander only seemed to be interested in seeing if Nix could maintain her winning streak.

Nix didn't belong here, not that these farmers belonged here either.

After almost a decade of silently watching Hakan trade people for protection, why had she suddenly cared? Kuno...Kaylo—whatever the lying prick's name was, wasn't worth it. And that little brat of his.

Too late now, she thought.

Sweat prickled against her skin as winter air cooled the droplets. The pads of her fingers had gone numb, clinging to the ashburn blade. The cold was annoying, but the sweat running down her frost-pimpled skin irritated her enough to make her drive her practice sword through the belly of the next unfortunate prick to step into the circle.

As Nix adjusted her grip on her practice sword, a northman stepped into the circle across from her, much younger than most of the lot they had stuck her with, almost wider than tall. If she stood still for him, he could probably swing the length of wood with a bit of hurt.

His brow furrowed, and he bit his lip like the pain could drive away his fear.

"Yaktan," Yansar said.

Neither of them moved much. Nix cross-stepped to the side and watched the bumbling footwork of the northman. She continued to circle, waiting for the right opening.

The northman didn't have the training for patience. He charged Nix with his blade cocked back. She crouched and waited. With a bit of discipline, his swing could have chopped clean through a tree trunk. Nix stepped aside, and his practice sword slammed into the ground.

Behind her opponent, the flaps of the tent parted, and a young woman in ragged robes rushed towards the Commander. For a moment, the Sonacoan servant looked up, peaking through the long, gnarled lengths of red hair dangling in front of her face.

The woman's eyes tugged on the inkling of a memory.

Those hard and dark eyes, sharp as a well-tempered blade—turns ago, those eyes belonged to a young girl who had been traded to Astile. One of Hakan's first. She had cried and reached after her mother as they stole her away. She had a song of a name.

What was her name?

The world went black as pain cascaded from Nix's cheekbone across her face.

Inexperienced he may have been, but the northman knew enough to take advantage of a distracted opponent. The flat of his blade met her right cheek with full force, and Nix crumpled to the cold sand.

When Nix's vision settled, the Sonacoan woman was gone. The northman danced around like he had won the war, and that wouldn't do. Nix didn't even take the time to pick up her sword as she pushed herself to her feet.

All eyes shifted from the braggadocios northman to Nix. He turned with everyone else, wearing a fucked-for-the-first-time grin. He reared back his sword, and Nix stepped into the opening.

As she drove her palm into the young man's nose, the crack vibrated through up to her elbow. He fell to the sand, clutching his nose—blood oozing between his fingers.

"Yield," Nix said.

He nodded furiously, holding up four fingers with his thumb pressed tight to his palm.

Nix had tried not to injure anyone more than she needed. Her shoulders drooped when she looked down at her bleeding opponent. Not because of what she had done, but because of how good it felt.

Despite the temperature, Nix wasn't ready to go back to her barracks. They had so little freedom, giving up her time to lie in an overcrowded box with a bunch of other unwashed recruits didn't appeal to her, even if her body needed the rest.

Tomorrow morning promised to be unbearable. The muscles along

Nix's neck, back, and arms already began to ache and pull. The pain in her cheek flared whenever she moved. Her sparring sessions with Hakan back in Dasoon had been playful. His strength had always been his words, not his sword work.

The cold air added another level of pain. It lashed out against her exposed skin. Astilean robes clung tight against the bitter climate, but the army didn't tend to give recruits clothing in the best condition, much less a winter cloak.

Lights peered out from the mountain entrances, making it glow like a giant lantern flickering in the night.

In her entire life, Nix had never been one to plan out the future. The present occupied her perfectly fine. If she had to fight, she would. If she had to wait, she would. Life happened to her, and she did her best to keep the shit off her robes. Of course, the first time she decided to interrupt life's endlessly messed up plan, it had decided to bring her here.

The crunch of snow under her boots broke through the silence as she contemplated her own melancholy. She took her next step, trying to consider what her life might be as a warrior in the Lost Army, when the snow crunched a fraction of a second before her foot touched the ground.

Again, she lifted and planted her foot, and a second, almost identical crunch mimicked her own. Nix had a shadow.

Maybe one of her fellow recruits had taken unkindly to being dropped in the sand by a kamani person. Ever since the Gousht washed up on the southern shores, the Empire's strict understandings about gender took hold with some Enneans. Those who didn't fit the mold, like her, found themselves in a more tenuous place in the world.

The way some of her people adopted Gousht ideals hurt far worse than the condemnation of some pricks from across the ocean.

Unless she had fallen out of practice, only one set of unwelcome footsteps trailed after her. And whoever it was, she didn't intend to run. She turned to face the sound. "What is it you want with me?"

The moonlight was barely a glimmer in the night—both Kana and Toka hid behind the mountain. Nix peered into the darkness. Nothing moved. No one spoke.

As Nix started to walk in the direction of her shadowy mimic, the darkness shifted and a figure ran towards the Citadel.

Whoever it was moved quick as a jackrabbit running for its life. The figure cast a slight silhouette in the glow of the mountain lights.

The muscles in Nix's legs wanted to constrict and seize up. Her tendons were tight and painful as she pushed herself to run after the silhouette in front of her. Light seeping out of one of the ground-level entrances grew closer. If Nix didn't catch her spy soon, they would remain anonymous.

She coughed against the harsh chill air. No way she could make it.

"Stop," Nix yelled, between labored breaths. "What do you want with me?"

The figure darted between the guards outside the mountain entrance, and in the brief moments before her shadow slid beyond view, the glow of the mountain chamber caught her face—the servant girl from the training tent.

Nix aimed to follow her, but a guard stepped into her path. "Where do you think you're going, recruit?" His hand drifted to his sheathed sword.

"I need to have a word with that servant."

"Funny."

"Let me in. I need to talk with her."

"You *need* to go back to your barracks," the second guard said. She didn't stand as tall as the first, but her expression was more eager. She wanted a fight.

"Can you at least tell me her name?"

The guards looked at each other and smirked. "Nameless don't have names," the larger guard said.

"What does that even mean?"

"Back to your barracks, recruit," he said as he drew the first finger-length of steel from his sheath.

CHAPTER THREE
CURRENT DAY ENNEA

Kneeling before the brazier, Kaylo prayed while a quieter part of his mind wondered why. There was the answer he had given Tayen so many moons back—tradition, a symbolic act of defiance. The more the Empire sought to destroy, the more he had to remember. It wasn't quite a lie, but it was the easier part of a larger truth.

His mother had taught him how to pray—small offering, name the spirit, speak true, kiss three fingers and touch them to The Mother. The ritual reminded him of her, and Munnie, and Jonac.

The strands of hay taken from his bed burned in a small plume of smoke as he offered them to the flame. "Ennea—Mother of all, land beneath us, and The Mist before us—survive this. The sixth—The Seed, we may be beyond forgiveness. Try regardless. The seventh—The Balance, what is there to say? I'd tell you to fuck off, but I'm afraid you would. And you may be the only one who can stop this mess. Why don't you..."

Three sharp thuds struck the door, reverberating off the stone walls.

"You know the rest," Kaylo said. He pressed his fingers to his lips, then to the stone beneath him.

Kaylo pulled open the door to his quarters only to find Wal leaning on the doorframe, looking at him expectantly, like a guest waiting for an invitation.

The Commander's freshly braided hair kindled the memory of a home that no longer existed. As much as Wal was the older version of the boy Kaylo had known, he also represented a piece of Tomak—braids woven tightly to the scalp to be bundled into a knot at the nape of his neck, rich cedar-brown skin, full lips curved into an easy smile. Though it felt more a dream than a memory.

The tattoos underscoring his eyes marred the visit from Kaylo's past. Patterns formed by lines and solid black shapes stretched from the bridge of Wal's nose to the rise of his cheekbone. Their precise meaning eluded Kaylo, but such markings told stories.

"Do you knock before entering all of your prison cells?" Kaylo asked.

"What a grand life you must have lived to call this a prison cell."

"Then, I'm free to leave?"

"I'm so glad you haven't lost your sense of humor, old friend."

And still the Astilean Commander did not enter the room. He rocked back and forth on his heels, exaggerating the silence between them.

In another symbolic act of defiance, Kaylo swung the door at his visitor and walked back into his quarters.

Of course, Wal caught the door and let himself in despite their exchange, then took a seat at the table in the middle of the room. He set the arrangement of winter honeysuckle to the side. In its place, he rolled out a tanned piece of hide and set down two leather pouches. Two sets of intersecting lines had been scorched into the hide.

"Are you serious?" Kaylo asked.

"Join me. It's been too long." The sincerity of his voice struck a sharp discord to their situation.

Kaylo sat down begrudgingly before reaching into the pouch closest to his chair. He brought out five pebble-sized pieces of ironoak dyed white, weighing them in his hands. They felt familiar. He flipped them over and ran his fingers over the runes carved into the wood.

"I kept them safe for you. I thought you might want them back if I ever saw you again."

"Wal...when I left...it was better for everyone."

"Is that what you tell yourself?"

"I was angry and dangerous."

"And I was happy and carefree." Wal placed one of his runes face down on the mat, the sharp click stating an end to the conversation.

For a moment, the man across from Kaylo ceased being a warrior, his tattoos and purple robes faded away, and he became the boy Kaylo had abandoned.

As Kaylo traced one of the runes in his hand with a finger, some of the white stain flaked away. He picked a rune and placed it on an empty crosspoint.

Wal challenged, and The Flame took The Shadow. He marked the victory with a new face-down rune and finished his turn with a third.

Runes was a stupid game of luck and memory. Good players realized the key was focusing on the opponent across from them, rather than on the runes in either player's hands. Wise players realized it was all a waste of time.

Despite the empty crosspoints, Wal attacked every piece Kaylo set down. When the crosspoints finally filled, Wal had six black face-down runes to Kaylo's three white runes. Neither of them spoke as they played. One challenge after another drew the game to a tie at three face-up runes each.

Reaching into his pouch to refill his hand, Kaylo pulled out a rune with a charred-black edge. A crack ran the length of it. *He kept it?* Kaylo thought. *All this time, he kept it.*

Kaylo tucked away the scarred rune and challenged with The Wind instead, winning another crosspoint. Then he marked the win with the charred rune, knocking his knuckles against the table to pass the turn back to Wal.

Wooden pebbles clinked about in Wal's hands as his eyes lingered on the burned bit of ironoak. He had always been a fiddler. "You know, I remember that rune."

"I thought you might."

"You really are a second-hand bastard of the worst sort," Wal said.

"I learned it from you."

"I thought I implied that with the second-hand bit."

"What am I doing here, Wal?"

A familiar smirk returned to Wal's face. He leaned back in his chair, adjusting his purple robes. "You're here to serve King Shonar."

"You are too smart to trust letting me loose on a battlefield. So, what in the name of The Mother am I doing here?"

"Don't get all excited. We have use of your particular set of skills."

"The Lost Nation can find another spirit dancer."

Wal smiled with all his teeth. "Oh, we have."

Understanding unfolded like a flower in bloom. "No. No way. I am not training a spirit dancer for you."

"Not for me. For your king," Wal said, letting his smirk fall. "The girl's name is Tayen, right? Well, she is going to be safe and cared for as long as you do your part in service of Ennea. I'll personally see to it."

Kaylo pushed himself up, and his chair clattered against the ground as it fell. Wooden pebbles scattered over the table and onto the floor. His hand went to his hip, but his knife wasn't there. The veins in his neck twitched. His mouth felt dry. If he wrapped his hands around his old friend's neck, Wal would turn the same ugly shade as his robe.

And then Tayen would die.

After all the lessons grief had taught him, he made the stupid decision to care again.

"You seem to be missing this," Wal said, like the smug little shit he was. He pulled Kaylo's knife from his belt and placed it on the table amongst the chaos of game markers. "I thought you should have your father's knife back, for an old friend's sake."

Kaylo looked from the knife to Wal. His old friend stood up straight, daring Kaylo to attack. The seconds drew out. When he didn't reach for the blade, Wal tipped his chin in farewell, opened the door, and closed it behind him.

The charred ironoak pebble lay face up, the rune of The Balance engraved into the wood.

———————

This morning's training was less eventful—not as much blood and equally as little excitement. Tayen followed along as Sola corrected the new recruits' bad habits. He displayed proper sword grip and stance; the correct way to parry an attack, accepting the weight of the blow in one's hips and legs; a simple attack, which in his words, "didn't look like a child fighting off a bee with a stick."

Kaylo had never taught Tayen formal sword work beyond a proper grip and stance. Mostly, they had sparred. He had corrected some mistakes and let Tayen learn from the others. It made her an agile and intuitive fighter who lacked an understanding of the fundamentals.

Under the tutelage of Sola's assistants, the recruits who had been there for several span ran through more advanced techniques. They learned combination strikes and practiced on each other, while she repeatedly hit an opponent made of straw.

At least they gave her a real sword, blunted but real.

"Concentrate," Sola said. He repositioned her head and her hips. "Your hips should face your opponent."

It took effort not to roll her eyes. Instead, she struck the dummy again. Harder. A killing blow.

"No, no, no, no, no. You think you're above this, but you're not. Stop watching what the others are doing and pay attention to what's in front of you. Your legs and your hips power your attack, not your shoulders. And strike through your opponent. You're stopping your momentum, like you're done when you make contact. Your goal isn't to break skin, it's breaking bones."

Hips centered, knees bent, sword angled forward in a strong, but malleable grip—she stepped into her strike and drove her blade through

the dummy until her sword dug its blunt edge into the wooden post.
The jarring stop crawled up the metal, and the hilt wrenched in her
hands.

"Better, you should have proper calluses within a week," the
Commander said. "Again."

Sokan crawled along the sky as Tayen continually crashed her weapon
into a stationary object, each strike hurting more than the last. She could
have eased off when Sola turned his back, but she was done hiding from
pain.

By the time the regiment broke for lunch, the ache starting in her feet
had climbed up through the rest of her body.

As Tayen stumbled towards the mess with the rest of the sullen
recruits, she massaged life back into her hands. *What in The Mist is a
proper callus?* She already had plenty of calluses.

The mass of recruits settled into a line stretching out of the tent.

Hunger failed to describe the pain in her stomach. The fire in her belly
threatened to consume her if she didn't feed it, and it only grew wilder
with each step she took.

Finally reaching the large iron pot, her hands shook with anticipation.
But then a servant slopped a ladle of grayish porridge into her bowl, and
the shaking stopped.

Same bland shit from yesterday.

She took her hunk of stale bread, thanked the server, and walked
away, staring down at the gruel. It looked simultaneously under and
overcooked. Congealed lumps swam in the watery substance.

Despite the unappetizing meal, recruits hunched over tables and
shoveled the contents of their bowls into their mouths. She wove her
way between the thirty or so tables jammed into the clay-brick building.
Each table stood at a different height. Whoever built them slapped them
together with whatever scraps of wood and rusted bits of metal were
available.

It would have been nice to sit down and rest her feet, but the army didn't believe in chairs or other such inefficiencies for recruits. A dozen training regiments rotated through the mess at any given time—an odd combination of the too young, the too old, and the ill-prepared.

Servants occasionally wiped down empty tables, but they had too few rags to keep up with the recruits. The remnants of past meals dried on the tables, giving Tayen all the more encouragement to eat quickly and leave. So, she stood as she ate, dipping her week-old bread in her bowl of slop. Whatever it was, at least they cooked with salt.

A low mummer of conversations filled the hall.

At the other end of the table, Daak shoveled his food into his bulbous face. He looked like he had run through a hornet's nest—the swelling around his right forced him to squint, black bruising sprawled out from the bridge of his nose, and a cut broke his upper lip open. Even if the medics snapped his nose back into place, the swelling wouldn't subside for some time.

Maybe she had taken it too far. Then again, the little prick deserved it.

The young girl who had stood next to her the day before leaned over the table and whispered, "You should watch out for tha one."

"Nothing I can't handle."

"You sleep, don't cha? I'm just sayin, a man wit pride is nah someone to antagonize." The girl offered a sympathetic smile, and her cheeks formed two small dimples. Tayen couldn't help but smile back.

"My name is Tayen."

"Vāhn."

"What brings you to this glorious army?"

"Oh, cha know, just doin my part to fight for the future King of Ennea," Vāhn said. "I figured tey could use a fighter of my skill." She wrinkled her brow, pouted her lips, and grunted.

If she was trying to hide her accent, which she very much was, she was doing a shit job of it.

"Very intimidating."

"Is it true cha came in wit Ennea's Thief?"

Of course, Tayen thought.

It shouldn't have hurt. What other reason would this girl have to speak with her? Tayen didn't know Vāhn any better than any other recruit. But whether or not Tayen would admit it to herself, Vāhn had a magnetism about her. Something about her that cut through Tayen's anger.

Life on the run hadn't left room for friendship, but Tayen's spirit took to Vāhn immediately.

Vāhn didn't drop her chin to the ground. She smiled like hope wasn't a dream she had left on the other side of the Lost Forest. The rest of the recruits either walked around like mourning processions or bullies looking for someone to show up, like Daak.

Regardless of all that, Tayen refused to be an extension of Kaylo. She scraped the last bit of porridge with her dry bread before shoving it into her mouth. "Finished," she said with a full mouth.

The gap she left at the table filled the moment she stepped away. Eventually, she wouldn't be so replaceable.

A bowl of slop fell to the ground just in front of her. Its owner apologized, not seeming to be overly distraught by the loss of his lunch. Looking at the runny lukewarm porridge splattered across the dirt, Tayen wouldn't have cared much either.

She stacked her bowl near the serving line, trying not to wonder if they cleaned the bowls after each meal. The servants behind the serving tables didn't look especially clean themselves. One of them came by to collect the bin of dirty bowls, and Tayen thanked him. But the young northerner didn't even look her way.

The bells hadn't chimed yet, which meant she had time before afternoon lessons. The choice was simple: a cold walk on her own or waiting with a bunch of other recruits in the training tent. At least the cold didn't smell like old sweat and other less-than-pleasant bodily odors.

Away from the training grounds and the overcrowded buildings, the scent of the forest broke through—snow dripping from pine trees in the sun. It was subtle. She had grown up surrounded by it, and the smell touched memories of simpler times.

She took a deep breath and looked around. The Citadel towered over the buildings to the west. The cliffs fell into the ocean to the east. In the distance, snow accented the colors of the trees.

Taking away the context, she couldn't deny Myanack's beauty.

Cool air teased her nose as she breathed in, trying to find a calm. There had been moments with Kaylo when she could find it. When they would whittle away at chunks of wood, watching the fire in silence. But she had left that calm back in Dasoon.

Tayen clutched at her sister's whistle hanging around her neck. At least she hadn't lost everything.

The snow crunched behind her, and she spun about to find a tall northern woman walking across the field.

Even now, Tayen couldn't be alone. Her days of having her own space died when the purple-robed bastards showed up.

At second glance, the woman fit Nix's build. She walked with a straight back and a long stride, like a predator, always alert.

Tayen's feet moved before she had a chance to think. She hadn't caught sight or sound of Nix since they arrived. But as the gap closed and Tayen got close enough to see Nix clearly, she stopped.

A bruise covered the left side of Nix's face from temple to jaw, turning her golden-brown skin shades of black and blue.

Life could be worse. There were always more bruises.

When Nix caught sight of Tayen, she started to turn away, then stopped with a heavy sigh. "Hey, kid."

"What happened?"

"Don't worry about it."

"Did you lose a sparring match?"

Nix's eyes went harsh, and her mouth formed a tight line. "There's not a single person here—recruit, warrior, or fucking king—who could beat me in a fair fight. Most of these pricks don't know a blade from their backside."

"Then, what happened?"

"Let's just say a small distraction can leave a lasting memory."

Tayen's lips turned into a sympathetic pout as she stared at Nix's injuries. "Sorry."

"Keep your sorrys, kid. I can take care of myself. Just make sure you do the same. Now piss off. I came out here to be alone."

───

A stick-thin Sonacoan woman waited on the other side of the door to Kaylo's quarters, and a sweet, greasy scent rose from the plate in her hands.

Is that duck? he thought as his stomach grumbled.

Fat glistened off the roast bird, running down into the bed of barley and vegetables underneath. It looked so good Kaylo forgot to invite the woman in.

The servant hesitantly raised her eyes, and he realized his rude behavior. Kaylo stepped out of the doorway, allowing her to scoot by him. He thanked her, but she did not respond.

After placing the food on the table and straightening up the vase of flowers, she walked back out the door without a word or a second glance. A sweet aroma lingered in the air after her, familiar, but the specific scent escaped him.

"Only the best for our guests." Kaylo turned back to the doorway to find Wal standing there, smiling. "May I join you?"

"Do I have a choice?"

"No, but I thought it would be polite to ask."

A second servant followed Wal into the room and placed a plate of food opposite the setting meant for Kaylo. Wal didn't say a word or acknowledge the man with the down-turned chin as he left.

Kaylo considered performing another minor act of disobedience, but it would have been pointless, and he was hungry. He sat down to marvel at the plate in front of him. The duck's skin was crisped to perfection, just a hint of black tracing the edges of the fatty adornment. And yet, somehow, the vegetables looked even more alluring. The vibrant oranges and purples of the carrots in contrast to the rich green of the snap peas.

His knife crunched into the duck skin, then slid through the meat like it wasn't there. As he took the first bite, Kaylo closed his eyes—hints of orange, salt, and rosemary. He had never tasted anything quite like it. Most of his life had been stews and spit-roasted meat, pot curries and vegetable soups.

"Mmm...good enough to sway even the most stubborn bastard in the room. Am I right?" Wal looked up to meet Kaylo's glare. "Guess not."

And like that, the food soured in front of him. Whatever enticing aroma had been there before faded. Maybe his father had been right. A meal without company was only food, but a meal with the wrong company could be poison.

Wal's lips smacked as he chewed his dinner loudly. "What is it you want?" Kaylo asked.

"Do you really want to have this conversation again?" Wal asked. "Listen, we both know you don't have a choice."

"I'm not training another spirit dancer."

"Three thieves, actually. And if you'd like, we can prove how little of a choice you have with your friend Nix."

"What happened to you, Wal?"

"I survived, old friend."

The silence that fell between them thumped in Kaylo's ears, and the world fell behind it. The room contracted until the walls locked around the table, and all that remained were two men, their history, and the wood between them.

What remained of their youth had vanished like the daylight. Wal had the beginnings of wrinkles across his forehead. Life left him tired. Yet, despite the turns, he remained the same stubborn boy. There would be no changing his mind. If Kaylo refused, Nix would die. If he continued to refuse, Tayen would die. Then they would let him rot in his grief for the principle of it.

"I have demands."

Wal's eyebrows lifted. "Interesting. And what would they be?"

"Tayen and Nix move into my quarters."

"Yearning for a more domestic life, are we? I don't think so. They can visit, one at a time, but they stay in the barracks and train with the other recruits. Warriors need to learn a warrior's life."

"I need to be able to leave my room."

"Oh, and shall I arrange for a trip beyond the forest as well?"

"You can't expect me to stay locked within these four walls forever."

Wal's face contorted as if he was considering whether that was true. "You can explore the common areas of the Citadel under escort," Wal said. "Anything else, great and wonderful Hero of Anilace?"

"I train the spirit dancers my way."

Wal took an obnoxiously large bite of his duck and then spoke through the meat. "As long as they fight for the King."

CHAPTER FOUR
CURRENT DAY ENNEA

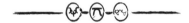

Tayen and Vāhn stood across from one another in near-mirrored positions, gripping their hilts at waist level, angling their blades across their chests, and waiting. The cold in the air could have been to blame for Vāhn's shaking ashburn blade, but it couldn't excuse her poor stance.

"One! Two! Three! Four!" Oakan shouted. The dusting of patchy facial hair over the warrior's face contrasted the age in his staccato baritone voice.

Sharp thwacks of wood followed each number, as the recruits practiced their attacks and guards to his count.

The seriousness with which Oakan took his position as Commander Sola's assistant was etched into his face. The morning light made his golden skin sheen and glow as he shouted the repetitive count. "Again! One! Two! Three! Four!"

Sola paced through the lines of recruits—inspecting and correcting. The only encouragement he offered came in the form of silence.

With her concentration focused on her grip and stance, Tayen attacked, rotating with her hips and torso. Each strike creeping towards to perfection. Her practice sword crashed into Vāhn's guard. They were near enough in height and weight for the match, but Vāhn's inexperienced guard shook with each blow. Her hands slipped, and her feet shuffled over the sand.

If Vāhn had held a sword before this span, she had probably gripped the wrong end. Her technique lacked a basic understanding of swordplay. She tried to use her arms to muscle through her blocks. Even if she had the muscle for it, which she didn't, she lacked form. She was more likely to kill her sword than her opponent with the way she strangled the grip.

Vāhn's inexperience only urged Tayen on. With each count, she drove her wooden blade into Vāhn's awkward guard. With each contact, Vāhn clenched her teeth and winced.

"One!" Vāhn raised her blade to the right—too high, putting the weight on her shoulders.

"Two!" Sliding to the left just in time to catch the second blow. Choreographed or not, Vāhn had difficulty keeping up.

"Three!" To the lower right, arms extended too far to absorb the attack properly.

"Four!" Vāhn's wrist buckled, and Tayen's sword crashed through Vāhn's guard into her shoulder. The force drove her to the sand beside her fallen sword.

Vāhn's eyebrows arched over her rich cherrywood eyes in a question. Whatever shame Tayen felt, she covered up with stubborn pride. Tayen existed outside of Kaylo's shadow, and everyone would know it.

"Get up, recruit!" Sola yelled.

The sand shifted under Vāhn as she grabbed for her practice sword and pushed herself to her feet. She rubbed her shoulder, then steadied her guard once again.

"No, not like that." Sola grabbed the girl's thin arms roughly and repositioned them. "Have you learned anything? Fight with your legs and hips."

Eyes drifted over to the commotion as Commander Sola bent Vāhn into place—moving her feet, her hips, forcing her to bend into her knees, straightening her back as if she were a lifeless doll.

"Now, block right," he shouted, even though he stood directly next to her. She shifted into position. "No, why are your elbows turned out like you're about to flap your wings? Elbows in." He smacked her elbow with the back of his hand.

Her eyes began watering, but she tucked in her lip and looked straight forward, over Tayen's shoulder. "If your elbows are in, you can absorb the force of the blow in your hips and your legs. It puts you in position to turn your opponent's blade and strike."

"Block left!" She shifted, keeping her elbows tucked into her torso. "Why are you turning your feet? Are you dull? Is that the problem? Are the terms I am using too complicated for you? I am right in front of you. Face me."

Vāhn's lips puckered, and a couple of tears ran down the soft curves of her cheek. Her nostrils flared as she stared forward.

When she found the correct position, Commander Sola nodded. Then, seeming to notice the attention he had drawn, he shouted for everyone to return to their drills.

As the count continued, Tayen and Vāhn traded roles. Tayen blocked effortlessly, looking at her opponent's arms and chest rather than her eyes.

Vāhn didn't lash out or break down. She didn't say a word, moving methodically through the drills. By the time the bells struck for lunch, her form had improved, mildly, but at least the flaws attracted less attention.

As the other recruits scurried off to the mess, Vāhn dropped her guard and waited for Tayen to look her in the face. Tayen could have walked away, but she refused to bow to that soft voice of cowardice in the back of her mind.

No more running.

The skin under Vāhn's eyes remained irritated, but her tears had stopped. "Why?" she asked.

That one word held the weight of a thousand questions.

The steady timber with which she spoke left Tayen without an answer or a voice. Moments stretched, as the few remaining recruits filtered out of the tent. Tayen looked down to the sand, then Vāhn left as well, leaving Tayen searching for an answer amongst the miniscule grains.

Why? she thought, her inner voice mimicking Vāhn's.

A presence jerked her out of her stupor. A short Sonacoan boy, one of the Citadel's servants from his ragged clothing, waited beside her. His chin remained tucked into his chest as he held a folded piece of paper in his small hands.

Your presence has been requested in the Citadel.

That was all it said. No reason why. No clue as to what awaited her.

"Who sent you?" she asked the servant boy, but he didn't respond. He didn't even look up to acknowledge she had spoken, simply turning towards the mountain, waiting for her to follow.

The Citadel loomed larger and larger as they approached the entrance. Ever since she first saw the massive structure, she harbored what she considered a justifiable fear of it. Here she was, a captive of a nation that had pulled a mountain from the earth and turned it into a city. It said that they had power, but more than that, it said that they would get what they wanted.

What rational reason could there be to build a city out of a mountain? None, except they could. And if they could do that, what could they do with something as small and fragile as her?

Tayen stepped through the entrance. Fear didn't control her, no matter how justified. She made her face a mask of passiveness, concentrating on the tapestries hung on the stone walls of the large hallway. The oil lamps flickered. Each tapestry bore the same geometric pattern with the rune of The Shadow at the center.

She stopped to study a tapestry, and her guide stopped as well. Six layers radiated out from The Shadow—each spirit rune woven into the intricate pattern.

Her secret stared at her, woven with delicate thread in an ancient language. The Song surrounded her as it always did. Shadows jittered in the light of the oil lamps. They called for her to dance with them and forget the Lost Nation, Kaylo, The Gousht. If she dropped her guard, the shadows would take her away from this nightmare.

"Move it," a warrior shouted behind her, shoving the servant boy out of the way as he walked towards the exit.

After glaring at the warrior's back for what she considered an appropriate amount of time, she looked to make sure the boy was alright. The servant didn't seem to notice. He kept his head bowed as usual—his closely cropped red curls catching the flickering light.

It was then, in the tight quarters of the mountain hallway, that she noticed the subtle sweet smell wafting off the boy. Tayen's brow furrowed, but she dismissed her suspicions. The drafty mountain hallways must have picked up all sorts of smells. It couldn't have been susu grass.

They came to a door not much further into the mountain, and the boy knocked. A guard stood beside the door, not bothered in the slightest by her presence. He was unusually large, as was the spear he held. Someone shuffled behind the door before pulling it open.

Kaylo stood there, smiling wide and draped in crisp, purple robes. *Of course,* she thought. *Kaylo.*

The servant boy scurried off before she could ask him to take her back to the mess hall. She looked from the guard to her kana. *What begins sooner, ends sooner.*

Whatever time she had spent worrying about Kaylo had been a waste. Light danced along the tapestries on the walls. The slate gray made every decorative flare jump into focus. The bastard even had fresh flowers in a vase on the table.

Two plates sat beside the flowers covered with large cloth napkins, which were immaculately white. How could anything meant to clean remain unblemished? Then the smell hit her, grease and herbs mingling with a sweetness.

"Are you hungry?"

Few questions could have made Tayen angrier. Did he think the army had pampered her like this? Did he think she slept atop a high bundle of soft hay with a brazier to keep her warm at night?

If a glare could communicate the complexity of her feelings, she had managed it. Her lips remained stoic, her brows turned downward, and her mother's green eyes aimed at the veins in his neck.

Kaylo ignored her, walked over to the table, and sat down. The napkin flourished in the air as he uncovered the plate and laid the cloth on his lap. The smell of the meal thickened in the air.

Despite herself, Tayen could not resist a proper meal. If she left now, she would have to scrounge the pot in the mess for the drags of another sloppy porridge. When she sat and lifted her napkin, the tension in her brow eased. A thick slice of pork over mashed root vegetables and a sticky sauce drizzled over the meat. It smelled of apples and spices.

In all of her brief life, she had never thought of such a meal. Who had the time?

The few times her father had hunted boar, he had carved off slices of meat and wrapped them around a slice of apple for her. As the fat from the boar coated her tongue, the tartness of the apple transformed it into something different. The flavors sung a harmony. Out there, boar was a rarity, but whenever her father got the better of one, she would eat until her stomach hurt.

The smells wafting from the plate in front of her twisted her lungs. She smiled in those memories, and it hurt all the worse.

"I've arranged for you to be able to visit my quarters when you aren't training."

"So we can chat over meal times?" Tayen said. "After you finish telling me stories, I can tell you all about being forced to fight other kids with wooden swords."

"Tayen..."

"No!" Her voice squeaked as she yelled. It made her sound young and foolish, but she wasn't. Not anymore. "You promised to take care of me. You promised to train me so I could settle the blood I owe. Now, I'm locked up in someone else's army, taking orders and sleeping between strangers.

"If you had just let me fight. If you had let me call The Shadow..."

"Keep it down. You don't want them to know."

"Secrets, that's right. You're all about secrets. Like, how is it that your friend, Wal, is a commander in the Lost Nation?"

"I don't know."

"Of course, you don't. For a kana, you don't seem to know much."

Kaylo hung his head, looking pathetic. As the soft feeling of sympathy started to temper her anger, she looked down at the meal. He had been here eating like royalty, while she scraped soggy porridge from a dirty bowl.

"Don't send for me again," she said. Her voice lowered, but it retained the same intensity.

He looked up, and his eyes watered. "If you change your mind, I'll be here."

"And I'll be in the shack below the mountain with a hundred other stolen children." She stood up and turned to the door. It didn't budge. She slammed her fist against the stormwood until the guard opened up the door. If she hurried, she could get to her afternoon lessons on time.

Her stomach growled. Because of Kaylo, she would have to wait until dinner to eat.

The air tasted stale. Kaylo's chest rose and fell as his breath flowed in through his nose and out through his mouth. The wood table felt cool beneath his hands. Cinnamon and pepper drifted up from the food in front of him. He concentrated on the physical distractions, as if he could master his emotions.

Before he could think better of it, he grabbed the wooden plate and flung it at the wall. It rattled against the floor. "I should be in my hallow!"

"I didn't ask for this!" He reached for the second plate and threw it harder. It twisted in the air as food sprayed in a circular pattern before the plate crashed into the stone.

As mashed vegetables and sauce slopped down the wall, he screamed from the depths of his belly. It wasn't enough.

He wrapped his hands around the back of the chair, swinging it with all his force into the wall. The impact traveled up the wood into his arms as the chair broke into several pieces and clattered to the ground. At least it had the decency to break.

A tickle climbed along his forearm.

When he turned his arm over, a bit of splintered wood the size of his small finger protruded from his left palm. Blood trickled from the wound, but the pain was too quiet for all of his rage.

The guard threw open the door, yelling something incoherent or unimportant. He leveled his spear at Kaylo.

With a simple thrust, this warrior could end Kaylo's pain. But he had responsibilities he couldn't leave behind.

Kaylo raised his hands, stepping away from the table towards the center of the room. The warm blood from his palm ran a trail down his arm.

Despite the early hour, Sokan fled the sky. Days grew shorter and grayer, which suited Tayen fine. She pushed open the flaps of their training tent and released a heavy breath when Sola and his assistants weren't there yet. Most of the regiment had already lined up, awaiting the Commander's presence.

Afternoon lessons took place in the same tent they trained in every morning. The fire did a poor job of keeping the cold at bay. If it had not been for her earlier trip to Kaylo's quarters, she would have mistaken Astileans for a simple people who valued function over form. Now, the loosely flapping tent walls symbolized the value the Lost Nation placed on those who inhabited them.

It didn't take Tayen long to spot Vāhn.

With a quick nudge to a scrawny kid from the south, Tayen claimed the spot next to Vãhn. Her fellow recruits offered Tayen a certain amount of deference after her temper had shattered in front of the whole regiment and she had beaten Daak bloody.

No one had ever feared her before. It felt oddly empowering.

Vãhn glanced at her suspiciously and shifted a little further away. Then the flaps at the front of the tent opened, and everyone straightened their backs.

Barely a span had passed, and already Tayen had fallen into an obedient pattern alongside her fellow recruits. Sola's quick discipline— physical abuse—had been effective on two fronts: no one questioned him, and no one liked him.

Oakan and Chitere, Sola's second assistant, entered first and marched to opposite sides of the room, monitoring the recruits like Sola's extra eyes. Then Sola walked in, robes as immaculately clean and straight as always. If he had new robes made for him each morning, Tayen would not have been surprised.

Behind the three of them, in such contradiction it appeared intentional, an older Tomakan servant walked in and stood in the corner. His robes looked dirtier than the swept sand beneath them.

Everyone seemed to hold their breath, stretching their backs as tall as they could while Sola inspected the ranks. When he motioned for the recruits to sit, none of them did so casually. Tayen carefully knelt, sitting on her ankles with her big toes crossing, as she had been taught.

The position put pressure on her knees and thighs. She would have preferred standing, but she had seen what happened when recruits showed a lack of self-control.

"I bring good news. As of yesterday, this regiment has reached capacity," Sola announced as he paced back and forth in front of the regiment. "In three moons, you will face the trials, a series of three tests designed to determine who is worthy to become a warrior in the King's army. The ninety-nine recruits beside you will be your competition and your collaborators. The proven will earn their mark." He pointed to the first tattoo under his left eye.

"The fallen will offer another type of service to King Shonar." All eyes shifted towards the dirty man standing in the corner with his chin tucked into his chest.

The manipulative bastard brought this poor old man here to scare us, Tayen thought. From the looks on the faces of the recruits next to her, it had worked.

"Some of you are scared, which is understandable. The task before us is great. The trials are but a step towards the battleground. You are here because our land is under siege. We face an enemy that would erase everything we are. They would usurp the spirits and The Mother with their false god. They would subdue the people. They inter our history in the ashes of our fallen warriors. That, our King will not allow."

As he stopped pacing, he swept his gaze over the regiment. "Are you worthy of fighting for Ennea's King?"

"Yes, Commander," the recruits all around Tayen responded, but she stared back in silence.

The lines on his face had gone soft and gentle, his words dripping with unadulterated sincerity. The prick believed every word. And maybe he was right.

Even Kaylo had admitted the Uprising lacked the numbers to face the Gousht armies. The Lost Army might be Ennea's last chance. Maybe Ennea needed a strong leader. Without one, the Gousht had conquered most of the continent in two turns.

Commander Sola stepped aside, and Chitere replaced him. Her thick black curls parted to one side, perfectly framing her soft features. Her full lips formed an unbending line, as always. She waited, and no one dared break the silence. No need for threats or glares. This young woman commanded attention without effort.

This pattern became routine. Sola addressed the recruits, then stepped back and observed while Chitere or Oakan led a lesson on military protocols—who took orders from whom and such, how messages moved from regiment to regiment, how to dig a field latrine.

Who cared? How could they expect Tayen to focus after what Sola had said?

In three moons, their skills would be tested. How? In combat? They could give her a sword now if they needed her to prove herself.

With a purple robe, she could claim the blood she owed. That much the army could give her.

Two sharp scratching sounds pulled Tayen's attention back to Chitere. The north woman held a slate high with two white lines meeting at a point. "This is the mark you will earn should you pass the trials. It represents the Citadel, the center of our power."

One-by-one, she drew symbols on the slate before explaining their meaning. An angled straight line indicated one turn of service. Every battle earned a warrior a pair of intersecting lines. And they marked every kill with a horizontal line ending in a vertical line.

Each warrior wore their deeds on their face for all to see. By the time she finished, Tayen's kills would cover her cheeks.

At this distance, the marks on Sola's cheeks blended into one another. All the battles and kills over the turns lined up in several rows over each cheek like a stain of black blood running from the round of his cheekbones to the bridge of his nose.

Chitere's collection stretched nearly as long, but only on her left cheek. For someone so young, she had killed her share of couta bastards, which made Tayen like her more with each kill she counted.

"Kills are how you earn a command." Chitere paused and let her words settle over the regiment. "Why would we do this? Why would we mark our faces with our kills?"

A recruit stood, as was customary, and answered. "To intimidate the enemy, let them see as we count their dead."

"What would a Gousht soldier know of our culture?" Chitere asked with disdain. "No. We don't do this for them."

"We mark our bodies so that when we pass into The Mist, we may be known as warriors," another recruit said.

"A pretty idea, but the spirits do not need markings to know what we do for them." Chitere waited, and the air stiffened with tension. "Not a single person knows?" Her indifferent stare moved from one recruit to the next. No one moved.

"When the Gousht enter a battlefield, they send their weak first. Their officers remain behind. They only bloody their pretty little tunics when the battle is dying down. It's pathetic," Chitere said. "The only way to be a commander in the King's army is to kill. When you look at your commander, you will know the person you fight for is forged of steel, tempered in the enemy's blood."

The tiny hairs on Tayen's forearms went tingling. She could picture the black ink lining her face, mapping her vengeance.

Vāhn rushed out of the training tent as soon as the lesson broke. Despite her slight frame, she moved quickly up to the front of the line of recruits heading towards the mess hall.

Tayen rushed after her, calling her name, but Vāhn refused to turn around until Tayen caught up with her and tapped her on the shoulder.

"What?!" Vāhn stared at Tayen with her reddish-brown eyes as the rest of the regiment broke around them like a river around a stone. "What is it cha want?"

"I want to apologize."

Vāhn closed her eyes and took a deep breath. "Do I look like a warrior?" she asked. "Do cha look at me and see a warrior?"

Tayen shifted back and forth, partly because her knees ached from sitting in the lecture, but mostly out of nervousness.

"You don, do cha? I am seventeen, on the verge of my swearin day, and I ave ta look up ta meet cha eyes." Her Renēquan accent grew thicker. "I'm older than almost everyone in ta regiment, but I don know how ta fight. I've never held a real sword before. Out tere I hid."

"You can learn to sword fight," Tayen said in a tentative voice.

"What happens when I fail ta trials?"

"You won't fail..."

"Do ta servants look happy ta cha?" Vähn bit her bottom lip and looked off to the side.

"No, but you won't fail..."

"Do cha know tha they aren't allowed a name?" Vähn asked. "Ta warriors call them ta nameless."

"What does that mean?"

"So, for no good reason, cha decided to show me up in front of Sola and put my freedom at risk?" Vähn said. Her voice shook, like she could barely control the breath behind it. "I am goin to go to the mess now and get some food before it's all gone because, even though it is ta worst food I ave ever eaten, I am hungry.

"Don't follow me. Don't sit by me. Just stay away." The slight woman turned and walked off.

Although Tayen's belly grumbled at her, she didn't follow. She stood in the middle of the snow-covered field, alone. The stiff wind blew over her face, and for the first time in several moons, she didn't have her anger to hold her up.

CHAPTER FIVE

CURRENT DAY ENNEA

Kaylo jolted upright in his bed and reached for the knife he kept beside him. The fog of his dreams still swam through his vision. The coals had long burned away, leaving the brazier as dark as the rest of his quarters. Nothing moved. The shadows were empty.

Thump. Thump. Thump.

The door slammed into the frame like someone thought they could break the stormwood by knocking hard enough. Muffled words grew louder and more violent on the other side of the door. He rubbed his eyes, stumbling towards the noise with his knife at his side.

As he flung the door open, he found two silhouettes wrestling in the dim lighting. The guard had one arm wrapped around Tayen, trying to restrain her while he reached to close the door with his other. She kicked and screamed, then suggested what the guard could do with his oversized spear. It didn't sound comfortable.

They both stopped, a mess of entangled limbs, when Kaylo stepped into the hall.

"I don't remember your commander saying anything about restricted hours. As long as she doesn't sleep here, she's welcome. Yes?" Kaylo waved the girl in as he held the guard's incredulous stare.

In truth, Wal hadn't been particularly specific in his allowances, but

the guard permitted her to pass all the same. The girl wore the luck
of The Mother around her shoulders. No one of any great importance
would've questioned the guard much if he snapped her neck.

And still she gave the guard one last look of defiance before pushing
her way into Kaylo's quarters.

"Good morning. Is it morning yet?" Kaylo asked dryly.

Despite the hour, Tayen's aggressively combative body language,
and his pride—despite all the circumstances—the muscles between his
shoulder blades relaxed. After their last encounter, he had expected her
to keep her distance, and it had held his heart frozen between beats.

He never should have allowed her this close.

"Where are the flowers? And the other chair?" Tayen asked.

"What are you doing here? How early is it?"

"The sun should reach the horizon soon. I need your help," she said.
"And you owe me."

The remnants of sleep still crusted over the corners of his eyes. His
back hurt. After sleeping on the ground for as long as he had, the soft
hay bed left him aching like an old man, feeling every turn twice over.

Kaylo moved towards the remaining chair, making all manner of
otherworldly noises, grunting and sighing like a forest full of animals. As
he took a seat, he pushed his tangled braids out of his eyes, waiting for
Tayen to explain herself.

Instead of taking the silence as an invitation, Tayen crossed her arms
and stared at him.

One day, somehow, her pride would find a way to wound her, maybe
even as deeply as her guilt.

"What is it you need my help with?"

"I need you to train me."

Was the world on a loop? Why did everyone want his training? By all
rights, he was a shit teacher. He rubbed at his forehead. "Don't you have
people training you already?"

"Why are you making this difficult?" Tayen asked. "You know those servants running around here in dirty clothes, smelling like susu grass? The lost assholes call them the nameless. If I don't pass the trials—and only The Mother knows what those are—I end up like them. Do they look like they are happy to you?"

Ever since he had arrived, Kaylo had been trying to ignore the little incongruities. The steady stream of servants who didn't speak or look up from the ground. The decadent meals he ate while the servants looked thinner than the plates they served. His quarters took up space for at least three more people. All this while a war raged on beyond the Lost Forest.

Whatever disparities he saw, he wanted to overlook. He told himself they had nothing to do with him. Tayen and Nix had to be his priority. They had to escape.

"I won't let that happen," he said.

"Just like you wouldn't let them take me?"

Kaylo cradled his face in his hands. "I'm sorry, Tayen."

"I don't need your apology. I need you to meet me and my friend on the training grounds every morning at dawn."

"So I can train you to be a warrior?"

"It's all I have left!"

He looked up from his self-pity, and the scared, angry child he had saved from the Gousht only two seasons past stood in front of him. She needed him in ways she didn't know. "I'll train you, but our old deal stands."

"No. No more story time."

"You want me to train you and your friend? You have to visit me here every night and listen." Her eyes were daggers, but he met them anyway.

Time stretched between them—two stubborn people testing wills like children. The actual child blinked first. She rolled her eyes, making sure that he understood the full distaste she had for his bargain.

"We start tomorrow. Don't be late," she said before leaving.

———

The sand begrudgingly gave way to Nix's feet. Winter's chill stung her nostrils with every inhalation, and each exhalation hung in the air for a halted moment before dissipating. In and out in rhythmed meter. And yet despite the winter winds and the frost-ridden sand, sweat beaded over her skin as she ran.

Commander Yansar set the pace, and Nix refused to fall behind, even as her newfound compatriots drifted farther out of sight. She matched the rise and fall of her commander's gait. The extreme temperature variance between her sweaty body and the air made her ears ache. Even as her muscles threatened to seize up, she drove herself forward.

Yansar had a decade or more on Nix, but she moved like her body had been crafted for battle.

Every morning, the regiment ran the perimeter of the training grounds, and they only stopped when their commander stopped. Nix counted the circuits. A dozen one day, three dozen the next, without reason or explanation.

The rhythm of her boots against the rough sand slowly coaxed Nix into a trance. The world quieted. Her aching body, the cold wind teasing her skin, the force that crawled up her leg with each footfall all faded into the distance.

When all else vanished, the face of the Sonacoan servant remained. The servant looked like the distant relative of a child she once knew in Dasoon. Her cheeks had hollowed out, her rich skin had paled, and her hair had become matted, but the slight indent in the middle of her chin endured the turns.

It took several days before the girl's name came to Nix. When the Lost Nation had taken her away, the girl had held onto her mother, and her mother had continued screaming the child's name as the soldiers ripped the two apart—Sosun.

Eight turns had passed since Hakan had struck his bargain with the Lost Nation. Nix had relented her objections too quickly. Dasoon was dying again. What little they had done to lift the city from the grave waned under the burden of each new mouth to feed. Raiding parties, harsh winters, and a poor autumn harvest had left them desperate.

Nix had clenched her fists and bit her tongue when the soldiers wrenched Sosun from her mother's arms. The girl had looked to Nix. She had pleaded for Nix to save her, even as Nix turned her back from the scene.

Sacrifices had to be made.

How many of them had died fighting for the Lost Nation? How many were still bound in its service?

If Sosun sought vengeance, Nix would let her have it.

Nameless, she thought. *The woman had a name, and I took it from her.*

Nix rounded the corner and almost toppled over her commander. Yansar stood with her arm raised over her head, signaling the end of their morning run. The Commander's eyes rolled over Nix as she fell into line, waiting for the rest of the unit to join.

"It's easy to lose yourself in the adrenaline, isn't it?"

"Yes, Commander," Nix said, still panting for her breath.

"Fight it. A warrior is control."

"Yes, Commander."

Yansar's eyes looked sharper than the knife that hung from her belt. Calculations and judgments jumbled behind the brilliant ochre of her irises. It unsettled Nix. If she met the Commander's gaze, she could take it as a challenge. If Nix averted her eyes, Yansar might mistake it for weakness.

This woman controlled her fate.

Reminding herself to continue breathing in and out, Nix lifted her gaze to meet Yansar's stare. They shared silent eye contact for far too long.

Finally, Yansar nodded, turned on her heels, and marched into their training tent.

———

The corridors of the Citadel blended into one another as Kaylo traveled deeper into the heart of the system of tunnels. How one marked the difference or remembered the path eluded him. The sheer size of the structure felt beyond comprehension. That the entire weight of the stone above him didn't come crumbling down around them was astounding. Luckily, he had his guard to accompany him.

A light at the far end of the tunnel grew stronger, and the passageway expanded. The angle of the light fell straight down like they had trapped a sun in the center of the mountain.

For all their vanity, surely, they had tried.

The light overwhelmed his eyes as he stepped closer, continuing to blink until he stood at the lip of the tunnel, staring out over the hollowed-out core of the mountain. Shadows and blurs faded from his vision as his eyes adjusted.

Much in the way a path spiraled around the outside of the mountain, a walkway spiraled around the grand central hub of the Citadel. Above hung an intricate series of oil-burning lamps dotting the ceiling of the atrium like stars in the sky in the middle of which hung a gaudy display of crystals reflecting light in every direction.

"How?" The word escaped Kaylo like a breath. His bear of a guard ignored him, standing a pace back over his left shoulder.

"Great talk," Kaylo said to the guard, then walked down the spiral path to the base of the atrium.

They passed several people on the way down, mostly northerners dressed in the finest of robes. War had not touched these halls. The people walked with a looseness in their gait, as if they didn't have to worry about rounding the next corner.

As he studied their presumed freedom, their eyes followed him in return. Apparently, rumors of his stay in the Citadel had traveled through the tunnels.

Only the servants ignored his presence, dressed in rags, scurrying up and down the pathway like dogs attending their masters. Some held large trays of delicious-smelling foods, others scrolls of parchment, and some nothing at all. However, they all shared one common quality—their eyes watched the ground two paces ahead of them. By luck and practice, they didn't stumble into anyone.

When the pathway flattened into the base of the atrium, Kaylo stopped to collect the grandness of his surroundings. How long had the dancers toiled to carve this perfection into a mountain? The mastery of The Song that this required humbled him. If The Mountain herself had stood on this very spot and called this hallow into being, it would have sounded more believable to Kaylo's ears.

His shoes scuffed over the ground. There was an unevenness to the floor. *Even in perfection, imperfection,* Kaylo thought. But then he looked down, only to realize that the floor of the atrium had a pattern carved into it.

Walking atop the carving, it was difficult to visualize the image. Then, in the center of the floor, the rune of The Shadow stood as clear as the lights that shone above. They had carved the same mural that hung on tapestries throughout the corridors into the floor—seven intertwining shapes with The Shadow in the center.

Something about The Shadow being the central figure of a hallow called from The Mountain seemed disrespectful. But that remained at the bottom of Kaylo's list of complaints. The Great Spirits could take care of themselves. They always had.

Several tunnels branched out from the atrium, but one eclipsed the others by comparison. Kaylo looked back to his jailor before continuing forward. The brute didn't seem to take any exception to his walking down the pathway, and so he followed his curiosity.

The short walk through the corridor led to a set of large stormwood doors. A lone guard waited outside the entrance, holding his spear upright in his right hand, his sword dangling from his hip.

"A friend of yours?" Kaylo remarked to his silent companion, who unsurprisingly said nothing. "You mind if I go in?"

The guard looked at him without affect. "You are quite the conversationalist, but you really should keep some of your thoughts to yourself," Kaylo said.

With silent permission to continue, Kaylo pulled open the heavy stormwood doors. What waited on the other side was far more beautiful than any mountain carving could be.

There, in a room four times the size of his quarters, stood the largest collection of books Kaylo had ever seen.

The outside walls of the chamber had been smoothed flat, with large sections dug away to create shelves in the stone itself. Between the walls, a dozen stormwood bookshelves formed rows, each shelf measuring at least twice as tall as Kaylo.

"Again, how?" Kaylo asked to the empty room.

When his astonishment subsided, confusion took its place. The mountain must have been a home to thousands of people, not even considering the thousands that lived in the homes and barracks surrounding the mountain. *How are there any books left on the shelves? How is there room to stand?*

He walked to the closest bookshelf and ran his fingers along the books' spines, as if to prove they were real.

"Quite the collection, isn't it?"

Kaylo jumped and turned towards the voice.

There, in the center of the library, at one of four tables, sat a solitary person. They wore fine Astilean robes, which hung disheveled on their slight frame. Long black curls hung from their head like tangled vines. A smudge of ink ran from their cheekbone to chin, in contrast to the soft golden hue of their skin.

The stranger sat in front of a collapsed pile of books spread across the table, with a mess of crumbled parchment accumulated on the floor around them. It all seemed such a waste.

"Where is everyone?" Kaylo asked.

"Access lessens importance," the stranger said. "I am Lanigan, resident poet and library hermit."

"Kaylo."

"Ah, Ennea's Thief." Lanigan's expression widened with delight. "A pleasure."

"All of this treasure, and only one person to appreciate it?"

"Sometimes others come in for a visit. Usually seeking an answer to some question or a momentary distraction from life's dull melancholy."

"You are quite an eccentric man, aren't you?"

"Eccentric kamani, actually. Not all of us fit so easily into one of those genders you all like to box yourselves into."

"My apologies, I didn't mean to…"

"Apologizing for ignorance is unnecessary," Lanigan said. "Now, do it again, and I shall challenge you upon my honor." A wide smile broadened across their face and fell into dimples on either cheek.

Kaylo raised his hands. "I would hardly risk such a challenge."

"In that case, shall we be friends? Too few care to discuss books. I'm afraid Ren doesn't even bother coming past the library doors anymore."

"The guard at the door?" Kaylo asked, and the poet nodded. "What makes a poet so dangerous they need a jailor?"

"Maybe he's there for my protection."

"Is he?"

"No, but it's a rude assumption," Lanigan said, smile stretching wider than it had any right.

"My deepest apologies."

"Sit, please sit. I would love to hear about the world. Sadly, these books are horrible references for current events."

The legs of the chair scraped the stone floor, sending the sound reverberating throughout the chamber.

In the haphazard collection of books that lay before him, one title stood out. A book covered in pitch-black leather, filigreed in gold— *What Lurks in Dreams?* The leather was worn and smoother for it. Inside, large letters wove daemontales through the pages. Detailed drawings of monsters causing mayhem interrupted the stories.

"Daemontales?" Kaylo asked with a raised eyebrow. "All these books at your reach, and you choose to read children's stories?"

Lanigan peered through the unkempt curls that fell in front of their eyes and spoke in a somber tone. "The truths in our fantasies are often greater than those we are willing to offer in plain language."

They brushed their hair aside as they leaned back in their chair. "These shelves hold all manner of secrets if you know how to search for the truth. These words are escapes, tools, distractions, lessons, lies, reminders, and weapons. What power you might hold if you could only see the difference?"

For a moment, this tousled mess of a library hermit commanded all the poise and grandeur of a wise elder. No more than fifty turns to them, yet they were captivating and terrifying. Then their smile broke the spell. Crooked teeth and genuine warmth dispersed the air of grandness.

"Then there are some books that make you smile," Lanigan said. "And that is enough at times."

"Know of any books that will help me change a stubborn teenager's mind?"

"They're words, not magic," Lanigan said, somehow grinning even wider. "Maybe a poem will do.

> *A flower planted in shade*
> *Still knows the need for sun*
> *Watch it creep and climb*
> *Bark and branch*
> *Watch it bloom*
> *Brilliant and out of place*

Cut its growth and it will wither
Crack and crumble into the dirt it was
Watch it feed the soil
Nurture the next seed to fight the shade.

"That doesn't rhyme," Kaylo said dryly.

"Songs rhyme. Poems are truthful," the poet said. "Do you only believe something when it rhymes?"

"This is why people hate poets."

"One of the many reasons, Anhil." Lanigan showed their crooked-toothed smile and picked up the book that was open in front of them.

"My name is Kaylo."

"I know." The poet winked, returning to their book.

The collective odor of a hundred stolen children in sweat-soaked robes saturated the air in the barracks, creating a stench reminiscent of a basket of rotting fruit. A wave of the scent made Tayen gag as she walked into the clay-brick shack. At least, the body-heat of one hundred child warriors-in-training kept the cold on the other side of the open doorway.

Most of the regiment had already claimed their bit of the ground and passed out, curled tightly around each other as they dreamed about better times and places. A few stirred as she crept through the mass of bodies, searching for Vāhn—one underfed, petite girl in a sea of similarly afflicted bodies.

Vāhn turned her shoulder away from Tayen as she approached. Gestures, no matter how blatantly obvious, would not deter Tayen from her course. She stuck her knee between Vāhn and the boy who slept next to her, and proceeded to roll the boy to the side. He snored on through as though nothing happened.

"Wha tis it cha want?" Vāhn said, her accent full of her exhaustion.

Tayen lay down beside her, eyes searching the unorganized pattern of the thatched roof. "I'm going to help you pass the trials."

"Who said I wanted cha help?"

"I don't mean this as an insult, but I've seen you with a sword," Tayen whispered. "You need my help."

"Be quiet, we are trying to sleep," an irritated voice called out from the crowd of sleeping children.

"Cha heard tem. Shut up and gota sleep."

"Tomorrow at dawn, we are going to the training grounds."

Vāhn didn't respond. She simply pulled her ragged blanket tighter over her shoulders.

If Vāhn didn't want her help, Tayen couldn't force her, and she wouldn't try. Too many people had forced Tayen's life down this path. She had no desire to control anyone's life, but her mother had taught her to set the world right when she tipped it off balance. That's what she meant to do.

Through a hole in the roof, bits of the night sky crept into the barracks. A star. A pinprick of light stole through the thatched reeds. So small. So far away.

In the infinite black of the sky, her hope was a faint star.

CHAPTER SIX
CURRENT DAY ENNEA

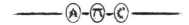

Wal relented and allowed Kaylo to partake in training with Tayen at sunrise, but he insisted that a guard be present to monitor the sessions. So, as Kaylo walked to the training ground in the soft glow of the early morning, his silent friend traipsed behind him like an anchor latched to his ankle.

The jailors rotated through the post, and yet they were all one variation or another of the same brooding warrior, none of whom were stunning conversationalists. Each of them carried their weapons and a sustained look of indifference, as if a smile would have betrayed their king.

Asking after their name proved as useful as spitting into the wind in winter. As such, Kaylo took to calling them after pretty flowers. This one he named Hibiscus, after the redness that crept up his tawny cheeks.

Sadly, Hibiscus gave no indication whether he enjoyed the moniker. Though he had turned when called on several occasions—to Kaylo's infinite entertainment.

In the distance, two silhouetted figures waited at the edge of the sand field. The taller of the two fidgeted with her hair, her robes, her belt. Stillness was not a quality Tayen possessed in great order.

As soon as he was close enough, Tayen called out to him. "We've been waiting."

"I see that," Kaylo said. He fed his inner child by slowing his gait. When he finally stood in front of Tayen and her friend, he offered her a full-toothed smile. "Aren't you going to introduce me to your friend?"

"We aren't friends." The young woman's thick, black eyebrows furrowed.

"Do any of us want to be here?" Kaylo asked Tayen.

She rolled her eyes. "This is Vāhn."

"Vāhn, it is a pleasure and a kindness to meet one of Tayen's not-friends," Kaylo said. "I'm Kaylo, and this is Hibiscus, also not a friend. At least, not yet."

The large northman's face remained unmoving as stone.

"Kaylo?" Vāhn asked with wide-eyed disbelief. "Ennea's Thief. Hero of…"

"Yeah, yeah, none of that. Just Kaylo." He looked over the slight woman. From the way her weight settled on her heels to the slump in her shoulders, her lack of fighting prowess could not be easily understated.

"What am I doing here?" Kaylo asked.

"She said cha were gonna train us."

"He is. It's the one thing he's good for," Tayen said.

Tension ran several circuits between the four mismatched people standing on the edge of the training field. Only Hibiscus seemed consistent in his feelings towards the others, his disinterest as steady as his expression.

Kaylo broke away from the standoff and walked to the third tent in the second row, allowing the others to trail behind. It was difficult to gauge which was worse: the seething anger from his toka, the adoration of a young stranger, or the constant knowledge that Hibiscus would cut him down with utter dispassion if ordered.

"Tayen, a fire if you would," Kaylo said.

Despite the cold and the relatively innocuous request, Tayen simply stared at him with disdain.

"You're mad at me. Trust me, you have made your feelings fairly evident," Kaylo said, abandoning his jovial tone. "But you are the one that asked me to meet you here before the seven bastards of The Mist even broke their fast. If I am going to train you, I would prefer that my blood doesn't freeze while I do it."

The two glared at each other for twice as long as uncomfortable before Tayen finally turned and walked towards the firepit.

"I love nurturing young minds," Kaylo said. "You, Vac, why am I here?"

"Vāhn, and we're here because I couldn't sword fight a drunk child to save ma life."

"Why would you want to?" Kaylo asked, then waved off the question. "Never mind that. Start by grabbing us two practice swords from the rack."

Kaylo massaged his palms to keep the blood flowing as he waited for his pupils to finish their assigned tasks. If worse ways to wake up existed, they involved blood and lots of it. Something had to be done to reset the tone of this encounter. As much as he hated the idea of making this training session routine, he needed more time with Tayen.

Finally, firelight danced over the training sands, and the two girls rejoined him at the center of the tent. Hibiscus settled into position near the entrance of the tent rather than his usual position over Kaylo's shoulder.

"Before we begin, let's get things in order. Whatever occurred between the two of you, forget it. Pick it back up on your way out of the tent if you must, but while we are here, you are partners," Kaylo said. He turned to Tayen and met her eyes. "The same goes for what stands between us."

Silence spread over them as Kaylo waited for them both to acknowledge his words. Vāhn nodded first, then Tayen quickly bent her head.

"Good, now take position opposite each other."

The two fighters gripped their swords and took position, with two paces between them. Tayen looked like a statue, body molded into form with her elbows tucked into her sides, hands wrapped in a perfect not-too-tight grip around the hilt of her weapon.

If Tayen emulated a statue, Vāhn would be best compared to a jittery mess of clay. Her grip strangled the wood. Her feet turned at odd angles, and her knees went with them. She stood like someone more afraid of the sword in her own hands than the opponent across from her.

"Have you ever held a sword before the Lost Army?"

"I'm nah a fighter."

"I can tell. Give me your sword," Kaylo said. "Both of you."

"You promised you'd train her."

Kaylo ignored the comment and focused his attention on Vāhn. "You're not strong. You aren't particularly fast. And you're not skilled with a blade."

"And you're an ass," Tayen said.

"Nah, he's right."

"Listen, you won't become the best sword fighter in your regiment— maybe not even as good as most, but you could be the smartest."

"How?"

"We train," Kaylo said. "We train like every opponent you face will be stronger, faster, and more skilled. Despite all of that, you are going to understand the fight better than they do. You are going to read their bodies. You are going to push your opponent into traps. Take advantage of every weakness."

He held out a hand to each student. "That all starts with footwork, so again, give me your weapons."

Vāhn placed her bit of ashburn in his hand without question. Tayen, however, took her time to glare at Kaylo before dropping her practice sword to the sand at his feet.

"Seed and fucking Balance," Kaylo muttered.

He took a deep breath and smiled—becoming far more used to

swallowing his pride than he would care to admit.

"Picture a square below you, as wide as your shoulders. The ball of your left foot will fall on the front left corner of that square, and the ball of your right on the back right corner. Does that make sense?"

Vähn looked at him with the blankness of a clear sky in the second moon of summer.

"Follow me." The sand resisted as he dragged his foot through it. The outline of the square below him was faint, but visible. "Place the ball of your left foot there and the ball of your right foot there. Now, bend your knees. Just enough bend that you could easily push yourself whichever way you want to go." He demonstrated as he spoke.

If the woman had been drowning in water, she would have looked more comfortable. "Tayen, take position opposite Vähn," Kaylo said. "Keep your feet planted and face Tayen. Make sure that your hips are parallel to hers."

Slowly, Kaylo guided Vähn as the two young women moved in circles around the tent. When Tayen stepped back, he prompted Vähn to step forward. They danced as mirror images of one another.

It would have been nice to say that Vähn stepped with more confidence each time they moved or that her body adapted to the movement, but neither was true. Kaylo drew square upon square in the cold sand below her feet. When they finished their training, a quilted pattern of overlapping lines and angles filled the tent.

The problem was not the physical movement, rather what the movement represented. Every step dug Vähn further into conflict. Every turn of her hips embodied another part of a fight she would rather avoid. If her performance hadn't made it clear, the way she ran from the tent at the end of their session did.

Four nights had passed since Nix last saw Sosun. Every time she began to dream, warriors ripped the girl from her mother's arms again as Nix stood by watching. What little sleep she got carried her through the day, but her mind slowed pace. Training mistakes led to bruises. She ate less of the slop served in the mess halls. Any moment of freedom, she patrolled the perimeter of the Citadel, looking for Sosun.

The horizon tilted back and forth ever so slightly as Nix walked between the barracks and storehouses at the base of the mountain. A handful of homes filled in the outer city pathways, most likely belonging to the farmers who tended to the livestock and storehouses.

Nix placed her hand on a wooden home to help balance herself, but her vision wouldn't settle. She took another step, and her foot fell into a divot in the ground. As her ankle rolled, pain jolted up her leg.

"Fucking Mother and her seven bloody twat spirits!" She leaned against the wooden shack of a home, sliding to the ground.

She hadn't eaten since supper the night before, which was thoughtless. Nix had gone without enough times in her life to know that food—even the awful slop they served recruits—shouldn't be turned down.

Her head pounded, and her ankle throbbed. *I'm a fucking mess,* she thought.

Penance never solved a damn thing. It was self-indulgent—starving herself like her pain would make up for the suffering she caused, or at least allowed.

She rolled her ankle back and forth. The joint cracked. She would be fine. Training would be a bastard in a burning building, but no bones broke, no blood spilled.

Maybe if she hopped herself back to the mess, she could get the dregs of the pot. At least it would stop her head from spinning. Might even taste less like warm snot after skipping a few meals. Absences and fondness and all that bullshit.

As Nix pushed herself up, using the wooden house for leverage, a middle-aged Tomakan man turned the corner. He wore in the ragged robes that she had come to know marked him as a servant—the nameless, as the warriors referred to them. Someone had shaved the man's gray hair down to uneven stubble against his brown scalp.

A folded piece of paper shook along with his outstretched bony hand. The cold could have snapped him like a twig.

Another person suffers because I'm not where I'm supposed to be, she thought. *At least, I'm consistent.*

The note read:

Nix *(tall woman, new recruit, mid-thirties, northerner).*

The nameless servant hesitantly met Nix's eyes. Behind the glassy stare of an addict, there was a question in the man's gaze. She nodded. "Yeah, that's me. I'm Nix." He waved for her to follow.

For a shaky skeleton of a man, the servant moved quite quickly through the narrow rows of homes towards the Citadel. Occasionally, he glanced back, but his eyes remained trained on the ground.

"Who sent for me?" Nix called out, to no acknowledgement.

The mountain throne of the Lost Nation loomed large. In all her aimless wandering, she had witnessed a constant flow of people come and go from the Citadel—finely dressed northerners, soldiers, servants, even a few of the local farmers and villagers, but never a recruit.

She patted her hip until she found the lump buried in the fabric. Of course, recruits weren't permitted weapons. So, the rock knotted to the end of a bit of loose fabric that lay tucked away in her belt could get her in trouble. But no one met old age these days without a healthy amount of caution or luck, and based on her current circumstances, Nix had ruled out luck.

The servant handed the entrance guard a note, and she waved them both inside the Citadel with a sneer of disgust, particularly aimed at the servant.

Pathway upon pathway veered off in every direction inside the lavish mountain tunnels. The servant hurried to an unspoken route. If Nix lost this man, she would be stuck in the middle of the Citadel, out of place, with only a rock to defend herself.

When she turned the corner, he stopped in front of a large, dark wooden door, then shrunk into the shadows on the wall.

"Who is in there?" Nix whispered. Still, he didn't answer.

She could either try to find her way out and hope the guards let her leave without a notice of permission, or she could find out who had called for her and why. With one hand, she clutched the handle of her homemade weapon, the rock still tucked away in her belt, and with the other, she knocked.

After a moment, the door peeled open.

"What the fuck do you want?" Nix said.

"The pleasure of your lovely company, of course," Wal said, greasy smile flashing. He stepped back from the door and left it open for her to follow.

The bastard—the tricky fuck who had cracked her in the back of the skull and ordered her conscription in Dasoon—had his sword at his hip and two warriors standing in the middle of his quarters.

To one side of the door sat a table, set with clean cloth napkins covering two plates of food and two wooden cups. Wal walked over, taking a seat on one side of the table and gesturing for Nix to sit across from him.

The smell was the only reason she entertained the idea of eating with the two-faced bastard. Grease and fragrant herbs clung to the air. The very thought of what awaited her under the napkin made her salivate. When she lifted the napkin, she dropped her grip on her homemade weapon.

Crispy brown skin wrapped tightly around a juicy chicken quarter, roasted with figs, chiles, and corn flatbread. Nix couldn't help but close her eyes as the smell wafted up from the plate.

"Sadly, it's not as warm as I would have liked, but I think you'll find it more appetizing than what they serve in the recruit's mess."

"What do you want?"

"I want to talk," Wal said. "It is truly unfortunate that we haven't had the chance to get to know each other. Your commanding officer thinks you have great potential."

"You sure you have enough back-up?" Nix said, nodding towards the warriors standing guard.

"Don't mind them. Please, eat."

It took all of Nix's willpower and a helping hand from her anger not to eat the food in front of her. She sat silently, staring, waiting for a clear answer.

"Fine," Wal said. He switched the plates and took a sip from both cups. "If you are worried about any tricks on my part, I assure you, there are easier ways to kill you."

It occurred to Nix then that her pride and restraining herself from eating wouldn't change a thing. What was the saying? Pissing into the wind only dirtied your boots, or something like that.

The chicken was lukewarm, but that didn't make any difference. Her teeth tore through the bird as easily as a ripe mango. Salty, spicy, with a hint of sweetness at the end. Wal could have thrown the rest of the meat into the snow outside, and she would have been happy to clean the dirt out of her teeth after finishing her meal.

Wal ate at a gingerly pace as Nix ravaged her way through the food. When she had finished everything else on the plate, she snapped the bones and sucked on the marrow before finally downing a large gulp of the barley wine.

"Well, now, don't you feel better," Wal said. "I will admit, I had alternative motives for inviting you to dine with me?"

"That's a fucking surprise."

Wal genuinely laughed. "I like you. In all my runs to and from Dasoon over the last two turns, I don't think we've said more than a handful of words to each other. Had circumstances been different, I think we may have been friends."

"From what I can tell, you're a shit friend."

"If you're referring to my relationship with Kaylo, you're missing quite a bit of context," Wal said, the levity draining from his voice.

"Care to fill me in? I would love to hear how you became the bastard you are today."

"Another time, perhaps. For now, I have a proposal to make," Wal said. "From all accounts, you're a skilled warrior. You might even do well as an officer in the army."

Wal took a long sip from his cup while he stared into Nix's eyes.

"Kaylo is well-known and has a certain set of skills that could make him an integral part of our plans, if he behaves," he said.

"What does that have to do with me?"

"As you said, he and I aren't on the best of terms. I'd like you to keep an eye on him."

She pointed at him with a broken chicken bone in her greasy hand. "And I'd like you to shove a hot poker up your ass."

"As colorful of an image as you present, I'm afraid I must decline," Wal said. "Though I would like you to consider my offer. Life as a recruit can be quite difficult." He picked up the cloth napkin and dabbed the grease from his lips.

"I'll let you ruminate on it," Wal said. "Astile is not your enemy. Why suffer when you could contribute so much more?"

Three knocks rapped against Kaylo's door in a lackluster rhythm. He smiled. If the sound of knuckles on stormwood could communicate angst, Tayen had managed it.

He opened the door, and she stood at an angle with her eyes averted. "Thank you for coming," he said. "Please come in."

"You didn't leave me much choice." She strode past him into his quarters.

Kaylo nodded his thanks to the servant who had brought Tayen to his door, but the northman didn't look up from the ground.

"What is the point of this?" Tayen asked.

"You know exactly what the point is."

"You're trying to convince me vengeance isn't the answer? Here? A little late for that."

Kaylo walked over to the brazier, sitting cross-legged next to the contained fire. A three-pronged stand held aloft a smooth, dark iron basin caged in a cross-stitch pattern of iron weaving. No filagree. It was the least ornate thing in the room, and for that reason, Kaylo had grown fond of it.

Lifting the small door in the cage, he added a few more coals to the fire. The flames stirred and spat ash into the air. A small plume of smoke rose where before there had been a gentle stream. He enjoyed the simplicity of the exchange, ashburn coals for fire and smoke. The brazier didn't offer any answers, but it didn't cause any new problems either.

"When we first struck our deal...I was afraid that you were going to go down the same path I had. I saw you as a chance to make better decisions," he said. Then he turned from the fire to meet her eyes. "That wasn't fair.

"I told you I was going to tell you a story, and you could do with it as you pleased, but that was a lie. I didn't intend it to be, but it was. I wanted to scare you towards the decisions I wanted you to make."

"Look where that got us," Tayen said. The bite in her words was as lackluster as her knock.

"You're right," Kaylo said. "I'm sorry."

The confusion on Tayen's face would have been funny had the moment not been so serious. She stared at him, wide-eyed and lips parted, and he knew how he had wronged her. That she would be surprised by his apology only spoke to his arrogance. He pinched the bridge of his nose and sighed.

"Would you join me? I want to tell you the rest of my story, but this time I want to offer it honestly. When you get older, you want to be known—understood. You want someone to see you, especially when you can't see yourself."

Tayen looked at him, then back to the door.

"I'll train you and Vāhn regardless of your decision, but if you would stay, I would like to tell you my story."

"Only because I have questions. But if you get preachy, I'm done."

The next breath came easier. "I shall do my best to restrain my abundance of wisdom."

Like two waves rising before they crested and crashed into the ocean, Tayen's rolling eyes brought a familiarity to their interaction that had been missing. He didn't fight the curve working its way through his lips before he cleared his throat.

CHAPTER SEVEN
KAYLO'S STORY

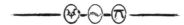

FROM THE MOUTH OF a cave below the peak of the Gentle Dagger, the moons scattered their light over a sea of bare ironoak branches, reaching into the night like needy hands. My home. Tomak. What were we if not a sea of outstretched hands reaching for the light?

My backside started going numb against the lip of the cave as I fiddled with my father's knife. The Missing were hiding somewhere in the forest, yet we had searched for four span. They had been as good as their name. In this much snow, they shouldn't have been able to hide their tracks so well.

Time drained away as we searched. The Priest had murdered my second family, and I stalked around the forest with a bunch of bickering asses hunting for a rumor.

Even in the solitude of this scene, voices crawled over the stone and found their way to me. Whenever the opportunity presented itself, Wal and Adéan nipped at each other like a pair of puppies—no matter the subject.

That none of us had bled one of them out in the middle of the night was a testament to our restraint.

Beneath their quibbling voices, Liara's echo crept closer, her light footsteps ticking against the stone.

"Can't sleep?" I asked, without turning around.

"Do they have to argue every night?"

"I don't know. I might be concerned if Wal wasn't pestering someone. Be glad it isn't you."

As Liara settled next to me, her shoulder brushed against mine. The heat of her body chased the cold away, sending a tingle up my spine that made me shudder.

The moons' light draped over her like flowing fabric. Her onyx skin caught the light with a subtle shine on her cheeks as she smiled. I smiled back, hoping the darkness would mask the redness in my face.

Her hair had grown steadily since we had escaped the mission school. Rows of tight red curls lined her scalp. As much as her locs suited her, they hid the shape of her face. Her strong jawline softened into her high cheekbones and rolled into her full-moon eyes.

When I caught myself staring, I turned my head back to the forest at the base of the mountain. The light touch of winter's wind tickled my neck, making me shudder again.

Liara and I shared far too few moments, so when they came, I shut off the parts of myself that kept guard. The River sang through her as The Seed joined in harmony. Her shoulders moved in rhythm with her breathing, and I felt as free as the wind.

Then my stomach twisted, as it did whenever I allowed myself a reprieve. After what I had done, I didn't deserve this soft joy.

When I closed my eyes, Junera's burned body flashed in front of me, giving me back my dull ache. She lay face down on the ground, her body rising and falling twice before stopping forever.

"Are you cold?" Liara asked. "Just now, your body went...stiff."

I bit my lip to redirect the pain. "What happens if we can't find the Missing?" I asked. "We've been searching too long. We don't even know if they're still here."

"Are you saying that we should give up?"

"I'm saying maybe we don't need them. There are six of us, three of us are dancers."

"So, what? We are going to start our own militia, Kaylo's rebels?"

"Mock all you want," I said, as The Song soured into a harsh melody. "The Gousht owe enough blood to fill all the rivers that run through Ennea."

"Why are you trying to fight with me? You know, I know what the Gousht owe," she said. "Adding our blood to their tally won't help anyone."

"If I die, I plan on taking The Priest with me."

"Great. Kill a descendant of their one true god. They will kill hundreds in retaliation just to prove they can," Liara said. "Don't be short-sighted. Your pride and anger aren't the only things at stake."

"Let them keep the rest of the red-hooded couta. The one that killed Nomi, Soca, and Junera needs to die. And I'll make him suffer before I send him into The Mist. Then the spirits can take their turn. After, I don't care what happens to me."

"Kaylo, it wasn't your fault." She placed her hand on my arm, and I pulled away.

"But it was. Mine and his." I stared into her eyes. She wouldn't change my course.

Several long moments held between us in a chilled silence. The green flecks in the deep brown valleys of her eyes vanished when she got angry. And still her gaze softened my resolve.

Then I closed my eyes to watch Junera die again, stoking my anger.

"Stubbornness isn't strength, and if it gets me or my sister killed, you won't be able to hide from me in The Mist," she said, enunciating each staccato syllable.

"If you want to go, go," I said.

"The others look to you. They need you," she said. "I need you. If you are too angry to be the person we need, tell me and I will take my sister and leave."

At least if she left, I could stop worrying about killing a third family.

She pushed herself up from the lip of the cave, looking down at me. "If there is anything you can trust, trust me when I say I understand. There is a reason I'm out here looking for the Missing. I want to make those green bastards hurt as much as you do. But there is a difference between fighting back and getting yourself killed," she said. "You'll have to forgive yourself, eventually."

"Maybe, but not tonight." I turned back towards the forest as she returned to the others, her footsteps reverberating off the cave walls.

The forest ran slick with fresh snow from the night before. Each step I took crunched into the relative silence of a Tomakan winter. Most of the creatures had taken shelter or migrated south for a gentler version of the season, leaving me the wind and a few strong-willed foragers for company.

I pulled my robes tighter, hoping to keep myself from freezing over like everything else. A brown blur crossed my peripheral vision. *A deer,* I thought. After too long with nothing but fruits and vegetables, the thought of venison made my heart race.

It took every bit of training not to chase after the animal. *Slowness and stillness are your greatest allies when you are hunting.* The phantom cadence of Jonac's words added to the tension in my shoulders.

Reminders of what I had lost slipped into quiet moments like a blade.

The doe stopped, not twenty paces out, as if waiting for me. A soft dusting of snow coated her fur as she bent her neck towards the ground.

Slowness and stillness, I thought.

Snow crunched beneath the first step I took towards my prey, and my heart stopped its rhythm. The doe looked up, craning its neck to and fro. After a moment, she returned her attention to the snow beneath her, and my heart raced to account for the missing beats.

After moons of failing to find the Missing, I needed a small victory.

As shit as I was with a bow, I needed to shorten the gap as much as I could, but a sheet of icy snow glazed over the forest floor. "Blessed Mother, soften my feet," I whispered, as I took another step.

When I got as close as I would dare, I crouched down in the nook of an ironoak and reached to pull my bow off my shoulder, only to find nothing there.

My quiver didn't hang at my hip either.

How the fuck could I have forgotten my bow? I thought, always finding a new way to fail the others.

When I looked up, the doe had vanished. No tracks in the snow where it had been. No tufts of fur or broken branches. Just an unbroken sheet of icy snow.

An overwhelming presence loomed over me like eyes crawling over my skin from every direction. My heart pounded in my chest. Each breath felt like too little, but I had to keep calm. I fought the drive to gasp for air.

A speck of brown disrupted the white-blanketed forest where the doe had been. As I crept forward to see it more clearly, hard lines and sharp edges took form. The snow made no effort to keep the wood as I slid it from the frozen divot.

My breath caught in my chest.

"It is a pleasure to meet someone touched by The One True God." The slow, deep crawl of The Priest's voice came from every direction.

"Where are you?" I screamed.

"Patience young one," The Priest said. "We know what happens when you forget patience."

The presence, like everything else, disappeared, leaving me alone with the carved ironoak rabbit in my hands—slightly burned and splashed with dried blood—then I collapsed into the snow and sobbed.

———

When I opened my eyes, Sionia, Liara, and Adéan stared at me from around the fire. The looks on their faces could have been concern, but I took it for pity.

I rubbed my eyes dry. "What are you looking at?" I said roughly, sleep caught in my throat.

"Are you okay?" Sionia asked.

"No, but what does that matter? We are wondering around the mountains looking for a rumor because we have nowhere else to go. None of us are okay."

"No need ta be tha way. She wa jus askin a quession," Adēan said. Either his accent had settled or my ear had grown more comfortable with it, because I actually understood him the first time he spoke.

"Well, it was a stupid *quession*."

Adēan jumped to his feet, looking down at me where I sat. What he lacked in height—and he wasn't short—he made up for several-fold in his broad form. His shoulders and chest swelled and receded with each breath. "Whadid cha say ta me?"

As I thrust myself from the floor, a thin layer of dirt and dust kicked up. Height, I had on him, but I had no illusions that I could win hand-to-hand. A twig might as well challenge a foot to a fight. If he stepped on me wrong, I could have mildly irritated him.

I had no wish to fight. More accurately, I had no wish to defend myself as Adēan pummeled me.

Time trickled away as his brown eyes held as steady as the rock under our feet, neither of us moving. The tension slacked until standing so close together, staring at each other became uncomfortable.

"Wal, get your things. We're going hunting," I said, attempting to maintain my bravado.

Wal hadn't gotten up from the comfort of his bedroll on the other side of the fire. "Okay," he said in a long groan.

No one said anything else as I gathered my knife and bow.

It had taken me two span to carve a bow from a branch of ironoak. It lacked the craft of my father's work, and the wood made for a shitty weapon, too stiff and easy to break, but it felt good to have something powerful in my hands.

With all three arrows I had carved in my left hand and my bow settled over my right shoulder, I walked out of the cave and down the sloping rocks to the forest without saying a word. Wal's scrambled footsteps followed after me.

The cold morning air ran through me like water through a riverbank. Not a single track marred the perfect plane of white snow stretched over the forest floor. It had been two span since I had come across a pair of squirrels outside of their cozy nook. The land appeared as barren as it had in my dream. The wood bit back against my dry skin as I squeezed the arrows in my hand to make sure they hadn't disappeared.

Even if there had been game to hunt, Wal's uncoordinated steps crunched through the snow loud enough to scare it off. Though, to his credit, he didn't say a word. Not this time.

A child in a city as big as Nomar could make it to their swearing day without ever needing to hunt. And the mission school had done little to improve Wal's self-sufficiency. I tried to teach him what I could, but my patience didn't lend itself to teaching.

The underbrush stirred, not twenty paces ahead of us. I tried to focus on the thought of greasy meat turning over the fire—the fire flaring as oils dripped from the animal into the flame. But all I could think about was The Priest.

His voice grumbled in my head, "A pleasure to meet someone touched by The One True God."

I closed my eyes and gripped my bow until the wood etched into my skin. *He's not here,* I told myself. *It was a dream.*

While I notched an arrow. Wal crouched beside me. Of course, it wasn't The Priest in the brush, it was a meal.

Hunting demanded time, the slow ebb of waiting. I did as my father had taught me and split my mind from my spirit. My physical being stayed behind, feeling and observing everything. He understood the difference between a branch shifting in the wind and an animal pushing its way through the brush. He knew how to wait until the right moment to draw back the string and loose the arrow.

As my mind focused, my spirit escaped into an endless ocean of possibilities—what had been and what had yet to come.

My father had been the first one to take me out into the forest. He insisted that I join him as he hunted for our dinner to understand where our food came from.

The forest had been empty and still. My young mind full of questions. The Song walked with me, and I wanted to know everything about the trees and the plants. My father listened, answering my questions as best he could, not caring that I scared all the animals off.

As he sat on the forest floor with his back against a tree, we talked. His easy baritone strummed a melody in my head. I couldn't remember his words, only the gentle thrums of his cadence.

Eventually, I ran out of questions, and he picked up his bow. When he caught a rabbit in the hindquarters with an arrow, he had me watch as he finished the kill with his knife. "The food we eat had a life," he had said. "When we usher it into The Mist, we should try to make it a quick death. Every creature deserves that respect."

As I processed his words, he studied me with his umber eyes, as if trying to figure out who his son would become. His gray curls formed a tight crown atop his head. He preferred to keep his hair short, much to my mother's dismay. Long hair got in the way of his wood and metal work. Even in that moment, as serious as he had been, his expression bore a gentle kindness.

The branches of the bush flickered. My mind awakened as I drew back the notched arrow and let it loose, pinning the squirrel to the ground.

The small creature twitched in its last throes of life. Quickly, but gently, crouching next to the dying animal, I finished the kill with my father's blade.

"Blessed Mother, accept this creature's spirit into The Mist. May it find a home in your ever-present embrace." I placed three fingers to my lips before touching them to the ground.

"A whole squirrel. If we split that between the six of us, we can each have a bite."

"Don't disrespect its sacrifice," I said firmly.

"Sacrifice? Did you have a good talk with it before you speared it with an arrow? Was it honored to be your lunch?"

I closed the gap between us until I was nose to nose with Wal. He was nearly my height, the same warm-brown complexion, wearing the same long gray braids. We could have been brothers. For all of that, I could only see the antagonistic, quippy asshole in front of me.

While we stood there staring blades at each other, a high noise cut through me.

An echo whistled through the air, then engulfed me. As I turned towards the sound's origin, the ground froze under our boots. Wal grasped my arm as he lost his balance, bringing both of us crashing down on to a thick sheet of ice.

The River, I thought, as I searched the forest for green and yellow, still prone on the ground.

The echo receded. I couldn't see anything.

"What in the name of The Blessed Mother was that?" Wal shouted, shoving my shoulder.

"It wasn't me, you twit. Get off of me."

Three new echoes rose into the sky to join the first, which had again filled the air with its sharp pitch. The echoes came from several directions.

"Gousht?" Wal asked, his voice suddenly small and scared.

"I'd assume so," I said, pushing myself to a fighting stance.

"Steal their spirits."

"Shut it and grab your knife."

Everything slowed except for my heartbeat. I dug my heel into the slick ice to anchor myself. Wal found his feet, imitating me and planting his back to mine. I raised my bow and notched a new arrow, scanning the forest for any signs of movement.

One of the four echoes surged past the others—low and quick, a furious clatter, gluttonous rhythms consuming the silence. To my right, a bright red crystal glowed in the shade of the forest, then fire crawled along the ground, melting the snow in its wake. The flames crept from one tree to another, encircling us in a white-hot cage. Whoever wielded the crystal knew how to command the spirit trapped within.

"Kaylo!" Wal shouted, fear singeing the edges of his voice.

The corner of my lip raised at the thought of killing the green fuck hiding in the forest. As I shifted my bow and arrow to one hand, I reached out with the other to grab The Flame spirit from the sky. The familiar rage and torment filled my insides as the spirit clashed against their new prison.

The image of the soldier's confused face flickered in my mind, and it helped to salve the pain of the stolen spirit.

With a quick gesture of my free arm, I pulled on The Flame's echo, smothering the fire.

The invaders didn't wait for another demonstration. The crescendo of a second echo crashed into a third. Heavy torrents of wind shook the trees before crashing into Wal and me from two different directions.

Wal's head cracked into mine as the two currents lifted us from the frozen ground and spun us like a pair of winged seeds falling from a maple tree. My bow clattered onto the ice moments before I did, and the world continued to churn even after I came to a stop.

Then it all halted.

The tormented spirit in my gut fed my anger as I reached up to steal the second spirit from the air.

My muscles all contracted at once. I wanted to retch. I wanted to tear my flesh apart to free the spirits. Instead, I found my anger under the fresh layers of pain and took solace in the blood that was to come.

As I stood, I turned around, making sure they all had a chance to see me. They might as well know who would kill them. "Is that all?" I yelled. My fingers felt for the leather hilt of my father's knife, and I slipped it from its sheath. "Our spirits will not serve you, you couta fucks!"

Steps rustled through the silence. Black and brown faces peered out of the forest in confusion. *Blood banners,* I thought and gripped my knife even tighter. *They will do.*

"What are you?" a Sonacoan boy asked softly. His hair was brushed into red waves crashing atop his dark umber skin. He might have been ten—twelve turns at most. A long, thin sword hung from his hip, but he stood upright and unprepared, staring at me in wonder.

"A spirit thief," said a deeper, older voice.

To my left, a northman stood. He looked the image of a warrior, but smiled like a friend. His head was shaved down to the grain. The hard leather vest atop his robes clung to him like a second skin, showing all the definition of his well-muscled form. The leather extended over the shoulder of his right arm—his sword arm—and the hilt of his sheathed blade crested over his shoulder. All of his teeth were showing.

Whether he wanted to kill me or greet me, he appeared to enjoy the prospect.

The northman raised his hand and flicked his wrist. The children receded into the forest at the gesture, except for the small Sonacoan boy. It took a repeated gesture and a long stare to force him off.

The Flame and The Wind still stormed within me. Even with Wal beside me, this warrior could kill us both without losing his smile.

Without a word, the northman walked several paces back, sitting down at the base of a large elm tree. He waited and watched as Wal and I measured him. Half of his turns were past him, but he still carried himself as a young man. A scar cracked through his forehead, just over his left eyebrow.

Wal looked at me as if I knew what to do next, so I did what came naturally. I asked questions.

"Why did you attack us?"

"You were trespassing in our forest."

"Your forest?"

"This half of the Kenke. Everything from The Gentle Dagger to the Sanine River."

"A forest doesn't belong to anyone."

"Tell that to the Gousht," the northman said. "Besides, my warriors and I weren't trying to attack you at first. We were trying to contain you. Your little trick scared them a bit, and they don't have the best impulse control."

"Your warriors? Your land? Who in the name of the seven fucking spirits are you?" Wal said, apparently comfortable enough to contribute.

"A mouth on you, huh?" the northman said. "You are right, though. It is well past time for introductions. I am Zusa, third regiment-commander of the Missing. I would stand to greet you, but I'm under the impression that you might be more comfortable if I stay where I am for the time being."

"The Mother's tits you are," Wal said.

"You blaspheme a lot, don't you?"

"He's lying, Kaylo. Why would a commander of the Missing be running around with four brats carrying spirit crystals? Where are the rest of them? Where are the other adults? This guy's a wet nurse with a sword."

Children with spirit crystals wasn't exactly what I had imagined we would find.

"Can you explain why you're the only one that is bigger than their sword?" I asked.

"I don't know what you expected, but most of Ennea's warriors died in the invasion. Those who didn't were sent to the mines. If you lined up the continent from youngest to oldest, there would be a big fucking gap in the middle. The Missing take in those who can fight, whether or not they are old as they should be," Zusa said, the smile fallen from his lips. "As for the crystals, we will fight the enemy with whatever resources we find. War has no place for morals."

"The war is over," I said. "We lost."

The corner of Zusa's mouth tilted into a smirk. "Then we ought to start another, don't you think?"

CHAPTER EIGHT

KAYLO'S STORY

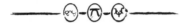

SOKAN HUNG TWO FINGERS from the horizon by the time we reached the base of the mountain. Wal complained the whole way back. Although I didn't join his self-pitying rant, my spirit agreed with the sentiment. It had been a long day of hunting, made even longer by an ambush and the subsequent interrogation.

The sight of the climb up to our cave—no matter how short or easy a slope—sent a spasm through my back. Every muscle from my shoulders to my calves clenched. And still, with the weight of a dead squirrel hanging from my belt, I urged my legs forward.

Both Adēan and Sionia stood watch at the entrance to the cave. The relief that flooded their faces was strangely heartwarming. But relief soured to anxiety as Adēan's eyes shifted back into the darkness of the cave.

"Where ave cha been?"

"We found them," I said. "We found the Missing."

"Well, they found us," Wal said.

"That's amazing!" Sionia said with a bright smile, which I couldn't help but return.

"Yah, tis, but don be too excited. If cha wan ta see tem again, cha gotta survive tonight."

The sisters sat as silhouettes in front of the fire. Liara's larger presence loomed over her sister as she stared towards the cave entrance. Though the shadows masked her face, I knew she didn't look relieved.

With a heavy sigh and heavier feet, I walked towards the fire and the darkness peeled away from the sisters' faces. Tomi simply looked at us before turning back to the fire. Liara didn't move.

"I know you're angry, but..."

"Oh, you know. You know how I pictured finding your bodies in the snow? You know how scared I was that whatever bastards got to you would find us next? You know that..."

"I love these examples, but we have really great news to tell you," Wal said.

In one fluid motion, quicker than any rapids flowing through the countryside, Liara stepped forward with an extended hand and smacked Wal upside his sizeable head. The resulting sound broke through her boisterous echo, filling the cave.

Wal looked up; his right ear redder than the sunset. His mouth hung wide open, but no words came. He blinked, and his breath tightened into a hissing noise.

"Fuck your news," Liara said, enunciating her words in quiet, staccato syllables.

When she looked at me, I did the only thing I could. "I'm sorry we scared you," I said. "I shouldn't have left the way I did. It was childish and selfish." I met the fullness of her brown eyes—flickering in the firelight—and I held them in mine.

She took a long breath, and the green flecks in her eyes shined through the anger. "You're right, it was childish, and selfish, and blockheaded. And if you do it again, I am walking off and finding somewhere safer for me and my sister."

"Wait, you aren't going to hit him?" Wal said.

I stepped in front of him before she could smack him again. "Wal was right about one thing," I said. "We have good news."

"If your news is that you caught a squirrel, I'm going to hit you harder than I hit him."

As Wal and I recounted our interaction with the Missing, the group gathered around the fire. Whether out of stubbornness or trepidation, Liara sat still as a rock as she listened, hiding her thoughts behind a stoic expression. If she opposed meeting with the Missing, the others might as well.

Sionia and Adéan leaned forward as I described the ring of fire that had raced around us like the walls of a prison. I told the story like my mother would have, embellishing the right moments and pausing for effect. If I peppered in too much hyperbole, I did so out of a sense of self-preservation.

"The Flame screamed as the fires raged around us. I reached out," I said, reenacting the gesture, "and stole The Song from the air, and the fire stilled."

As I heard my own words, the cave walls closed in around me until only my heartbeat and the stone remained. Since when had I become so free with talk of The Thief and echoes? They all knew what I was, but that didn't mean we openly discussed it. One didn't speak about the malitu living in their skin.

I slipped my knife into the squirrel's joint, separating it with a loud pop that broke the tension as I severed one of the hind legs from its torso.

"They use spirit crystals?" Liara asked with a thin layer of disapproval.

"Why wouldn't they? Killing couta with their own weapons sounds like justice to me," Tomi said.

"You've said it yourself, Kaylo," Liara said. "Those spirits in the crystals are being tortured."

"None of us trapped them in there, and none of us can get them out," Tomi said. "And tell me, why are you worried about the spirits that let this all happen in the first place?"

"The Thief let this happen, not The River," Liara said before she caught herself, and her stern demeanor slipped.

And there, as inevitable as the rising sun, came their pity.

None of them could understand. No matter what words I might use—I hated The Thief more than they ever could. Yes, she had betrayed us all, but I carried a part of that traitor in my spirit. And I would until the day I died.

"The Missing aren't who we imagined," I said. "They use spirit crystals, and the 'warriors' we met were children, but their commander seems to know what he's doing."

"We're just supposed to follow him because he *seems* to know what he's doing?" Wal said.

"Tat's wha we came out here fa," Adéan said. "Did cha expeck an army? Ta army's dead, boy. Ta Missin is wha we got."

"If they kill couta, they are good with me." The firelight fluttered across the scowl etched into Tomi's face.

"What do you think, Sionia?" I asked.

The soft-spoken Sonacoan girl looked up from her lap and met my eyes. "I'm not the one who spoke with them," she said. "And I didn't come out here because of the Missing. I came because I trust you. What do you think?"

My pulse thumped under my jaw like it would rattle the bone from its socket.

As they waited for my answer, firelight contorted the shadows along each of their faces. Somehow, without trying, I had convinced these people I had answers or some deeper understanding beyond my anger.

Why? I thought. *Why me?*

The responsibility stood too tall. I couldn't see beyond its presence, and I never asked anyone to follow my lead. At least the Commander of the Missing had a title. Maybe he had a plan too. Maybe he could be what I couldn't. Then I could be free to claim the blood I owed for the wrongs I had done.

The squirrel's last joint popped under my knife before I added the meat to the water. "I think Adêan is right. We came here for a reason. Let's see what the Missing have to offer."

───────

As I sat on the lip of the cave, taking the first watch, questions filled my head. With complete disregard for my exhaustion, they came like water dripping into an empty pot—one becoming hundreds, then thousands, then thousands of thousands, each eventually indistinguishable from the last.

From this vantage point, the forest was as it should have been. An occasional gust of wind blew over the trees. An owl hooted into the night. Kana waxed and Toka waned in the sky. Yet, somewhere in the peaceful forest, a band of militia waged their quiet war.

If I made the wrong decision, I could be damning five more lives. If Zusa led us to our deaths, it would be my fault.

I closed my eyes, and The Priest waited for me; his red-veiled face surrounded by darkness.

In a strange way, Zusa reminded me of The Priest. Neither recoiled nor hesitated when they discovered what I was. The Thief intrigued them. They appraised me like a weapon, to be honed and wielded. Zusa tried to hide it, but the tone of his voice betrayed his ambition.

And so what?

If Zusa wanted to use me and The Thief, fine. I could be his weapon as long as he pointed me in the right direction. Maybe it took a man of ambition to cut another down. Blood for blood. No sacrifice too large.

My mother's book sat on the cold stone beside me. The blue fabric I kept wrapped around the book had grown patchy with faded white spots. After we left the Jani, I had started reading little bits of my mother's writing.

As I opened the book and flipped to the last page, the leather binding creaked. The first time I had opened the book, I had cried too much to read anything through the tears. The second time, I had scrawled the names of my mother, my father, Shay, Nomi, Soca, and Junera on the last blank page with a coal from the fire.

My well-deserved pain helped me to focus.

When I finally explored the book, I realized it was more of a research journal—my mother's notes for a book that would never be. She had explored the truth behind Ennean stories. Some pages outlined ideas she wanted to develop more. Others contained essays on the historical significance of one story or another. While, between the pages, she stuffed loose scraps of paper full of notes, new thoughts and perspectives on older writings, and questions—so many questions.

As The Waking and The Mist continued their endless dance, my mother's writing helped me step apart from it, if only for the length of a page.

I grew up hearing her tell most of the stories in her book. But each story she wrote down had at least one deviation from the version she had told me; some meaningless, others changing the story completely.

She would always say, "We are our stories," and apparently, she wanted to root out the truth behind who we were.

The pages fanned out under my thumb, coming to rest at a natural stopping point. In the crease of the opened pages, a piece of folded-up paper waited. Small notes like this lay scattered throughout the pages, but most were scraps of paper barely large enough to contain my mother's thoughts. Whereas this note claimed a full piece of paper, folded neatly.

My breath paused with anticipation. Every word of her writing mattered more to me than anything else in my small world, but I cherished the scraps of unbound paper the most. They read more like her voice—like she had simply spoken, and the ink had appeared on the paper.

She wrote one word at the top of the unfolded note, underlining it three times with a question mark beside it. I smiled at the rushed and messy writing. When she got excited, her penmanship vanished.

<u>Sinkara ?</u>

I hate the Gousht a little more with every half-burned
book I am able to get my hands on. How many stories are ash
because these assholes have a childish need to burn things that
they disagree with? The vast majority of the text from this latest
find is completely destroyed, but I found something interesting.

At first, I thought it was nothing. Everyone knows the story
of Sinkara. And all evidence points to it being based on real
events, though how well those events have withstood the test of
time is up for question.

This version starts out like all the others. A group of ever-
growing numbers laid siege to village after village in what were
contested lands between Tomak and Sonacoa. Their leader was,
by all accounts, a young woman who offered to fight for control
of each village in single-combat. Depending on the source,
by the time she died, she had between eight to twelve villages
under her rule.

The thing that is different about this version is that the
leader of the conquering army was given a name. She is
always referred to as The Thief, the deceiver, or some other
villainous term. But in this story, the people call her Aniki—a
pre-common tongue dialect word which translates roughly as
liberator.

Of course, this is only one version. The person who wrote it
may have had some bias. But I find it strange that none of the
other stories mention her name. What would happen if those
other versions were wrong about her?

As I read the note, a strange harmony of voices gathered in my head. My mother's voice clashed with Nomi's as they told the story of Sinkara.

For a long while, I stared at my mother's words. Reread them several times. A spirit thief, a liberator? If The Thief were a liberator, then why did my mother die? Why wasn't Nomi sitting by the fire telling her children stories? Why would she give The Priest the weapon he used to burn Junera and Soca to death?

Whatever story my mother had uncovered had to be a poor translation. Maybe the woman who had written the diary had bad handwriting. If spirit thieves acted anything like The Thief, we weren't worth the ink my mother soaked into the paper.

Some things are exactly as they seem, I thought. *I lost two families to The Thief. Some half-burned story can't redeem her.*

A lodestone stood in the crooks of a bend in the Sanine River directly east of the Gentle Dagger. If we had any intentions of joining the Missing and their rebellion, we were to meet Zusa at the stone the third dawn after we parted. He made it clear—we would not find them again.

With two full days of walking to the river, we left as soon as Sokan broke through the mouth of the cave, marking the first dawn.

After more than two span of gray skies, the First Daughter pierced through the cloudless day like a gift from The Mother herself. It had to be a sign. Maybe, for once, I had made the right decision.

Though the more I contemplated, the more doubts formed.

The Song and echoes chased after each other through the forest. Their persistent call grew louder as I lowered my barriers. If any spirits apart from Liara's or Tomi's sang out, I needed to be ready.

A strange man leading a group of child soldiers had claimed to be a leader of the last rebellion, and we had decided to take his word. Or rather, I had, and the others followed. We left behind what little shelter we had to trudge into the winter, hoping a rumor could be real.

Wal clung to my side, as he had grown accustomed to. He occasionally broke through the silence with stilted conversation, but each time, the silence settled again.

For all the tension between Liara and me, I wished she would walk beside me the way we used to walk the perimeter of the Jani encampment, talking about everything. I would make some silly comment, and she would stare me down from the sides of her eyes until we both broke into laughter. Our conversation had been as easy as the night sky. It just was. No need to question it.

That all changed after we escaped the mission school. As distance grew between us, Tomi had filled a gap in her sister's life—the space where I had once fit. They shared laughter and small confidences. They walked side-by-side. What had I thought would happen when she got her sister back?

"Kaylo." Wal shook my shoulder and waited wide-eyed.

"What?"

"What do you think?"

"About what?" My annoyance seeped into my tone.

"Do you think I'll be able to pick which spirit crystal I get? I mean, no offense, but The Seed isn't the best weapon," Wal said. "Now, The Mountain. I could do some damage with The Mountain. Everyone's first thought is The Flame, but if you control the ground, that's it."

"What are you even talking about?"

"It might not seem like a big deal to you, but some of us were born bound," he said. "You don't think that it's hard to watch you dancers play with the spirits? For once, I could know what it feels like to touch one of The Great Spirits."

"It's not the same. The spirits in those crystals are filled with rage and hatred."

"So am I." All amusement and levity vanished from his voice.

His sarcasm usually made it difficult to take Wal seriously, but he had lost family too. He had as much blood to balance as I did.

"I know, Wal." I offered him a small smile. "Let's get there first. Then we can figure out exactly how we are going to hurt the green bastards."

He returned my smile and nodded. We walked in silence for a good while after that—the voices of the other four drifting over us as we imagined our revenge.

The Song rang out as a series of small pings and chimes that, on their own, would be insignificant, but together, created a polyphony that swept me up. I shifted my stance, bent my knees, and flicked my wrists over the soil, as if beckoning a small child. Two thick tendrils pushed through the soil and grew. Bark formed, and each tree divided, jutting out in sturdy branches, until two adult ironoaks loomed over us.

I smiled at the new lives and ran my hand over the bark of the nearest tree. Everything Jonac had told me about giving into The Song had become true. Since I had allowed myself to open up, dancing had become my nature, and The Seed kept us safe.

We hung the few blankets we had over the low branches to create a makeshift tent. It didn't stop the cold, but it trapped the heat from our bodies and our small fire. The cave had been far more comfortable, but we made due.

No one was interested in another helping of vegetable soup. A combination of nerves and exhaustion eclipsed my hunger, but we needed to eat. I pulled potatoes from the ground and sat them to roast in the coals of the fire. Then, for good measure, I coaxed a blackberry bush from the soil.

As our meager supper cooked, I rested against one of the ironoaks and ran my knife over a fallen branch, stripping away one thin layer after another until nothing remained but wood shavings. The fire stirred as I threw them into the flames, then I grabbed another length of wood and repeated the process.

Liara walked over to me, hunched down to avoid the low hang of the makeshift tent. When she placed a hand on my shoulder, the soft heat of her body spread from her touch. My knife jumped a cut as I tried not to react.

"We should talk," she said before walking out into the night.

After such a long day, the thought of leaving the relative heat of the tent was about as enticing as another fight with Liara, but I couldn't leave her waiting. I managed to groan my annoyance as I followed her out of the tent.

She stood there with her arms crossed and her breath forming small clouds of vapor in the night. "Liara, I don't need another lecture..."

"I want to apologize," she said.

"What?" I looked back to the tent, but no one else was there to hear her words. "What for?"

"That night, after the Shunanlah festival..."

"You already apologized for that," I said. "Can we get back to the fire?"

"I forced you to come with me to the mission school." Moonlight glinted off the tears in her eyes. "When you said you wanted to come, I told myself I believed you, but I made you go."

"That's not how it happened."

"Maybe if I hadn't forced you—fuck, if I hadn't gotten myself in trouble with the guards, maybe they would still be alive."

I stepped forward to close the gap between us. "You can't do that to yourself."

"Why?" She rubbed her sleeve over her cheek to catch her tears. "You do."

"That's different."

"Because you're a thief?"

"Yes," I said, far louder than I had intended to. "I told you what she did. The Thief is the reason The Gousht won the war. She is the reason the dancers couldn't drive them away. And she is a part of me."

"When are you going to stop defining yourself by what others do?"

My lips turned up in a broken smile as tears ran down my face. "Fine, let's stick to what I've done. I let the Gousht kill my friend. I left my parents to die. I led The Priest to the Jani. And I couldn't stop him from killing Nomi, Junera, and Soca."

I bit my bottom lip, and the pain felt right. "That's why, whatever I have to do, I am going to join the Missing. I'll be the malitu I always worried I would become, and I will unleash all the evil in my bones on the Gousht."

"It won't bring them back."

"No, it won't." I reached out my hand to brush away a tear from her cheek. "But maybe I can keep the couta from doing it again."

CHAPTER NINE
KAYLO'S STORY

A SOFT GLOW FELL over the lodestone, its shiny black surface reflecting the purple-red dawn.

It stood exactly where Zusa had said—an obelisk-shaped stone protruded from the earth at the peak of the river's bend. Its perfection defied nature's chaos, either wrought by a dancer or The Mountain herself.

I had never considered the oddity of the lodestone on the outskirts of Nomar. It had been there my entire childhood. Shay and I had played on the stone, snapping metal against the magnetic surface. But our squat stone lacked the flair of the obelisk. I had dismissed its smooth, even faces as minor miracles of nature.

Adēan brought his belt knife close to the stone. The metal jerked forward and collided with the surface, creating a high-pitched *tink*. The northboy smiled and pulled his knife against the stone's attraction.

"Quite a magical ting, huh?"

"The nomads called them up," a voice said from behind us.

As I spun around, Zusa stood there with his arms crossed over his chest. The Sonacoan boy, with red waves of curls spiraling around his head, mimicked Zusa's posture. "Before the Conclave—before they named themselves Jani, the earth dancers amongst them called up the lodestones all over the continent, marking safe meeting places."

Zusa strode over to the stone, pulled out his sword and allowed the lodestone to take it from him. "During the Great War, nomads would meet with leaders from different nations. They would all give their weapons to the stone. Then they could speak freely. Of course, it's mostly ceremonial. Anyone could carry extra weapons, but I still think the symbolism matters."

"The Jani struck peace at the Conclave, not in small meetings all over Ennea," Tomi said.

"Young one, peace is a much slower process than war. It took time and sacrifice to convince the four nations to meet. Time and sacrifice."

"We didn't come here for a history lesson, old man," Wal said, safely behind Adēan and me.

The boy with Zusa stepped forward and spat on the ground. Only one or two paces separated us from the boy. One hand found the crystal hanging from his belt and the other found a sword.

"Now Boda, we don't start violence near the lodestone," Zusa said before he looked over my shoulder to Wal. "But we will not refrain from answering like with like."

As I slid my knife from its sheath, Boda's eyes followed me like a hawk. Slowly, I moved the blade towards the stone, giving it to the magnetic pull.

"Wal, place your knife on the stone," I said.

"That's ridiculous. None of us are nomads here."

The red hue of The Flame spurred under the clear surface of Boda's crystal, and the echo of the jailed spirit flared. If I had to steal the spirit, I would be ready, but the thought alone made my abdomen constrict.

I took a step towards my knife.

Liara smacked Wal on the back of his head. "Give me the blade."

"But he..." Wal started, pointing at Boda.

"Him? He's what, twelve turns old?" Liara asked, sounding every bit the mother of our small band.

"Thirteen!" Boda shouted.

Liara sighed as she held out her hand. "Give me the knife," she said. And just like that, the rest of our small band added their blades to the lodestone's collection.

Zusa knelt, and his companion followed in turn. They waited and watched until we did the same—two small groups kneeling on opposing sides of an invisible line.

"Can I take your presence to mean that you would like to join our cause?" Zusa asked.

"How do we know you are who you claim to be?" Liara's tone betrayed her impassive expression. She liked him even less than before she had met him.

"What else would we be?"

"That's not reassuring," Tomi said.

"Sister, right?" Zusa asked with a smile. "Family is important. You're lucky to have each other. Me, I have my regiment." He locked eyes with me. "Family knows, right?"

"You didn't answer my question," Liara said, rallying control over the hostility in her voice and straightening her back. She never responded well to threats, veiled or not, leveled at her family. And still, her demeanor carried the poise of an elder. "How many are in your regiment? How many regiments are in the Missing? What is the plan to reclaim our home?"

"We don't have to answer your damn questions," Boda said.

Zusa placed a hand on the back of the boy's neck and squeezed, making the boy wince. "What Boda means to say is, we don't tell every stranger the intricate workings of the militia. It wouldn't be a sound strategy."

"Then we are at an impasse because we don't trust strangers with our lives," Liara said.

Irritation and respect combined in a smile on the older warrior's face.

"What I can tell you is that the Missing has regiments spread all over the continent. Our numbers are too small for warfare—in a traditional sense. We do what we can to thin their numbers and strip the Gousht of their power."

"The crystals," I blurted out.

Zusa gave a non-committal nod. "We live like nomads and fight like thieves. Their confidence and comfort are our strength."

As he stared at me, his eyes betrayed his façade of indifference. He wore the look of a man measuring a new blade, weighing the hilt and testing the tempered metal.

"And if we want to leave?" Tomi asked.

"Leave Kenke Forest now. No one will stop you. But if you join our regiment, there is no leaving. Our militia has survived because we are a rumor. Our regiments are small, our missions are precise," Zusa said. "If the Empire knew the strength of our network, they wouldn't rest until they killed the last of us."

He took a breath as if to pause for effect. "No, if you join us, you don't get to leave."

"I believe we need a moment to speak amongst ourselves," I said.

Zusa waved his hand in an offering gesture. "Take the time you need."

We collected ourselves as close to the river as possible, which only gave us twenty paces of separation. The Commander's eyes followed me as if I were prey.

"Let's leave now," Wal said.

"Wha did we come here fa, if we jus leave now?" Adéan asked. "Before I even knew ch'all, I was lookin fa ta Missin. I have blood ta settle."

"We all made sacrifices to be here," Liara said. "I can't believe it, but I agree with Wal. The Missing were supposed to be the answer, but the rumors are bigger than they are. So far, we know there are at least five of them, four of whom are young enough to remember the taste of their mother's milk."

"Zusa seems to be telling the truth," I said. "If we leave now, we are on our own. We have our bedrolls, a few knives, and a bow. Between us, we might have enough experience with a blade for one adequate fighter."

"Then, we hide. We practice," Liara said.

"Four span have already passed!" I bit my tongue to stop the words that wanted to follow. Liara didn't deserve my anger, but I had nothing else to give her. "Soca was six. Junera was FIVE TURNS OLD!"

"We all know how old they were," Tomi said.

At her dismissive words, the full locus of my anger found a new home. The Song rumbled loud enough to drown out my better judgement. If she thought that her anger could match mine, she was mistaken.

Sionia stepped next to me, placing a hand on my shoulder. "No one here is the enemy. We are only trying to decide if we can trust Zusa."

"I don't have the luxury of trust," I said, far too harshly. "Every one of the kids who ambushed us yesterday knew how to wield their crystals better than most couta. They each had swords—odds are they knew how to use them too. They moved as a unit. Yes, they were young, but they were more prepared than we are.

"I don't care if he's telling the truth. I don't care if they call themselves the Missing or any other stupid fucking name. All I care about is paying blood owed," I said. "Zusa can help me do that. With or without any of you."

Sokan peered over the trees and filled the riverbank. The babbling water and a steady breeze rounded out the picturesque scene, in deep contrast to the hostility hanging between us. Liara's and Tomi's echoes intermittently pierced through The Song, but they were whispers compared to my screaming rage. The heat of it ran through my veins.

Auntie Munnie's voice fluttered through the noise. "Wrath is a powerful thing, but so is a tornado. In my experience, both tend to cause aimless damage."

For all her wisdom and twisted sayings, she never mentioned how good it would feel to give into my anger. The relief would be like a salve on an open wound.

When what remained of the Fallen Rock Clan exiled me, I was prepared to leave the others. If I had to, I would leave them now. It would hurt, but I could bury that next to the rest of my grief.

As if she knew my thoughts, Sionia broke the silence. "Lodestones are safe ground and they are waypoints. We have to be that for each other because, no matter what we choose, fate will test us." She looked at me and her calm breached the storm of my anger. "Kaylo, you will need a safe place—somewhere to turn when hatred isn't enough. Whatever Zusa can offer you, he doesn't care about you. For people like him, the cause will always be greater than the people who fight it."

I looked at her as if for the first time. The bridge of her nose flowed into her full cheeks, that dimpled when she smiled. She carried an age beyond her turns in her chestnut eyes. No wonder I heard Munnie's voice in my head. Her matching spirit stood in front of me, younger, but just as full of kindness and grace.

Liara nodded, and I followed suit.

"So that's it? The quiet one says some pretty words, and it's all decided?" Wal asked.

"Fa once, shut it, Wal," Adéan said. "We move forward togeta."

Nothing about our chaotic, intertwined relationships made sense. But the pieces didn't have to fit. Every single one of us had blood to settle.

I broke from the group first, prying my father's knife from the lodestone. Boda reached for his imprisoned shard of The Flame. The echo screamed just beyond my reach, but if he pulled on the spirit, it would be mine in an instant.

"Calm down, kid," I said as I sheathed my blade.

Zusa placed his hand on the boy's shoulder and squeezed. "You made your decision, then?"

"We came here looking for you," Liara said. "Don't disappoint us."

The others began collecting their blades from the stone as Zusa and Liara stared each other down. Zusa's smile ran wide, then he nodded and brought a small length of wood to his lips.

Three short whistles pierced the air before the brush rustled and three young warriors emerged from their hiding places along the tree line. As they settled their bows over their shoulders, they fell into line beside Zusa and Boda. Their age took nothing away from their disciplined movement.

"They were there the whole time?" Wal shouted.

"We have a long walk ahead of us before we make camp." Zusa walked forward to collect his sword from the stone. "You made the right decision."

Although he spoke to all of us, his eyes lingered on me. Then he turned on his heels and walked off into the forest without another word.

"Are you sure about this?" Wal asked. The combat and mischief abandoned his eyes and left him small.

"I'm not sure about anything, except that this path will bring us blood." I clapped him on the shoulder, then broke through the tree line.

The small regiment of freedom fighters fell into formation behind us. A single echo walked with them—The Flame crystal hanging off Boda's belt. They had all carried crystals two days prior. This northman knew something about thieves.

He knew something about power as well.

The Commander could have ordered his archers to sneak away unseen. The show by the lodestone—stripping himself of his weapon, approaching with a single companion—it had all been a tactic. He had allowed us our illusions as long as it suited him. For all any of us knew, there could have been others stalking us through the wood.

No matter how we had operated before, Zusa had taken command the instant we had stepped out onto the riverbank.

Clever lived long, as Munnie liked to say, and Zusa had undoubtedly earned his turns.

Pine and spruce needles filled in the gaps left by the barren limbs of the ironoak and ashburn trees. Snow clung to branches from the storm that had blown through the span prior.

As the sun traversed the sky, I made note of what few markers I could. If we had to leave in a hurry, we couldn't run carelessly into the wood. Kenke Forest stretched below the border into Sonacoa and almost as far north as the Lost Forest, even continuing beyond the Sanine River. It would not do to be lost.

The hours passed as we walked. Sokan peaked, then started to fall. Zusa turned us in subtle circles, but the sky didn't care. Munnie had taught me to look up.

One who knew the sky, knew the land.

Based on Sokan and the mountains peeking through the treetops, we had traveled towards the northern edge of the forest. Every step became the furthest north I had ever been.

A gathering of echoes pierced the night's air. Twilight settled over the sky. Zusa stopped to dig his whistle out of his leather vest, blowing the same pattern of high-pitched whistles as before, reminiscent of a blue jay's call. A moment later, two quick notes and a longer, sustained pitch responded from the same direction as the echoes.

As we steered towards the responding call, the trees opened into an unnatural clearing. Three tents surrounded a small fire walled within a ring of rocks to quiet the light. Foliage wove through the canopies of their tents, blending them into the surrounding forest.

Where the Jani built their encampment to celebrate life, the Missing did everything they could to hide all signs of it.

No wonder we had never found them. We would have had to stumble into their borders to find any trace of them. Or at least close enough that I could have heard the echoes.

"You can come out now," Zusa said.

A young man, a turn or two older than me, walked out of the forest into view. He stood tall and full, like he knew a hard day's labor. His red braids fell loosely over his shoulders onto his onyx skin. Even though his bow remained trained on the dirt at our feet, his fingers waited, poised perfectly at the arrow's nock—ready to draw.

"You sure?" he asked with an honest smile. It felt odd to be at the whim of such a cheery-looking person.

"Yeah, I'm sure," Zusa said.

"He said he's sure. Now put down the bow, asshole," Wal said.

"Don't tell my brother what to do, prick," Boda said, shortening the gap between him and Wal with two large paces.

"Brother? I knew there was a reason I didn't like him."

"Sounds like we could all do with a good meal and some introductions," Zusa said, slapping his hand down on Boda's shoulder, causing the boy to wince once again. "Boda, why don't you and Niven make up a pot of pepper bon?"

Boda looked up like the frustrated child he was before putting himself to work with his brother.

"This doesn't look like much," I said.

"What did you expect? We don't announce ourselves. Our luxuries are fire and dry bedrolls. If you were looking for better accommodations, it's time to adjust. But if you're here to make green bastards bleed red, you're not completely out of luck." Zusa said the last bit with a greedy smile, and my anger reveled in the thought.

"Our camp is as big as it needs to be. As I said, we move like the nomads. Warriors come and go as needed. Right now, there's some doing needing done elsewhere. So, you're left with the likes of us to greet you," Zusa said. "Aren't you fortunate?"

"Like The Mother granted my prayer," Tomi said flatly.

"Sit. Eat. We'll make introductions," he said. "We have a spare tent you can set up for tonight. There is no reason to be growling at each other like rival packs. As of this morning, you are all part of the Missing."

The brothers from the south worked over the pot as we settled our belongings on the ground and formed a semicircle around the fire.

As Zusa made introductions, members of each party tore flatbreads with each other. The symbolic tearing of grievances did little to erase suspicions, but everyone kept a pleasant tongue—well, nearly everyone.

Wal was Wal, and we could never apologize enough to change that.

Adéan broke the divide between our groups first. Chêta was younger by a couple turns, but she hailed from the island nation to the north, which was all the invitation Adéan needed. The two of them rambled back and forth in what he called proper tongue, their words speeding up until they tumbled into a clatter of sounds.

Bowls were filled and passed around the fire until the silence of good food settled over the camp.

I scraped the bottom of my bowl for the last remnants of gravy. The saltmeat had gone stale, but Niven knew how to season a pot, the chiles keeping the cold away better than the fire.

Across the firepit, Talise and Mahli huddled in conversation. If they hadn't expressly said they weren't related, I would have mistaken them for sisters. The Tomakan girls added a sense of home, but nostalgia cut a dangerous path.

For some reason, the others looked to me as a leader. If I had led them into a trap, I had to be ready to pull them out of it.

While we ate, and some few of us attempted to cross the divides that made us strangers, Zusa sat on the outskirts of the firelight. His eyes scanned back and forth over the tense gathering.

Every time I met his gaze, my body jerked away as if I had gotten too close to a flame. As much as the man smiled, he wore the aura of a killer. Wherever his skin broke from his robes, a collection of scars alluded to battles long since passed.

Spirits being the tricksters they were, he probably got them tripping over a stone in the forest.

"Kaylo," Zusa said, causing my shoulders to jump. "Could I have a moment of your time?"

He didn't wait for a response, simply getting up and walking into the largest of the three tents.

As I looked for my companions to lend the confidence I lacked, I met a series of questions in their eyes.

A moment passed, and Adéan made a move to get up and come with me, but I waved him down. Even if I didn't feel it, I needed them to believe I had the situation under control.

But of course, when I nodded and winked, I garnered an eye roll from Tomi.

"Do you want me to..." Wal let the half-finished sentence hang in the air.

"Stay here. It will be fine," I said, and the relief on his face put a genuine smile on mine.

Inside the Commander's tent, untidy stacks of maps spread over the swept dirt, barely leaving room for a bedroll and a small metal brazier.

A thick chest of stormwood stood apart from the clutter. Heavy as stormwood was, it would take at least two people to lift it while empty. But it wasn't empty. The imprisoned spirits inside battered against my barriers.

"I'm glad you decided to join us," Zusa said, breaking my focus on his collection of caged spirits.

"If we hadn't, would you have let us leave?"

"Our plans here are delicate, and I think someone like you can set the balance in our favor," he said.

"You didn't answer the question."

"No, I didn't," he said. "I knew a thief once. Not well. We grew up in the same village. When our neighbors found out what she was, they ran her out that night with nothing more than the robes over her shoulders.

"Doesn't seem right, does it? The Thief is as much a Great Spirit as the others. Damn useful skill to take The Song from a dancer. Wish I could do that."

"I doubt that," I said. My anger overtook whatever fear I had carried into the tent. He didn't know what it meant to be a thief. None of them did.

"Is that what happened? Did they run you out of your home?"

"What do you plan to do with us?"

"You didn't answer my question," Zusa said.

"No, I didn't."

Zusa smiled even wider and chuckled from the back of his throat. "I like you, Kaylo. You have a head on your shoulders. So, how about this? We answer one for one. What are you willing to do to kill the Gousht?"

The fire reflected off his soft brown irises, and I refused to look away this time. I held his eyes for several breaths. "There is nothing I won't do. I owe blood, and there's a red-cloaked bastard out there who will pay it," I said. "Now, what do you plan to do with us?"

"Oh, my boy, I plan to give you what you want." The northman nodded towards the entrance. "Now, go get some rest. You look like The Mist would take you if a strong wind hit you wrong."

By the time I stepped out of Zusa's tent, the others had secured the canopy of our new quarters. They had made rushed work of it, but the heavy leathers and furs would stave off the cold well enough.

Talise and Mahli still sat by the fire, jabbering away under the glow of the younger Daughters. The sight touched a memory long since passed, Tomakans gathering around shared firepits before the Gousht arrived.

Maybe this won't be such a terrible place to call home for a moment of time, I thought.

After two days of hard walking, I needed sleep. My feet had grown accustomed to the punishment, but it still took its toll on my body and my mind. Thoughts broke in my head, scattering into tangents when I tried to collect them.

As I reached the threshold of the tent, something moved in the darkness. Sionia looked up at me from the ground and pulled her blanket tighter over her shoulders. "I don't trust our hosts yet," she said, making no effort to lower her voice. "Figured someone should keep watch."

"Not a bad idea."

"Go, get some rest. You look exhausted."

"Can I ask you a question?" I asked, and she nodded. "It never seems to get to you. Aren't you angry?"

"Angry about what?"

"Everything," I said. "What the Gousht did to your village. What they did to you. This isn't the life we should be living."

"No, but it's the life we have," she said. "I get angry. I get sad too. My grandmother used to say that anger was like driving a nail through wood with your thumb. After my second turn in the mission school, I finally understood what she meant."

Her rich ochre eyes did not waver. We looked at each other, and her calm humbled me. Without my anger, I couldn't take another step.

"Then why are you here?" I asked.

The fullness of her lips stretched into a smile. "The nail still needs to be pounded into the wood. I'd just rather not use my thumb."

CHAPTER TEN
CURRENT DAY ENNEA

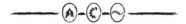

Kaylo welcomed the sting of the winter-morning breeze touching the sheen of sweat gathering across his forehead. Training two novice fighters shouldn't have left him this worn. Maybe the turns had finally found their way into his bones. The rich meals from the Citadel kitchens and his hours sitting amongst stacks of books hadn't helped the matter. He inhaled the winter, inviting the cold to stir his blood.

Little by little, Vāhn had improved. Though, to be fair, gripping her practice sword properly while settling into a passable stance marked improvement. Still, the young woman took to instruction well. And her presence certainly made teaching Tayen easier.

Each morning, the three of them focused on sword skill as the First Daughter signaled a new day. Kaylo imparted what he knew, and the girls moved in his footsteps. He slipped back into his failed parental role, and Tayen let go of her animosity—for an hour.

Maybe he hadn't lost her completely.

With a single step past the threshold of the Citadel, the sting of the wind ceased as if it knew better than to enter these walls. An endless series of rules dictated the inner workings of the mountain hallow. Why would they leave the wind to its own devices?

The quiet of the mountain halls underscored the inequity of life in

Myanack.

About this time, Tayen and Vāhn would be gathering in ranks for their morning drills under Commander Sola. While children toiled, playing the part of warriors, bureaucrats and other powerful, lazy citizens slept deep into the daylight.

They slept as if blood wasn't soaking into the soil on their behalf.

Chrysanthemum's heavy gait resonated off the stone walls behind Kaylo. Even in his brooding, Wal's warriors loomed in Kaylo's shadow.

The pathway curved as they walked deeper into the heart of the Citadel towards the true treasure of this wayward nation. Every day when he pulled open the oversized doors to the library, the aisles remained empty and the books untouched. Thousands of people had access to the surviving knowledge of Ennea, and they left it be.

Once or twice a servant had rummaged through the shelves, gathered a tome or two, and rushed away to deliver them. But no one else, besides Kaylo and the poet, gave this treasure the respect it deserved. Had it not been heartbreaking, his near uninterrupted access to these books would have been a beautiful dream.

Lanigan, peculiar as they were, had become something of a friend. Their conversations wove through the tomes surrounding them as they discussed what they read and their thoughts on the world, but never themselves.

Some stories were better offered than asked after.

Yet, their conversations did not suffer the absence. Whatever topic Kaylo brought up, the poet had read at least one book on the subject, usually several.

Kaylo had never considered himself uneducated. Even if his kanas had not reinforced his curiosity for the world around him, which they had, his mother instilled an undying need to investigate life. He had read more books than most Enneans had seen since the invasion. But Lanigan practically lived in the library.

Yet, for all their wisdom, Lanigan's world had distinct boundaries. The pages could never replace the feeling of the shore under one's feet or the taste of the waters from Lona Lake.

The two of them explored through each other what they hadn't been able to on their own. Of course, they read. The books called to them, after all. But the conversations they shared helped Kaylo escape his imprisonment far more than the ink-stained pages.

As he crossed the textured floor of the atrium, with Chrysanthemum in tow, he considered exploring the shelves for a book on sword defenses. Surely, words left by masters of the art could offer more than his fading recollection of trainings from decades past.

One of the poet's rotating guards watched Kaylo as he approached, wearing her distaste, either for him or her station, plainly. Her nose scrunched up like she had smelled a rather insidious fart, which brought a smile to Kaylo's face. If he could make her day just a little worse with his presence, he had used his time well.

Munnie would have scolded him for his pettiness, but there were some things Kaylo had no interest in outgrowing.

He pulled the heavy stormwood doors open as he walked into his sanctuary. The air smelled delicately of old paper and leather. The small slit windows in the far wall allowed daylight to creep into the dusty room, and an oil lamp chandelier spread light to the corners daylight couldn't reach.

Around the bend of the first bookshelf, the poet sat in their usual seat. They met his eyes, and the wonder of the library disintegrated.

Instinctively, Kaylo reached for his knife, but of course, it wasn't there. Wal didn't permit him to carry it outside of his room.

Soft footsteps filled the empty library chamber, and Kaylo turned to meet the ambush.

"I thought it would be harder to catch you off guard, thief." A decorative leather vest covered the woman's standard military robes. Gray streaked through her black hair, pulled into a ponytail, which highlighted the sharpness of her cheekbones. Rows of small tattoos covered most of her face, the black ink stark against her golden-brown skin.

"I thought you would be bigger, General," Kaylo said. "Can I help you find a book? I am rather new here, but I have done a fair amount of exploring the shelves."

"A very kind offer, but I have more important matters to attend to. There is a war, after all."

"You might be surprised what you would find in a good book."

"Enough. I am not here to banter with you like a child," she said, her expression emphasizing her point. "If it were up to me, you wouldn't step foot out of your quarters."

Kaylo's eyebrows lifted in a question before he could ask it. "Who is it up to, if not you?"

If her glare was any indication, this was a sore subject. "Commander Wal seems to think you and your kind would be of great benefit to our cause, and King Shonar agrees, for now. I personally don't see the use in infecting our ranks with malitu, but in all things I bow to the King's wisdom.

"And yet, despite the claims of your value, you spend your days in the library with the King's shame." She nodded towards Lanigan. "Why haven't you started training the little thieves?"

"General, I..."

"I apologize. I don't know why I framed that as a question," General Tanis said. "Tomorrow, after morning mess, you meet the bastard dancers on the training grounds to start their instruction. There is no 'or else.' There is no threat. Because it will happen."

They stood facing each other for a long moment. Kaylo let a hint of a smile curve through his lips. The High General of the Lost Army had scolded him and stared down at him like one would a child. It should have been frightening. And maybe it was, slightly. But his mere existence rankled her, which amused him.

Eventually, he nodded, but not before reveling in the moment.

"Don't make an enemy of me, thief," she said. "I can be far less kind."

If the sound of her boots against the stone floor provided any indication, he had not made a pleasant first impression.

Kaylo slunk into the chair opposite Lanigan, releasing an embellished sigh.

Lanigan smiled. "Odd as it may sound, her wife is actually a very pleasant person. At least from what I can recall. It has been a spell since I last dined with them."

"It's time for you to fill in some of the context, poet."

"You should take her seriously," they said. "Tanis didn't rise to the top with smiles and heartless threats."

"Why did she call you the King's shame?"

"I'm glad that you are giving my warning serious consideration."

"No, really, what could a poet do that could shame a king? Dirty limerick?"

Lanigan's eyes fell to the wood table. "Shonar and I grew up together. In another life, we were best friends, inseparable. This poet once served as an advisor to a young king.

"When the invasion started, I begged him to heed the calls for aid. Of course he didn't, and I wrote about the shame of a surviving nation. Then he declared himself the King and uniter of Ennea, and I wrote about the four pieces of a soul that were sacrificed for the ego of one.

"My words found the eyes and ears of the people as talks of an uprising were stirring. If I had been anyone else, he would have executed me. Tanis offered to swing the blade. But Shonar spared me, to his everlasting shame. Now, my words and I are restricted to the Citadel."

The poet looked up with a strained smile and tears trailing down their face. "It really is a pity. I would have made a wonderful martyr."

There were no words to offer to calm the sting of their story. Kaylo slid his hand down the table and rested it palm up in front of Lanigan. After a moment of staring at it, they placed their hand in his.

The hundred recruits sat in immaculate rows waiting for Commander Sola to begin his afternoon lecture, none of them adults in The Mother's eyes and all wearing signs of their harsh training—bruises, cuts, torn robes. In less than two span, they had learned not to bemoan such trivialities. Tayen sat amongst them and waited, as she had been trained.

Once he was finished lecturing on the minutiae of military policy, Sola started in on tactical theory. The Gousht relied on numbers. They continually reinforced the immense army with supplies and soldiers from their homeland to the south.

What had begun as an invasion of fifty thousand soldiers grew to an army of over one hundred thousand. Even if every living spirit within the bounds of the Lost Forest picked up a sword, they didn't have the numbers to meet such a force. Not to mention the Empire's vast stock of spirit crystals. No, if Astile meant to win this war, they had to out-strategize the Empire.

Sola stood at the head of the training tent. He had shorn his hair down to the stubble again. The change drew more focus to his eyes, making his glower all the more intense.

"In the Writ," Sola waved a copy of the enemy's holy book, "the Gousht claim they met another people who wielded magic. A century ago, during the reign of Emperor Candor II, while the Empire fought armies throughout the continent, they encountered the Deawndien. One in a thousand of these people had the gift of sight. They could see the futures that might be.

"The Emperor pulled troops from the skirmishes all around their expanding border. He lost battles and swathes of soldiers to his enemies. The nations surrounding them reclaimed previously conquered land and threatened to push in further. Even so, the Emperor pulled more soldiers from the walls protecting his borders.

"The full force of the Gousht army met the Deawndien in battle. Even if the seers amongst the Deawndien were few, they proved resourceful. The Gousht forces suffered extreme losses. Yet, their numbers eventually overran the Deawndien. When they forced the Deawndien to surrender, they killed the seers first," Sola said. "What did the Emperor do next?"

A young Tomakan woman near the front stood. "Emperor Candor II ordered his people to kill every single person of Deawndien blood, so that none would bear a child with the seer magic."

"Correct." Sola nodded to the woman. "He erased a people from The Waking to destroy the possibility of another seer. Why didn't they do the same here?"

A soft murmur ran through the ranks, which Sola allowed. He let them weigh his words and accept what could have been.

When the tension grew to be too much, Tayen stood. "The spirit crystals, Commander."

"Expand, recruit."

"The seers could only be a threat to the Empire, but with the crystals, we can be a resource. The more spirit-marked people they control, the more power they can take for themselves," Tayen said.

From the earliest lessons her parents had taught her about the Gousht, she understood she had something they wanted to take from her. When the Gousht saw her, they saw a mine or a forest of strong timber. Still, saying it aloud gripped the muscles in her gut.

The Song rattled in the distance. If only she could pull it closer and wrap herself in the shadows. Instead, she pushed it further away.

Sola nodded and Tayen sat back down. "We share a complicated relationship with spirit crystals. It is true that we may have beaten back the invasion if the Gousht hadn't discovered them. It is also true that we would likely all be dead if the Gousht had won the war without the crystals.

"The Uprising would have us believe that no good can come from a stolen spirit." Sola removed a smoky gray crystal from his robes. "I do not wield this tool lightly, but I will not let moral superiority be the reason we lose the war of our reclamation. You will learn to use these crystals, and we will turn their weapons against them."

He had a point. But then why did her upper lip curl at the sight of the crystal in his hand?

Maybe Kaylo had described the spirits trapped within their stone prisons one too many times. She had spent hours imagining their cries— the nimble music of the shadows eroded into a primal scream. If Kaylo hadn't saved her from the soldiers who had killed her family, her sliver of The Shadow's spirit would be trapped in a crystal just like the spirit in Sola's hand.

Sola, Oakan, and Chitere gathered the recruits into three groups and spread out as best as they could in the tent. Tayen followed the rest of her group to the back of the tent as they formed a circle around Chitere.

Of the three instructors, Chitere had the least patience with words. She spoke simply and directly, and she didn't repeat herself. If one took Nix and removed her dry humor, Chitere would be standing in her place.

As young as the northwoman appeared, she controlled the attention of the recruits with ease. She waited in perfect posture, her thick black curls pulled back into a tight knot, stretching her forehead taut. An eagerness swept through the children.

"I will explain this once, then I will demonstrate twice—once to each side of the group," she said in a low, reserved tone.

"In order to use a spirit crystal, you must be physically touching the stone. It is not enough to have it in a pocket or strung around your neck," Chitere said. "You have to know exactly what you want the spirit to do. Then picture it in your mind.

"The limits to the stone are your imagination and the nature of the element. The Flame will not cause rain to fall from the sky. It will not give you the power to fly or throw fire. Fire will act like fire does, but you can direct it."

If I'm directing the fire, then it's not acting like fire, Tayen thought, but she kept her words to herself and her face neutral.

Chitere reached into her robes, pulling out a deep blue crystal. As the recruits leaned in, the circle constricted. The color slowly churned beneath the surface of the stone.

"With the picture in your mind and the crystal in your hands, you can make the spirit control water. Some find it easier to move like they want the water to move, but you are not dancers. It is not necessary," Chitere said.

"Why aren't there any dancers in Astile?" Tayen asked.

"They give their spirits over for the greater good. A power that can be shared is greater than a power controlled by an individual."

Chitere retrieved a pot of water from the edge of the tent and brought it to the center of the circle as if she hadn't said anything earth-breaking. But the cavalier tone behind Chitere's words only made Tayen's blood pulse faster in her neck.

The crystal glowed in Chitere's fist, and the water at the edges of the pot turned cloudy and froze. As she manipulated the trapped spirit, the frost crept towards the center of the pot. "You will all have one chance today to freeze and unfreeze the water in this pot," she said. "Do it slowly and give the water a chance to adapt without shattering the clay. If you break the pot, you will fetch another."

The ice melted in an instant, the contents sloshing against the rim of the pot. Then she turned to the other side of the circle to demonstrate.

"The River is weak," Daak said from the other side of the circle. "Freezing and unfreezing water?"

Chitere bent down and dipped her hand into the now-liquid water and then slowly removed it. As she pulled her hand from the water, she clutched a cylinder of ice, which kept growing from the surface of the water as she drew her hand higher. Eventually, the cylinder narrowed to a point and Chitere held an icicle the length of her arm.

"Spirits are not weak. Sometimes their users are." She drew the short spear of ice over her shoulder and threw it into the ground in front of Daak. Despite the cold sand, the spear pierced the ground without breaking. Daak scuttled away from the spear along with the recruits to either side of him. "Go fetch another pot of water."

One by one, recruits attempted to freeze the pot of water as Chitere had. None had been overly successful.

A large, baby-faced Sonacoan boy handed Tayen the crystal. It sparkled like ice in the sunlight, but it warmed her palm. If she closed her eyes, it could have been any other stone that had sat out in the sun. But it wasn't. The crystal in her hand held a part of The River, which used to reside in another dancer. This stone was a prison with boundaries as real as the Lost Forest.

Somewhere a dancer knew this piece of The River as Tayen knew The Shadow.

With a moment of silence and proper concentration, she could feel The Shadow within her. It wove through her own spirit, and yet it belonged to something greater, like a small story that fit into a larger one. Without it, she would be someone entirely different.

Somewhere, a dancer was incomplete—maybe trapped in a dark mine shaft digging more crystals from the earth. More likely dead.

The Song swirled about the tent, reacting to her fear. The shadows flickered against the natural fall of the light. It took all her will to still herself against The Song's pull. If anyone noticed the movement, they didn't show it—likely blamed it on the flames flaring in the firepit.

She quickly passed the blue stone to Vāhn, who grabbed at the crystal with eager hands. Her fingers mapped out the surface of the stone. As a smile twisted her face with curiosity, she grasped it tight. Shards of the clay broke from the pot in a high-pitched clatter, leaving a block of ice poking through the gaps.

Her smile vanished as she tried to apologize, but Chitere waved her off. "Pass the crystal and fetch another pot."

None of the recruits had the subtle control the task required. When the crystal had made its rounds, only three of the thirty-five recruits had stirred the water. Vāhn and another girl managed to break the pot, and a northboy had accidentally boiled the water.

As they left the tent, Vāhn wore a smile unencumbered by her usual stress. "Did cha see tat?" she asked. "Is tat wha it's like to be a dancer?"

"How would I know?" Tayen said.

"It's rhetorical, smart one. What's wit cha? Cha look abit pale?"

"You know, your accent gets thicker when you're happy. When you're mad too." And quick as lightning through the sky, Vāhn's smile vanished. "No, I mean...no, it's not a bad thing."

"My father hated it. Said it reminded him of my mother," Vāhn said, forcing each word apart from the next.

Of course. She had lost her mother too. The questions waited on the tip of Tayen's tongue. Had the green bastards killed her mother too? When? Had they been close before it happened? But once she asked, Vāhn would ask her in kind. And that opened up doors that remained shut for a reason.

"Heading to the mess?" Vāhn asked.

Tayen rolled her eyes and shook her head. "I have to go see Kaylo."

"Yeah, you have a hard life. Fine food and a story no one else knows," Vāhn said, forcing her accent away. "I'll pray for you over my lovely meal of slop."

The two exchanged lackluster smiles, then parted ways.

As Tayen walked, the way the spirit moved and twisted under the crystal's surface stuck with her. The ground beneath her feet shifted from sand to frozen dirt without her noticing. In all her turns, she had never held a crystal before.

Holding it made the daemontale real. One of those fucking things could cut her off from The Shadow and bind her spirit to The Waking.

Still, Sola made a certain sense. If Astile had a chance of winning the war, they couldn't abandon weapons. But how could she use the crystals, knowing what she knew?

Raised voices yanked her from her thoughts.

A tall northwoman lumbered over a guard at one of the Citadel entrances. But not any northwoman. Nix. The guard moved his hand to his sword, shaking out of anger or fear, as she yelled and lorded her size over him.

A second guard joined the first and backed Nix down. Apparently, she knew better than to start a fight with two armed guards in the middle of the Lost Nation capital. She might have won, but even then, she would have lost.

Nix stalked off away from the Citadel and Tayen followed her. She had to jog to catch up with the older warrior's strides. "Nix, wait."

"What is it?" Nix yelled as she spun around.

"What happened back there?"

"A disagreement," Nix said. "What are you doing spying on other people?"

"It looked like a serious disagreement."

"Shouldn't you be in the mess? For a recruit, you never are where you should be."

"I have to go see Kaylo. What's your excuse?"

"Listen, you sassy little bug, I'm not being questioned by a girl ain't finished growing," Nix said. "And what do you mean, you have to see Kaylo? Recruits aren't allowed in the Citadel."

"Kaylo made me promise to visit with him if he continued to train me."

"You realize you are horrible at communicating necessary information."

"My friend Vāhn is one of the worst fighters I have ever seen, so I convinced Kaylo to help train her and me in the mornings. He agreed, as long as I visit him every night," Tayen said.

"And why do you seem so upset about that? Sounds a shitheap better than being trapped in the mess and the bunks with hundreds of other smelly recruits until you pass out."

"I have my reasons."

"I'm sure you do, kid, but tell me one thing. Have you forgiven me? I made the deal with the Lost Army in the first place. Kaylo had nothing to do with that."

"You never promised me anything. He did." Tayen met Nix's dark brown eyes and held them with all her stubborn grit.

"You should get going," Nix said, then walked away without another word.

———

Kaylo drummed his fingers on the table as he waited for Tayen to arrive. By the time she slumped through the door and into her seat across from him, the food had cooled.

They peeled the cloth napkins from the bowls, and Tayen dug in without hesitation. Stewed chicken, potatoes, roasted leeks, and fresh bread—a fairly tame meal from the kitchens, but delicious all the same.

"I'm close to a way out," Kaylo said. He had meant to work his way up to the conversation, but he had never been one for idle chatter, and Tayen's posture didn't invite it anyway.

"What?"

"Keep it down," he whispered at her, tilting his head towards the door. "Stormwood is thick, but not soundproof."

"What are you talking about, old man?" Tayen said with an over-emphasized whisper.

"I'm working on a plan to get us out of here. I need you to be patient for a little longer, but I think I can do it."

"Why would I want to go?"

"What are you talking about? Are you enjoying your prison that much?"

"I asked for one thing from you—train me so that I can avenge my family. Astile is giving me that chance. They are teaching me how to kill green bastards, and none of them are trying to convince me not to."

"They are using you. The King will use anyone and everyone to get what he wants."

"As long as it means that I get to kill Gousht, I don't care," Tayen said.

"Are you that short sighted?" Kaylo asked, no longer whispering. "The King wants to rule Ennea. That means no more Tomak, no more Jani, Renéqua, or Sonacoa."

"What's so wrong about that? Maybe the Gousht wouldn't have conquered one nation so easily."

Kaylo could only stare in response to his toka. He had failed her more than he thought possible. "When you look at this city, do you see equality? Justice? Opportunity?" he asked. "There are reasons you are desperate to make sure your friend doesn't become one of the nameless."

"Don't call them that."

"The name isn't worse than what the Lost Nation does to them."

There was a momentary hesitation in Tayen's eyes, then her eyelids settled around her glare. "I've met my obligation. I came here to listen to your story. If you don't want to tell it, then I'll go back to the barracks," she said. "I'll see you in the morning."

She wiped her mouth on the soft cloth, got up from the table, and walked out the door.

Well, Kaylo thought. *That could have gone better.*

CHAPTER ELEVEN
CURRENT DAY ENNEA

This is a mistake, Kaylo thought as he loitered around the entrance to the tent. The winter lashed against his skin and threatened to freeze the sweat from his earlier training session. And yet, he preferred it to what awaited him inside. *What have I done to convince these people I know enough to teach anything?*

Given the chance, he may have waited in the frigid air until his flesh froze as solid as the sand under his feet. Summer Thistle, his jailor for the day, was less apt to lose her appendages to the winter. She shoved him forward, and he stumbled into the tent.

What his entrance lacked in grace, it made up for in visibility. At least he caught himself before tumbling into the sand.

The three would-be spirit dancers knelt in a line, staring at him like a herd of startled deer. The youngest of the three quickly righted his expression to something more befitting a recruit in the King's army, or whatever. His immaculate robes fit his trained disposition. The boy reeked of the Citadel. Probably some bureaucrat's brat ready to command older, more experienced soldiers to their deaths.

The Lost Army may have prided itself on battle-tested leadership, but the tattoos across their cheeks didn't mean shit in the face of nepotism. Even ink had a price. Only fools believed that every commander and general earned their marks, and those fools rarely lived long enough to learn the truth.

A young Sonacoan woman on the opposite end of the kneeling recruits had painstakingly twisted her red hair into spirals, which meant she had the potential for patience, even if the look in her eyes indicated otherwise. Her robes lacked the fineness and quality of the boy's. Several scars marred her dark skin. This one hadn't come from a pampered life.

In between the motley pair sat a northwoman with at least a decade on Kaylo. Wrinkles had settled around her eyes, and gray hair salted her black curls. She wore an inoffensive expression as she waited for him to speak. Age had a way of tempering expectations.

Kaylo had taken as much measure of the trainees as he could while standing there. As much as he desperately wanted to, he couldn't remain silent forever. Not with Summer Thistle, who had far more barbs than her namesake, standing over his shoulder.

"My name is Kaylo, not Commander Kaylo, not kana, just Kaylo. You have undoubtedly heard me referred to by other names—heard stories about my past—forget all of that. I am here to teach you how to control The Balance.

"That is the proper name for your spirit ancestor. As much of a bitch as she is, I won't have you refer to her by any other name in this tent. Understood?"

The boy on his left nodded with his whole torso, while the other two tipped their heads forward.

"Controlling The Balance is difficult, and it takes time. Some of you have lived with the seventh spirit longer than others, so it is time that I know what you know," Kaylo said. "What is The Song?"

The boy stood up, pulling the ends of his robe taut. "My name's Pana, sir," he said. "The Song is a bridge between The Waking and The Mist. Dancers are a medium, and they are able to direct their spirit ancestors to interact with the world around them."

"Okay, Pana. You can sit down. Do any of you have an answer you didn't read in a book?"

"It's an annoying noise that flares up around the spirit-marked when they get emotional," the Sonacoan woman said.

"Name?"

"Euri," she said with the same level of disdain as she spoke about The Song.

"And how about you?" Kaylo asked the third.

"Rūnka," she said. "I'm old nough ta know I don know. I ave lived wit The Song ma whole life 'n done ma best to shut it up."

Kaylo closed his eyes, his chest swelling with a sigh before deflating. If they knew what they were doing, Tanis wouldn't have bothered with him.

"We will start at the beginning," Kaylo said. "What you hear is not The Song—not as other dancers hear it. You are hearing the reverberations of what they hear, not a direct connection to the spirits, but a second-hand one. An echo.

"I want you to picture a hallway with a door at either end. One door leads to The Mist and the other door leads to The Waking. When a dancer is open to The Song, the door to The Mist is open. That is when you hear their echo. When the dancer pulls their spirit ancestor into The Waking, that is when you can borrow their gift."

"What about spirit crystals?" Pana asked, genuinely eager to learn.

"The crystals trap a piece of a spirit in the hallway," Kaylo said. "You can always hear their echo, if you listen for it."

They sat for an hour as he rambled on about The Song and the echo. Whether anything he said made sense, he didn't know. He had never tried to instruct another spirit dancer before. When he tried to parse the difference between borrowing a spirit from a crystal and from a dancer, it became clear none of them had taken a spirit from a dancer before. It shouldn't have come as a surprise.

This far into the occupation and war, there were likely more spirits trapped in crystals than freely walking with spirit-marked people. These three spirit dancers would never understand the feeling of moving with a natural spirit. Instead, every time they pulled an unwilling spirit from its prison, they would experience its pain and rage.

When he finished rambling, he dismissed them for the day. They could wait one more day before they practiced enduring that pain.

———

"Remember your footwork," Tayen mouthed to Vähn.

The slight girl stood opposite Daak in the sparring circle, while he turned with his whole body, searching through the recruits surrounding them. When he found Tayen, his lips pulled back into a smarmy, chip-toothed grin.

His bruises had faded to patches of yellow and purple against his stormwood skin. The bastard had spent every day since she beat him senseless staring her down. Whenever he found an unfortunate recruit who would listen, he swore Tayen had fought dirty—throwing sand in his eyes and swinging for his nethers. Even though they all saw the fight, some of them had started to believe his lies.

Between the Gousht, the Lost Army, and little shits like this, most of the recruits only knew second-hand versions of someone else's truth.

Still, it didn't make much difference how many people dirtied Tayen's name behind her back. She could take care of herself. Vähn, on the other hand, shook from knee to neck. Her left foot bounced arrhythmically in the sand. She strangled her sword until the tips of her fingers turned reddish-purple.

Commander Sola had the clever idea that fair matches couldn't prepare the recruits for the realities of war. He had arranged three separate sparring circles under the tent, then he and his attendants started pairing up uneven fights—taking into consideration skill and size. Somehow, Daak had convinced Oakan to pair him with Vähn.

In a span of early morning training sessions, Kaylo had helped Vähn improve her grip, stance, and footwork. But the lessons hadn't had an opportunity to seep into her bones. She wasn't ready to face Daak—not that anyone would confuse him for a sword master, but his size, strength, and attitude made him dangerous.

Oakan stood between the two fighters. He lifted his hand like a blade. Vāhn's foot stopped bouncing. As she settled into her stance, she pulled her elbows into position.

"Yaktan." Oakan said, and the word cut through the air as swiftly as his hand.

Daak moved like a predator circling his prey. He showed her his teeth and drew out the anticipation. And yet Vāhn mirrored every step he took, remaining squared up, facing her opponent.

When he attacked, Daak yelled out with all the air in his lungs. Maybe he meant to intimidate, but that would assume a level of forethought he had never displayed before.

The boy charged, and Vāhn side-stepped, the momentum of his wild swing carrying him past her, their wooden swords never touching.

Several of the recruits chuckled, and Daak's smile transformed into a scowl.

They circled each other until he yelled again. But this time, he didn't charge. He closed the gap between them and swung his sword like he was chopping lumber. She angled-out and parried, one blow after another. Each movement she made was minimal, but effective.

A skilled sword fighter would have defeated Vāhn immediately. She painted her intentions across her face before every movement, like she had to reach for her training instead of letting it come to her. But against a brute with more muscles than ideas, she held her own.

The energy around the circle shifted. Vāhn controlled the match. She had yet to attack, but her opponent panted for air. His chest heaved in and out, sweat covered his face, and his attacks lost their ferocity. He swung downward in a desperate move, which she easily parried.

The lost sleep had been worth it.

Vāhn needed more time and practice, but she showed the beginnings of true skill after only a span. Given more time, she could master the sword.

Vāhn opened her guard and stepped back to let Daak's wild attack through. A smile filled her cheeks, and she reared back to take a swipe at her opponent.

The wooden blade would have cracked Daak in the ribs, but Vāhn stepped poorly on the uneven sand. As she caught her weight on the back of her heels and shifted her stance, her guard opened.

Even winded, Daak managed to knock her blade to the side, and Vāhn lost her one advantage—her footwork.

She still saw sword work as a procedure. The feel and memory hadn't worked into her muscles yet. She recovered too slowly, becoming an open target, and Daak took full advantage. He slammed the flat of his blade into her ribs with all the power from his shoulder.

Her rib snapped with a subtle pop, followed by her high-pitched cry. She grabbed her side before collapsing to the ground.

When she looked up, sand clinging to her face, she lifted her four-fingered forfeit into the air.

As Tayen returned her friend's gaze, pain stretched Vāhn's expression, disappointment sinking into her eyes. Tayen forced herself to smile for Vāhn's sake.

It had only been a span. She would get better. They would train twice as hard if need be.

Daak's blade came down before anyone realized what was happening. The edge of the wooden blade crashed into the base of Vāhn's skull.

The sound that emanated from wood striking bone started with a pop. Then the noise rounded before breaking off with a jagged edge, crunching with a finality that forced the tent into a silence. The silence became a dam, restraining the moment from moving forward until the weight grew too large to bear.

As if watching a sunset rush through the motions of an ending day, the disappointment dimmed from Vāhn's eyes until they were hollow pools of honey brown.

Her eyes remained open as her body lay in the sand.

Even as chaos erupted all around them, she and Tayen never broke
eye contact. The flames cast hectic shadows running through the tent.
Daak stood like a stunned child over his victim the moment before Oakan
tackled him to the ground. Recruits cried out in horror. And through
it all, Tayen didn't move, as helpless as when she had seen her family's
burning bodies.

Again, I did nothing, Tayen thought.

After a long stretch of forever, Tayen crawled over to her friend and
gathered the lifeless girl's head off the sand. For such a slight person, the
weight of Vāhn's head on Tayen's lap felt like enough to break her.

The tent emptied. A couple of recruits dragged Daak away. Sola sent
the rest of the regiment back to the barracks. If anyone had tried to
encourage Tayen to leave, she hadn't noticed.

She was too busy picking grains of sand off Vāhn's face. Several
granules stuck in her eyelashes, and Tayen blew them away as gently as
she could.

All the while, Vāhn's eyes remained open. Closing them would be too
permanent, so Tayen brushed the sand out of her friend's curly black hair.
When her hands came back red and sticky, she wiped them on her robes
and continued her work.

The Song waited like an open doorway to The Mist, begging Tayen to
step through. If not for her responsibility to care for her friend's body, she
may have taken the offered escape.

"You knew her well?" Chitere asked as she sat down on the other side
of Vāhn's body.

It was a silly question. She and Vāhn hadn't come here of their own
accord. They didn't pilgrimage to the lovely capital of Astile. They had
been captured and thrust into each other's lives.

Captives didn't know each other well. They clutched onto the
people beside them to save themselves from the stark reality of their

circumstances.

Tayen didn't know Vāhn's story. She didn't know if anybody on this side of The Mist would mourn Vāhn like she deserved.

"This shouldn't have happened," Chitere said. "She was under our protection, and we failed her."

At that, Tayen looked up.

Of course, it shouldn't have happened, but Tayen bore as much guilt as anyone else. If she hadn't beaten Daak in front of the entire regiment—if she hadn't tied herself to the girl...

Daak knew. When he swung his sword, he swung hard enough to hit Tayen through Vāhn.

She ran her hand through Vāhn's hair. No apology would do.

"She will be buried in the Honored Fields. Recruits who die in training accidents are given the rites of a soldier," Chitere said.

"Accident?" Tayen said. She swallowed the hoarseness of her voice. "That was not a fucking accident. Daak murdered Vāhn in front of all of us. So, where are they going to bury him?"

"The recruit will be punished, but you should focus on yourself right now."

"Punished? Anything less than a slit throat is too good for him."

"This is not your concern or your decision, recruit," Chitere said, the stoic tone returning to her voice. "Vengeance is not justice. The army doesn't throw away recruits so easily."

"Oh, I forgot, you have your precious war to win. You wouldn't want to let a silly thing like murder get in the way of that."

"I understand your grief, but if you think you can speak to me in this manner, I will show you a more visceral pain," Chitere said. Then she looked down at Tayen's hand gently combing through Vāhn's hair. "We all have lost people. Let it drive you, but don't let it consume you."

"Is that an order?"

"Take it as friendly advice. With your strength and talent, you could do great things, Tayen. But you have to decide to care."

"You don't think I care?"

"Anger isn't caring. Anger is destruction," Chitere said. "Go. Take the rest of the day to settle your nerves. I'll take care of Vāhn."

When Tayen didn't move, Chitere leaned forward and pulled Vāhn's weight from her lap. "That is an order."

───────────

Kaylo stared at the book in his hands as he hunched over the table in the middle of his quarters. He hadn't turned the page of his book in several minutes. Ever since he had left the other spirit dancers, echoes throughout the Citadel had started to slip through his barriers. Hundreds of spirits trapped in The Waking. Their anguish became a sharp and discordant chorus undermining his every thought.

If he could only reach out and dissolve their crystal cages, he would be free of their horrible refrain. And then he would be freed from this body in a rather bloody fashion.

The Lost Nation wouldn't overlook the destruction of their weapons cache. Yet dying itself didn't stay his hand. What lay beyond dying did— the dead that waited for him on the other side.

He turned back to the page, but there were no words that could keep his dead from him. They appeared at even the slightest tangential thought. Mostly faceless apparitions. The turns eroded their features from his mind, silhouettes trapped in the moments before their dying. Shay on the singed forest floor, his parents awaiting the soldiers on the other side of the door, Junera's hand resting upon the wooden rabbit. If only he could see them in happier moments, but that was not how they appeared to him.

He returned the book back to one of the stacks lying on the table and leaned back into his chair. "Seed and Balance," he muttered to himself. "What am I supposed to do?"

The table had progressively collected more clutter over the past few span. There were three stacks of books, a dirty basin of water next to the vase of flowers, and a collection of scrap wood he had been whittling during his empty hours. A series of small messes gathered throughout the room. The routine that had given his life shape and kept his thoughts in place stayed behind in Dasoon.

Whether he called this jail a home for another day or for the rest of his life, he needed a new routine. He bent forward to empty the water basin when the door swung open.

Tayen strode in, the guard behind her grabbing at her arm. Kaylo barely looked up, waving the guard off. "Back off. Your commander approved her visits, did he not?"

The wiry northman stopped pawing after the girl, but he didn't move.

"I promise we won't slip out the slit in the mountain, Daffodil," Kaylo said.

The guard glowered at his given name before walking back out the door.

Tayen erratically paced the stone floor, the lantern behind her flashing and dimming as she moved between him and the light. When he finally took the sight of her in, he shot up to his feet, his chair grinding against the stone floor as he pushed it aside.

Dried blood clung to her robes. Her eyes were puffy. Streaks of blood and tears ran down her cheeks.

"What happened to you?" he asked, rushing to his toka. "Whose blood is that?"

She slapped his reaching hand away. "You promised!"

"Are you okay? What happened?"

"You promised!" she screamed again.

"I need you to tell me. Are you hurt?"

"You promised to keep me safe. It's all your fault. You should have just let me die," she said. Her breath stuttered as she exhaled. Then she stepped forward and pushed him hard in the chest.

"Tayen, what happened?"

Anger filled her voice, but her eyes begged him for comfort. Kaylo stepped towards her again, and she tried to push him back, but this time he didn't allow her. Instead, he wrapped his arms around her. She struggled for a moment, then the tension disappeared from her body, and she fell into him.

"Vāhn's dead," she said like it was a breath of air she had held onto for too long.

"What?" He had seen her only a few hours past. She had been smiling when she left, some sarcastic quip about becoming the greatest sword fighter ever to grace the sands. The sprite girl with the half-hidden accent and fully bared spirit had been so alive.

For all the questions he had, despite his own shock and pain, all he could manage was, "I'm sorry."

He shifted his weight and swept Tayen from the floor. To his surprise, she let him.

Her anger and boldness made it easy to forget her age, only a moon over fifteen. She fit in his arms, and despite his grief, he enjoyed her closeness.

As he walked her over to his bed, her heart thumped against his stomach. She fell asleep by the time he tucked the edges of his blanket around her. He brushed a loose braid from her eyes and let her rest.

Light shifted over her face in gentle waves.

How can Vāhn be dead? he thought.

When they had first met, he had tried to warn Tayen. He hurt everyone around him. He should have made her believe him. It was too late now.

―――――――――

Whatever they called it, the barracks was a cage. The whole damn country was a cage, but at least, out in the snow-covered fields at the foot of the Citadel, Nix couldn't see the bars.

Small bumps covered Nix's exposed flesh. Nothing new. After turns walking the perimeter of Dasoon, she had grown accustomed to the chill burrowing its way into her body. The numbness calmed her thoughts, slowed the world. Her problems became smaller beneath the wide-open field of stars in the night sky.

She wondered after the people she had taken care of all these turns. Hopefully, Tisda had kept enough of her own harvest to last the winter. The old woman gave away too much too quickly, and rations had gone thin even before they had taken Nix away.

Winter in Dasoon stole too many people from them, people looking for safety who found the freecity instead. Hakan always promised the next turn would be better. They would save more grain to last the cold. They would fix the cracks in the stone that let in the freezing winds. But his promises always outmatched their harvest stores.

Despite how things ended, Nix couldn't make herself hate the bearish man. History connected them. Hakan had been her family. Unreliable, manipulative, and self-centered, but family. She wouldn't likely see him again.

No, she would die in some battle. He would die in a raid. And when they met in The Mist, she would bloody his lip before she hugged the ugly bastard.

A second pair of footsteps joined her own, crunching the snow. Sosun rushed towards her, dried blood caked under her nostrils and in the split of her lip. A black circle ringed her eye.

The young woman stopped short and reached out a piece of folded scrap paper. The white of the paper was browned with dirt and age.

"What happened?" Nix asked.

Sosun pushed the paper into Nix's hand, her expression a mixture of rage and frustration.

Leave me alone.

That was all the paper said. Nix flipped the scrap over to see if there was any more, but it was blank.

"What happened? Who did this to you?"

Sosun pointed violently at the piece of paper, but Nix persisted. "Tell me what happened to you."

Sosun jabbed her boney finger into Nix's chest and pushed with all her effort.

"I know it's my fault you're here. I am trying to do whatever I can to help you now. What happened?" Nix asked, softening her voice and looking into the deep brown eyes of the girl she'd traded away so many turns ago.

Sosun grabbed Nix's wrist and pulled it up, shaking it and pointing at the slip of paper in Nix's hand.

"Seven spirits and The Great Fucking Mother, speak. I know that you're not supposed to. I can see what happens when you break their rules, but there is no one else here." Nix swept her arms wide in a grand gesture. "Please, Sosun. Tell me what happened?"

Leaning her head back, Sosun opened her mouth wide to reveal a stub of pulpy flesh hanging in her mouth where her tongue had been. She left her mouth open for longer than necessary, forcing Nix to see what her betrayal had wrought.

When Sosun finally closed her mouth, she met Nix's eyes. Her lips pulled back into a snarl, opening the cut on her upper lip further.

The young woman ripped the paper from Nix's hand, and with her other hand, Sosun pulled out a piece of writing coal and scrawled something on the back of the paper. She held it open in front of Nix's eyes, long enough for Nix to read her message. Then, the paper drifted down to the ground at Nix's feet and Sosun walked away. The sound of her boots breaking the crust of the snow over the field rang out against the silence of the night.

The girl's silhouette in the night shrank until she became no more.

Nix bent down to pick up the piece of paper and looked at the hastily scribbled words.

I have no voice.
I have no name.
Stop asking about me.

The sister moons moved through the sky above, the wind swept over the fields, and Nix's chest rose and fell, but nothing else moved. She stood there as the cold crept deeper into her body, looking at Sosun's words.

When she finally moved, tiny pricks stabbed up and down her legs. She didn't walk towards the barracks like she should have. Instead, she made a direct line to the nearest Citadel entrance.

The two guards watched her approach and straightened up from their slouched positions. "What do you think you're doing, recruit?" the shorter Tomakan guard asked.

"Tell Commander Wal that Nix needs to speak with him. He'll know what it's about."

CHAPTER TWELVE
KAYLO'S STORY

THE LEAVES FROM THE scarlet cypress tree feathered out from the stem in an asymmetrical pattern. Its subtle red fur tickled my fingertips.

As often as I visited The Seed, the peculiarities of the flora still delighted me. I had never seen a cypress tree this shade before, but the intrigue lay deeper than that. The idea that trees grew in The Mist amongst the spirits led to so many questions, like how could I feel the prickle of the leaves without my body? Why did I still perceive a body where there was none?

"That's how you wish to perceive The Mist," The Seed said, without a greeting. "In fact, the tree in your not-hands is only a reflection of my perceptions."

"That doesn't make any sense."

"Everything in The Waking is a limit. The tips of your fingers. The shore where water meets land. The distance between one place and another. Those limits only exist here as a matter of perception." His deep, slow voice calmed me until I realized the sound of his voice was another choice of perception.

"Does that mean that you choose to look the way you do?"

The Seed's long body stretched up like a man roughly cut from a stormwood tree—the grain of the wood running like tattoos across his dark polished skin. His body had been carved with the most intricate detail, yet like all Great Spirits, he did not have a mouth. And still, I heard his voice. Different flowers bloomed from his body every time I saw him. Today, purple and yellow daffodils rolled in a diagonal across his chest—at least in my perception.

"Ah, now you are starting to understand," he said. "It is the same for all of us in The Mist, great and small spirits alike, even The Balance."

I thought about The Thief, her two-toned face of porcelain white and midnight black. *Why would she have chosen to cast such a stark figure?*

"Because she is used to being seen as ominous. She embraces it rather than being forced into the role."

"Stop listening to my thoughts. It creeps me out."

"Thoughts and speech are no different here. And you are avoiding talking about her," he said.

"No, I'm not letting you twist the facts like you always do. She isn't a tragic figure. She knew what she was doing, and she gave the spirit crystals to the Gousht despite the consequences," I said. "Boohoo, people told stories about her. She put us in shackles for her bruised ego."

"You are angry, and you have the right to be, but..."

"But nothing. Anger is the right response to betrayal."

"There is also compassion," The Seed said. "You hid your truth for a turn, and it nearly broke you. Try centuries. Think about being cursed by the people who carried a piece of your being—all because of twisted stories."

"That doesn't forgive what she did."

"Perhaps not, but you could. If you chose to," he said. His cheeks rose in what would be a kindly smile, if he had lips for such a gesture. "Forgiveness is the root of our nature."

"Some things are unforgivable."

The tent hummed with the sounds of sleep when I pulled away from

The Mist. I should have tried to rest for whatever remained of the night, but even though my body ached with exhaustion, my spirit teemed with energy. The Song sang through every plant, and the distinction between where I ended and they began seemed meaningless.

Once I maneuvered through the tangled sleeping bodies of my friends, I reached for Zusa's bribe. The warrior had given each of us a cloak of mismatched, patchwork skins and furs to keep the winter at bay. It hugged my shoulders like an old friend but smelled as stale as the gesture.

If he thought he could buy our trust for the price of some tattered pass offs, he severely underestimated our collective stubbornness.

Where I had my doubts, Liara studied every action the Commander took for missteps, and her sister followed in kind. Yet, for all our watchful eyes, his words and his actions moved as one.

None of his regiment hid their apprehension either. The tentative alignment of our two groups balanced on an edge finer than my father's most well-crafted blade, a fact which many on both sides of the line openly discussed.

Of course, Wal and Boda had nearly come to blows several times.

Outside the tent, Sionia perched next to the communal firepit. The six of us decided we needed to keep watch over them as long as they watched over us.

Niven, the only one of Zusa's band beyond his swearing day, nodded to me from across the outskirts of the campsite, where he leaned against a tree bundled in his cloak.

"It's only been an hour or two." Sionia looked into the sky, squinted, and measured the distance of the traveling moons with the width of her fingers.

"I can't sleep, so I figured I would let you get some rest." I settled down next to her, holding my hands up to the fire.

"Bad dreams?"

"Something like that," I said. "Do you believe there are things people do that can't be forgiven?"

"As vague as that question is, I am assuming there is something much more specific behind it." She studied me for a moment, then sighed. "You've been walking with The Seed again."

"Don't tell Liara."

"Why? Because it's dangerous and shortsighted?" she asked.

"It would only be dangerous if The Seed tried to stop me from coming back."

"That's comforting," she said. "Kaylo, as self-deprecating as you can be, I hope you know we need you."

I smiled and nodded. She was wrong, but she meant it, which made it worse.

"You should get some sleep," I said.

She lingered next to me as the fire licked at the cage of stones surrounding it. Then, when the silence had truly set, she got up and made her way into the tent.

"A mistwalker?" Zusa said, stepping in from the shadows. "You are full of surprises."

"An eavesdropper? Not surprising at all."

The older warrior had sleep caught in his eyes when he stepped out into the night without his leather vest, which struck an odd image. He perpetually wore his guards, like the next battle was waiting for an opening.

A cadence of stifled claps sang from beneath the soil as I struggled to settle The Song. It knew my discomfort and mistrust. He watched me like a predator as he strode over to a rock on the opposite side of the flames and sat. Hunger lashed out behind his eyes.

"Paying attention and eavesdropping are hardly the same thing. After all, I am responsible for what happens here—even if you don't trust me." He let the statement breathe before continuing. "Your friend isn't wrong. Mistwalking is dangerous. Then again, we are rebels fighting an army that has conquered our homeland. What do we do that isn't dangerous? The real question is, is it worth the danger?"

Beyond Zusa's shoulder, Niven made no effort to avert his gaze.

"So, are your journeys to the other side worthwhile?" The Commander waved his hand in a circular fashion, and Niven stood up without complaint before taking leave to perform a routine perimeter check.

"What do you mean?" I asked.

"Is the risk worth the reward? Are you stepping into The Mist for a reason?"

"The Seed understands me—what I've gone through." My hand rose to my chest. "He is the only one who knows the full story."

Zusa leaned closer and lowered his voice, pulling me into an intimate conversation. "What piece of the story are you keeping from the rest of us?" His words sounded genuine, like he had an eagerness to know me. *But why?*

Silence pulled at me until the words fell from my lips. "The Thief."

His brow arched, but he remained silent.

"I walked in The Mist with her before I even understood what I was doing. All the stories I grew up hearing...I hated her. But she isn't evil, not exactly. She's in pain." I fiddled with my fingers as if touching something physical would ground me.

When I met Zusa's eyes, his head tilted and his brows lifted with curiosity.

"Can you forgive the unforgivable if you understand the reasons?" I asked.

"That's a heavy question for a kid to carry. I don't know that there is an answer," he said, leaning back, anchoring his hands in the dirt behind him. "I have done some awful things, Kaylo. I always had reasons, but I can't say I've forgiven myself, not fully."

As he spoke, the image of rabbit ears poking out from under Junera's limp hand crawled into my mind. The ear on the left bent at an odd angle where my hand had slipped while carving. It ruined the proportion between the two ears. I should have spent more time making it perfect for her.

"We have all done things, made choices we regret. That is human. If forgiveness isn't possible right now, can you move past it?" he asked.

"The Thief created spirit crystals and showed the Gousht exactly where to find them."

Zusa nodded slowly. "Stones that can steal spirits from dancers like spirit thieves do. Can't say I'm surprised. It's not the first time I heard someone blame The Thief for all this, but it may be the first time I believe it."

"And part of her lives in me."

"That doesn't mean the occupation is your fault. Damn kid, the moons aren't shining as brightly I as I would like—is that your fault too?"

I smiled wearily. "I'll talk to the Daughters about that tomorrow."

"Ahh, Kaylo," he said. "What am I going to do with you? You might be more broken than I am."

"Glad I could make you feel better about yourself."

As Zusa straightened up and looked into my eyes, the smile left his cheeks. "Listen. There's nothing wrong with you. No spirit can make you what you're not, and the way those other kids look at you tells me something," he said. "It tells me that you are someone to believe in, even if you don't believe in yourself."

"I don't think..."

"Stop. I'm done hearing you belittle yourself tonight. You can start again in the morning if you need to, but not tonight."

I couldn't look at him any longer. If I did, I would have started crying and, even if he left his armor in the tent, I wasn't ready to drop mine. Instead, I studied the tips of the flames stealing through the gaps in the rock wall that surrounded the firepit. They snuck through their cage for a moment of freedom before falling back.

———————

Boda bit his lip and furrowed his brow as he swept the snow from the clearing with a makeshift broom. The circle separated this empty patch of dirt from the rest of the forest—a world onto itself. Obviously, a trick of The Seed.

Somewhere in Zusa's chest of crystals, one of my brother spirits screamed out endlessly. *What happened to a spirit of forgiveness after turns of being caged within a spirit crystal?*

I wanted to find the stone and smash it to pieces, but once a crystal got hold of a spirit, it never let go.

At the northern edge of the circle, Niven and Sionia stacked wood for a fire. Soon we would be moving and the cold would fade from our minds, but until then, the rest of us stood shivering, waiting for Zusa to begin his instruction.

Morning training usually began with standard drills, sword stances followed by sparring. Every few days, Zusa would work a new skill into the routine, and we would sweat as Sokan climbed higher into the sky. From the look on his face, today was one of those days. He cradled something heavy wrapped in fabric and gently set it down.

"Swords are essential in war. They are versatile weapons." Zusa held up his sword, catching the glare of the sun along its edge. "A blade like this favors piercing strikes, whereas heavier blades batter an opponent's guard. The weight of a blade can change the way it moves through the air and how hard it lands against an opponent's guard. This is a weapon of finesse, not force."

Many things could be said of Zusa, but he controlled an audience even better than he wielded his blade. He bent down slowly, drawing attention to whatever he had wrapped in the fabric at his feet. With a flourish, he tossed the fabric open to reveal a cache of weapons, from which he hefted a large axe.

The grain of the ironoak ran the length of the axe handle, which measured as long as Zusa's arm. The smooth steel head arched out to a sharp curved edge on one side and jutted out like the flat of a hammer on the other. Zusa held the axe in two hands, jostling it back and forth to feel the weight of the weapon.

"This, on the other hand, may not be as versatile, but it has its uses. What it lacks in finesse, it makes up for in force. Speed is an advantage in combat, but so is strength," Zusa said, then handed the axe to Chêta, who stood closest to him. "Pass it down once you have a chance to feel the weight in your hands."

All eyes followed his hands as he reached down for the next weapon. His hand settled around a spear. The triangular blade perching atop the long staff reached a head taller than Zusa. Far less intimidating than the axe.

"The spear is all about speed. The adaptability of a spear is in its length. It can allow you to strike from a greater distance than a sword, or reposition your hands," he said and demonstrated. "And you can engage in closer combat."

He passed the spear down the row. "Lastly, the bow and arrow. I'm sure all of you have used this weapon to hunt, but it is an entirely different weapon in combat. Your opponent understands the weapon in your hands. They know that if they can shorten the distance between the two of you, they can cut you down," he said. "But there is no greater weapon for long distances.

"Today, you will each rotate through, practicing with each of these weapons," he said, then paused for a moment. "When you have a choice, I want you to know what weapon fits you best. When you don't, I want you to be able to use what is available. Too many times, you won't have a choice."

Zusa grouped us in twos and threes, assigning each group to a section of the training grounds. Niven, as usual, served in an apprentice role. He walked Adêan and me over to our assigned section, carrying a spear in each hand.

As intimidating as Niven's presence could be, his smile softened him. His arms were thick as ironoak branches, and his legs were larger still. Yet, he moved with a gentle grace. The two times I had the misfortune of sparring with him had left me uninterested in repeating the experience. As soon as the matches had begun, his smile had dropped, and then I did.

Adēan nearly matched Niven's bulk, but he lacked the agility and skill Niven had. If Adēan learned how to move his body properly, he would be a daemon on the battlefield.

"A spear is a challenging weapon to master," Niven said. "You must learn how to fight with it as a lunging tool, to keep distance between you and your opponent. But you also must understand how to wield it like a staff when your opponent breaks past your guard."

Without warning, he tossed me a spear. The ironoak clapped against my hands and fell to the ground. Niven smiled and shook his head.

"The first thing you need to learn about a spear is that your offense is your defense, especially against someone with a sword. By thrusting forward," he said as he forced me back with a quick thrust. "You can keep your opponent at a distance."

Over the next hour, Niven showed us both how to grip the spear properly, how to angle the shaft so that the tip of the blade shielded our faces, and how to make simple short and long thrusts. Once he deemed our basic mechanics passable, we paired off against two trees and practiced thrusting.

Pain spread from my shoulders to my biceps. Each attack demanded that my body move in a way it wasn't accustomed to. The spear grew heavier and heavier in my arms, but I refused to complain or rest—not while Adēan continued to push through the drills without slowing.

Niven moved back and forth between us and Talise and Sionia, who worked on sword drills. Each time he came back, Niven tipped the blade of my spear back into position. "Don't get lazy," he said. "If this blade drops, so does your defense."

"At this point, I think the tree is dead," I said, maintaining my defensive stance.

"The more you train your body to fight through the ache now, the more likely—"

A sudden crack and moan broke through the training grounds. Everyone turned to see Boda clutching his head, leaning forward, and Zusa standing over him with his unsheathed sword.

"This isn't a game, boy," Zusa yelled. "Pick up the axe and swing the bloody thing, or I will teach you what pain is."

The small boy hefted the axe in his hands and positioned it diagonally across his body. The length of the handle made Boda seem even smaller. He glowered at Zusa and breathed deeply through his flared nostrils.

"You're angry," Zusa said. "Good. Attack me!"

Boda didn't need further prompting. He yelled, reeling back and slashing forward from his right shoulder. The attack moved as if the air were made of sap, and Zusa easily parried with his sword. Regaining his balance, Boda thrust the hook of the axe. The weight of the weapon carried the boy forward.

Zusa stepped aside and blocked Boda's foot with the flat of his blade, causing the boy to tumble to the ground. "Never let your anger throw you off balance," Zusa said, as Boda lay in the dirt below him.

As if noticing the silence around him for the first time, Zusa looked up and around. "That's enough of a break. Leave your weapons where they are and move to the next section. Niven or I will come by to start you on your drills."

With that, Zusa sheathed his sword before walking over to Wal and Tomi to collect the other axes. Niven rushed over to his brother, but as soon as he touched the boy, Boda pushed him away.

When Adéan and I exchanged looks, we didn't say a word, but my concern reflected back at me in his eyes. What if it had been Tomi or Wal? Would we have allowed the scene to play out the same way?

Apart from Zusa and Niven, we were the oldest. And yet, until the spring equinox, when we were to swear ourselves to Ennea, we were both children. And we behaved like children, saying nothing.

CHAPTER THIRTEEN
KAYLO'S STORY

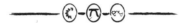

IF I HAD TO rely on anything other than a sword in battle, I would be dead. Picking up an axe would be tantamount to stabbing myself in the gut and twisting the blade.

But Zusa insisted, and as with all things, he got his way.

After a span of weapons training, the skin on my palms started to peel away to rough red flesh. The edge of the axe blade caught Sokan's light in a fine line, as if to prove it could have been a worthy weapon in the hands of someone more capable.

The damn thing weighed too much. I planted my feet exactly as Zusa had shown me a dozen times over. The axe head rested in front of me at a defensive angle. I reeled back and then drove forward in a crosscut. The blow would have cleaved away a hunk of flesh had anyone been on the other end of it, but as it was, the momentum of the blade tipped me forward, causing me to stumble after my balance.

"Blessed Mother, no! Let the axe do the work," Zusa said. "You're swinging the thing like it isn't sharp." He motioned for me to put the weapon down. "Look at Adéan. Watch how he positions himself."

Only a pair of moons separated Adéan and me, but he measured more of a man than me by far. His shoulders stretched his robes to the edge of tearing as he took a deep breath. Then in one smooth motion, he drew back the axe blade and slashed downward, stopping when the axe head reached starting position across his chest. The grace of his attack could only be outdone by its power.

"You see? Now do it like that," Zusa said.

A slight smile crept along Adéan's mouth as he continued to run the drill.

Several uncouth words ran through my head as I lifted the weapon. I needed a new drill partner.

"Right now, starting position," Zusa said, and I did as told.

"No, no, no. You aren't doing lunges." Zusa's annoyance crept into his voice. He smacked my front leg, and I repositioned it. "That's better. Now, slash."

As soon as I brought the head of the axe down, Zusa grunted his disapproval. "Fucking Seven Spirits. Why are you attacking with your shoulder? Give me that thing."

Without giving me the chance, Zusa yanked the axe from my hands and got into starting position. "When you slash, your high hand is a guide and your low hand snaps into your chest. That is where the power comes from. If you lean your shoulder into your attack, you'll be slow to recover, and you'll open up your defenses."

A sharp sound broke through the forest, followed by a dozen more. I whipped my head around towards the echoes to find something flashing between the trees. The echoes moved closer.

Suddenly, I longed for the weight of the axe back in my hands. Whoever was out there moved amongst a horde of caged spirits.

"Where the fuck are you looking?" Zusa asked. "This is the difference between life or—"

"Someone's coming."

Zusa paused and narrowed his eyes, then followed my sightline.

Moving shadows and shapes formed into a horse, then another, and another still. We had to escape. The trees would slow them down. *Too many echoes. Too many soldiers.*

"We have to run," I said, but the words came out like a whisper.

Zusa's fingers clasped my shoulder and held me in place.

The horses ambled closer, and the riders came into view—northmen wearing gray, threadbare robes and leather vests. Beyond them, the forest stood still. No flickers of green and yellow. No soldiers to be found.

"We don't run." A deep frown creased Zusa's face. "Go back to your drills." He shoved the axe handle back into my hands and walked towards the approaching riders without another word.

My tongue dried in my mouth. *We have to run?* The sound of my own whining voice repeated in my head. After all my bravado and declarations, my first reaction was to flee.

Adēan went back to perfecting his form with the tree chopper, but I couldn't. Drills couldn't erase the shame that hollowed out my chest.

Zusa greeted the riders warmly, helped them hitch their horses, and escorted them into his tent.

Eyes closed to the world, I searched for my rage. The image of a small hand clutching for a bloody rabbit was never far from reach.

The snow crunched after my third step towards the tents, and I caught myself. *This could end badly.* Zusa didn't tolerate disobedience.

Then again, we were rebels.

If fear resided in the unknown, I needed to know who they were and why they had come. So, despite the feverish pace of my heartbeat, I crept towards Zusa's tent.

Several people called after me in hushed tones, but I waved them away until their pleading words stopped. Maybe their own curiosity stilled their tongues. Or maybe they didn't want to be rolled up into whatever mess I created.

With each step, the echoes grew fuller and louder, like the sound of a waterfall plummeting into the valley below. The new stones added their own chaos to Zusa's collection of crystals, growing into a torrent of clashing spirits.

It took a turn's worth of discipline to silence the violent storm as I settled against the mismatched collection of furs and hides forming Zusa's tent. Light from the brazier inside shined through the thinner of the skins.

My breath caught in my ears, louder than their voices, but not so loud as my thumping heart.

"Can you trust the boy?" a loud grumble of a voice asked.

The boy?

"Trust or not, this is an opportunity." The second voice pitched up and cut through the chaos.

"You just tell the General she would be foolish to ignore it," Zusa said.

"Foolish? You want me to lose my tongue?"

General? Who the fuck is this General?

"Pick whatever words you like, but tell her. Now, you should get going. The light won't be on your side long."

Bodies rustled and wood clanged against something hard on the other side of the fabric divide, but the thoughts in my head spoke louder. *Was he telling them my secret?* Zusa had eyed me like a weapon since the first time we had met.

Pimpled flesh covered my arms under my robes.

The secret that had cut me off from everyone around me had slowly seeped out into the world, growing beyond my control.

As I craned my neck beyond the tent's canopy, two of the riders walked towards their horses carrying Zusa's stormwood chest between them. Neither of them had seen two decades. Leather armor hung loosely over the smaller man's shoulders. These warriors were little more than children themselves.

Snow cracked under the chest's weight as they dropped it unceremoniously to the ground. They popped the lock and began transferring the crystals into their saddlebags by the armful. A case filled with stolen shards of the Great Spirits, and they tossed the stones into their bags without care or caution.

Anger drove away my insecurities as the crystals clanged together.

They had no respect for the spirits trapped within those crystals.

A third, much older, rather hairy rider waited beside Zusa right outside of his tent. "We ride north for another two days. That should be our last stop before we cross," the warrior said. "I'll give your regards to the General."

"Yeah, tell that arrogant daemon she can kiss my sweaty undercarriage," Zusa said.

"I'll try to pass your words along verbatim," the rider said, then paused. "You never answered me. Do you think you can trust your young thief?"

"Why?" Zusa asked.

"Is that him?" The rider gestured in my direction without looking.

Zusa turned, and his face drooped as he sighed. "Maybe trust is something we'll have to work on."

Whatever the consequences, I had no intention of hiding myself. I stared at the strange man who knew my secret.

"Reminds me of a young man I knew once," the older rider said. "Be well, friend. I'll give your kindest regards to the general."

"Till next we meet. This side of The Mist..."

"Or the other," the rider finished.

Without ceremony, our visitors trotted off, carrying the bulk of the echoes deep into the forest with them.

The screeching spirits had almost vanished when Zusa rounded the tent. His face was placid as he stepped uncomfortably close, leaned down, and whispered into my ear. "If you're going to eavesdrop, you need to be better at it. Now, get back to your drills. You'll need all the practice you can get."

Fear held my words at bay, but I managed to meet his gaze before he turned back towards the training grounds.

The hours passed as I continued to display the futility of learning this useless weapon. Muscles from my shoulder blades to my fingers seized into a fury of hardened tissue until three successive whistles pierced the air.

"Let's to it," Zusa yelled.

Same phrase every day—the routine of it carried weight. And nothing mattered more than routine to Zusa.

The stiffness in my shoulders settled into a slow burning as I placed the axe back in the pile of weapons. The burning sensation swept down my neck, through my shoulders and down my sides.

My body wasn't used to this level of demand. It wanted to wilt and settle into the dirt, but there was work to be done.

Without exception, chores before food and rest.

The training grounds needed to be cleaned, the weapons tended to and stored, food needed cooking, and water needed fetching. Yet no one needed orders. We fit in where work needed doing.

As soon as Niven volunteered to gather water, I offered to join him.

The half-hour walk to and from the pond sounded about as enjoyable as picking up an axe again for another round of training, but Niven knew this place. And he, if anyone, would have the answers to my questions.

So, despite my rumbling stomach and sore muscles, I hefted up my share of waterskins and followed after him.

Sokan hung about four fingers above the falling horizon, and for once in too damn long, the clouds allowed her light to fill the sky with something other than gray. The wind ran cold death over every bit of exposed skin, but the blue in the sky made it more tolerable.

Neither Niven nor I spoke a word on our way to the pond. Apart from his skills on the training field and his annoying little brother, Boda, Niven was a series of unanswered questions. The others talked, some of them too much, but Niven kept his own council.

He walked with an affable smile and broke the silence by humming a tune I had never heard before.

"What song is that?" I asked.

"Actually, it's a drinking song from the south. My father and his friends would sing it after they finished a mug or three of his ale." He held out an invisible mug.

> *Drink one for all the spirits,*
> *drink another for the sun,*
> *when you've had one for the Daughters,*
> *you've only just begun,*
> *for The Mother needs a cask or two,*
> *so hold your mug up high,*
> *if you drink enough to meet her,*
> *then here's to our last goodbye.*

I chuckled. "It's much prettier when you hum it."

"Yeah, and that one was more pleasant than most," Niven said. "We've almost reached the pond, so you might as well ask me what you came to ask me."

"How did you come to join up with Zusa?" I asked.

"I guess we'll get to the real questions later. My mother died when she gave birth to Boda, then my father left to fight off the invasion." He held his smile in place, but it lost its truth. "After that, our neighbor raised us as best he could, but when age took him, we ran from our village.

"We hid out in the forest for almost two turns before Zusa found us—bone thin and threadbare. We weren't looking for a fight, just a safe place. Zusa gave us that."

"He found you by accident?" *Like Jonac found me,* I thought.

"Well, we saw his fire and were hungry enough to risk it. When Boda ran straight for the pheasant cooking over their fire, Zusa and his trainees damn near fell over themselves pulling their weapons."

"I wish I could've seen that."

"Boda wasn't a day over ten, and he started wailing when one of the older rebels pointed a knife at him. Zusa calmed everyone down before offering us the bulk of the bird," he said. "That's the Zusa I know."

"He's a bit harsh with Boda."

"Boda is a handful, and he knows how to push Zusa's buttons. Sometimes it goes too far, but Zusa loves him." His voice trailed off at the end.

"What's up with Boda's hair?" I asked, and he smiled again. "I don't think I've seen him sit down without brushing it out."

"If you want to see him lose control, touch his hair. You don't even have to muss it up, and he will go wild," Niven said, laughing.

"I'll take your word for it. My mother taught me never to mess with anyone's hair."

"Our father used to wear his hair in waves. He'd say, 'Other people will see you, make sure they see what you what them to.' I don't even think Boda can remember him, but I've told him stories. Ever since he was big enough to hold a brush, he's been working his hair."

Niven stopped and smiled wider, though his eyes turned into a sad memory. "He really does look like Daddy did."

I smiled at the story, despite the sadness underneath it. My parents used to argue over which one I looked like, but I could never see it. I ran my hand through my braids. They had gotten long and needed rebraiding. My mother would have read me up and down about how disheveled I looked.

We fell into a different kind of silence for the rest of the walk to the pond. When I was little, I used to beg my parents for a brother or sister. All my friends had siblings. Some of them fought constantly, but they always got back to even ground the next day.

My thoughts turned on me. Junera and Soca had been as close as any siblings I had known. Junera constantly pushed against Soca's boundaries, but for her little sister, Soca bent. The tiny, responsible, guarded girl allowed herself to be freer, to play and abandon her anxiety for a time.

Tears gently rolled down my face by the time we reached the pond. We filled the waterskins in silence. I didn't offer any reason for my tears, and Niven didn't ask for one.

My stomach roared to life in the thick of our silence.

Despite my stubborn need for guilt, I couldn't help but giggle at the silly sound. Everything about my life, from training to walking through The Mist, held such a weight. The gurgle of my belly cut through the heaviness of it all.

A giggle turned into a belly laugh, and I couldn't stop myself. Then the fact that I was laughing over something so juvenile made me laugh even harder.

Niven's judgmental expression cracked until he too began laughing at my ridiculousness.

Eventually, I caught my breath, and Niven and I exchanged wide smiles. We slung the heavy waterskins over our shoulders and began walking back, lighter on our feet, despite the weight on our shoulders.

If I was going to get the answers I wanted, I needed to ask my questions now. "What happened earlier with the riders?"

"And there it is. The real reason you volunteered to walk to the pond. I knew it was something."

"No, that's not why…" His eyelids narrowed, and the look itself was enough to stop my excuses. "Okay, it is, but I'm glad I came anyway."

"Me too," he said. "You all seem to think that it's you and your friends against Zusa and the rest of us. But we aren't your enemy."

"You know what it's like out there. Trust is dangerous."

"That's where you're wrong. Trust is the only thing we have left." His lips settled into a straight line, and the roundness of his cheeks fell. "Without trust, we're all on our own. Without trust, the couta outnumber us a hundred thousand to one. But we aren't alone."

"What about Zusa's secrets?"

"Ask him. Zusa isn't hiding anything from you. He may not have made a detailed presentation regarding every plan the Missing have, but he's not keeping anything from you," he said.

I was about to counter and remind him that not sharing information and hiding it formed two edges of the same blade, but he cut me off before I formed the first word and repeated himself. "Ask him."

We returned as the others gathered around the firepit. Niven joined his brother in the circle. The sound of Boda's brush lightly sweeping through his hair joined the crackling of the fire. People engaged in their own small conversations or settled into the night.

No one crossed the invisible boundary between the two groups as we ate. After my conversation with Niven, the division seemed juvenile. We had trained side-by-side, eaten from the same pot, and kept guard over this camp for near a moon.

Eventually, we would have to decide to abandon our apprehension.

As everyone finished their meals, the smokey, sweet scent of our dinner lingered in the night. Roasted sweet potatoes, salt meat, and fresh blueberries—compliments of The Seed.

Gravity pulled harder on my weary body. If I could stand and make it to the tent, it would be a small gift from The Mother. There would be no searching for sleep tonight. Hopefully, that meant it would be dreamless.

Sionia broke the circle first, making her way to our tent. After that, people stretched and grunted, then pushed themselves up from the ground to seek the relative comfort of their tents. Adéan and Chêta lingered behind with Zusa and I. They had both drawn first watch, which seemed to happen with some regularity.

Maybe some of us had already given up the tensions of our original loyalties.

Slowly, they began speaking to each other in their native dialect. Their conversation sounded like a call and response of a song I couldn't understand. It must have been tiresome to force themselves to slow down and change the way they spoke for the rest of us.

How could I begrudge Adéan this small comfort?

"Kaylo," Zusa said. "Follow me." Without waiting for a response, he got up and walked into his tent. I took my time following suit.

Inside the tent, the brazier flickered off the canopy skins. Zusa waited, sitting atop the chest filled with echoes. The stormwood box imprisoned fewer spirits than it had yesterday, but they screamed all the same.

"You need to work on your spy-craft," he said.

I opened my mouth to make an excuse, with no idea of what to say. But he saved me from my lies. "You're curious. Curiosity isn't necessarily a bad trait. What do you think is in this chest?" He slapped his open palm against the wood.

"I know what's in the chest."

"Now I'm curious. How?"

"I can hear them—spirits locked inside crystals."

His eyebrows arched. "You can hear The Song from the crystals?" His eyes shined with a hunger, which sent a chill crawling over my arms.

"Where did you get the crystals in that chest? Who were those riders this morning? Why did you give away most of the spirits?"

"So many questions. It's natural, I guess. You and your friends are still wary of us, but it's no secret," he said. "We stole the crystals from the Gousht, and those riders take the crystals to people who can make better use of them."

"The spirits inside those stones are suffering."

"You are a fascinating young man, Kaylo," he said. "If I am correct, you don't even know the bounds of your power—a mistwalker, a descended of The Thief and The Seed."

"I'm not your tool."

"No. No, you aren't. You're much more than that." The corner of his mouth crept up into a sly smile. "Do you hate The Thief?"

My lips tightened, and my nostrils flared. What a stupid question. The black and white bitch was a curse worse than words, but that anger belonged to me. Zusa could take his answer from the silence.

"Then why don't you use her? Let me train you to dance with The Thief. Use her power to destroy your enemies," he said. "Without their stones, the Gousht are worthless."

"I'm not a malitu."

"Fuck that. Be a malitu. Be the cruelest, most dangerous spirit thief the couta have ever met." He leaned forward, lowering his voice. "When they tell the story, be the fire that burns an empire to the ground."

The voices of everyone I had ever trusted and loved screamed warnings in my head. As much sense as it made, it went against everything I had ever learned. But those voices belonged to the dead and gone. Their faces filled the space between Zusa and me like a burial ground.

"How do we start?"

CHAPTER FOURTEEN
KAYLO'S STORY

THE TIME HAD COME. As I walked into the field of near-black, I took stock of my surroundings. No runes to line the ground. No manipulative visions to put my tragedies on display. The space was simply empty—save her.

The Thief waited, covered in her shadow cloak, larger than I remembered her. Her mouthless face hid within the shadowed hood of her cloak. And yet, without question, her stark white eyes watched me from the darkness.

A vestige of The Seed's voice spoke softly in my head. "Limits only exist here as a matter of perception."

The blackness that surrounded her, the shadows that draped over her, the mask that was her face—they only existed as a matter of perception. She projected it into The Mist. She wanted me to see her in this stark world.

"Oh, young one," The Thief said. "Just because it is a matter of perception doesn't mean it isn't real."

"Why didn't you tell me?"

"What does it matter to you how I shape The Mist around me?"

"You know that's not what I mean."

"Ah, after these long moons, you came here to demand answers? Why do you think I owe you anything?" she asked. "You are only alive because I gave you the power to protect yourself."

"We are not having this argument again. Not when it's your fault that the Gousht won the war."

She peeled back her hood and paused for a moment as her brow rose, wrinkling the perfect black of her forehead. "If your people willingly turned me into their villain, why should I be anything else?"

"You destroyed my people because they told mean stories about you?"

The Thief's eyes thinned to small lines of white against her onyx-black skin. "They killed my descendants for those stories. They cursed me and called me by a false name. Have you forgotten the look in Shay's dying eyes, how she recoiled from you?" she asked. "Tell me, did the stories feel insignificant to you at that moment?"

"You're a liar! It's all you do—lie and steal. Did you steal your cloak from The Shadow too?"

"Watch yourself, boy. If you leave this place, it will be by my goodwill."

"Then tell me, Balance, what is it you want? You trapped pieces of your siblings in cages to suffer. Why?"

"I found a way to allow anyone to dance with the spirits. For so long, The Song only belonged to the marked. Most weren't even deserving. That was not balance."

"You've seen The Waking. Does that feel like balance to you?"

She met my question with silence. We stared accusations at each other in the void that was her corner of The Mist. Then she lifted her hood back in place before turning to walk away. "You should leave," she said. "Next time, I may not be so generous."

"Questions only feel like attacks when you don't want to admit the truth," I called into the blackness as she walked away.

———

My chest constrained against each breath, the veins in my neck pulsing small vibrations through the back of my jaw. Morning's first light slid through the cracks of the tent's opening, but everyone else slept, blissfully unaware.

Even if my body got what rest it needed, my thoughts moved as if they carried the weight of a sleepless night. I couldn't keep this up much longer.

When I slept, the dead haunted me. When I walked The Mist with spirits who could change this world but didn't, I woke up with a different kind of weariness.

At least in The Mist, I could control the burdens I had to face.

Zusa and Boda huddled around the firepit, briefly pausing their conversation as I stepped out into the early morning. Wal didn't stir at all, slumped against a tree, staying vigilant through his watch.

Let him sleep, I thought. *If I could, I would.*

"He's been out for over an hour," Boda said with a smirk.

"Is there anyone else you would like to tattle on?" I asked.

"If you all can't handle a watch, that's not my problem."

"Boys, there is no reason to fight this early in the morning," Zusa said. "Kaylo, I know you all have lingering trust issues, but having two people on watch all night is not a long-term solution. Tired people shouldn't be swinging axes."

"I'll talk to the others," I said.

"They couldn't swing an axe even if they rested all day," Boda said.

"Are you really the one to talk?" Zusa said. "If you are going to taunt someone, make sure you can carry the weight of your words."

Boda's upper lip turned up into a sneer, but he didn't bother saying anything else. He dipped his spoon into his porridge, struggling to maintain his dirty look as he ate his breakfast.

"I've been thinking about our talk last night," Zusa said. "The whole point of training with multiple weapons is that you need to discover your strengths and lean into them." He looked at me expectantly, as if he had finished a full thought.

"And?"

"You're a spirit thief. That's the training we need to focus on," he said. "It's not like you're showing much of an aptitude for spears and axes."

"It's been a span."

"Ten long rough days," he said, and Boda snickered with a mouth full of porridge. "Finish your breakfast, then wake up your vigilant guard. We are going to need someone for you to train with."

Zusa scooped the last of his breakfast into his mouth, clapped the dirt from his hands, and walked off to his tent, leaving his dirty bowl for Boda to tend to.

What did I get myself into? Zusa ran weapons training like a series of torture drills. Now he would concentrate all of his focus on me and The Thief.

My expression must have made my apprehension clear because Boda's smile spread wide—the cocksure little nuisance.

"Go brush your hair or something."

Boda winked at me. "Enjoy your training, thief." The prepubescent child collected both his and Zusa's bowls, then walked back to his tent.

Wal's snoring filled the space Boda and Zusa left behind. If I had been mentally exhausted before, my faculties were completely depleted now.

The cold papery bark of the ashburn tree tickled my skin as I pressed my palm flat against its trunk. Leafless and gray, the tree floated like a soft whisper in The Song. As if it was biding its time until spring's renewal, a thin melody within the tree sang a prelude.

But Zusa needed a second training ground.

For the fifth time this morning, I moved my arms inward and outward in opposing motions, and the slow march of time sped up. First, the branches of the tree turned paler. Then they shriveled. Some pieces of dead wood fell to the surrounding ground. When death crept into the tree's core, the trunk arched. Finally, the last remaining pieces of the tree aged beyond death, crumbling to ash and scattering over the snow.

No matter how many times I had used The Song to kill a living thing, it never stopped hurting. I pressed three fingers to my lips, then to the frozen soil in mourning. We needed flat earth where I could train to kill, and for that, I sacrificed these peaceful lives. The ugliness of it settled in my stomach beside my breakfast.

Wal stood beside Zusa as I finished clearing the grounds—a circle about ten good paces from any end to the other. The sagging bags under Wal's eyes and the paleness in his cheeks made him look sick. He and the others had escaped an indoctrination camp, got caught in an ambush, trekked through the winter, and then picked up weapons to train for war. They all needed some rest.

Blessed Mother, I needed some rest too.

"Tell me how this works," Zusa said. The casual way he asked about The Thief toyed with my nerves.

"How are you going to train me if you don't know anything about dancing with spirits?"

"We are going to learn together and test The Thief. She has bounds like anything else. Let's find them," he said. "Now, tell me how it works."

"If a dancer can hear The Song, I hear the reflection of The Song through them. I call it an echo. With crystals, the echo never goes away—it's trapped. Then, when someone pulls on a spirit through The Song, I can take that spirit into myself."

"That's it? You just take it?"

"If it's a spirit from a crystal, it feels like a raccoon is trying to claw their way free from my gut, but yeah, I just take it."

"Alright then, let's see it," he said and handed Wal a smokey gray crystal.

"I don't know what to do with this," Wal said. He held the crystal like it might burn him.

"Wal, given your ability to turn everything into a quip, I am going to say this as clearly and concisely as I can," Zusa said. "You are shit with a sword, and yet, it's your best weapon. Now one day, you might be slightly better than shit, but that won't be enough. Learn to use every advantage that comes your way. You won't win because you're more skilled. You'll win because you're a scrappy little bastard who will do anything to survive."

Wal's gaze shifted between Zusa and me. He took several long breaths and then nodded. "Fair enough. How does this work?"

"The Wind is trapped in this crystal," Zusa said. "Through you, it can move the air around us. But it is only air. You can make the air do anything you can imagine air would do. It can gust, it can spin into a funnel, it can cool you off on a warm summer's day, but it can't turn into a blade. It can't set a fire or crack the earth in two."

"Got it," Wal said. "So, how does it work?"

I waited and listened as Zusa painstakingly taught Wal the basic mechanics of spirit crystals. In theory, it wasn't difficult to understand—one imagined the wind doing something, then willed the wind through the crystal. In practice, it required a finesse that didn't come easily to everyone.

Sokan slowly crawled higher into the sky. I held my hand up to measure the hours. At least six fingers had passed by, and Wal could only make a stiff breeze. That or a stiff breeze just happened to coincide with his flailing about.

"Can I make a suggestion?" I asked.

They both froze in place, their faces marked with two different stages of annoyance—Zusa held murder behind his eyes, and Wal would rather be napping.

"Wal, you aren't a dancer. You'll never be a dancer..."

"Thanks for the helpful tip."

"Close your mouth and listen for once," I said. "The spirit in that crystal belongs to a dancer. When a dancer calls The Wind, they move with it. The separation between the dancer and the spirit shrinks, and they move together."

"You want me to dance like wind?"

"I want you to get the fuck out of your own way and move like you want The Wind to. There is no one here to impress. Zusa thinks you're a waste of the air in your lungs, and I am going to be on your side regardless of what happens. Try it."

Wal waved his hands in front of his face and blew through his sprawled fingers.

"What do you have to lose if you take this one moment seriously?" I asked and leveled my gaze until he met it.

He nodded, taking in a deep breath. With tentative steps, he moved forward like the ground beneath him had frozen solid and a wrong move would send him tumbling to the ground. One foot followed the other as he circled the edge of the clearing. His hands fell into a simple pattern, waving through the air while tightly clutching the crystal in his left fist. The echo built, and then the wind started swirling through the clearing. As the wind caught the snow from the ground, it lifted a small cloud of white powder into the air.

The left side of Zusa's face tugged into a smirk as he watched Wal move. His gaze grew possessive, like he had added a new weapon to his cache.

The snow cloud fell all at once, the echo receding as Wal stood up straight. He looked to me with his mouth held partially agape. His eyes went wide. Then he nodded to himself. "Did you see that?"

"How did it feel?" I asked.

"Like power," he said. "Like, for once, I wasn't the target. I was the arrow."

"Do you want to try again?" Zusa asked.

Wal didn't wait. He moved again, faster than the last time. The snow-filled wind stung as it rotated around the open circle. If it moved any faster, the wind would have threatened my stance.

"Kaylo!" Zusa's voice barely penetrated the wind. "Now! Do it Now!"

The echo screamed louder than the wind whipping across my face—there for the taking. A strand of light, a wisp of light gray floated in the air—a line between the crystal and me.

There was no subtlety to The Thief.

I reached my arm into the air and, as soon as I closed my fingers around the thread, the snow dropped back to the ground, and the air stilled.

The familiar wrenching of my gut and searing pain made me bend slightly forward. I gritted my teeth. Zusa and Wal both looked at me like I had played a trick on them, which they could not figure out.

"You have the spirit?" Wal asked.

I took my turn to smile. As I looked over the forest, I imagined a gust of wind pushing through the trees behind me, building speed. My body understood what to do. I rotated my arms, one over the other. A circle that pushed and pulled. And then I leaned forward, and a gust blew over my right shoulder straight into Wal, sending him tumbling feet over head to the snow-covered dirt.

"Oh shit!" I said as I ran to him.

He lay splayed out, face down in the snowdrift. His body didn't move. Zusa and I shared a concerned look before I dropped my hold on the spirit and rushed to my friend's side.

"Wal, are you alright?" I turned him over with all my strength.

A smile pulled his face wide. "Teach me how to do that."

We didn't stop to eat. Zusa had to force us to drink water. Wal and I passed the spirit between us, moving the air in every conceivable way.

It became a game, and I forgot to worry over the stolen spirit or The Thief's crystals. The power of pushing and pulling the wind sent adrenaline coursing through my body.

As Sokan dipped behind the treetops, Wal folded in half, panting for air with sweat rolling down his forehead. "This is exhausting," he said.

"Of course it is," Zusa said. "The Wind is on the other side of The Mist. You are pulling him into The Waking; you are giving your energy to move the air."

"Makes sense," Wal said. "Maybe that's why I'm so hungry." He stuck his bottom lip out and tilted his chin down in an exaggerated pout. "Could we please be done for the day, Commander?"

Zusa shook his head at Wal. "At some point, you are going to have to realize life isn't a joke."

"Maybe," Wal said. "But for now, can we go eat?"

The others had already begun their meal by the time we joined them. Wal rushed to the pot and found an open space around the fire.

Camp had settled into the two regular factions as always, but the tension didn't hang as thick.

People had paired off, focusing their attention on their companions. Wal's head bobbed periodically as he struggled to stay awake, which may have accounted for the lack of off-putting comments. And Zusa held to the outskirts of the firelight, sipping his soup, wearing a contemplative look on his face.

I pulled Wal away from the others, and we finished our soup over a game of runes. If I left him to his own devices, he might have broken the delicate balance the group had found, and I needed to focus on something. Too many thoughts clattered around in my head.

Wal learned quickly. Each time we played, he put up a harder battle.

As I waited for him to choose his next move, I rolled the runes around in my hand. He stared at the crosspoints like they would move if he waited long enough.

When I cleared my throat, he flinched, then challenged one of my pieces with The Shadow. Given all the pieces that had cycled through the game or lay face up, it was a thoughtless play. The probabilities leaned my way. When I turned my rune over, The Seed marked another crosspoint in my favor.

"Where are you right now?"

He looked up at me. "What are you talking about?"

"Are you thinking about the crystals?"

"No, well, yes and no. I was thinking about...it felt good to have something I always wanted," he said. "You don't know what it's like to be bound."

"I know what it's like to be hunted and have to hide."

"I'm not saying I have it worse." He rolled his eyes. "I'm just saying it's hard to be average. Today, I got to feel what it's like to have the power to move the world," he said. "It felt good."

Part of me wanted—no, needed to remind him that the spirits in those crystals had been stolen and imprisoned, but he knew that. It didn't mean that he didn't have the right to want something that he could never fully have.

Three quick bursts of Zusa's whistle gathered everyone's attention. He stood next to the firepit, the light wavering over his face. "Tomorrow, we move camp. Make sure you're ready in the morning. We don't leave anything behind, understood?"

Heads nodded in agreement in each of the small groups, but Wal remained still. A small smile turned the corners of his lips.

"Get some sleep." Zusa stepped back from the light and went off into his tent.

"Do you want to finish the game before we hit the bedrolls?" I asked.

"Sure, sounds like a plan," Wal said, but his gaze lingered across the firepit. He reached into his hand and placed a rune down next to one of his own crosspoints, as if to challenge himself.

"Are you okay?"

Wal's attention snapped forward as he chuckled. "Sorry, my mind was somewhere else," he said with a stammer. A flush filled his cheeks as he drew back the wooden marker. "What do you think of Adéan?"

Across the fire, where Wal had been staring, Adéan sat close to the flames. He leaned back on his arms, the firelight bright against his soft tawny skin as he stared up into the sky.

"What do you mean, what do I think of Adéan?"

"He has nice shoulders, doesn't he?" he asked, looking at the Renéquan boy. "But his accent is the worst."

"It's getting easier to understand him."

"Yeah, I guess it's not so bad," he said, more to himself than to me. "Maybe it's kind of nice."

Since my family moved to Nomar when I was seven, I had known Wal in one small way or another, and he had never stammered before. His quick wit and quicker tongue kept him in constant conflict with the people around him. But next to the fire, his reddened cheeks and breathy tone softened him.

As people broke away for the evening. Wal adjusted himself, turning his focus to the game when Adēan got up and started walking in our direction. The stocky boy nodded to us as he passed, and I returned the gesture. Wal ignored him all together.

After the non-encounter, Wal proceeded to make several mistakes that wrapped up our latest match rather quickly. It took some of the joy out of winning, but seeing a bashful Wal made up for it tenfold.

When I reached down to collect my runes from the crosspoints, someone tapped me on the shoulder. Liara looked down at me with a grave expression. "Do you have a moment to talk?" she asked.

The look on her face made me want to say no. Today had been a good day. Serious late-night conversations didn't ring out a pleasant ending, and Liara and I had been at odds lately.

Despite my reservations, I nodded.

"Go get some rest, Wal," I said. "You earned a good sleep."

After a nervous smile, he pushed himself off the ground and walked into the tent. Talise had first watch and took off to patrol the perimeter, leaving Liara and I alone on the outskirts of our camp grounds.

A heavy silence descended over us as Liara took Wal's place in front of me. Her eyes watched me as if she could find answers to whatever questions she had if she looked at me long enough. Her mouth formed a stern line. The little contour that ran from the base of her nose and puffed up her cheek when she smiled lay flat and sullen—and perfect.

"What are you doing?" she asked. "You're the one who told me the spirits in those crystals are tormented, and now you're playing games with them?"

"Games?" The peaceful feeling I had flew away with the night breeze. "I'm training. If you hadn't realized, we're fighting an army."

"And this is how you want to fight?"

"Oh, I see. When it meant your sister's life, you were perfectly comfortable with me stealing spirits, but now it's shameful?"

"That's not what I meant," she said, the energy falling from her voice.

"What did you mean then?"

"I don't trust Zusa." Her voice lowered to almost a whisper. "You've seen how he gets. The way he treats people when they don't measure up."

"So, he's hard on Boda."

"It's not just Boda," she said. "Maybe you don't see it because you're his precious weapon."

She clutched her hand to keep it from shaking. Her chest heaved like she was ready for a fight. But I didn't want to fight. The soft wind blew over my exposed neck, and I let myself feel the chill.

"I get it. He's not the most stable person, but he doesn't look down on me because of what I am."

The edges of her mouth turned down, and her lips puckered slightly. "He's using you," she said, with a genuine gentleness.

"Maybe I'm using him."

"I've known men like him, Kaylo. Charismatic when they want something and abusive when they don't get it."

"He isn't your father."

She flinched as if I had poked a fresh bruise. "Maybe not, but he isn't yours either," she said. "I just don't want to see you get hurt."

"Trust me, I won't."

"That may not be up to you," she said. "Just be careful, Kaylo. I need you." With that, she got up and walked into the tent, leaving me alone.

The fire was too far away to reach me, so I sat with the cold.

Everyone wanted something from me. They all imagined I could become some version of the person they needed. No matter how I changed, I would never be enough. Not for all of them. Maybe not for any of them.

All the competing ropes pulled me in different directions. Zusa wanted a weapon, Sionia wanted a leader, Wal wanted a confidant, but Liara said she needed me. Not 'all of us', not 'the others'—*she* needed me. That silly, maybe unintentional phrasing, erased everything else and made the next breath easier.

"I need you too," I whispered into the emptiness of the camp.

CHAPTER FIFTEEN

CURRENT DAY ENNEA

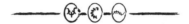

No matter how much Tayen prayed, cursed, cried, or screamed, her mother and Vāhn haunted the dark side of her eyelids. They stared at her through the darkness as if they were waiting for something. And of course they were. Blood owed blood.

She shook the sleep from her eyes, gripping her practice sword until the pain in her palm stirred her.

Their unblinking eyes lacked color and depth, as if they had lost the essence of what they had been.

After all her training and her lofty words of revenge, Tayen had failed again.

If the army didn't intend to use their training tents during meal times, Tayen damn sure would. She hadn't even bothered to start a fire. Winter could try its best. Nothing under the Blessed Mother's eyes could keep her from honing her skills.

Her arm felt as loose as mud on a rainy day. Still, she slashed the blade of her practice sword through the air and snapped back to standard position—perfect form, as it had been hundreds of times before.

They had buried Vāhn with full honors. The regiment watched as Oakan and Chitere lowered her wrapped body to The Mother, but not Tayen. Her eyes had clung to Daak as he knelt amongst the rest of them, head bowed and dirty.

The little fucker hadn't been taking care of himself. His usual arrogance diminished, leaving this frail thing behind.

If he thought that would earn Tayen's pity, he thought wrong.

Tayen swung her blade as the visage of Daak stood in front of her, eyes wet and lip quivering like a fucking child.

There are no children in war, she thought. *You proved that.*

Her strike caught the imaginary boy where his neck sloped into his shoulder.

At night, when the regiment huddled in the barracks for warmth, she thought about it. It would be so easy to find him with his eyes closed and slip a blade across his throat. Or bash his skull in with a rock. But then he would be buried in the same dirt as Vāhn, and Tayen would never be able to honor her parents and her sister.

The muscles from the underside of her arm flowing back to her shoulder blade twitched whenever she went still. Her body hadn't become what it needed to be. The sword wasn't even metal. She shifted her grip on the wooden hilt and began practicing her thrusts—full extension, small step forward, return to center.

After the funeral, Daak had approached her, whimpering like a baby. Wringing his hands. This was the thick-headed, baseborn vermin who killed her friend? He couldn't even look Tayen in the eyes as he cried through an apology she didn't listen to.

It took constant reminders to stay her hand, to continue to allow him to breathe.

Secrets might have been a small power, but sometimes the truth held more weight. She told Daak what she intended to do the first time she saw him after he killed Vāhn. "From now until the trials, I am going to do everything in my power to assure that you fail," she had said. "I am going to tie you to the Citadel so you can walk around like the other mindless drones and serve food to the next round of recruits with your eyes lowered to the fucking dirt."

That would be his first punishment—knowing his future and not having the means to stop it.

Tayen shifted her stance and repositioned her hands on the hilt of her sword before starting her drills over with the new grip.

Nothing would be left to chance. In the morning, she trained with Kaylo. She ate a quick meal and then arrived at the tent before anyone else. When they broke for midday meals, she stayed.

The entrance to the tent flapped open behind her, far too early for the regiment to be back from lunch. She whirled around, fully prepared to beat someone senseless, then she dropped her guard.

"Nice form, but your elbow is moving too much," Nix said. Steam rose off the bowl of porridge in her hands.

"You're not supposed to take food from the mess."

"You need to eat." Nix walked further into the tent.

"Be careful. They'll give you a lashing for that. Maybe a few more if you killed someone. You know how strict they are."

"I heard what happened," Nix said. "I'm sorry about your friend."

"Don't be sorry. You didn't do anything," Tayen said. "And they took care of it. Five lashings for murder seems fair, doesn't it?"

"They are training killers. They can't be surprised when it works."

"She wasn't the enemy!" Tayen screamed as tears ran down her face. Stupid tears that had no right to make her look weak.

"You can't kill him."

"He deserves it."

"But you don't." Nothing about Nix was soft but the pity in her eyes, and Tayen didn't want it.

"You've been talking to Kaylo, huh?" Tayen asked. "I've already heard that lecture."

"No lecture. Just a bowl of lukewarm, bland porridge."

"You want to help? I could use a sparring partner."

Nix sighed, her shoulders slumping in resignation. "Only if you eat something first."

The cherry wine tingled sweet and tart on Kaylo's tongue, then burned softly as it ran down his throat. In all of his turns, he had never tasted something so pleasantly stinging. The lightness in his head offered a welcome distraction from the constant maneuvering. Politics was not a game for direct people. Liars and charmers more often won the day—not that much difference existed between the two.

Wal met his eyes over the rim of his cup. "It's good to see you enjoying some benefits of life in the Citadel."

"If you insist on these visits, I might as well let my brain swim in alcohol," Kaylo said.

"If you continue to say such cruel things, I may start thinking you mean them." Wal turned back to the runes in his hand and quietly selected a marker to place face down on an empty crosspoint.

For all his complaints, he caught his anger slipping, and the context of their meeting faded away. He could only read and train so much. What harm could come from an easy moment? And, like that, Kaylo sat across from an old friend playing a game of wit and luck.

He pulled The Mountain from the collection of runes in his hand and set it down in challenge. The wood rattled against the leather mat. The anticipation before an opponent revealed their rune was the best part of the game. Nothing could be done. In that moment, cleverness ceased, leaving only luck in its place.

The Mountain. Wal winked at Kaylo before returning his rune to his pouch while Kaylo placed a fresh marker face down on the crosspoint.

The balance of probability tipped in the challenger's favor. Each rune was strong against three others and weak against three others, yet the challenger always won a draw. One could lay a long-winded analogy atop this trivial game, make implications about which spirit was stronger than the others, but that would be a waste of time. It was a fucking game, as arbitrary as the rules of life.

"So, my friend, how goes the training?"

There he goes, ruining the moment, Kaylo thought.

"Report time, is it? Well, it's been a span, and they know as much about dancing with the spirits as I know about cherry wine." He lifted his cup in salute and nodded his head towards his friend before taking a large sip. "Drinking it doesn't mean I know shit about how they make it."

"While I do enjoy your clever words, and trust me, I do—would you mind answering the question?"

Kaylo leaned back in his chair. "Pana is young and thinks he knows everything he doesn't. Euri doesn't care to know. And Rûnka has spent five decades learning how to block out echoes in order to not lose her sanity."

"Well, isn't it lucky that they all have such a wonderful kana to guide them through this arduous journey?" Wal asked. "Tanis is itching to...how do I put this? Clear the board. She doesn't think there's a damn thing that you or any of them can do that a crystal can't."

"Is she wrong?"

"You know she is. I know what you can do. And you better start showing it. If she has her way, she will execute the lot of you. Spirit thief—spirit dancer, it won't matter what you call yourselves."

"What do you care?" Kaylo asked.

Wal sighed, and it looked like he was ten turns older. "Despite how you abandoned me, we were friends once."

Kaylo's heart became a slow drum in the hollow cavity of his chest. "Wal, I never meant to..."

"I don't want your apology," Wal said. "When I brought you here, I called in every last political favor to set this up. If you fail, I can't protect you. What do you need to make them proper dancers?"

"At a minimum, I need one of each spirit," Kaylo said.

"And I want to sit on the Citadel throne with my bare ass."

"I'll try to forget that visual. Thank you," Kaylo said.

"I'm not handing you the key to escape."

"You have Tayen. You have Nix. What am I going to do—steal The Seed, incapacitate the guard, find the two people you have enrolled in your little army, and run off into the Lost Forest unnoticed? You realize you have a literal army, right? Give the crystals to the guard. Add another guard for all I care."

Wal slumped forward, hiding his head in his hands. After several low grunts and sighs, he lifted his head from his palms. "And you think, if you have all six spirits, you can train these little shits to be what we need them to be."

"Just like Zusa," Kaylo said with a sad smile.

"Don't make me look like a fool."

"I am curious. Why didn't you let us have The River? Did you think I was going to climb down the cliffs, freeze the ocean, and walk off?"

"I had considered it." Wal's smile returned, but the worried lines in his face lingered on.

———————

Nix was shit with spirit crystals. She had no interest in trying to control a spirit. That work was better left to dancers. A sword, a spear, a fucking tree branch—anything would do better than the little glowy gemstones.

Today, she almost burned down the training tent.

The fire sprang to life in the pit, as she intended, when the assholes in the tent's corner began messing with the nameless servant. The big one, Dunnin or some other equally ridiculous fucking name, repeatedly called The Wind to batter the servant back and forth. He moved around, graceful as a bear wearing shoes, as gusts of wind blew the poor girl off her feet.

One absent thought and enough anger, and the flames escaped the firepit. Fire swept across the sand, charging at Dunnin.

In the forest, the fire would have moved faster and spread, but over sand, the line of fire dwindled to a halt several paces before it reached its target. Although not before it caught most of the regiment's attention.

Dunnin and his weak-willed followers all backed into the corner, staring at Nix like frightened rabbits.

Rather than looking inept, she twisted her mouth into an unabashed smirk and quenched the fire as if she had complete control over the spirit. Better they feared her and assumed her competent than see her weakness.

Commander Yansar sent everyone back to their drills, letting her eyes linger on Nix as the rest of the regiment turned away from the scene. The Commander squinted, making the wrinkles around her eyes deepen. If not for the slight quirk of her lips, it would have been a threatening expression. In its stead, a begrudging respect flickered within her gaze.

Nix waited until the rest of the regiment left for the mess before leaving. Hakan always said, "If you have enemies, never give them your back." He had forgotten to mention that giving your back to friends could be every bit as dangerous.

The crystal left her drained in a way that training with a sword never had, like the fire had consumed all her energy. Still, a part of her wanted to give more. The crystals drew her in, despite her disinterest and utter lack of skill.

If she hated anything more than the Gousht, it was not being in control of herself.

Her choices led her to this place and her predicament. She could accept that. But a rock toying with her head wouldn't fucking do.

As she ambled through the cold, snow drifted down on the breeze and stung her cheeks, sending shivers down her back. The snow thickened until it blotted out the horizon, and she was alone. Behind closed eyelids, she sat in the sensation as the cold prickled her skin. These small pains belonged to her.

When she opened her eyes, whiteness covered the world, except for a lone figure moving through the field. In all this open space, they walked a straight line towards Nix.

She had been dull to think that Dunnin wouldn't make a move.

The middle of a snowstorm was the perfect time to lose a recruit. She cracked her knuckles along each hand, awakening them from the chill. If he wanted to come for her, she would be ready.

The figure got bigger and clearer the closer they came. Then they swayed with the changing wind and stumbled into the snow.

Fucking fool, Nix cursed herself, dropped her fists, and ran towards the faltering figure.

"Sosun!" she yelled.

The girl shouldn't have been out in this blizzard. Not in that threadbare cloth. Not this bone-thin and fragile.

"What are you doing out here?" Nix yelled into the blizzard. "You'll catch sick." She pulled the young woman under her arm and rushed over to the nearest building.

Under the cover of the wooden wall, Sosun shook. Her cheeks were dark and dry. "What are you doing out here?" Nix asked again, slightly softer than before.

The shaking woman handed her a note.

> *Whatever you did, thank you. They moved me into the Citadel, permanently. I'm assisting in the kitchens. No more running errands for the army. No more warriors. I am grateful. Now, please leave me alone.*

Nix hesitated to look up from the paper. Wal kept his part of the deal. Now she would have to keep hers. When she looked up, Sosun shuddered with cold, but her expression held her conviction. She nodded and started to turn, but Nix stopped her.

"I want to help you."

Sosun sighed. She took the paper back from Nix. Even as the writing coal shook in her hand, she continued to write.

I don't want your help. I want to be left alone.

"What if I could take you from service? What if you could leave the Lost Nation?"

A long moment held between them in which only the snow moved. They both stared at each other, Nix's face hopeful and pleading, Sosun's face doubting and standoffish.

"If I could make it happen, would you leave with me?"

Sosun looked around her as if it was a trap, then she leveled her eyes on Nix and nodded.

"Good. I need you to deliver a message." Nix held her hand out for the writing coal, then wrote her message on the only blank patch of the paper.

As soon as she finished, Sosun took the coal and paper back from her, a question persisting in her eyes.

"You can trust me," Nix said.

The slight woman swirled two fingers at her temple, tapped her fist over her heart with her pointer finger and thumb extended, then swiped her open hand over her chest. As her hands stopped their dance, she turned and walked off into the snow.

The walk to the mess was brief, not nearly enough time to gather all her thoughts. Rowdy banter filled the mess, along with the stench of several hundred recruits.

Nothing she could do would earn Sosun's forgiveness, not that she deserved it. But if she could, she had to undo one of her many wrongs, in whatever small way possible.

When she reached the front of the food line, she held out her bowl for a scoop of the same runny porridge she ate three times a day. The nameless servant ladled her food without looking up.

"Hey," Nix said and repeated when it didn't catch the servant's attention.

The nameless man raised his gaze only slightly. Then Nix mimicked the same gestures that Sosun made only minutes earlier. The server looked up, tilting his head in confusion.

"We all would like to eat," the recruit behind Nix said, and the server dropped his head down to ladle out another serving of porridge.

———

Kaylo opened and closed the scrap of crumpled paper in his hands.

We need to talk.
-Nix

A moon had passed since he last saw her. He should have called on her sooner. Even though Wal granted him permission, he hadn't. What was he supposed to say? Apologies couldn't encompass his trespass.

Three gentle knocks wrapped against the stormwood door. *Why do all the servants knock the same way?*

With a deep breath, Kaylo stood up and opened the door. A short boy around Tayen's age stood there in worn robes, looking down. Nix loomed over him like a tree, tall and slender. Her cheeks had grown hollow, but she had the same piercing, light brown eyes.

"Can you bring us something from the kitchen?" Kaylo asked the servant boy. He tilted his head further down before striding off, deeper into the Citadel.

Kaylo stepped back, opening his body from the door and gesturing for Nix to step inside. As she did, she looked around the room, taking stock, probably comparing luxury to austerity.

"I didn't come her for a meal." Nix bent down over a stack of books and shuffled through the covers.

"Didn't expect you did, but that doesn't mean you shouldn't have one," Kaylo said, forcing a smile into his voice. "Take a seat."

The table was bare, except for the flowers. For some reason, Wal continued to have servants come and change them at least once a span. He had set all the books and the runes aside.

They sat opposite each other for several moments of silence. Nix's eyes turned down and to the side, like an all-encompassing thought occupied her.

"Is it too late for an apology?" Kaylo asked.

Her eyes squinted at the comment. "I didn't come here for that either."

"Still, for what it's worth, I am sorry."

"You and that kid of yours are too damn similar. The only people to blame are those Lost Army bastards and myself. I knew the deal when Hakan and I parleyed with the Lost Nation."

"Have you seen her lately?" Kaylo asked.

"This morning. She's not doing well," Nix said. "But why am I telling you that? You see her more than I do."

"She doesn't talk to me. I'm an obligation to her. That's all."

"You are as dim as the forest on a moonless night."

"Excuse me?"

"That girl cares more about you than anyone with a heartbeat. You'd have to be a fucking fool to not see that."

"She hates me."

"Maybe, but that doesn't mean she doesn't care about you," she said. "If half of what I'm told is true, she lost her family, the Gousht took her home from her, and a kid killed her best friend in front of her. She might have a few emotions right now."

The vein in Kaylo's neck pulsed, and the pull of it ran up the left edge of his jaw. His mouth hung open without a thing to say as Nix waved his ignorance in front of him like a flag flapping in the wind.

Three knocks broke the tension.

"Come in," Kaylo said.

The servant boy walked in to set a tray of bread, cured meats, and two mugs on the table. The grease wafted off the meat with a salty sting.

"They treat you pretty well in here." She broke a piece of bread from the half-loaf and brought it to her nose. "Bread in the mess doesn't smell like this. Shit, it doesn't smell like anything."

"What did you want to talk about?"

Nix grabbed a mug of ale to wash down a large chunk of bread. "We've been talking about her. Listen, Kuno—Kaylo, whatever the fuck you're calling yourself nowadays."

"Are you still upset that I lied to you about who I was? We were on the run."

She waved away the comment. "Tayen is a good kid."

"I know that."

"Do you?" She grabbed a sausage from the platter and took a large bite. "Why are you letting her suffer?" The meat muffled her words, but they were clear enough.

"What am I supposed to do?"

Nix took a sip of the ale and leaned forward. "Get her out of here."

"I'm working on it." The words slipped out of his mouth before he could stop himself.

The edge of her lips lifted for a flash of a second. Maybe they hadn't at all. "Tell me about it," she whispered.

They leaned in and stared at each other, like two wild animals sizing each other up. "Nothing to tell, not yet," Kaylo said.

"First smart thing you said tonight," she said. "Trust is a hard commodity in a place like this. But when you decide you can't do it on your own, send for me." She leaned back, taking another gulp of her ale.

CHAPTER SIXTEEN
CURRENT DAY ENNEA

Rúnka sat next to the other trainees with her legs out front, leaning back with her arms like stilts in the sand. It was a posture that said, "I'm old. What the fuck are they going to do that life hasn't already?" Kaylo tried not to smile.

Pana and Euri sat in standard Lost Army fashion—back straight, knees forward, legs tucked under their hindquarters. Not only had they taken the training more seriously than Rúnka, they had made much more progress.

The old Renēquan woman had built her walls so completely over the turns that the echoes quieted to a whisper. She had only used her gift when her life depended on it, as the warriors who had stolen her away into the service of the King could attest—at least, those who had survived.

A second and a third guard accompanied the heavy canvas sack of crystals. It said something of the resources within the Lost Nation that the army could spare two extra guards to make sure Kaylo didn't run off with the crystals in an escape attempt. Either that or it reflected the depths of Wal's stubbornness.

"What do you hear?" Kaylo asked.

"Echoes," Pana said. Regardless of the dispassionate aura filling the tent, his eagerness pushed through like an annoyingly bright light.

"Cha hear echoes eh'ry fuckin day, kid," Rûnka said. "Read ta subtext."

Pana's shoulders slumped and his lip pouted, but he didn't run from the question. "More echoes?"

When Kaylo nodded, the boy perked back up as if Rûnka hadn't said a word. It was exhausting. Cute, but exhausting.

"There are six crystals with all six spirits trapped in that sack the ornery fellas are guarding," Euri said.

"You are going to train with each of the six crystals," Kaylo said. "When you call them, I want you to listen for the differences in the way they sound, feel the different ways your body moves with each spirit."

"When are we finally going to start..." Pana paused. "Borrowing the spirits?"

"As soon as you can wield each one with a crystal. You need to be able to tell them apart before you start pulling them into your body," Kaylo said.

Over the next two hours, the three spirit dancers called on the imprisoned spirits in their own separate corners of the tent. Kaylo offered small guidance as he walked around to each of them.

Rûnka barely moved in her corner. When he came by to check on her, she would harden a small patch of sand or stir the air for a moment. She knew how to use crystals. She didn't suffer a lack of knowledge; she simply had no interest in taking down her walls.

"I can't imagine what it must feel like after thirty turns of hiding, but I need you to try listening," Kaylo said.

"I ain been hidin," she said. "Nothin wrong wit bein who I am. I just don care ta hear all tem screamin spirits, got me?"

"Do you think these guards are only here to protect the crystals? They have eyes, and they certainly have mouths. The army knows everything that's happened in this tent the moment you leave it. If you don't start acting like you care...Well, they have two other spirit dancers."

"I heard cha," she said. "But I don know if I can thinka much worse ten being ta army's thief."

Neither her posture nor her voice carried any judgment, but her words held a weight all the same. He nodded to her. Each of them had choices. Shit choices, yes, but choices all the same.

He left her to her corner of the tent and her intermittent manipulation of the air.

After exchanging her crystal with the guards, Euri walked back to her corner. Kaylo didn't have to see the green crystal shimmer in her palm to know which spirit she had taken from the sack. The diluted version of The Seed's call sounded like cries of an old friend.

Kaylo had the power to free The Seed, this small sliver of him. He had the power to free each of the six spirits screaming their agony into the tent, but that would have consequences. Instead, he forced himself to walk to the young woman and help her manipulate the life trapped in the translucent prison.

"It helps if you think about a plant with all of your senses. Think about the scent of the flowers. Are the petals waxy? If it bears fruit, what does it taste like? Then picture that plant in the echo and pull it out."

As Euri nodded, she gently brushed each of her fingertips against her thumb rhythmically. The pads of her fingers touched the slight movements of the echo. The cold, barren sand bulged, then a single sproutling poked through. It grew, and the green tendrils unfurled into leaves with a single bud sprouting from the top of the stem. It bloomed into a rose where there had not been one before, with petals redder than blood.

"Why a rose?" Kaylo asked.

"They used to grow in my mother's garden." Euri smiled down at the life she had pulled from the sand—a speck of beauty in an otherwise drab scene.

A shrill scream shattered the subtle trance of the flower.

Pana doubled over in pain, holding his belly like a wound. Rūnka rushed over to him first, abandoning her empty crystal.

Shortsighted little shit, Kaylo thought.

"What's wrong wit him?" Rūnka asked, cradling Pana's head on her lap.

"I'd say he's a few bunches short of a bundle," Kaylo said. "Bored with the crystals, were you?"

Pana only grimaced deeper, baring his chattering teeth.

"Help him," Euri said.

Kaylo knelt down to brush the beads of sweat from the boy's brow. "You need to let the spirit go."

"I can't," he said. "Take it away. Take it away."

The echo wailed like a daemon from inside the boy's body. The small thread that yoked the spirit to its prison lingered in the air. It would be a simple thing to grab it, but for the guards.

"Please!" Pana clutched his belly, whimpering.

"Seed and Balance," Kaylo mumbled, then he snatched the echo from the air.

The tension abandoned Pana's body, and he unfolded against the sand.

The familiar rage and pain of a stolen spirit clawed at Kaylo from the inside. Then he reached out to the shadows from every corner and crevice of the room. He formed his mouth into a circle and exhaled into the shadows. They grew with his breath. All eyes focused on him.

As the guards exchanged glances, they reached for their weapons. Then everything went black.

Small sounds filled the darkness. The spirit dancers scuttled around on the sand. Despite the lack of light, the fire still crackled. A twang of metal sang as one of the guards pulled their sword from its scabbard.

"Stop this thief," Calla Lily called out, but her voice lacked authority.

If the guards tried to fight in the darkness, they would just as likely spear each other as anyone else.

No one could see it, but Kaylo's shoulders loosened. He smiled at the small control he had. His stomach moved in and out with the soft push and pull of air. There was pain, of course, but it was a pain he could control.

Then, after reveling in his momentary power, he let it go.

As the spirit fled back into its crystal prison, the shadows snapped back into place. Everything returned to as it had been, except now the guards approached him with their weapons bared.

"On your knees," one guard said, leveling her sword in his direction.

"Calm yourselves," Kaylo said. "Demonstrations are necessary, especially when students do something foolish." He looked down at the boy. "Before you decide to drag me before your superiors, ask yourselves, what did I do wrong? Commander Wal tasked me with teaching these three how to spirit dance. What are you going to charge me with? Spirit dancing?"

Hibiscus wore his uncertainty openly, and Kaylo focused his attention on the red-faced guard. "Do you want to waste your commander's time complaining that I am doing what I've been asked to do?"

Looking at his counterparts, Hibiscus' eyes formed a wide question.

Calla Lily's sword bounced in her hand, and her nostrils flared. "Don't do that again. If you need to provide a demonstration, you will ask permission."

"No, I won't," Kaylo said. He didn't offer a challenge in his voice. He simply spoke the truth. "I have a task that has been given to me. In this tent, I am kana to these three. I cannot teach them properly if I have to ask your permission to do so."

Kaylo and the guard stared at each other. No one said a thing. The fire crackled. The soft sound of seven people breathing filled the space between them. Then Calla Lily sheathed her blade. "There will come a time when you are no longer necessary, and the commanders won't care what happens when they aren't looking."

"Maybe," Kaylo said. "But today, we have a lesson to continue."

Opening the doors to the library felt like opening a book after a long day. The smell of leather and old paper washed over Kaylo, and despite the trials from earlier in the day, it made him smile.

Beyond the first bookshelf, Lanigan sat at their table. They nodded to each other, and Kaylo sat next to his friend. "It has been too long."

"A handful of days," they said.

"A full span."

"You can't hold ten days in your hand?" they asked with a smile. "So much for the Hero of Anilace."

"Such a clever tongue. Are you going to use it to continue avoiding the question?"

"And what would the question be, Anhil?"

"You're not going to distract me with your little nickname," Kaylo said. "Where have you been?"

Lanigan's smile lessened as they took a deep breath. "Our captors enjoy flexing their grip once in a while. When they feel the need, privileges can be revoked with a word."

"How long?"

"As you said, a span." They exchanged a glance. "Oh, you mean, how long have I been a guarded resident of our fair nation-state?" They made a show of counting their fingers with a sad smile. "Twenty-one turns. You'd be amazed at the amount of reading you can do in two decades of captivity."

"Twenty-one? Sorry. I didn't know."

"Kaylo, there are sadder stories than mine. Every turn or two, the scion of The Shadow, my old friend King Shonar, joins me for a meal and offers me my freedom. All I have to do is recant, show my support for the kingdom that Ennea would become.

"And when we eat, I consider it. I look at my old friend, wondering if it would really be so bad—unite the five nations under his rule. Then I see the pendant swinging from his neck, a piece of The Shadow locked inside crystal, hung like jewelry, and I thank him for his kind offer. Then I decline.

"To his credit, he never raises his voice or threatens me. He nods, then we eat and reminisce over our childhood. At this point, we have rehashed all our stories several times over."

"He carries a spirit crystal?" Kaylo asked.

"The royals may be descendants of Shunanlah, as they claim—I don't know—but the spirits left their line several generations back. That is unless you read the official records of Astile," they said. "Enough about me, Anhil. Tell me about your days."

"Tayen is a mess," Kaylo said. "When I think about the decisions I've made, I can see them, like an endless tree. They climb further and further away, splitting off, one branch after another. Each new branch is another consequence."

He idly pulled a book from the stack in front of Lanigan, running his fingers over the leather binding. "And now, look at me. I'm speaking like you."

"I will take that as a compliment, my friend. Though, I think you are making it too simple—one choice leading to one consequence or the other. But the truth is complex. Each consequence is the product of too many decisions to chart its origin." Lanigan reached their hand over and stilled the book in Kaylo's hands. "If you hadn't taken Tayen in, if you hadn't decided to train her, she might be dead. Or she might have ended up in the exact same place, only without someone looking out for her."

"Interesting way to avoid responsibility."

"Maybe. Or maybe there is a way to take responsibility without punishing yourself," they said. "Just a thought."

Lanigan leaned against the high back of their chair and watched Kaylo with a subtle smile. They had been someone different in the beginning. Twenty-one turns had to change a person.

"Why don't you take the King's pardon? You don't owe your life to anyone."

"My friend, that is what you don't understand. This isn't about owing anyone. Regardless of the consequences, I am choosing to follow my beliefs. I am choosing myself," they said. "If the rain turned around and rose into the sky, it would no longer be the rain."

"Is that from some obscure poem?"

Lanigan smiled, the weight lifting from their expression. "Probably."

Nix waited between a pair of guards until Wal opened the door, his braids draping down the sides of his face. He usually kept them pulled back. Then again, she hardly knew the man well enough for usually.

"Ah, what a pleasant surprise. Come in." His grin showed more teeth than any person had a right to have. She could knock several out, and the asshole would still have a full smile.

His sword rested on the table next to a whetstone, a rag, and a water basin. At least she could respect something about the man. Some warriors walked around this city with dull blades begging for rust. A well-cared for weapon could live as long as a family tree.

She sat across from him and his sword. It would be easy to reach out and take it. He might be a capable warrior, but if luck moved with her, she could slit his throat before he made a sound.

Of course, if she did, she would probably die in a very painful, very public fashion. Several examples already hung in the middle of the village at the base of the Citadel.

"You kept your word," Nix said.

"And I will continue to, if you keep yours." Wal dipped his rag into the basin and rewet the stone before slowly sliding the blade across it. Some people hated the abrasive sound, but to Nix, it sounded like the tide coming in.

"He's planning on escaping," Nix said, and Wal's sword stopped mid-wave. "He doesn't have a plan yet, but he's not going to stay put like a trained puppy. You knew that, or else you wouldn't have asked for my help."

The waves began again. "You're right, of course. I knew my old friend wouldn't listen to reason, but I had hoped. What did he say exactly?"

"This place isn't healthy for Tayen."

"Is that your opinion or his?"

"He loves that girl. You know he does, and he won't let the army chisel her down into a weapon," Nix said. "Some of us are beyond saving. We stopped crying over dead bodies long ago."

"Maybe you have. Maybe Kaylo has. But some of us remember the dead every time we have to kill again."

"I didn't realize you were such a sensitive spirit, Commander."

His grin remained, but his eyes changed. The playful brown irises hardened into the gaze of a predator. "We all have our reasons for the choices we make," he said. "I am sure there are reasons you protected that nameless girl."

"She has a name," Nix said with a bite in her words.

"She used to, and she might again, but now—in the Citadel's belly— she doesn't. No one would notice if she were replaced by any of the other servants. She could cross into The Mist, and nothing would change. Just another day. More dust swept out the door."

The strain of Nix's bite ran from the back of her jaw to her temples.

"Why do I say these things?" Wal asked with a feigned lightness in his tone. "Because I agreed to help you in exchange for information. I helped you, and yet, I have no information."

"I told you..."

"That Kaylo is going to try to escape, but you don't know how? Would you like to tell me the color of the sky next?" His sword clattered against the table. He leaned forward, placing his palms flat on the wood. "I need Kaylo. I need Tayen to keep him in check. If this is all you have for me, I don't need you."

Finally, he showed his true face, the face he hid behind the fog of his smile and quick wit.

She leaned forward to match him. "If you want details, I'll find them. And when I do, you'll honor our agreement, or we'll see how sharp your sword truly is."

The fog returned with a new smile. "I look forward to it."

Daak stood in a void in the middle of the mess hall, everyone giving him a wide berth. Their stares and whispers were his only company.

Tayen walked in a direct line and stood across the table from him. He looked up at her, then his eyes shifted left and right. She didn't need to look to know the other recruits were watching the scene like a hungry audience. In fact, she counted on it.

A bit of porridge slopped off his spoon back into the bowl. *That's too bad,* she thought. *Could have had one more bite.* She reached across the table and took his bowl. Then she held out her hand for his spoon.

There was a moment of hesitation. A question in his eyes. A slight flare of defiance. Then he placed the wooden spoon in her hand.

"I can get another bowl," he said.

"You could. I'm not stopping you."

"How long are you going to keep this up?" His voice quivered.

The blank expression on Vāhn's face flashed in front of her, and whatever pity Tayen had for the boy died. "Oh, the trials are about five span away."

"I'm not going to fail the trials."

"I think you will, but if I'm wrong—well, accidents happen on the battlefield." Tayen took a bite of the porridge. "I'm giving you a choice, your name or your life. It's more than you gave Vāhn."

Daak backed away from the table before walking off. Whether or not he returned to the serving line made no difference. If she had to see her friend die over and over again, she didn't intend to allow him to forget what he had done either. Not for a moment.

CHAPTER SEVENTEEN
KAYLO'S STORY

THE DAUGHTERS OF ENNEA chased each other through the sky. Zusa continued to push the bounds of our training, exacting new levels of pain as we explored my abilities. The days grew longer, and the snow began to melt. Nearly a season had passed since we parted with the Jani.

What boundaries existed between the Missing and our small group of runaways had thinned to nearly nothing. We trained together, shared the nightly watch, and laughed around the fire over stories and meals.

If any differentiation between the two groups remained, it vanished the night Tomi and Mahli returned from their hunt, dragging a wild boar between them. The damn thing weighed nearly as much as the pair of them.

The long winter made meat a rarity. We shared the occasional squirrel or game bird, but most nights consisted of meals I called from The Seed.

That night the air about camp hung thick with the scent of charred fat. Grease dripped from the animal to the hot stones surrounding the fire with a sizzle. Tomi cursed and carried on about how her body ached after dragging the beast for an hour, every foul word brimming with pride.

Fourteen or not, she had grown into a fierce warrior. Her arms were slender and strong. She could wield a sword as well as most. But none of us could loose an arrow with her precision, as the boar could attest.

I gathered a chunk of greasy meat from my bowl with a bit of frybread. Spice tingled along my tongue, gathering at the back of my throat. Adēan had a heavy hand when it came to pepper, but he could cook.

"Do you think there is something going on between them?" Wal's voice barely cut through the boisterous conversation, but the look on his face and his heavy stare across the fire clarified his meaning. Adēan and Chêta leaned into one another, waving their arms about as they spoke in their heavy accents.

"Why don't you just talk to him?"

"I do talk to him."

"Stop staring. You look like you're stalking prey," I said. "You talk to him when you have to. You don't have genuine conversations. How do you even know you're interested in him?"

"Have you seen his arms?" Wal said with a smile.

"Seriously, nothing is going to happen from across the firepit. Talk to him, and when you do, can you try to get him to tone down the pepper?"

Wal pushed me playfully, going back to watching Adēan and Chêta with a minimal amount of tact.

Ever since we had begun searching for the Missing, Wal had clung to me. He never asked any interrogating questions, and neither did I. Our relationship was based on shared sarcasm and pessimism. This doting infatuation he had begun to harbor started throwing off our delicate balance.

When Adēan got up to clean out his bowl, Wal pushed himself off the ground and made his way to intercept the northboy. He fidgeted like a nervous child as he approached, but he didn't veer away.

The distance and noise obscured their conversation as Wal gestured with every movement of his lips. Adēan remained still as he looked up at the taller, skinnier boy. He leaned in as he listened.

Whatever happened between them, Wal didn't need an audience. I sopped up the last of the gravy with my bread, my mouth tingling with heat as I got up to clean out my bowl.

All around the firepit, people moved with an energy that hadn't been there the day before. It paled in comparison to the gatherings in the Jani encampment, and yet, I found myself back there, watching the clan laugh and smile as if everything were right in the world. But there was an absence—Liara.

The closer our group of runaways got to the Missing, the more she sought solitude. Maybe I should have let her have it, but looking at Wal blush made me want to find her all the more.

After a quick search, I found her sitting in the tent, running her hands through the new growth of her hair. The brazier turned her body into a silhouette as she stretched a tight curl taut.

After having to shear it all off, it had finally reached the length of a finger. She dipped her hand in a bowl of oil and separated out a small section near the nape of her neck. In long strokes, she applied oil from root to tip, then twisted.

"Do you need help?" I asked.

As her spirit tried to jump from her body, she nearly knocked the oil over. "Don't do that," she whisper-yelled at me. "Creeping in the shadows like a damn daemon."

"Where did you get the oil?"

"Boda makes it from sunflowers, 'to get the waves right,'" she said, mimicking his cadence.

"Do you want help?"

"What do you know about locs?"

"Whatever you tell me," I said. "You're pretty good at giving directions."

She raised her eyebrows and looked at me from the corner of her eyes, then tilted her head in relenting agreement.

Sitting so closely behind her, the smell of sunflowers filled my nostrils, mingling with her natural scent. The scents played together like freshly tilled earth and raspberries. Her head tilted to the left, her neck gently curving into her shoulder. The light from the brazier accented her rich, black skin in the darkness of the tent.

"Dip your right hand in the oil. Only the fingertips. I don't need to have pimples popping up all over my scalp." She parted her hair, leaving only a section free. "Take a segment about the width of your small finger and separate it from the rest. Now, use the oil and moisten it as you stretch it out. When that segment is clear of any snags or tangles, twist it tight."

The lengths of her copper hair shimmered in the oil. I picked up the hand-carved comb and pulled it through her hair, smoothing out the tangles. Then, pinching the ends of her hair between my thumb and the comb, I twisted.

The first segment took forever, but then my hands fell into a pattern of movement. We didn't speak as I separated out one small section after another. Instead, I reveled in her closeness.

She stretched her neck, and a loc slipped out of my grip. "Stop moving."

"Stop tugging at me," she said.

I took a breath and looked down at her in the soft glow of the brazier. "Why are we always fighting?" I asked.

"Because you're stubborn."

I laughed at the suddenness of her answer. "I'm stubborn? You're the one hiding away from the rest of us."

As my hands rested on her shoulders, her smooth skin teased my fingertips. Without a thought, I started rubbing her muscles with my thumbs. A gentle pressure of skin against skin. Her shoulders let go of the tension, then they locked.

"I'm not Shay," she said.

At the mention of Shay's name, I froze, my hands resting on Liara's shoulders. "Is that what you think? Is that why you're so distant? I know you're not Shay."

She took hold of my right hand with her left and slid it off her shoulder. "I'm not sure you do," she said. "It's barely been a turn, and you loved her." There wasn't any anger in her voice, just a small hurt.

"You have no right to bring her up," I said. "Shay has nothing to do with us."

Even as the words left my mouth, the visage of the girl I had grown up with appeared beside Liara. Shay's auburn curls fell down to her warm ochre skin.

Liara's lips rounded down into a frown full of pity. "I can finish on my own."

My left hand fell from her shoulder, and I sat stunned for a moment. I should never have told her about Shay.

The oil still clung to my hands as I left the tent.

Under normal circumstances, Wal couldn't match my skill with a sword—not that I was especially talented, but he lacked basic mechanics. Put a blade in that boy's hand, and he lost all sense of spatial awareness. However, the two spirits rolling around inside me gnawed on my organs like gristle, forcing me back on my heels.

I raised my sword at an angle to parry his shoulder-heavy attack, and my short blade in my off-hand to block another. Backstep, parry, backstep, parry.

Every exercise Zusa concocted pinpointed the limits of my body, mind, and spirit. When we found pain, we embraced it and forced it back one step at a time. And as long as The Priest continued to breathe, I would suffer it.

Wal slashed again, and his front foot extended too far in front of him, pulling him off-balance and open. But the pain kept me from countering his attack.

If I couldn't withstand stealing one or two spirits, I wouldn't be any use on the battlefield.

I swung my wooden blade towards a gap in Wal's defense, but my attack lacked power and speed. Wal easily knocked it aside.

During the Gousht attack on the Fallen Rock Clan, I had stolen at least half a dozen spirits. Now I struggled to contend with two.

Wal launched a series of attacks in quick succession, but he sacrificed speed for control. I sidestepped and blocked with my short practice blade, which Zusa had encouraged me to wield. Splitting my focus between the two blades and the stolen spirits forced me to hone my concentration.

"Stop gritting your teeth and attack the bastard," Zusa yelled from the edge of the sparring circle. "His form is worse than a child drunk on barley wine."

Several expletives ran through my head, but I attacked regardless. As I caught yet another heavy swing with my sword, I turned it, then with my short blade in my off-hand, I thrust at Wal's kidney. He twisted away in time.

Dull as the practice swords were, it still would have laid him out moaning.

"Good, good. Now, here comes another friend," Zusa said.

Another echo surged awake before I could question what he meant. Despite my pain, I reached for the spirit as I sidestepped Wal's thrust.

Every muscle from my groin to my neck constricted. The air crawled down my throat like a storm of flames. The morning light dimmed to black, and the forest disappeared. My weapons vanished from my clenched hands.

And I was alone.

The blackness parted for one figure whose red cloak billowed in the non-existent wind, the stark absence of light sealing around the two of us. Two spirit crystals dangled from large chains around his neck. Between them, the divided circle fell in the dead center of his chest.

Veiled face or not, it was him. The Priest. My Priest. The man who took Nomi, Soca, and Junera. The man who owed me blood.

The Wind swirled within my gut, and I pulled on the spirit with all my rage. A torrent of air carried The Priest from his feet, landing him flat on his back in the blackness.

As I reached for The Flame, I spread my arms wide, then pushed forward. The ground erupted in fire, and it crawled towards The Priest.

"Kaylo!" a voice called out.

"Kaylo, stop!"

With a blink, the blackness withdrew, but the flames continued to rage. The fire crawled over the forest floor towards Wal, who lay flat on his back. As he skittered away as quickly as he could, the flames shortened the distance even faster.

He screamed, then I snapped my hands closed and pulled them back to me. The fire receded into itself, snuffing out into wisps of gray smoke and a trail of embers.

Still lying on his back, Wal craned his neck, his eyes as wide as the whole of Ennea. Zusa stood off to the side, his chest moving up and down rapidly.

I released the spirits back to their crystal prisons and collapsed onto my hands and knees. "I'm sorry," I said, and my breathing became staccato puffs of air in and out, until I started sobbing.

Whatever thoughts I had about turning The Thief against the Gousht were lies. This curse would corrupt me—another malitu.

A presence drifted over me. Wal knelt down, draping an arm over my shoulders. "It's okay," he said. "I'm okay."

"I'm sorry," I said, still weeping. "I didn't mean to."

"I know, I know," he whispered.

———

Long after Zusa collected the crystals and the practice blades and left, Wal stayed by my side. We sat with our backs against a tree and didn't say anything. I cried until the tears stopped coming.

Sokan moved through the sky above, marking our hours sitting there in the quiet. I could have left. The snow-covered forest waited for me like an invitation. Everyone would be safer without me. No goodbyes. No reasons.

If I had protected the Jani from the threat I was, they would still be alive.

"I wish I could do what you do," Wal said. His soft voice barely broke through the ambient noise of the forest.

"No, you don't."

"Take away the part where I almost died, and what you did was pretty fucking awesome," Wal said. "When I have one of those crystals in my hands, I'm not weak anymore. For once, I'm not a liability. I'm powerful."

"You aren't weak."

"I'm the worst fighter here. The best thing I can say about my sword fighting is that I know not to hold on to the pointy end," Wal said.

"You'll get better. You're already getting better."

"Do you know why all the stories are about spirit-marked people? Because you are the powerful ones. You are the ones who do things worthy of stories." Wal stared into the forest as he spoke.

"You know that book I keep tucked under my bedroll?"

"Your mother's book?"

"She collected stories," I said. "She liked the stories that didn't fit anywhere else. The stories that contradicted or stood out."

"And?"

"You've heard about Kalani, the Tomakan general from the Hundred-Turn War?"

"Yeah, the earth dancer," Wal said.

"Yes, but General Sione wasn't." Wal looked at me, waiting for my point. "Sione was bound and the only general who ever defeated Kalani.

"Kalani was a strategic genius. She always seemed to know what the opposing force would do. Sione had lost nearly half her forces to Kalani's attacks. Kalani had a spy in her camp. So, Sione enlisted spies of her own."

"Does this story have a point?" Wal said.

"You're the one who brought up stories, jackass," I said. "When Sione informed her commanders their next plan of action, she had them followed by warriors who had lost family in Kalani's raids—warriors who wanted vengeance.

"All the commanders informed their regiments and set to preparing their battle plans, except for one—Retan. He returned to his tent, lay down, and went to sleep. The warrior following him reported the strange behavior, and Sione smiled. She called the potential traitor back and informed Retan that a spy infiltrated their ranks. She gave the Commander alternative orders to surprise the enemy.

"Retan listened, making all the right promises. Then he left with his new orders, lay down in his tent, and took another nap, or so it seemed. But Retan had been passing messages in The Mist. When he returned from his mistwalk, he opened his eyes just as Sione slit his throat.

"The next day, Sione used the subterfuge to her advantage and decimated Kalani's army. Kalani escaped and went on to other victories, but never again taking ground from General Sione."

"What is the point of your story?" Wal asked.

"You are dense as a too fresh melon," I said. "The point is that, as long as you're smart, you can defeat the strongest enemy—dancer or not."

"It still would be nice to be a dancer."

I punched him in the shoulder and shook my head. "You're helpless."

We sat there for a while longer before walking back to the heart of the camp.

After chores, we sat down for dinner. The camp smelled wonderful, thick grease clinging to the air. Boda and Niven used the bones and scraps of boar meat to make a rich stock. The peppers and vegetables they cooked in it soaked up the heavy liquid and burst with every bite.

We hadn't known the luxury of fresh meat in far too long. Whatever meat remained would be dried and salted, but it would never be as good.

So I ate a second bowl even though my stomach threatened to rupture.

On the other side of the fire, Wal sat close enough to Adēan for their shoulders to touch occasionally. All the false bravado Wal carried with him vanished next to the stocky northboy. His eyes continually veered off into the woods, his fingers drummed along the outside of his thigh, and he brushed an unwieldy braid behind his ear a half-dozen times. For one so full of words, he seemed to misplace them when he needed them.

Adēan kept his subtle smile and leaned in closer to the fidgety young man.

The sound of Zusa's knife tapping against his wooden bowl cut their clumsy flirtation short.

"The equinox will fall in three days. A new season will begin, and the forest will return to life. What was once young will grow wise. The life that was will pass on to the life that will be. And Tanonta will see three of our family become adults—Adēan, Talise, and Kaylo." He smiled and nodded in my direction. "Occupation or not, we honor the traditions of our people. We will celebrate their promise to The Mother."

Wal whistled into the air, then the rest of the group joined him. The shrill sounds cut into one another in a clash. Liara sat on the other side of Wal, whistling with the rest of them. Her cheeks were high and full, caught in a smile that made me smile in return.

As the ruckus faded, Zusa sat next to me. "Don't let what happened today weigh you down. It was my fault. I pushed you too hard."

"I should have more control."

"That's what we are working on." He clapped his hand on my back. "We will find the right pace. Don't worry about it."

"I almost killed Wal."

"Yeah, but it's only Wal," Zusa said with a smile.

"Zusa?" Boda stood beside him, looking down.

"I'm in the middle of a conversation," Zusa said. His voice lost all the joy it had held only moments ago.

"But, I need to ask..."

"Boda," he said with a harsh edge. "If you interrupt me again, you will get all of my attention. And I am certain you do not want that."

The boy waited for a moment, as if he was unsure of how to move. His breathing grew heavy and quivered in time with his bottom lip. He looked as if he wanted to hit Zusa and run away at the same time. Eventually, he turned and walked away.

"I'm sorry about that," Zusa said. The smile had returned, but the edge in his voice hadn't fully softened.

"It's okay."

"No, it's not. Discipline is all we have against our enemy. You'll learn that. In a few days, you won't be a child anymore." He pushed himself up and walked to his tent.

I couldn't remember the last time I felt like a child.

CHAPTER EIGHTEEN

KAYLO'S STORY

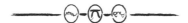

ADÉAN'S AXE CRACKED AGAINST the trunk of an ironoak with a deep thunk. He withdrew the blade and swung again until the pattern became a steady rhythm.

All the others had taken up their standard positions and proceeded with their morning drills. The noise of weapons clanking and arrows finding their targets overlaid The Song rumbling through the soil beneath my feet.

I don't belong here, I thought as I loosely gripped the handle of my axe.

After what had happened with Wal, Zusa hadn't permitted me to return to my training. He said I needed a break.

In truth, if the incident had proven anything, it emphasized how much more training I needed with the spirits. A metal blade could dent a tree. A spirit could light it ablaze or tear the ground beneath it asunder.

I cocked the head of the axe over my shoulder, then buried it in the tree in front of me. Vibrations crawled through the handle and bit into my hands.

Pain helped the anger burn.

From the first moment I had met Zusa, he looked at me like a weapon to wield, then at the first sign of imperfection, I became a broken thing to toss aside. The bastard had promised to help me hone my skills.

I didn't need a break. I needed to become the weapon he saw.

The blade of the axe clung to the tree as I pried it from the wood before resetting my stance and swinging again. Stealing spirits required controlling pain, so I swung harder and clenched my teeth as my calluses burned.

"Don't sacrifice form for force," Zusa said from over my shoulder.

Even in this, I couldn't meet his expectations.

Instead of turning around, I pulled the axe from the meat of the tree and swung harder. Slivers and chunks of wood sprang away from the tree as the blade sunk deeper.

"Kaylo," Zusa said louder, and several heads swiveled in our direction. "If you can't use a blade, it won't matter what kind of control you have over the spirits. What happens when you meet soldiers without crystals? The Seed isn't going to take care of them for you."

When I spun to meet him, the early spring light glinted off his hard leather vest. The tension in his jaw underscored the tone in his voice.

"I won't lose control again," I said.

"Tomorrow night, you will sit before The Mother and pledge yourself to her. You don't have the luxury of throwing tantrums." His lips lifted into a begrudging smile. "If you want power—true power—it will demand your patience, not your anger."

Zusa knew nothing of my anger. The Song and its misborn children pounded in my skull, feeding my fury. And as his placid mask withered away into a scowl, I held Zusa's gaze.

"I am a patient man, but even I have my limits," he said, then leaned forward and lowered his voice. "I am not here to nurture your delicate pride. I am your commander. If you want to find out the bastard I can be, continue to stare at me like that. Now, run the drill correctly."

As soon as I lowered my eyes, Zusa walked away. He hadn't been entirely wrong. The spirits would offer The Priest too kind a death. When I met him again, I would bury my blade into him until the blood ran slick on my skin. An axe would work as well as a sword.

Adēan adjusted his stance next to me, and I mimicked him to the best of my abilities. As he attacked, I did. The axe handle scraped my calluses, and they burned, but the pain faded faster.

The closer I watched Adēan, the more differences I counted between our attacks. He didn't cock back the blade before he attacked. He lifted it. The weight of the axe head never fell over his shoulder. Then he turned his torso and drove the heavy metal into the tree.

Each swing drove deeper into the heart of the wood.

"Is that mud on my sword?!" Zusa yelled from the northern edge of the training circle.

On the other side of the leather-armored warrior, Boda furrowed his brow. "It's a training blade."

"Of course," Zusa turned back to the center of the circle as if performing for the regiment. His mouth stretched into a wide, false smile. "It's only a training blade."

The warrior spun back to the boy, unsheathed his belt knife, and brought it to rest under Boda's chin. "Your weapons are your life. If you care so little for your life, what use do I have for you?"

The boy raised his chin higher to avoid the edge of the knife, but Zusa grabbed the back of his head, locking him in place.

All other noises ceased to exist. Boda rose on the balls of his feet to create distance between himself and the blade as Zusa lifted the edge higher.

"You've made your point," Niven said from ten paces out, his fingers wrapping around the hilt of his sheathed sword.

Zusa looked up with a wild grin, his knife still a fine line against the boy's throat. "Have I?" he asked before turning back to Boda. "Have I?"

"Yes," Boda said, the word shaking in his voice.

The moment stretched, then Zusa released Boda's head and sheathed his knife. "For those of you who need it spelled out—you disrespect my weapons or my training, and you disrespect me, your compatriots, and yourself." His gaze shifted towards me as he finished his announcement.

Boda's chest stuttered as he exhaled, but he didn't cry.

"With that unpleasantness out of the way, we have proper lessons to teach." Zusa walked to the center of the training circle with the poise of a showman. "These trees have served well, but for all their wonderful qualities, they cannot strike back.

"It's time to show me what you've learned. And for all of you reaching for your favorite blade, it won't be that easy. In war—AND THIS IS WAR—you cannot predict the weapon your enemy will attack you with. You need to use whatever you have at hand to defeat whatever they bring to bear."

A wild look settled in Zusa's eyes. In his paused silence, each of us exchanged looks.

"Everyone, make rank," he gestured to the western edge of the training grounds.

No one moved immediately. A heavy silence captured us. Then Boda walked to the edge of the circle and knelt. One by one the rest of us gathered in a line.

Zusa's eyes swept over us as we waited. "If I call your name first, you get to pick your weapon, but you won't know who your opponent is. Those called second will have the benefit of knowledge when they choose their weapon, but they may not choose the same as their opponent."

Whatever point Zusa set out to prove, I had a point of my own. I wasn't weak, and I didn't need his coddling. In little more than a day, I would swear myself to The Mother and the spirits she bore. If Zusa or anyone else needed to learn that lesson, I would force whoever he paired me with to yield.

Niven wouldn't be participating, which left nine potential opponents. Adéan and Talise both preferred the axe. Tomi wouldn't be allowed her bow and quiver. And the rest of us would reach for a sword first. Whoever had to settle for their second choice would likely lose.

If the northman stayed true to form, I would face Wal. And, friend or not, I would put him on the ground if I needed to.

Zusa pinned his arms behind his back as he paced up and down the line. He stopped in front of Boda. "Why don't we get this out of the way? Pick your weapon."

Boda stood, walked over to the weapons laid out on a strip of worn leather, and picked up one of the practice swords.

"Why, of course," Zusa said. "And Tomi, what weapon would you choose?"

Tomi only had one turn on the boy, but he barely reached her shoulders. She strode over to the weapons without a moment's hesitation, bent down, and pulled the spear from its resting place. The blunted tip had been wrapped in fabric. It wouldn't pierce flesh, but it would damn sure bruise.

The length of the spear only added to Tomi's advantage. Where her flesh showed through the tears in her robe, her body was coiled muscle. She had strength and reach on her side. But Boda had something to prove.

Each fighter stood, legs shoulder-width apart, bent with their right foot slightly forward, crouched and ready to strike.

Zusa took a moment to appraise the two. "Yaktan!" he shouted, and the match began.

Boda charged, abandoning his stance and his form.

Despite the boy's scream and his raised weapon, Tomi did not move. She waited as Boda closed the gap between them, then lunged forward. Her body leaned into the attack. Her eyes followed the target. Everything about her form made her strike obvious, easy to defend.

Boda swiped his blade to block the spear thrust, but Tomi drew back to center.

The feint left Boda off-balance. Before he could scramble to square his body towards his opponent, Tomi had taken position. Her spear flashed forward, crashing into Boda's right shoulder.

The boy collapsed, and his wooden blade skidded across the swept dirt.

Before he could get up to retrieve his weapon, Tomi leveled her blunted blade at his throat. He looked up at her, baring his teeth as if he were in a position to threaten her.

"Yield." She prodded the same shoulder she had struck him in, and he yelped before raising a single hand with four fingers extended and his thumb pressed to his palm.

"We have our first winner." Zusa stepped in between the two fighters, kneeling next to Boda as the boy rubbed his shoulder. "Pathetic." He spoke loud enough for the sound to carry over the ranks, though quiet enough for it not to appear intentional.

Sparring matches were nothing new, but a somber air hung over these proceedings. No one cheered for Tomi, and everyone but Niven avoided Boda's eyeline as he rejoined the line.

The matches continued. Mahli pulled a sword from the cache of weapons before waiting at one end of the circle for Liara to face her. The moons of training had changed the way Liara moved. As she picked up her blunted and wrapped axe, she held herself taller.

We may have been on even footing in our days under Jonac's watch, but no longer.

As soon as Zusa called for the match to begin, Liara moved over the ground like a river. No longer fluttering on the balls of her feet, her footfalls took on purpose—strong enough to anchor a strike and light enough to bound to the next series of movements.

As they exchanged blows, Liara hooked the head of her axe around Mahli's sword guard and ripped the weapon from the young girl's hands.

When did I become the liability? I thought as I watched Liara accept surrender.

One match made way for another. Sionia and Chêta found opposite sides of the circle. Our quiet companion moved with more speed and grace than I could have imagined. If she had carried a sword in her hand rather than a spear, she might have won. But, as it was, Chêta made her way into Sionia's guard and claimed victory.

"Wal," Zusa called out without looking at the line.

If I intended to prove that I could be the weapon Zusa saw in me, I would have to do it now. I cracked my knuckles and shifted in place. Kneeling for such a long time had a way of seizing up the muscles.

Wal stood up and winked at me before pulling a sword from the cache. He tossed the practice blade in the air, and it spun before he caught it.

Both he and I knew I was utter shit with anything other than a sword, but it wouldn't matter.

"Talise," Zusa said.

The Tomakan girl, soon to be a woman, slapped her hands against her thighs as she stood up. The smile on her face said it all. She intended to crush the smaller boy in front of her. She hefted the blunted axe and took her position. Her legs anchored her in place like solid tree trunks rising from the earth.

The small current of energy that remained amongst the ranks dissipated. I had no interest in testing my mettle against Adêan, and no one cared to watch me try. The matches between Talise and Adêan had become the highlight of these sessions.

Zusa truly was a bastard of immeasurable proportions.

Wal looked like a child standing across from Talise. Her size added to the effect, but that wasn't it. She settled into her stance, and her raging spirit fought the restraint of her practiced discipline.

"Yaktan," Zusa said.

Wal dashed forward to everyone's surprise and slashed at his opponent's belly.

The attack lacked form and power, and Talise knocked it aside like a fly. She hacked away at the weak guard he managed to pull back into place, then swung straight through his poor attempt at a block. The force set him on his ass.

His hand went up before she could level her axe at his throat. "Yield," he said. "I yield.

"Well, that truly was a lesson in the mighty versus the meek. It seems that you have some more training to do, boy," Zusa said, shaking his head. "And then there were two."

If Zusa thought pairing me against Adēan would humble me—make me shake in fear, he didn't know my will. Adēan had size, strength, and skill on his side. But I was as thickheaded as they came.

"Kaylo, why don't you make the first choice?" Zusa said, with that cocky fucking smile.

The ten paces to the collection of weapons stretched into hundreds. Each weapon lay against the leather roll, weighing more than the sum of their parts. If I picked the sword, I would at least know what to do with it. I knew how to move, strike, and protect my fragile parts. But if I took the axe, it would force Adēan to use another weapon.

It came down to one simple fact—he knew how to fight with a sword, and I had no idea what I was doing with an axe.

The practice blade felt different in my hands than it had all the other times I had run drills. As I twisted the sword around, the smooth hilt brushed against my palms. If I moved well and took advantage of whatever opportunities appeared to me, I could win this.

Adēan shifted his grip on his axe as he moved to starting position across from me. His expression gave away nothing, not that he ever emoted much.

As my fingers dug into the wooden blade, I shifted back and forth in my stance. *No yielding*, I thought. *No surrender.*

"Yaktan!"

One leg over the other, I moved along the perimeter of the circle. Adēan mirrored my movements, and we circled the ground like a flock of vultures over fresh meat.

Zusa's eyes peered into me from over Adēan's shoulder. I would become the weapon I needed to be, with or without him.

When Adéan stepped closer to the center of the circle, so did I. I wouldn't run. The force of his strikes pushed me back as we exchanged parries and attacks like we were drilling.

Only a fool would continue to exchange blows with a fucking daemon.

The moment his guard left a hint of an opening, I lunged.

The bastard sidestepped as if he had anticipated my attack. My weight carried me forward. A pinpoint of concentrated pain stabbed into my cheek, then expanded, as the hammer side of his axe crashed into my face.

The sky and ground swapped places as I rolled to a stop. My cheek burned and a trickle of blood ran down my face, but I pushed myself to standing regardless.

I lunged. He parried.

He slashed. I dodged.

The axe bounced gently in Adéan's hands, even though it weighed several times more than the practice blade in mine.

Sweat ran rivers down his face. At least I had forced the water from his pores.

He pushed me back with three quick swipes. I dodged the first two and had to catch the last one with my sword. His blow vibrated through the hilt, shaking my bones.

My heels brushed the edge of the circle. He swung with all his strength in a downward arc. I shifted to the side—thinking to take advantage of the opening he had left, but when I looked up, he met my gaze with his unaffected stare.

He had recovered from his attack much quicker than I thought he would. Then he thrust the blunt tip of his axe into my sternum.

All the air wrenched from my lungs, forcing me to my knees, coughing.

The fabric-wrapped edge of the axe looked me in the eye, demanding me to yield.

Zusa stood at the edge of the circle, smiling. Everything had gone according to his plan.

"No!" I screamed as I knocked Adēan's axe to the side with my sword and speared my shoulder into his gut.

As we tumbled over each other, I lost track of the sky. His weight fell on me, then mine on him. I thrashed out with my elbows and fists, hitting dirt and flesh. His fist plunged into my side, beneath my ribs. Then we crashed to a stop—me on my back and him atop me.

I had found the sky.

"Yield!" he yelled, his hands pinning my shoulders to the ground.

When I yanked from his grip and tried to slam my head into the bridge of his nose, he tucked his chin and my nose crashed into his thick forehead.

My stomach swam. A jagged line of pain ran from behind my eyes to the back of my head. "No," I said, thrashing against his weight.

Adēan pushed himself off me, leaving me sprawled out on the ground.

The sky wavered like an ocean got stuck behind the clouds. Then Zusa stepped into view, wearing a gentle frown. "What are you trying to prove?"

"I'm not giving up. I'm not broken."

"Broken or not, that was stupid. You were supposed to be a leader. Leaders know their limits."

After the others had cleared the weapons from the training ground, they left me behind at Zusa's order, going back to the campfire for water and a midday meal.

When I breathed in, the pressure behind my eyes pulsed like they might pop out of my skull if I breathed too deeply. My cheek ached and my right side screamed when I tried to straighten up.

The pain flared as I coughed. *At least it's not angry spirits*, I told myself. *No, this time my friend beat the shit out of me, and I deserved it.*

The earth shook under my feet, and my vision flashed white hot before returning. I hobbled a few paces beyond the edge of the training circle and listened for The Song. The Seed remained constant in chaos. It sounded low and thrumming, a steady heart beating within the soil.

I called the willow tree first. It's full drooping branches and leaves were out of place amongst the early budding ironoak and ashburn trees. I missed green. The winter had taken so many things, but at least the green would return.

"Sorry, friend," I said as I snapped a twig away from one of the lower branches, drew my belt knife, and peeled away a section of bark. It coiled around itself as it came loose from the twig.

The bark's bitterness coated my tongue more with each bite, the grit sticking in my teeth. Even if chewing exacerbated the pounding in my head, eventually the medicine would come.

While I worked the willow bark into my system, I reached into The Song again. My hands sounded like gentle waves as they brushed against each other in a dance without pattern. As they moved, a sprout reached out of the soil. It grew taller before one stem became two and three. Then the bud bloomed into a crown of vibrant yellow.

"There is an answer in nature for everything. Arnica is a pretty decent answer for stupidity." I heard Jonac's soft, low voice, like he was there with me.

I crushed the arnica with a pair of stones, forming a much rougher grind than I would have liked, but it would serve its purpose. Mixed with soil and water, it made a quick salve to soothe my bruised sides.

If only there were a plant to soften the sting of a bruised ego.

As I lay there alone, staring up at the canopy of the forest for a while, my emotions modulated between anger, shame, and grief. I did my best to focus on the anger and shame.

Hopefully, spirits in The Mist had better things to do than watch the living. I hadn't behaved as my father's son. My mother would have some proverb or parable to explain what I should do. But neither of them were there.

"Are you okay?"

Liara stood several paces away.

"I'll be fine. I'm just lying here contemplating my stupidity," I said.

"We don't have that long," she said, a soft smile on her lips. "Apologize and do better."

"I'm sorry."

"Not to me. You really are dense."

"No, really. I'm sorry. I don't remember how to be myself anymore. Every time I think I can move forward, I think of Nomi and the girls, or my parents, or Shay. I don't want to be this angry, but I am," I said. Looking at her was too difficult, so I kept staring into the sky. "Do you think they're ashamed of me?"

Clutter on the ground shifted as she sat beside me. "I think they wish they were here with you."

"Is Adēan okay?"

"He's confused. He doesn't know why his friend tried to break his nose with a fucking headbutt," she said, a small touch of levity touching her words. "What were you thinking?"

"I didn't want you all to see you were wrong. You shouldn't have followed me."

"I don't get it," she said. "How is Adēan still walking upright after getting hit with your thick fucking skull?"

I pushed myself to sit up, and the world spun as I did. "I'm serious."

"So am I. Whatever Zusa has been telling you, none of us are looking for a savior right now. If we were, we wouldn't be looking at some seventeen-turn-old boy with anger issues. If you want to be a leader, lead. But don't lash out at us and call it anything else. Don't be a man who needs to abuse those around him to feel like a leader," she said. The green flecks left her hard brown eyes. "I won't stick around for that."

She was right, and I knew it.

"Can you help me up?"

Standing aggravated my injuries, but I had to stand at some point. I collected a few more shaved coils of willow bark and hobbled back to camp, holding my side. Liara didn't offer a helping arm, and I didn't ask her to.

An odd tension hovered over camp when I arrived. At first, I assumed it had to do with me and what I had done, but then I saw the horse tied to a tree on the other side of the firepit.

Adéan walked up to me, his face stoic. He reached out his hands and waited. After a moment, we exchanged small smiles. Then I took his right hand between my hands, and he did the same.

"I'm sorry. I took it too far."

"Yea, cha did," he said.

I pulled a coil of willow bark from my robe and offered it to him. "Your head hurt as bad as mine?"

"Cha gotta hard head." He accepted the bark with a nod.

I tilted my head, and he followed my eyes towards the horse. "Got here a coupa minutes back," he said. "In the tent wit Zusa."

———

Hours later, Zusa emerged with a woman bearing the same light-brown complexion, with the same hard leather vest. Her long black curls fell to her shoulders. They could have been family for all their likeness.

She mounted her horse, nodded to Zusa, and rode off into the wood without a word.

Zusa's focus followed the rider until the trees swallowed her. When he finally turned to see the lot of us waiting around the firepit, his head bobbed up and down. "After the ceremony," he said. "It can wait another day." His voice carried a solemn note, a feeling of finality.

CHAPTER NINETEEN
KAYLO'S STORY

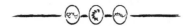

THE GROUND HAD THAWED, but winter still clung to the air like the last fading note of a song. It was a day of three vows, the first being silence, and I had never been happier for the quiet.

Various cracks of pain ran from the center of my forehead to the nape of my neck, from under my right eye through my cheek to the back of my jaw. My throbbing injuries gave a rhythm to the silence. Each breath I took pulled at the bruise in the middle of my chest like a threat—if I breathed too deeply, my skin would tear away from my ribcage.

With all the chaos contained in my body, I had no need for noise.

As I sat in front of my firepit, crafted from rocks as like in size as I could find, flecks of burning ironoak sparked into the air. Soft wisps of gray smoke rose even higher, smelling of bitter earth.

Tomorrow, spring would be here, at least in name. And I would be a man, at least in name.

In all my turns imagining this day, a child wanting not to be a child, I had been sitting in front of the fireplace in our home in Nomar, feeding wood into the flames. My mother should have been settled into her seat at the table with a book, enjoying the quiet, bringing me water when I needed it. At night, my father would have come home from the workshop with another load of firewood. He would have smiled, and I would have almost broken the silence before I thought better of it.

Instead, I sat in the middle of Kenke Forest on the outskirts of a small rebel training camp.

Adéan sat not far off to my left and Talise to my right, the three of us forming an asymmetrical triangle. They had probably dreamed of their swearing day. They probably had family who could only watch on from The Mist as well. Not that any of us spoke of such details.

The rest of the camp left us to our contemplations as they saw to their chores.

Today was a day of service and small sacrifices. I had hated it since the first time my mother made me join in the celebration, if it could even be called a celebration. Though, I never would have told her that.

As I fed another log to the fire, it danced with ash. I rubbed my hands over the stirred flames, and the slight sound made the silence all the more present.

The second vow was one of fasting.

Sokan hovered two fingers from its peak, and my stomach growled with a low ache, as if counting the long remaining hours.

Common wisdom said to know hunger was to know the importance of feeding others, of offering life. Those of us born to Ennea brought an obligation with us. One was many, and many were one. Where our eyes told us we were separate, our hunger reminded us of our connection.

I reached down for my cup and drank down the remainder. Hopefully, the others would bring more water soon.

A blue jay in the tree above called out with a sharp squawk. The ironoaks had begun to bud, but through the nearly barren branches, the bird's bright coat stood out against the brown tones of the forest.

Though I had little love for fasting, at least it meant color would return to the forest with the spring. Life would blossom as the animals returned.

Tanonta was a word that grew from a time before the nations, meaning the first new day—the spring equinox. It celebrated rebirth as well as a transition of life. As the day closed, when the moons reached their highest, those of age pledged themselves to The Mother.

That promise would become the third and final vow.

Once, I asked my mother what she had promised. She smiled at me. "That is between her and I, young one," she had said. "Not even your father knows."

"If we are all connected, then there's no reason to keep your promise secret," I said, childishly thinking I could outsmart my mother.

She smiled and beckoned me to her. Her warmth gathered me up as I sat in her lap. "It is a fair point," she said. "There is a more difficult truth. Connection and separation are not opposites. They are part of the same whole. We till the land and give life to new crops. They, in turn, feed us and provide the fabric for our clothes. Yet, we are not the crops."

"So, we are different, but we need each other?" I asked.

"Yes. Every choice you make will affect the world around you. The world around you will affect your choices. We are part of it all. Yet, we still get to choose what we will do and how we will change the world. Does that make sense?"

"You aren't going to tell me what you promised The Mother, are you?"

A soft chuckle bounced her shoulders. "No, my heart, I am not," she had said.

I always assumed her vow had something to do with stories and history, but as I sat, staring into the flames, I wondered who she had been at seventeen.

The brush to my left rustled, and the blue jay soared off into the sky. The others approached, carrying waterskins and armfuls of firewood. Liara dropped several logs into my dwindling pile. Even though I watched her do it, the abrupt sound made me flinch.

She smiled, and I smiled back, but it turned into a grimace as the movement pulled at the cut on my cheek.

Her chin tilted up, and I followed her glance. Wal knelt next to Adéan, taking extra time to fill his cup. They didn't speak, but they focused on each other with a deep intimacy.

Eventually, Wal stood up and made his way around to filling Talise's cup, then mine. I winked at him and nodded, then he and the others left us to our meditations.

———————

As Sokan slowly dropped behind the treetops, my body ached to move. The tingling in my knees and lower back turned to needle pricks. I stretched in place, which helped for a matter of minutes. Too long sitting in the same place staring into the fire.

When I got up to feed another log into the flames, even though it didn't need it, I let myself linger longer than necessary. Then I sat down and stared back into the heat.

Supposedly, the fire contained answers. Our vows lingered between the stone, burned coals, and flames, but I only saw a carved rabbit charred on one side. Then again, maybe that was my answer.

I didn't need a day of silence and fasting to discover my vow. Over two moons had passed since the day we left the Jani, and I had made a promise—whether or not it cost me my life, my knife would spill The Priest's blood. And for good measure, I would take as many Gousht into The Mist with me as I could.

My mother and father would have wanted me to make a different vow, something less violent, but they weren't here. When Toka and Kana crested the sky, I would whisper my vengeance into the flames and solidify my pledge to The Mother.

———————

My eyes had gone as dry as my water cup. Most of the others had gone to sleep over an hour ago, but the pledged needed to wade deeper into the night. I raised my hand to count finger lengths. Another hour and a half before the sisters reached the top of the sky.

Each blink lasted longer than the one before it.

No matter how I shook my head or rubbed at my temples, sleep pulled at me. My body ached for it—and for other reasons.

Only my stubborn need to tell Ennea exactly what I planned to do to The Priest propelled me forward.

I blinked and snapped alert. I blinked. I blinked. I blinked.

Light streamed through the forest. The last bitter touch of winter had vanished. As had the rows and rows of ironoak and ashburn trees— replaced with a fully bloomed array of trees and plants from every forest in Ennea.

My pain stayed behind with my body in The Waking.

The Seed sat on the ground in front of me. His wood-carved legs weaved under one another. Even sitting, he loomed over me with his long torso and great shoulders.

"I shouldn't be here," I said.

"Why? You are still sitting in front of the fire. Your spirit is allowed to seek answers outside of the flames," he said. "Who made up all these rules anyway?" His voice rumbled through the air, stirring my chest.

"I don't need to seek answers. I know my vow. I have known it since The Priest massacred the Jani. I have known it since the Gousht killed my parents. Since they killed Shay."

The Seed rubbed his chin. Under his thumb, a small yellow flower bloomed from his cheek. I had never seen the particular flower before— five petals sprawled out from a collection of orange seeds tightly gathered in the middle.

My anger almost slipped away from me. So I tightened my grip around it.

"Your people say that the vow a person makes to our Mother will determine who they will become. Many of them see this as a type of mystical work, like the words somehow bind a person to their path. This isn't the case. People change their paths all the time.

"However, there is some truth to their superstition. The choice you make, whatever promise you give, will likely drive you. If you let vengeance drive you, you will become one man. Whereas, if you let forgiveness and hope drive you, you will become another."

"I don't need forgiveness," I said. The volume of my voice was controlled, but my resentment cut through the tone.

"We all need forgiveness." He hunched his shoulders forward and met my gaze, the warmth in his soft cherrywood eyes begging me to forfeit my anger.

"Send me back." I intended to make a demand, but my voice stumbled out of my lips.

"Little seedling, you are free to go back to your body and your pain whenever you like. I did not call you. You came to me."

I stood and walked around the forest, brushing my hands through the feathered leaves of a fern. Even though this was only a projection of my body, I felt a flood of relief with each movement.

"Do you feel pain when trees die in The Waking?" I asked.

"Pain isn't the right word for it. There is loss, but loss is temporary."

"Death isn't temporary!"

"Are you not walking through The Mist right now?" he asked. "Has anger hidden the obvious from you? You are standing in the eternal."

"And so that makes murder permissible?"

"Anger like yours has led too many of my sister's descendants astray. Your righteousness, it is a blade without a hilt. Swing it at your own peril."

"The Thief. It's always about The Thief with you."

"If that is what you must call her." He stood up before walking to a nearby great oak tree. Its trunk stretched wider than The Seed stood tall. Where he touched it, moss grew. "When one seeks balance, anger is natural. The world, especially people with their wants and desires, is constantly at odds with balance."

I thought about my mother's book and the questions she posed. "Is that what happened with Aniki? Was she a liberator or a tyrant? Was

Sinkara a hero?"

"Ahh, Aniki...the truth is beyond simple answers. She lived before the nations drew out their borders—before The Balance wore any other name," he said. "Are you certain you want to hear this story? The answers you find might not be the answers you seek."

"I want the truth," I said, and he shrugged.

"Aniki grew up in a small village, and when she was still small, a band of raiders came. They killed a handful of people as an example, then declared the village a part of their clan. Without a militia of their own, the village conceded, as did many others.

"The raiders took grain, and crops, and strong young villagers to fortify their raiding parties. They took Aniki and trained her to fight, but she kept her gift secret. After she took what she needed from their training, she organized a rebellion from within their ranks. The rebels formed a militia and set out to free villages from the rule of the clan.

"As the story goes, she went to one village after another to challenge clan leaders in single combat. They underestimated her, and she beat one dancer after another, liberating villages. The villages fed her growing rebellion until nearly all those under the tyrannical clan's control came under her protection.

"And if the story were to end there, we would call her a liberator. Many did. However, she continued the work the clan started. She approached new villages. In a way, her rebel militia had become a band of raiders. Eventually, she lost at the hands of Sinkara, but not before her clan became the beginnings of the first nation."

The Seed fell quiet. Without animals scurrying about or wind blowing through the trees, the silence formed a complete void. Where it was peaceful, it was also overwhelming. To hear nothing. Absolutely nothing.

"She became what she hated," I said.

"As do many who follow anger." He bent down to touch a small laurel bush. When he drew his hand back, the white and blue flowers grew towards him until the plant flourished to nearly double its previous size. "Tonight, you will make a vow, and tomorrow you will walk the path you've set. Make sure it leads you to where you want to go, young seedling."

———

The flames had eaten away at the last of the wood when I returned to myself. Kana and Toka straddled the highest point in the sky.

I fed two more logs into the fire and sat back down.

To my left, Adéan leaned forward into the fire, whispering his first words in a day. The desire to know what he had promised swept through me. He had set out from Renéqua in search of the Missing before we had even met. Did he seek vengeance as well?

"She became what she hated." My own words rang between my ears.

My mother and father wanted me to live. Shay wanted me to fight. Nomi wanted me to find peace. The Seed wanted me to forgive. And I... didn't know what I wanted.

What vow would I have given if I had never left Nomar? If the people I loved hadn't died? If I hadn't been a malitu? If the Gousht had never arrived on our shores? Who would that person be?

Tears ran down my cheeks, and I wiped them away with the sleeve of my robe. Tears had their use, but I needed my anger, not self-pity.

Toka pushed closer to the height of the sky.

Aniki made a vow, I thought. *What path did she speak into the flames? Did she follow it or falter from it?*

Then I knew. I closed my eyes, took two deep breaths, leaned closer to the fire, and whispered my promise to Ennea.

CHAPTER TWENTY
CURRENT DAY ENNEA

Tayen sat with her back against the outer wall of Kaylo's quarters with a blanket covering her feet. The brazier held back the darkness of the late hour.

Kaylo had gone quiet and still, staring into the flames.

"What was your vow?" she asked. "What did you say?"

"Weren't you listening? The words we offer The Mother on Tanonta are sacred. When we speak them, we lay a path before us. It is a choice that defines us. A choice that connects us."

"If you aren't going to tell me, just say you aren't going to tell me."

He faced her and smiled softly. "I'm not going to tell you."

CHAPTER TWENTY-ONE
KAYLO'S STORY

I WOKE UP TO an empty tent the day after Tanonta. Voices buzzed in the air on the other side of the patchwork leather. No matter how many hours I had slept, it had not been enough. Either the lack of sleep or the beating Adéan had given me the day before yesterday left my head cracked open like a canyon. Even the soft light pushing through the tent stung my eyes.

As I pulled the furs from the tent's opening, the sunlight flared, and I shielded my eyes. Spots of bright light peppered my vision, making it difficult to focus.

If not for Boda grabbing my arm to steady me, I would have stumbled over a stone and into the firepit. He looked at me with a tilted head and raised eyebrows. All contention had disappeared, replaced with genuine worry. We had either become part of this family or I looked a pitiful mess.

Adéan and Talise sat on the other side of the fire. Dark semicircles underscored their eyes as they sat hunched, but neither looked nearly as bad as I felt.

"Here." Boda set his waterskin in my palm. "You need to drink. There's plenty of broth, but you should take it slow."

I nodded, partly because my mouth had become a desert and I had no desire to speak, but mostly because I didn't want my gratitude to come out sounding like a question. Boda had only ever shown me contempt or indifference.

As I moved to take a seat, everyone watched, some less conspicuously than others, all wearing some version of the same concern Boda had expressed. Wal outright stared.

However bad I thought I looked, I must have looked worse.

The water ran cool and clean over my tongue. I drank too quickly and coughed, only to immediately drink more.

"Now that we are all here, it is time to discuss the messenger we received," Zusa said. Even though I kept my head down and eyes shielded from the brightness of the day, he had my full attention.

"We have orders." He paused, giving me time to imagine which outpost we would attack or who we might assassinate.

Bloodlust served as a passable remedy for all the aches and pains.

"In three days' time, a shipment of spirit crystals will cut through the Kenke Forest on the other side of the Sanine River. They are headed north to supply their outposts nearest the Lost Forest, and we are going to intercept the shipment."

Not the blood-filled mission I had hoped for, but there would be soldiers to kill.

"You are no longer just trainees. You are warriors of the Missing," he said. "We will need to move quickly. The ambush location is a day away, and we have much to do. Break your fast, pack a travel sack, and meet back here in two fingers."

Zusa stood up and began walking away. Then he turned and looked down at me. "Kaylo, a moment."

My body didn't want to move. The muscles in my back felt as rigid as stormwood. It might have been my imagination, but I could have sworn my body creaked as I stood up and walked over to the edge of the camp where Zusa waited.

His eyes scanned me from head to toe. "Are you ready for this?"

"Yes." My answer didn't require explanation. He should have known that.

"Have you been wrestling with a bear? You look a mess," he said. "Let me see your eyes."

Before I lifted my gaze to meet his, I tried to blink away the pain and blurry spots.

"I need you." His eyes were probing questions. "They need you. We can't know the exact path of the shipment, and there will be guards."

"Good."

"This is not the time for your vendetta. The soldiers will be armed with good steel and spirit crystals. If you lose concentration, your friends will die." He paused and let his words sink in. "It is not a question of if, but a question of who and how many."

"This is what we have been training for. It's the reason we came looking for you."

His head bounced up, and a smile filled his cheeks. "Good, we have some planning to do."

The report the messenger had delivered left much to be desired. We didn't know how many soldiers would be escorting the haul, how many spirit crystals they would be carrying, or even exactly which path they would take through the forest. But they were coming. I didn't need to know anything more than that.

Zusa and I sat in the center of camp, leaning over a map of the forest while the others crowded behind us.

The map detailed the forest more vividly than any I had ever seen. Every rock formation and open field had been notated in painstaking detail. Munnie's hallow was only two days hard walking from where we stood. For the others, it may have blended into the rest of the rock formations on the map, but it jumped off the paper at me.

Zusa shook my shoulder to grab my attention. "How close do spirit crystals have to be for you to hear them?"

"If I drop my barriers and concentrate, two hundred or three hundred paces. But I won't be able to tell our crystals apart from theirs," I said. "Are we certain they are going to be on the far side of the Sanine?"

"I've never known our scouts to be wrong about these sorts of details. If they don't know, they say as much."

"Where are we taking the crystals after we are done?" Liara asked from behind us.

"That is a question for later," Zusa said in a curt tone, not even bothering to turn around.

"No, it's a question for right now." Liara matched his tone. "If we're putting our lives in danger, we need to know why."

Now he turned. His face was placid, but his eyes were arrows notched and drawn. "My say so should be enough 'why' for you, girl."

"Don't talk to her that way," Tomi said.

"There is no need for any of this," Niven said. "We are all serving the same cause. When the Missing give orders, we follow. However, there is no problem in asking a question, is there?" He looked at Zusa, but Zusa kept his eyes aimed at Liara.

"The primary concern isn't where they're going," Zusa said. "The goal is to get them away from the Gousht. More weapons in Gousht hands means more dead Enneans. Afterwards, we will keep them in our camp until the Missing come to collect."

Neither Liara nor Zusa broke eye contact.

Something about Zusa's response made me eye him sideways. If he didn't know every detail about where those crystals went after they left his care, it changed everything I knew about the man. The man I knew understood how all the pieces fit together at all times. When he didn't know, he found out. Either his faith in the Missing outmatched his need to know or he was hiding something.

"I'll go," I said, and both Liara and Zusa looked at me. "We need a scout."

"No, it's too dangerous," Liara said.

"Can you do it?" Zusa asked, ignoring Liara's objection.

"Like I said, I can hear their echoes two or three hundred paces out. I'll never be close enough for it to get dangerous."

"And how will you send word that you've found them? They'll see smoke signals." Liara's mouth settled into a firm line of disapproval.

"The river," Wal interjected. "The Sanine flows north. Send a message with it."

Every single head turned towards the boy with the bitter tongue. Wal never spoke up in meetings, at least not with anything productive. His shoulders lifted in a question, as if he hadn't stepped outside of his character.

The plan was simple, yes, but also effective.

"You said it yourself, Kaylo. Kalani had the stronger forces, and she could wield the spirits, but Sione out-thought her," Wal said.

"Read a lot about the Great War, have you?" Zusa turned back to the map and nodded to himself. "This could work."

———

Adéan, Niven, and Tomi agreed to join the scouting party with me. Liara's dislike for our plan only grew with her sister's involvement, but the sway of the group pushed through her objections.

We packed up and broke down camp within the hour. After the mission, we would set up on a new stretch of land. No need to test fate and return to an unguarded camp.

I hitched my sword and scabbard to my left hip, and my father's knife on my right. The weight of the sword disrupted my gait, but I would have to get used to that. If I meant to kill Gousht, I needed to be prepared to bear far more weight than a sword.

As I slung my waterskins over my shoulder, Zusa approached me wearing a heavy expression.

"Remember, you're going south to scout. There will be plenty of killing when we snare them in our trap." He reached into his robe and brought out a hollow wooden cylinder. Inside, a bit of writing coal clinked around. "We don't have much paper, so use it well. You'll need to whittle a stopper to seal it shut, but I figure you'll have time for that tonight."

Liara walked up behind him and stood there silently. Zusa clapped me on the shoulder and nodded, then left Liara and me alone.

"You better protect her."

"I will."

"You better protect yourself."

"I will."

"You are such a fool, you know that."

"I know," I said and smiled.

As we stared at each other, her lips remained stiff as a board.

In the depths of our silence, she grabbed me by the shoulders and yanked me into her. The pressure of her body pressed against mine calmed something within my spirit. I squeezed her tighter.

For the first time, her touch didn't stir my nerves. I didn't question what it might mean. Her echo sang a series of gentle waves washing over me. The sunflower oil in her hair lingered in my nostrils.

When she let me go, she touched my cheek, held my eyes in hers, then walked away. A wiser person wouldn't have left, but as she said, I was a fool.

The small scouting team gathered near the edge of what had been our camp. We had said our goodbyes. Despite our words to the contrary, we knew we might not return.

"Wait." Wal rushed over to us.

"Wha brings cha ova here?" Adēan said with a smile.

"Impending death," Wal said, as if he were out of breath. "This is dangerous. Ambushing the Gousht. I mean, it's not like we aren't prepared. But we might die. One of us. And if that happens, you know, death, I don't want to regret not saying something."

"Is tere anyting cha don't say?" Adēan said, a small laugh in his voice.

Wal flushed and looked around before biting his lip. "I like you."

"Tha's nice. I like cha too."

"You're not going to make this easy, are you?"

"It wouldn't be annae fun." The stocky Renēquan man offered a wink and a smile. "Come here." He grabbed the front of Wal's robe and pulled him forward.

Their lips met in tender need. Wal cupped his hand at the base of Adēan's neck, his shoulders relaxing as they held each other.

Instinctively, I looked for Liara, but she had walked off.

The two young men held their embrace in the middle of our small militia. Wal gripped the fabric of Adēan's robes like he couldn't let go.

"Thanks for the show and everything, but we should probably get going." Tomi said.

Adēan pulled away from the kiss. "No one's gonna die, cha hear me?"

Wal nodded. Our scouting party turned away from the camp. Adēan hesitated for a moment, then joined our march east.

The last lingering light of Sokan cast a brilliant orange and yellow backdrop as we crossed the Sanine River. Waters ran shallow here, babbling against the protruding rocks. The cool current eased the wear of a long day. We made camp just beyond the tree line, encircled within a thicket of bushes I called from The Song.

The calm of the night prickled the hairs on the back of my neck. If plans worked as plans should, I would be tracking a convoy of soldiers by midday tomorrow.

As I slid my father's knife over a bit of wood, it gave way to my blade and curled in strips that fell to the ground at my feet.

The container lid didn't have to be pretty, just tight enough to survive the journey downriver. Slide the scrap of paper in the cylinder, strap the lid on with a bit of rope, and let the waters carry our words back north.

Niven shifted closer towards me as I carved away at the wood. "How does it work?" he asked. "Do you always hear the spirits?"

He wore an unassuming look on his face, as if he had asked about something trivial, instead of the inner workings of a cursed spirit.

After a moment's hesitation, he filled the silence. "If we don't want to die, I need to know how The Thief works."

"If I'm close enough and I'm listening for it, I can hear a spirit as long as it's on this side of The Mist," I said. "And spirits trapped in crystals are stuck on this side. Is that enough?"

"That should do."

I held his gaze for a moment, waiting for his eyes to flash with disgust or judgment, but neither came. "You should get some sleep. I'll take the first watch."

"Nah, tha's not gonna happen. Cha need ta rest," Adēan said. I tried to object, but he cut me off. "We're countin on cha, and I ain dying because cha too stubborn to sleep."

That was all there was to say. I lay down, covered myself with a blanket, and watched the sky darken. Niven and Tomi did the same.

Even if the air remembered winter too fondly, there would be no fire tonight. We shifted closer towards each other until we were a heap of bodies sleeping under Ennea's younger Daughters.

———

"Oh, little thief," The Priest said from within a field of black. "You fret too much. It is an honor to be touched by The One True God."

His shape formed out of the blackness, the blood red of his robes contrasting our surroundings. "Don't be scared. After all, we serve the same master. As the Writ tells us, 'You have no family under the sun, but the father and his children.'"

"The Thief is not your god. She just pretended to be!"

"Do you think that matters? Your Thief gave us power. Call her whatever name you wish, that makes her our patron, our God."

I took two steps and launched my body into his, but he evaporated into the blackness, sending me crashing to the ground.

"Now, now. That is no way to treat a friend," he said from behind me. His voice grew lighter than his normal low rumble, like he was smiling behind his veil.

"We aren't friends." I picked myself up and reached for my knife, but my hand fell against my empty hip.

"If you want to kill me, find me." The illusion shuddered in front of me. Then one Priest became two, then four, then eight. Too many red hoods to count encircled me. "You can't kill us all, little thief."

The joy lifted the register of his deep voice. Rage boiled in my belly, and I threw my fist through a red-cloaked figure, which turned to vapor and absorbed back into the dark void.

One after another, they vanished under my fists and my kicks. I charged through several with my shoulder. My screams filled the void. The insult multiplied with each false priest.

By the time I finished attacking the empty cloaks, I could no longer scream or curse. Tears ran down my face. And then, only one remained, standing tall with his shoulders back, unmoving.

I walked up to him, but this time, instead of attacking, I reached out and grabbed the fabric of his veiled hood. It didn't vanish. The soft material bunched up in my fist as I yanked it clear from his head.

A generic Gousht face with tightly cropped silver-white hair, icy blue eyes, and pale skin greeted me. Then his thin mouth vanished. His cheeks grew paler, and the skin above them turned black until his face bore the two-toned coloring of The Thief.

"I told you we were brothers," he said, without a mouth.

I awoke in a fit. Tomi hunched over me, her face caught between annoyance and concern. "The others are refilling the waterskins. We should get moving soon." Her lack of critique bordered on comforting.

The two of us cleared our marks from the land. If the Jani and the Missing had anything in common, they shared an abundance of caution. The land had to look as if we had never touched it.

As soon as Niven and Adēan returned from the river, we hefted our travel sacks and took off south, following the river from inside the tree line.

Before the Conclave of Spirits, this section of land had seen more war than any other—the Bloodline of Ennea. For every battle that pushed the border of Tomak farther south, another expanded Sonacoa. The storied battles had contradicting tellings, but all ended in an overwhelming amount of blood.

To look at it, the land and the forest showed no signs of the history. Blood didn't bother the soil. The forest grew despite our political squabbles.

What was it all for? I thought. *More land to farm? Better access to clean water? The simple ability to call more land our own?*

Our peoples, despite our differences, all belonged to Ennea. If we had given up our infighting, we would have been more prepared for the Gousht. We could have met their armada with a force unlike anything they had ever seen.

Instead, Tomakans and Renēquans took their time to answer Sonacoa's call while the Jani hid, and the Lost Nation tightened their borders.

Had we fought them as hard as we fought each other, maybe my parents would still be alive. At the very least, I wouldn't be traipsing through the forest, listening for echoes of stolen spirits.

"Bad dream?" Tomi asked, and I jumped at the noise. Tomi walked in lockstep beside me. Yet, in the chaos of my busied and bitter thoughts, I had noticed her there.

"Something like that."

"You have them a lot," she said.

"What of it?"

"When I was a kid, I used to dream about daemons. You ever hear of the face stealer?"

"I wasn't dreaming about daemons." My tone bit at the question, but if she heard it, she ignored it.

"Of course you were. What are the couta if not daemons? Pale-faced, blood-thirsty creatures who crossed an ocean to kill us, steal our spirits, and take our land—sounds like a daemon to me," she said, all the while staring straight ahead.

"They locked me inside that compound for more than four moons. They tried to convince me they were saviors and beat me when I claimed otherwise," she said. Her cheeks pulled into a pained smile. "I still dream of daemons. But today, we hunt the daemons."

When I looked at her, she ceased being a child. She stood level with my shoulder—skin, bone, and muscle. Only fourteen turns, and she had already lived too much pain.

We walked in a shared silence of understanding, our anger binding us. The history and the blood that fed this soil were done. Those warriors moved on to The Mist. The blood to come mattered far more.

In the next few hours, we would find the pale daemons, set our trap, and add their blood to the soil. The fucking crystals didn't matter. I wasn't searching for them. I hunted those who carried them.

CHAPTER TWENTY-TWO
KAYLO'S STORY

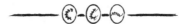

ECHOES CAME LIKE A swarm of bees. One faint buzz followed another, then dozens more until the noise became a collective of high-pitched screams—each individual and yet inseparable from the others. The sound grew until my vision rattled amongst the chaos. I fell to my knees, clinging to fistfuls of the earth.

Voices, too muffled and distant to be understood, reached for me.

Every instinct told me to wall myself off from the echoes, but instead, I focused on my breathing. The anxiety and pain—this was no different from hunting or training. I split myself in two, like my father had taught me. While my spirit reached towards the cacophony of echoes, my mind focused on the steady push and pull of my diaphragm.

The sound of the screaming spirits formed a reflection of my rage. We understood one another, and it put the pain in context. Despite my throbbing temples, the world settled.

The others huddled over me in a mixture of fear, confusion, and concern. "I'll be fine," I said, though my voice shivered. "They're close, hauling more crystals than I've ever heard before."

After Niven helped me to my feet, finding the soldiers became a simple matter of walking towards the center of the noise.

Silhouettes moved through the forest, then light caught the silver helm of a soldier. We crept closer. Six green-clad couta escorted the horse-drawn wagon—two driving, two walking behind, and two out front. They made no effort to blend in. The Emperor's seal lay draped over the covered wagon, yellow stitched into a field of green.

The snake stared at me between the trees.

"Fucking couta," I whispered on impulse.

They had torn countless spirits from dancers—dancers who would never again hear The Song—then tossed the crystals into the back of a wagon like a harvest.

Niven rested a hand on my shoulder. "I'll mark the location, then Tomi and I will send it north with the river," he said. "You two, stay here and keep an eye on our friends."

"Why me?" Tomi whispered harshly.

"We are the fastest, and Kaylo looks like he would probably run into a tree if he went. Is that a good enough reason?"

"We can take them ourselves," I said. "There are only six of them."

"That's not the plan," Niven said.

"What difference does it make if we kill them now or later?" My fingers encircled the hilt of my sword.

"No reason to even think it," Niven said. "We have orders. Tomi and I will deliver the message while you two keep watch. Understood?"

"Don worrae, we will keep our distance." Adēan smiled, subtle and self-assured.

"Watch out for him," Niven said, gesturing towards me.

My protest died before it reached my lips as another wave of pain ran through my head.

"Go'aun, we'll be fine."

Niven turned first, carefully walking back towards the river. Tomi waited as if to prove she didn't have to follow anyone's orders, then turned and crept away. Small movements in the trees and brush followed them until they vanished into the treescape.

"You sure you want to wait for the ambush?"

"I mae be able to take my half of tose men, but cha look like a sharp glare could knock cha down."

"Fuck you," I said with an attempt at a smile.

He successfully smiled back.

The soldiers moved slowly through the forest—navigating the cart between gaps in the trees where they could and using the crystals to remove trees that stood in their way where necessary. We stalked after them through the forest, always keeping our distance.

The flashes of silver, yellow, and green through the trees made the world turn on end, so I focused on the ground and followed Adéan's footsteps.

Eventually, the echoes unraveled. Together they were too discordant and jarring, but as I focused on the individual sounds that made the whole, the ache in my head subsided. They ceased being the chaos they had been. If I had the time, I could have counted the echoes one-by-one and sorted them into like spirits.

One spirit jumped apart from the collective. I looked up at the soldiers, searching for the outlier. The cart moved along the same path as before. The two soldiers out front plodded out a course for the wagon and the soldiers in the rear focused on their surroundings.

Wait! Only one soldier sat on the cart driving the horse.

The deviant echo drew closer. I spun to find the noise and found the missing soldier, a smiling pale face lined by his shining helm. He reeled back his hand and cracked me in the jaw with the hilt of his short axe.

As I fell to the ground, the echoes broke into all out chaos once again, and I lost control over the world.

Harsh noises scuffled back and forth over my head. Spirits screamed, the noises wrapping around each other into one tangled mess. The forest faded to a blur of shapes, shadows, and colors.

I tried to push myself up from the ground. Then the heel of a boot crashed into the back of my head, and everything went black.

I woke up staring at my feet with a crick in my neck, and my hands lashed behind my back and anchored to a tree. A numbing tingle crawled beneath the skin on the right side of my face from my jaw up past my cheekbone. Which felt pleasant compared to the throbbing coming from the back of my head.

Now, instead of being on the outside of the swarm of echoes, the swarm enveloped me. The throaty sound of Gousht words occasionally cut through the sharpness of the screaming spirits.

"It looks like the konki is awake."

Gousht soldiers only toyed with our language to insult us, twisting a tart fruit into a slur because of its coloring. They lacked the imagination of a proper insult.

The soldier sat on an upturned bucket only two strides in front of me. Thin strains of silvery-white hair fell to either side of his pale face, covering his ears. Wrinkles along his brow aged him. He wasn't the one who had beaten me senseless, but he had my father's knife. He flipped it back and forth in his hands, admiring the blade.

"Give me back my knife," I said in their curt and ugly words.

He smiled and waved the knife in front of me. *"No, little konki. This knife is mine. Just like you and your friend with the axe and the bad attitude are mine."*

When I lunged forward, the ropes around my wrists yanked me back into place.

The couta fuck's smile made his wrinkles more pronounced. If he thought his age or these bindings would save him from my wrath, he had underestimated my will. The Mother could take me once The Priest died, not before.

"You have courage," he said. *"Good. It's no fun breaking cowards. What are you doing spying on me and my comrades?"*

The wagon almost entirely shrouded Adēan, who sat about twenty paces away, similarly bound to a tree. The flesh on the left side of his face swelled into a bloody mess. If he had any other injuries, I couldn't tell—not from my vantage point. But he wasn't moving.

Another soldier sat in front of Adēan, much like the soldier in front of me. Not far from him, a third soldier tended to the horse, brushing its mane and feeding it an apple. The rest of the lazy bastards sat around a small cookfire, watching a pot of water boil. They idly chatted, their helms littering the ground around them. The asshole who had knocked me out smiled and laughed with the rest of them.

Apparently, our presence had not overly concerned any of these bastards.

The cold touch of my father's blade against the underside of my chin brought me back to the couta bastard in front of me. *"My questions are not optional. What were you doing spying on us?"*

"We weren't spying. We were headed to the river when we saw you."

"Oh, I see. You happened upon us. What is that expression? 'Water drowns the curious.'" He nodded to himself. *"What about my demeanor gives you the impression that I'm stupid?"*

"How could I pick just one thing?"

My interrogator smiled, then he placed his hand on my forehead and thrust me backwards. The crown of my head slammed into the tree they had bound me to. The forest dimmed. I blinked several times until the daylight returned.

The pain that had been throbbing sharpened into a series of cuts that radiated out from the point of contact.

"I appreciate you think that you're clever. Your kind always does, but you're not. Minds as muddy as your skin. You are an insect with grand ideas of importance. No, no. You and your kind need guidance," he said. *"You will answer my questions and whatever guidance you need, I will be happy to provide."*

He wasn't The Priest, but he would do.

This pathological need they all had to be superior made them vulnerable. I glared at him with all my will.

His body spasmed and jerked forward as he coughed up blood. A globule tickled the hairs on my cheek as it slid towards my chin.

At the moment, I could only think about how much younger he looked without his face pulled into a smile—the lines on his face slackened.

The arrowhead protruded from his throat like a slick, red curiosity. What remained of the shaft and the fletching stuck out of the other side of his neck. He jerked again and an airy squeak fumbled in his throat. Blood bubbled over his lips and ran down his chin before his pale blue eyes lost their keen focus.

For a breath, none of the soldiers realized what had happened. Then he collapsed onto the ground, the bucket toppling over beneath him.

A second and third arrow launched into the group of soldiers sitting around the fire. One lodged in the eye socket of a soldier, who collapsed as if his muscles had given way. The second went wide and cut into the quilted fabric of another soldier's padded armor.

The lucky soldier screamed, *"Ambush,"* and then chaos erupted.

Soldiers clamored for their weapons and sought cover as arrows continued to rain on them. Several bolts crashed into the wagon or flew into the forest behind them, but one caught a soldier in her shoulder, turning her green fabric armor a shade of brown around the injury.

Their fear was a lovely sight.

I pushed myself back against the tree anchoring me in place, reaching into The Song. As soon as I began aging it, the screams of two echoes grew louder. I yanked my hands towards the threads of the spirits, shining translucent silver waiting to be taken, but the ropes held me at bay.

A young soldier with a pulsing red crystal started a trail of fire that jumped from plant to plant, tree to tree, towards the archers. The second called The Wind, carrying the fire faster until it grew into a ravenous beast, feeding on whatever it could.

When the remaining soldiers recovered their wits, they notched arrows and began releasing them in quick succession.

My breath quickened. I blinked away the image of Tomi and Niven blackened by fire, punctured by several arrows.

Not again! I thought.

With my hand planted against the rough bark behind me, I reached for the life at its core and churned it forward. It aged, brittle branches crashing to the ground around me until the tree collapsed into a billow of ashen debris.

When the tension around my wrists vanished, I rolled to my back, reaching the rope binding my hands over my legs. Even if they were still bound, I could grab the translucent tethers linking the spirits to The Mist.

Two spirits rushed into me, spitting rage and fury, but my anger outmatched theirs.

As I pulled The Flame, the fires consuming the forest extinguished, leaving wisps of smoke in their place.

The cookfire in front of the soldiers was inconsequential, barely reaching over the stone border lining the pit. Hues of orange and yellow flickered low to the ground, yearning to be more. The reflection of The Song begged me to feed them, and I answered its need with all the rage contained within The Flame.

A pyre flared up higher than the oldest trees in the forest. The surrounding air shuddered an instant before a wave of heat swept over the battlefield.

Soldiers fell to the ground, shielding their faces from the sudden burst of light. One rolled in the dirt screaming, flames devouring her tunic and hair.

My interrogator's heavy sword winked at me from its scabbard. The bastard wouldn't be needing it any longer. As the blade slid free, its weight tested my grip.

I may have trained with lighter swords, but any sharp edge would do.

The three remaining soldiers pushed themselves off the dirt, drawing their steel. The bastard who had cracked me in the jaw with his axe led the charge.

Good, I thought.

He charged in recklessly, reeling his short axe over his shoulder. Stepping to the side, I swept my hand from one side of my body to the other. A gust of wind swept his feet out from under him, and he crashed to the ground like a sack of grain.

The heavy sword slowed down when it met his padded armor, but the fabric couldn't repel the weight of my thrust. He shuddered and blood gushed from his gut as I yanked my stolen weapon loose.

One of the two standing soldiers still had an arrow buried in her shoulder. A dark purple crystal glowed in her good hand before the shadows surrounding us expanded to block out the light.

The world went dark for a moment, except for one silvery thread.

When I stole the third spirit, the two soldiers stopped, eyes full of terror.

"Thief." The soldier with a now-empty crystal in her palm drew a line down her chest in a symbol of their god.

Her spine stopped the heavy blade, then she collapsed to her knees as blood sputtered from the open wound in her neck.

All the spirits trapped within me roared with the carnage, their rage feeding into mine and mine into theirs.

Only one pale man remained unblemished, staring at four slain companions and one half-charred soldier writhing on the ground.

The spirits wanted more blood, and I had no reason to deny them.

The last uninjured soldier looked at the crystal in one of his hands and his sword in the other before dropping both and running towards the horse.

His fear made my anticipation of the kill sweeter. The heavy sword no longer weighed me down as I paced after the fleeing man.

"Kaylo!" Tomi yelled out.

The Flame, after turns of captivity, tingled with a lust for vengeance beside the pain. The soldier's flesh would bathe in fire, pale hues burning black as coal.

"Kaylo, please!" Tomi's voice pitched sharply.

All three stolen spirits joined in chorus with my rage, demanding this man's life. Tomi could wait. His death would be quick enough. But not too quick.

"You better protect her." Liara's voice cut through the violence.

"Kaylo, hurry!" Tomi screamed.

The soldier hoisted himself onto the horse. The Wind could break him from his mount and make him easy prey. *Only a few more moments.* The spirit stirred.

"Kaylo, I need you!" The desperation in her voice turned Tomi into the fourteen-turn-old girl she was.

As I turned to run towards Tomi's cries, the sound of the horse galloping away grew fainter.

Burn marks scorched the brush and the trees. Quiet embers flickered from branches above my head. Then the damage to the forest ceased to matter.

Niven lay in Tomi's lap as she sobbed and brushed her hand through what remained of his braids. An arrow jutted out of his chest. Burns marred the right half of his body—the fabric of his robes fused with his burned flesh.

His chest still rose and fell—slowly, but he wasn't dead.

Tomi met my eyes. Soot blackened her hands. The skin over her knuckles had peeled away, but she continued brushing his hair like she could sooth the wounds.

"Help him," she said. "Save him."

It took soft tones to convince her to let me move him. We hefted his body into the wagon, where we laid him on the wooden surface next to the chest of crystals and a crate full of firestarter. At least it was cleaner than the ground.

Most of his burns were limited to his limbs, his right side far worse off than his left.

"He pulled me out of the fire when I fell down," Tomi said.

"I need you to check on Adéan. Let me handle this."

"Don't let him die." Tears streamed down her face. "He can't die. He saved me."

I nodded, though I couldn't offer a promise or even much hope.

Before I could tend to Niven, I made sure the soldiers were dead. The soldier I had burned stared blankly into the sky, her burned-paper skin flaking away at my touch. No pulse.

She had earned every last flare of pain the flames had wrung out of her, but Niven hadn't.

Burns had insidious ways of setting every system in the body off-balance. Jonac had taught me burn remedies, but plants could only do so much.

Goldenrod. Moonlight hazel. Aloe. Green cabbage.

I stole the helm from one of the dead soldiers and muddled plants with water and dirt in the cold metal cap. "Better correct and slow than fast and careless," I said to myself in Jonac's cadence.

As the individual plants melded into a thick greenish-brown paste, the smell of rotten fruit and grass filled the air. I slathered it on one side of several cabbage leaves and gently placed it on Niven's burned flesh.

The second skin formed a protective layer to stave off infection, but it had to be seamless. Any exposed burns would leave him vulnerable. One leaf at a time, I applied the paste, lined it up so that it overlapped with the previous leaf, and eased it into place.

When I finally finished that process, I still had an arrow wound to contend with. It pierced high enough towards the shoulder that it might have missed his heart and lungs.

No puss or discoloration—not yet. But if infection didn't take him, blood loss would.

I heaved Niven into a sitting position to get a better look at the wound. Of course, the bolt didn't have the decency to pierce through to the other side. Pulling it out would only do more damage, so I snapped off the fletching and pushed.

Every instinct begged me to be gentle, but his flesh resisted, and the unconscious young man groaned. Helping meant hurting, for now. I put my weight behind the length of wood, and it slipped through his body until it caught the tension of his skin.

"I'm sorry," I whispered to Niven before I drove the arrowhead through to the other side. A cabbage leaf smeared with a poultice was a poor replacement for skin, but I had to seal his body from the world somehow.

"Wha can I do?" Adēan asked from over my shoulder.

"Sit down. You're only slightly on the right side of The Mist as it is," I said, but he didn't move. Even with one eye swollen shut, he managed to glare at me. I sighed. "If you're going to be stubborn, you can take care of Tomi's burns."

After I showed him how to muddle the salve ingredients together and apply them, he went to work. Tomi complained, but she didn't have the energy to fight us.

I spent the next few hours applying salves and poultices to each of our various wounds. As long as I kept my hands in motion, I didn't have to think about how badly I had fucked up.

If I hadn't let myself get caught, Niven would still be alright.

His chest rose and fell. I pressed my fingers to his neck and his pulse thumped against my fingertips in a faint, erratic rhythm.

"For Boda," I whispered into his ear. "Hold on for Boda."

———

The moonlight guided our travel through the forest. None of us had any interest in waiting for the runaway soldier to return with friends. Adéan and I pulled the wagon with the harness meant for a horse, though we didn't move nearly as fast, and we had to take far too many breaks.

Tomi sat in the wagon with Niven, trying to feed him water. He still hadn't opened his eyes, and he wouldn't. Eventually, his chest would settle, and his spirit would slip away into The Mist.

And when he did, it would break her.

When we rescued her from the mission school, it had wounded her pride, even if she never said as much. That Liara had been hurt and the Gousht had followed us back to the Jani made it worse still. No one hated themselves as much as I did for what happened. But Tomi came close.

Now, a young man would die after saving her from the Gousht's fires.

At this point, all we could do was get Niven to his brother before his final breath.

With so many echoes swirling through the air, I barely recognized Liara's.

I stopped, and Adéan looked at me. "Need nother break?"

As my emotions washed over me, the air abandoned my lungs. I was still alive, and my gratitude for whatever days I had left churned the bile in my stomach. Niven deserved this life more than I did.

I collapsed to the ground, sobbing.

"Wha is happening? Cha okay?"

All I could do was point towards the familiar echo.

After a few moments, the rest of our band of young rebels stepped into view. Liara and Wal rushed towards us, trailed by Boda, the rest following close behind.

Boda's eyes scanned over us again and again as he approached.

"Stop him," I whispered to Adéan.

The broad northerner limped towards Boda and intercepted him before he made it to the cart.

"Where's my brother?" he yelled. When Adéan didn't respond

immediately, he screamed the question again. The boy pushed Adēan and must have hit a wound, because the sturdy northerner stumbled back.

Boda couldn't be protected from this, but he could be cared for. I picked myself up off the ground and wiped my tears on my blood-stained sleeve.

By the time I reached the back of the wagon, Boda sat hunched over his brother. He turned to me. "What happened? What did you do?" he asked in a strangely calm voice.

"It wasn't his fault," Tomi said.

"His plan, right?" Boda asked louder. "What happened?"

A pair of hands latched onto my shoulders and moved me away. Zusa wrapped his arm around me, guiding me to the side of the wagon before he began doling out orders.

They set a guard rotation immediately. Someone built a fire. Someone else constructed a tent, and laid Niven within it. The air smelled of broth. All the while, I sat with my back pressed against the wooden planks of the wagon.

Sionia pressed a bowl of soup into my hands, but I didn't have the stomach for it. So she sat next to me as Sokan rose into the sky.

Before Sokan climbed above the treetops, violent wails came from the tent where Niven's body lay. I had no more tears. The words Zusa said to me before we left on our mission repeated in my head.

"If you lose concentration, your friends will die. It is not a question of if, but a question of who and how many."

CHAPTER TWENTY-THREE

THE THREE WOULD-BE SPIRIT dancers knelt on the sand in front of Kaylo, murmurs of pain escaping their lips. They bit down hard, cradled their stomachs—anything to soothe their pain, and yet, none of it would work.

"The man who trained me how to use The Balance wasn't a dancer," Kaylo said. "He didn't know the agony of carrying a tortured spirit or the anger that rolls off that spirit into your blood. But he understood one thing—if I was to be of any use, the pain couldn't stop me, and the anger couldn't distract me."

None of them met his eyes as he spoke.

"He put me through whatever twisted plan he could concoct in order to test my abilities and strengthen my endurance. I learned how to live as a cage for violent spirits for days on end. And so will you."

Rúnka buckled forward, catching herself before she collapsed face first into the sand. A crystal lay in the sand in front of her, glowing a warm chestnut hue. Her back arched and fell with each heavy breath. The path would only grow more difficult for her. She had trained herself to block out spirits all her life. Now the army expected her to wield and loose spirits like she had been born with them.

"Go get some water, then come back here and try again," Kaylo said.

Her eyes narrowed with an unspoken threat.

Even if he tried, he couldn't begin to count the number of times he had glared at Zusa with those same eyes. The rebel Commander had expected him to torture himself for the sake of the cause without complaint. Only a young boy's grand ideas of vengeance had driven Kaylo through his trials.

Rūnka didn't have the same hatred to motivate her. Hopefully, she cared about her own life enough to endure.

Two spirit dancers with a healthy fear of consequences held more value to the army than two and a half spirit dancers with an inflated sense of self-worth.

Threats lurked everywhere. Rūnka didn't need his empathy. She needed to make herself invaluable. Kaylo matched her fury and stared back until she broke eye contact.

It wrenched his gut, how easily he mimicked the man who had used him as a weapon. After a time, the excuses and rationale became meaningless, and the thin margins that separated Kaylo from Zusa disappeared.

The crystals lying in front of Pana and Euri remained empty.

Ever since Pana overstepped Kaylo's training and felt the pain of stealing a caged spirit, he had quieted down and become more focused. One failure sparked a fire that outmatched whatever concentration Kaylo once possessed.

He nodded to the boy, and Pana's face softened for a moment. *So much to prove,* Kaylo thought.

Euri didn't have Pana's drive or Rūnka's hatred. Her stomach moved slowly with each breath, nostrils flaring with each inhale. If not for her clenched fists turning her knuckles to pale stones, she might have appeared serene.

"Do not fight against the spirits," he said. "You can no more swim against the river's current than you can fight the spirits inside you. If you try, you will fail. However long it takes, eventually the current will win."

Rúnka returned to her place, kneeling back in front of The Mountain.

"Instead, realize an important truth. You and the spirit have the same goal and the same enemy."

"I have more than one enemy," Rúnka said. Her eyes shifted from the guards to Kaylo and back.

"As do the spirits," he said. "They want one thing. Freedom. Anyone who stands in their way is their enemy, including you, if you try to control them. If they cannot have freedom, they will settle for vengeance. Give them that, and they will be your partner."

As Kaylo sat in front of them, he reached towards each of the spirits, one at a time.

Relief washed over Pana's face. His breath stuttered as he exhaled. Euri opened her eyes, her shoulders loosening.

"Spirits that have been trapped will never stop hurting you." Kaylo's voice stayed even. "Their rage may be meant for another, but they will take it out on you unless you offer them better. Let them see your hatred. Become their ally, and you will learn to endure."

The three dancers looked at the crystals in front of them, two of the shards still translucent stone. "You can hear them still," he said. "Their rage is still there."

Back straight, stomach faintly moving with each breath, Kaylo allowed the spirits their thrashing anger within him.

"How?" Rúnka asked, the guard in her voice dropping for a rare honest question.

The crystal to the left burned with a red glow as Kaylo released the spirit. Then, a breath later, the center crystal turned a deep purple, joining The Mountain spirit in front of Rúnka.

"My hatred is deeper than theirs."

"In one moon, the trials will commence." Commander Sola paced in front of the rows of recruits, wearing his customary impassive expression.

"Those who prove themselves will join the King's army. Beyond your ability to wield the spirits and your ability to wield a sword, you will have to demonstrate your capacity to work as part of a unit.

"In preparation, half of this regiment with be facing off with the other half. Chitere and Oakan have already determined ranks," he said.

As Sola continued to explain the terms of their engagement, his voice faded to the background.

A sly smile crept over Tayen's lips. Ever since Daak killed Vāhn, they kept her from facing off against him. No sparring. No drills. Chitere and Oakan separated them at every opportunity. With everyone on the same battlefield, they wouldn't have that chance.

One by one, Chitere read off the list of recruits to join her regiment. She called Tayen's name, and Tayen's smirk grew into her cheeks.

She wouldn't kill Daak. No, he deserved worse than The Mist. She would embarrass him, make him look inept in front of Sola. If she hurt him a bit in the process, well, some accidents couldn't be avoided.

"Daak," Chitere called out, then went quiet.

Tayen's right eyebrow twitched slightly. How could Chitere put them in the same unit? What game was she playing?

The dark-skinned boy walked over to the group surrounding Chitere, looking everywhere but in Tayen's direction.

Watching him breathe, let alone walk, prickled the hairs on the back of her neck. If any kind of justice existed, that boy would hobble along in agony. Every step would torment him with the worst pains life had to offer.

Chitere thought she could keep Tayen in line by placing her and Daak in the same unit. She underestimated the depth of Tayen's hatred. Even if she couldn't hide behind the excuse of combat, Tayen only had one true opponent on the battlefield.

The two units gathered their wooden swords and donned colored leather vests—a worn yellow for Oakan's recruits and red for Chitere's. The smooth hide ran soft under Tayen's fingertips. She picked out the

darkest leather; the older, the better. The subtle fragrance of the worn
and tested hide filled her nostrils.

During the long nights in Dasoon, Tayen had read the two books she
had saved from Kaylo's hallow over and over again. General Kalani may
have written with too flowery a pen for Tayen's liking, but her memoir
dove into the minutiae of war. Old leathers moved and withstood
damage better than fresh cuts of hide.

The laces of the vest bit into Tayen's side as she pulled the
binding taut. When Kalani wrote of the battlefield, she repeated one
rule throughout the pages of her memoir—no matter how many
consequences awaited the results of a battle, a warrior had only one
purpose in the middle of a fight.

Tayen's purpose was having difficulty cinching his vest over his robes.

Sokan rose higher into the morning sky as Oakan's unit took position
on a series of snow-covered hills an hour's trek north of the city. The fifty
recruits guarded a single flag mounted on a spear and driven into the cold
earth.

Sola had tasked Tayen and the rest of her unit with claiming that flag.

But none of that mattered. Tayen hovered within ten paces of her
target at all times. The boy looked over his shoulder incessantly. A smile
pulled at her lips. He could worry all he wanted, eventually he would
have to choose to focus on her or their yellow-vested opponents.

"Oakan is a clever strategist," Chitere said, as her unit formed ranks.
"He will assume a split-unit attack. However, he prides himself on his
tactics. He will try to spring a trap, even if it requires sacrificing recruits."

"We will offer a counter-sacrifice." Chitere stopped and gave an
uncharacteristic smile. "Tayen, Daak, I have a special role for the two of
you."

Sola, Chitere, Oakan, and several other warriors moved through the
battlegrounds as observers. The hills rose out of the forest, bare and

white. The trees below obscured Tayen and her fellow recruits as they approached, but as soon as they reached the base of the hills, their cover would abandon them.

Daak trudged through the snow in front of Tayen. His boots crunched with each step as if he were on a pleasant stroll, and his breath came and went louder than the fucking wind. The buffoon could fail the trials without her help.

Death is too easy a punishment, she told herself as she loosened her grip on the hilt of her ashburn sword, still sheathed in her belt.

Vähn would understand why she had waited. When the army stripped Daak of his name and forced him to serve the citadel like a drug-addled workhorse, she would understand.

Beyond the tree line, the hills were empty slates of white. The land rose and fell like a sea of snow. Somewhere in those waves of winter, Oakan's unit stood guard over their bit of purple fabric latched to a spear.

The true Astilean flag was a series of six purple circles surrounding a seventh on a field of white. If the symbolism were any more obvious, it would simply be the words "The Shadow" sewn into fabric. Regardless of their lack of creativity, the Astilean Army considered their flag too sacred to risk on training exercises, hence the purple scrap of fabric.

Four other recruits trailed after Tayen and Daak. They had names and stories, but Tayen wasn't inclined to learn them.

For what? Recruits who survived the trials were sent to the front lines, where most died quickly. The lucky ones got a few tattoos scrawled on their cheeks before crossing into The Mist, and Tayen didn't need to carry more names and stories for the dead.

The six of them marched the long curve of the forest edge until they found it—Oakan's sacrificial offering. Chitere had described it perfectly. Tracks ran through the snow, not too obvious, but clear enough that they wouldn't be missed.

There, between the meeting of two hills, seven recruits in yellow-tinted leather huddled doing their best to look natural. Two of them knelt in the snow, while the rest of them stood around rubbing warmth into their hands, staring into the forest. The land obscured them enough to make their exposed position seem mistaken.

If Chitere's prediction held up, a couple dozen more recruits waited over the crest of the hill.

"I guess this is it," Daak said, his voice shaking.

A smile pulled at Tayen's cheeks despite herself, then the snow cracked under her boots as she charged at Daak.

As her shoulder crashed into his stomach, the two rolled over one another into the clearing at the base of the hills. Tayen landed atop Daak, pulled her fist back, aiming for his nose. But he rolled away at the last minute.

His eyes bulged. He crouched in a wide stance with his palms facing Tayen, like he had startled a wild boar and was waiting for it to charge again.

She drew her practice blade from her belt. "Fuck you, murderer!"

All of her training vanished. The carved bit of ashburn became a club instead of the facsimile of a sword it was made to be—perfect for pummeling this cowardly waste of Ennea's good air. She hefted it above her head and drove it down with all the power in her shoulders.

The carved ashburn crashed into the snow where Daak had been.

"What are you doing?" one of their comrades yelled as they all rushed out from the tree line.

Daak drew his own weapon and blocked a series of attacks in one sharp crack after the other. Tayen feigned an overhead strike, then jabbed him in the thigh when he moved to block. He clutched his leg, and Tayen tackled him to the ground again.

She raised her sword high. If she drove it down now, his face would collapse beneath the blow. His blood would soak into the snow. His body would twitch below her until his last struggled breath failed.

A hand wrapped around her wrist. Another set grasped her under her arms, ripping her off Daak. She and her compatriot fell backwards in a pile.

When she looked up, Oakan's sacrificial squad stood twenty paces away, enjoying the show. Several members of the auxiliary unit peeked their heads over the hilltop as well.

Three of Tayen's comrades lay in the snow beside her. Daak and a northboy stood with their jaws hanging open as the encroaching force charged down the hill.

Tayen pushed herself to her feet. "Run!"

Boots scrambling for purchase on frozen earth, nerves screaming, Tayen collected her wooden sword from the ground and ran. The footfalls behind them multiplied until the individual sounds became indistinguishable from the others.

By the time Tayen, Daak, and their four compatriots readied themselves on the other side of the tree line, thirty recruits clad in yellow leather clamored after them.

"This is going to hurt," Daak said.

"Good," Tayen snapped back.

Oakan's recruits crashed through the tree line all at once. Daak stepped forward, waving his sword over his head in an act of surrender. A large northboy at the front of the assault reared back his hand and slammed his fist into Daak's jaw.

The wave of yellow-vested recruits didn't allow Tayen any time to enjoy Daak's squeal.

A lithe Tomakan girl weaved through the ironoaks and charged at her.

Whether these stolen children were the target of her vengeance or the nearest receptacle hardly mattered. Tayen knocked the lights from the girl's eyes with the hilt of her sword. She preemptively lunged for her next attacker, but he parried. A third enemy interrupted Tayen's follow-up attack, so she drove her boot into his knee instead.

Pain shattered across Tayen's shoulder, throwing her face down into the snow and dirt. When she attempted to regain her feet, someone kicked her in the ribs, forcing the air from her lungs.

They swarmed her and beat her with their fists, boots, and swords.

According to the rules of this drill, any strike to the head or torso signified death—meaning no longer a combatant. But her attackers weren't satisfied. Maybe they realized their mistake, pouncing on an obvious distraction. Or maybe they relished in the power the moment gave them.

Tayen tucked her head and caught most of their blows with her arms and legs. Each new strike seared the shape of their weapons and boots into her flesh.

By the time the officiants stepped in, her body had gone numb. She looked up, and the Tomakan girl she had hit in the head stood over her with a smile before she kicked Tayen in the chin with the heel of her boot. The force vibrated through Tayen's jaw, and the world went black.

A collection of small sounds caught purchase and bounded off the clay-brick walls as fires cast shadows in contrasting movements on the thatched roof—the infirmary. Each flicker of the shadows twisted about in The Song for Tayen to hear, one motion playing against another.

Chitere sat on a chair beside Tayen's cot. "Would you have stopped if the others hadn't pulled you off Daak?"

The slightest movement set her arms and legs ablaze. The cut on her chin bled a bit, but in comparison, it was a small spark of pain. "If you didn't trust me to follow the plan, why did you let me go through with it?"

Chitere nodded with a slight smile. "They needed to believe the fight was real. Everyone knows you want to kill Daak."

"Why didn't you order us to charge the decoy unit?"

"The unit lying in wait might have been clever enough not to spring their trap for six recruits," she said. "They needed a proper distraction." Her cheeks bulged as if she were about to smile, but didn't. "It worked. Our main force took the day with only one casualty. We won."

"I didn't win."

"The objective of this exercise is to determine how well you follow orders, not for you to clear the field by yourself. You could be a great warrior, maybe more, if you gave your mind to it." She offered Tayen a waterskin, but Tayen shook her head. It would have been too painful to reach for the skin.

"I don't care about tattoos and titles."

"No, you're too focused on your anger for anything else." Chitere took a deep breath and ran her hand over her tight black curls. "Anger can be a tool. Many great things have been done through anger. Many terrible things too."

"What's your point?"

"I am going to dismiss that tone as a part of your pain, but if I hear it again, your pain will grow deeper than you know." The flat tenor of Chitere's voice made her promise all the more ominous.

"The point is, anger can be selfish, or it can be righteous," she said. "It cannot be both. You'll have to choose your path." The young warrior stood up and left Tayen lying on her cot.

———

The doors to the library opened as Kaylo sat on his chair with his focus buried in another book. He tilted the tome down to find a nameless servant moving through the stacks with a tray of stew. The aroma of wild game and fresh rosemary hung in the air as she placed the tray next to Lanigan.

"Thank you," they said, making a slight gesture of their hands.

As usual, the servant didn't acknowledge the pleasantry. Her footsteps filled the silence of the library at an even pace until the door shut behind her.

"How long has this been happening?" Kaylo asked.

"I get my midday meal in here every day, you know that."

"You know what I'm asking." He slipped a piece of paper into the book to mark his place and set it on the table. "The 'nameless.'"

Lanigan exhaled loudly. "An unfortunate moniker and a linguistic paradox, to name a group of people 'nameless.'" A sad smile crept across their face. "Nearly one hundred fifty turns ago, dancers pulled the Citadel from the earth. The Great War had ended, and our people locked themselves inside a wall of stormwood trees."

"Answer the question, poet."

"Answers are rarely straightforward, my friend," they said. "The Citadel required servants, and the nation provided. Young volunteers came to earn the honor of serving their nation. When their service ran its course, they left and raised families, and when their children were old enough, they came to carry on the work.

"Then, as with everything else, things changed after the invasion. The Citadel's need grew, but the volunteers tapered away." Their voice lowered to a hush. "That is when my childhood friend, Shonar, had an idea. Refugees from all the nations fled to the Lost Forest. The King invited the refugees in to serve.

"At first, most did so willingly, accepting food, shelter, and protection from the Gousht in exchange for service. But some wanted more than a life of service. Our dear General Tanis suggested susu root. 'The tactics of our enemies can be our friends.' Or however the saying goes.

"They lit braziers of the root in the servants' quarters. When that didn't put an end to the resistance, the King and his general took it further. They deemed the servants nameless and cut the tongue from any servant who stepped out of line. Eventually, it became their practice to remove the tongue from all servants."

"How could you ever be friends with such a man?" The timber of Kaylo's voice quivered with fury.

"Did you know that Enneans used to use susu root to mistwalk?"

"Stop avoiding questions."

Lanigan narrowed their eyes as they bit their bottom lip. "I have never avoided your questions. I have opened up the darkest chapters of my life and laid them bare for you."

"You're right. I'm sorry, my friend," Kaylo said. "Please continue."

A moment and a deep breath passed as Lanigan's shoulders settled back into place.

"Dancers would travel to the mountains to journey into The Mist. They would burn susu root in their fires, allowing their emotions to fade away. All that kept them separate from The Mist, vanished.

"Things change with time," they said. "What a thing was—who a person was can be far and apart from who they become."

Silence filled the space between them. The stew cooled and sat on the tray, uneaten. Kaylo stared absentmindedly at the pages in front of him.

If he couldn't escape, what would he become?

Who would Tayen become?

CHAPTER TWENTY-FOUR

CURRENT DAY ENNEA

"Are you sure we're safe here?" Nix asked, sticking her thumb out from her closed fist and touching it to her chin as she said 'sure'.

Sosun placed her hand over her heart, then held it open parallel to her body, and touched her thumb to her chin as Nix had. After only two span, Nix had picked up enough signs to understand this simple statement. *"I am sure."*

The dim light from the lantern flickered in the small stone alcove. Stacks of wooden crates lined the stone walls. The cold pushed through the floor and her robes into her thighs. At least the walls restrained the wind.

As Sosun scrawled something on her slate, the soapstone scraped the surface, sending small screeches echoing through the alcove. It was not a pleasant sound.

Only servants come back here.

Nix's hands moved slowly through the gestures. *"Sign it, please."*

Sosun's lips curled gently, and the young woman moved through each sign slowly.

Nix repeated an unfamiliar sign back to the girl. She extended her pointer finger from her fist and placed it over her lips, then curled it back into a fist and held it beside her right eye. Sosun grabbed Nix's hand, shifting Nix's fist so her fingers pointed away from her.

The chill from Sosun's touch remained after she let Nix's hand go.

The new word felt awkward in Nix's hand, but she repeated it the way Sosun had taught her. As she practiced the sign, Sosun scratched out another message on her slate. Each line and curve of her handwriting carried a grace of movement.

Silent watchers. It's what we call ourselves.

This girl had continued on despite all the violent acts visited upon her, most of which had been done by their own people. Nix swallowed and took a deep breath. If Sosun didn't want to pity herself, Nix wouldn't pity her either.

Scratches bounced off the stone walls as Sosun wrote something new.

How did you figure out you were Kamani?

"*Sign it, please,*" Nix signed.

Sosun acquiesced. When she brought her hands together, one hand cradling a fist in the center of her chest, she stretched her fingers apart like wings, then brought them back to the cradled fist position. This sign, which must have meant Kamani, stood apart with a particular beauty.

"When I was young, the idea of finding one way to define myself seemed ridiculous," Nix said, signing what words she could. "Since then, I've tried on a few words and labels. Each felt like a version of me, but this is the closest to the truth."

"*That's it? I thought there would be more to it,*" Sosun signed.

"When it comes to gender, I've always just picked the words that fit me best and kept it moving," she said. "How did the silent watchers develop this language?"

"Long story," Sosun signed.

"Tell me, please," Nix signed back.

Sosun bit her bottom lip, and her chest heaved up and down. Then she nodded. She wrote out the first bit, and then signed it as Nix read the words aloud. This routine worked slowly, but Nix tried to remember each twist of Sosun's hand and extension of her fingers. The key to the language was placement. One gesture at the chest meant something completely different when signed next to one's temple.

"When the King," Nix read and Sosun signed, though the gesture literally translated to bastard with a crown, "started silencing his servants, they didn't know what to do. They tried to write to each other, but not everyone knew their letters. They struggled for turns to build some semblance of a life. That life changed and became something more when the army forced a deaf refugee into servitude. She slowly taught people to sign. It took several turns.

"Then the guards discovered servants [*silent watchers*] signing. They tortured them until someone gave up the old woman [*first teacher*]. The bastards hung her outside a servant's entrance to the Citadel. Anyone they caught signing joined her.

"That was eighteen turns ago. Now we only sign in secret. When there is a word we don't know, we make one up. Our language and the signs they use outside these walls must be nothing alike."

Sosun's hands stilled to silence. Her chin tilted down, and the flame in the lantern shined in her eyes.

"Bastard with a crown?" Nix signed with a smile.

Sosun smiled and chuckled lightly. *"Yes, bastard with a fucking crown."*

Each stiff limp forward pulled more pain to the surface, but at least the healers let Tayen leave the infirmary. Two days of rest, for what? A headache and a couple of bruises.

The lump over her left ear throbbed, fiery streaks of pain ran

down her right side when she stretched the wrong way, and she kept
accidentally biting a cut on her lower lip. Still, every wound would heal
and blend into the rest of her collection.

The stench of sweat and overcooked grain greeted her as she walked
into the mess tent. Same line. Same chaotic murmur bouncing between
the tables. Same bowed-heads serving the same slop like every other
lunch. As much as she hated the mess, something about the familiarity of
it made her smile.

A servant plopped a heaping of bland porridge into her bowl. She
thanked him, even though he wouldn't respond.

Astileans treated their servants like shit. Stripped them of their names,
didn't permit them to speak, and plied them with susu root, but at least
they were safe from the Gousht. Astile wasn't perfect, but they didn't
have to be. As long as they gave Tayen her opportunity to spill Gousht
blood, she could overlook their internal politics.

Daak's voice carried over the rumble of the crowd. "And they
surrounded me, but I held my ground. It took seven of them to take me
down. Even then, four of them left with a limp."

"Is that how it happened?" Tayen sat her tray down in front of Daak.

A field of deep purple and bronze spread over his left cheek. The
swelling puffed up the flesh under his right eye, causing him to squint.

"I recall a scream and a moan that sounded an awful lot like your
whiney voice." The injury on the left side of her face cut deeper when
she smiled, but she endured.

"Who asked you, little girl?" A bulky Sonacoan boy asked from beside
Daak. Fuzzy red whiskers covered his jawline like a collection of dust.

"I assumed you might want to know the truth, but maybe stupid is
contagious. Do you share thoughts with Daak because it's too hard to
come up with your own?" Tayen shoved a spoonful of mushy brown stuff
into her mouth.

The fuzzy-chinned boy slammed his fist into the table, causing
everyone at the table to turn their attention to the commotion.

The Song slammed against Tayen's barriers, but she pushed it back down. Kaylo had warned her that the spirit dancers had been improving. If they heard her echo, the army would take The Shadow from her.

"Lan, there's no need to call attention to ourselves," a second, skinnier Sonacoan boy said, pointing to the warriors guarding over the mess. "One rude little girl isn't worth it."

"If you think my words hurt, you should see what I can do with a blade," Tayen said, then gestured to Daak. "This one knows."

Daak tucked his chin into his chest and glanced up like a tentative puppy as he stood between the two older boys.

"I wish you had introduced us to your mouthy friend sooner," the skinny Sonacoan said. "Name is Uccan. I would be happy to teach you manners. First lesson, don't interrupt someone's meal."

The usual ruckus in their corner of the mess dropped to a hushed buzzing as heads turned towards the four of them. Tayen smiled for her audience. Daak's new friends couldn't help him during training or the trials. If they thought a couple of tough words would scare her off, she had a lesson or two to teach them.

She lifted another spoonful to her mouth, holding Uccan's gaze as she chewed the slop and swallowed.

"Daak, Lan, I think we have attracted enough attention for one meal. It is only right that we offer Daak's little friend a pass. One ill-mannered interruption is hardly worth quarreling over." His eyes narrowed and his voice lowered. "However, repeated transgressions would have to be corrected."

"I hope she transgressions again," Lan said with a wide grin.

"Oh, big guy, you don't have to hope," Tayen said with a mouth full of porridge.

Uccan picked up his tray and walked away, followed closely by Lan. Daak slowly lifted his eyes up, looking to each side before following his new friends.

Each time Kaylo tapped the chisel, another sliver of stormwood peeled away from the branch. Lines of soft brown mapped the dark umber, almost black wood.

"Why do you do that?" Wal asked from a chair on the other side of the brazier in Kaylo's quarters.

"Stormwood is hard. If you drive the chisel at the wrong angle, you might crack the wood or the chisel. It's better to go slow. The shape in the wood will still be there. No matter how long it takes."

"Thanks for the woodcarving lesson," Wal said with an added layer of sarcasm. "I meant why use stormwood? Why carve wood at all?"

Kaylo placed the branch on the ground, along with his chisel and mallet. "You're right. There is so much more to life. I should go out and live it. Walk through the fresh evening air, visit with friends and loved ones, sit on the cliffs and watch the water wash against the rocks."

"Really? It's a genuine question. Why?"

True enough, Wal's expression and tone displayed an openness that he rarely had before.

Kaylo picked up his father's knife. The firelight flickered off the blade and the leather-bound stormwood handle brushed over his calluses as he turned it. "It helps me remember my father. Few people have the patience or talent to work stormwood. He did."

"Funny, I drink to remember my father. Then I drink more to forget him."

"Do you ever tire of making jokes and sarcastic comments?" Kaylo asked. "Not every conversation has to be a battle."

"That's not my experience." Wal pulled open the brazier's gate and dropped in a few more coals. The bitter smell of fresh burning filled the air, then the gate squeaked shut.

"Fine, if that's how you see it, I gave you an honest answer. It's your turn," Kaylo said. "You know what they do to the servants here; drug them, cut out their tongues, take their names. How can you abide that?"

Wal exhaled a quick puff of air, a humorless chuckle. "It's not a secret. We don't speak about it, but it's not a secret."

"That's not what I asked."

"Not all of us are true believers in Shunanlah's scion, my friend," Wal said. "I wouldn't make the decisions he has made. The Nameless. The Missing. The King and General Tanis have drawn out this war far too long. But I don't get to make those decisions."

"You're not answering the question."

"What? Why don't I fight the good fight? Why do I make concessions?" Wal's voice grew louder and filled the chamber. "Because I want the Gousht dead. Every single one of the couta fucks. I believe in that. All the rest—it may be unfortunate, but sacrifices must be made."

"Easy to call them sacrifices when you aren't the one suffering."

"Aren't you the noble one? Dying for a decade and coming back like you don't have blood on your hands." The chair legs scraped over the stone as Wal stood. "Some of us had to make hard decisions when you left."

"I'm sorry, Wal." Kaylo met his old friend's eyes, brown and hard with hurt.

"Even if I believe you, it's too late for that. I'm walking the one path you left me." The hem of his purple robes flared as Wal turned towards the exit.

Kaylo didn't say anything more. He should have. He wanted to. Then the door closed, and he was alone next to the brazier.

Tayen didn't need to call The Shadow to blend into the night. Daak and his new friends twisted their way through the cropping of buildings between them and the Citadel, and Tayen followed. Their feet broke the hard snow, creating a trail behind them. She stepped in the outline of the biggest footprints to quiet her movements.

Forty paces separated the last building and the mountain hallow. She waited, back pressed against the ironoak building as they approached a crack in the mountain that didn't appear to be an entrance.

Then they vanished.

Tayen bit her lip. If she ignored them, she could get a good night's rest. After all, her injuries called out to her with each step. She needed the sleep. Then again, if she didn't investigate, the questions would keep her awake well into the night.

The winter wind stung her cheeks as she ran towards the crack in the mountain, a soft light glowing through the opening. Voices bounced off the stone. No warriors guarded the entrance. No fancy sconces or woven tapestries hung from the walls of the natural fissure.

One last breath, then Tayen followed the voices.

The further she moved into the mountain, the more disorienting the journey became. The path turned without logic. Around one corner, a small room opened up. Shelves filled with supplies lining the walls—grain, rope, fabric, and more.

A wordless yelp traveled the jagged walls, followed by a second painful squeal.

Tayen moved faster than her brain. She wasn't supposed to be in these tunnels, yet she ran towards the strange sound. If she turned around and returned to the barracks, nothing would stop her. Yet, as horrible as luck treated her, she couldn't help herself.

A stronger light filled the tunnel as it opened into a large cavern the size of Kaylo's quarters. Boxes and baskets of supplies overran the space.

Slowly, she thought, placing a hand on her diaphragm as she breathed. *In and out.*

Howling and moaning echoed off the stone walls, but she waited with her back pressed against the tunnel at the lip of the cavern opening.

"Listen to it," a familiar voice said. Probably Lan, the big oaf. "It sounds like a wounded wolf or something. Maybe we should put it out of its misery."

"You mean he?" Daak asked.

"Nameless aren't people. Not really," Uccan said with a smile in his voice. "Besides, it's too far gone to feel anything. Look at those glassy eyes."

"I guess, but..." Daak said.

"Do you want our help or not?" Uccan said.

What the fuck are they doing? She needed to get closer, but there was only one way to do that.

When she dropped her barrier, The Song rang out like a riot of clashing tones and pounding thumps. She took a deep breath and allowed herself to appreciate the fullness of The Shadow's call.

The black fog rushed forth at her call like a long-absent friend, clinging to her skin as she crept along the wall into the cavern.

Lan stood in the middle of a cluster of crates bear-hugging a frail, old Tomakan man. His gray hair formed a small circle around his balding crown. Blood trickled from his nose, down his lips, and soaked into the collar of his ragged robes.

Only the small voice of Kaylo ingrained in the back of Tayen's mind, whispering a warning, kept her from rushing in. "When you're outnumbered, it's all about moments: the ones you let go and the ones you wait for."

She moved behind a large crate and crouched down.

"How does this prove anything?" Daak asked.

"Trust takes a long time to earn, my friend," Uccan said. "Except, in exceptional circumstances. If you do this, we know you're willing to fight through your hesitations—misgivings. You will do what is necessary."

He held a knife by the blade, offering the hilt to Daak.

The old man screamed out again, in a moaning wail. He kicked his feet into the stone floor. Lan squeezed tighter, and the old man bared his teeth in pain. Even now, in the Citadel's gut, with no warriors about, the servant refused to speak.

What was she going to do? What could she do? There were three of them, and they had a knife. If she attacked with The Shadow, she would have to kill all three. She swallowed.

"Remember, carve without killing," Uccan said.

"After the first letter, they pass out," Lan said. "The best place is the upper arm, but you want to make it clear. People should be able to read your name."

"Won't I get in trouble if they can read my name?"

"You think anyone cares what happens to these mules?" Uccan asked. "Most of the Citadel guards have claimed at least one nameless."

Daak grabbed the knife and moved it back and forth, studying the blade.

Everywhere Tayen looked, more crates. No decent weapons. Baskets of fruit, crates of beans, stacks of firewood.

Kaylo's voice broke through her busied mind. "Not every problem is a nail. Sometimes a hammer is the wrong tool."

As Daak drew the knife across his arm, the old man's screams cut through Tayen's better judgement.

Shadows surged forward to claim the light like flood waters rushing over land. The Song swelled as adrenaline quashed Tayen's fears.

"What the fuck is happening?" Lan yelled.

"Uccan is this part of it?" Daak said.

"How could it be..."

Tayen twisted her body and clapped all the shadows away in an instant. The small fires flashed a disorienting white light throughout the cavern in the sudden absence of darkness.

All four men yelled and clutched at their eyes, including the big oaf who let the servant go to tend to his pain.

Tayen moved as quickly as she could, running to the old man.

Lan's meaty hand clamped down on her foot. "Who is this?"

Before he could take firm hold, her elbow cracked into the side of his skull, toppling him to the ground. She wrapped the old man in shadows and threaded her arm under his.

Frightened and hurt as he was, he limped alongside her. As Uccan had said, exceptional circumstances created quick trust.

The tunnel stretched through too many curves. It hadn't taken this long to reach the cavern. Footsteps and voices bounced off the walls behind them.

"Get them."

"How?! I can't see."

The servant stumbled in the shadows, but Tayen did her best to guide him through. The rough wall cut through her robe, scratching her arm.

Footsteps grew closer.

The night outlined the tunnel entrance.

Tayen welcomed the frigid wind that crashed into her as she emerged from the Citadel.

Forty more paces.

As Tayen and the servant reached the first row of buildings, the bumbling fools squeezed through the crack in the mountain.

The shadows unraveled and crawled over the ground back to their rightful place, leaving Tayen and the servant standing face-to-face.

"I'm sorry," she said. "I should've moved quicker."

The old Tomakan grasped her hands in his, his skin scraping against her like raw leather. He shook his head and tears fell.

"You can talk to me. I won't tell."

He stopped shaking his head and frowned deeply. Then he opened his mouth. The soft glow of the moons glinted off his yellow teeth, and a fleshy nub hung near the back of his throat where a tongue should have been.

Tayen sucked in a quick breath. "Everyone? They do this to all of you?"

The old man nodded, and Tayen pulled him into her embrace. "I'm sorry, uncle," she said. "I'm so sorry."

He pulled back and touched her cheek. His smile was weak, but he tried.

"Do you have somewhere you can go?"

His hands fell to his side, he nodded, then stepped back before shooing her away. Then he turned and walked through the next alley over.

Only a broken kingdom could do something this cruel. As much as she owed blood for blood, she couldn't take it wearing this King's colors.

She walked through the small city towards her usual Citadel entrance. Her thoughts weighed heavy on her. Too heavy to notice the small spirit dancer watching her from around the corner of a clay brick building.

Kaylo opened his door to find Tayen standing on the other side, her face hanging low and tears brimming over her eyelids.

She marched in without a word and made her way to the far wall, where she sat at the foot of his bed.

"What happened?" he asked. The door closed behind him with a hard slam. "Tayen, talk to me, please."

When he got close, she faced him. "Do you have a plan? Truly, do you have a way out?"

CHAPTER TWENTY-FIVE

KAYLO'S STORY

IN STRANGE CONTRADICTION, the forest offered as much silence as an autumn day had any right to, while a horde of echoes screamed in my head. No matter how many times we ransacked Gousht supply runs, the sheer bulk of spirits screeching with pain slipped the world off-kilter. I steadied myself with a hand on Liara's shoulder, filled my chest to the brim with breath, and held it for a moment before releasing it. She barely reacted to my touch. We had our routines.

The forest dipped into a valley on the other side of a heavy thicket. The trees seemed to lean into the center of the basin like an archway, the perfect site for an ambush.

Two pinpricks of light glinted off arrowheads through a swell of faded orange and yellow leaves in the treetops. Tomi and Mahli had become as deadly as any archers in the five nations. From their perch, they could pick a battlefield clean like vultures.

On the opposite side of the valley, Adēan, Sionia, Talise, Chêta, and Boda waited amongst a patch of bushes, comprising the main force of our attack. From my vantage point, the brush opened up enough to see Boda kneeling as he stared down on the lowland.

The night we gave his brother's body back to The Mother, Boda had shaved his head to the quick. In two seasons, he hadn't allowed the slightest stubble to linger on his scalp. If he wasn't sleeping or eating, he was practicing with one weapon or another. As he filled out, he began looking more and more like Niven.

If you lose concentration, your friends will die, I thought, and gripped the hilt of my sword tighter.

Wal knelt beside me, rubbing his thumb against the smooth edge of his dim red crystal. He had grown partial to playing with The Flame— even managed to come up with a few tricks I hadn't thought of. The bigmouthed jerk had the makings of a strategist.

"They're getting closer," I whispered, and Liara nodded.

Mere moments later, flashes of metal catching the sun pierced through the dense forest. Creaking wagon wheels and clomping horse hooves interrupted the imperfect silence. Then came the footsteps stirring the brush.

As the wagon drew closer, the drivers came into view—two Sonacoan's dressed in green and yellow tunics. Neither wore padded armor nor carried a weapon. I grabbed Liara's arm, and a scowl bloomed over her face.

We had never faced blood banners before.

Every ambush played out differently. No one could predict the violence, but a line of eight soldiers marched on either side of the convoy. The increase could have been a reaction to the missing convoys, but we had done our best to keep our attacks varied and random. They couldn't know which we would attack next.

For all their force, the wagon carried fewer echoes than any previous run we had encountered. Yet, the weight strained the rear axle. It was carrying something more than supplies.

"When the fighting starts, light up the wagon immediately," I whispered to Wal, but he didn't look away from his crystal. "Did you hear me?"

"What?" He shook his head as if pulling himself from a dream.

"As soon as the first arrow flies, turn the wagon into a pyre."

A wicked smile twisted his mouth, and he gripped his favorite new toy, a hollow wooden cylinder filled with firestarter. With all the supplies we had commandeered, Wal had begun experimenting.

Fifteen more paces. Ten. Five. The soft whistle of an arrow cut the air, and the last soldier to the right of the wagon collapsed. The second arrow grazed off another soldier's helm with a sharp ting.

"Now!" I yelled.

Echoes filled the forest with chaos, soft lines of tethered spirit rippling through the air.

As soldiers reached for their crystals and their bows, Wal tossed the wooden cylinder.

In all the madness, no one paid any mind to a bit of wood falling to the ground and rolling under the wagon's rear left wheel. It lay in the dirt for a moment—harmless. Then wooden shrapnel jutted out in every direction.

A plume of flames erupted into the air as the back of the wagon sprang off the ground before crashing back down, covered in fire.

The blaze spread like a hungry beast. Screams broke through the pandemonium. One soldier leaped from the back of the covered wagon, fire swallowing him even as he tried to escape it.

There was no time for soaking in my brilliance. I clutched one translucent thread out of the air after another, and the world flashed to black. A whole host of enraged spirits lashed out against the walls of their new cell.

The pain meant these spirits wouldn't be used against my friends. It meant the Gousht would die, so I dug my fingers into the earth beneath me and endured.

Metal clashed against metal. Adéan roared, and his axe slammed into a soldier, lifting the pale man from his feet only to slam back into the dirt.

Boda raced past Adéan, wearing all his fury on his face and meeting another soldier's blade.

Hoofbeats clamored against the earth, but the horses were still strapped to the wagon. The brush on the lip of the valley parted as two riders emerged from the forest, set on a course directly towards me.

"Thief!" the first rider screamed in Gousht as she raised a spear over her shoulder.

As I tried to push myself off the ground, the rampaging spirits tore my strength from me.

An echo surged over my shoulder. Liara combed her hand through the air, and it shimmered in her wake. As her fingertips brushed over the vapor, it crystalized and glinted in the sunlight. The small ice crystals bound together in a long, pointed shaft.

She hefted the icy javelin over her shoulder, and it shattered against the soldier's quilted armor, the shards flickering in the light as they fell. Several large fragments protruded from the soldier's shoulder.

To the soldier's credit, she leaned back with the force of the blow and immediately righted herself before launching a spear of her own. The tip barreled towards me, but I couldn't move.

Wal crashed into me at the last moment, and the spear tore through his calf instead of my chest.

It didn't matter. The second rider readied his spear, and neither Liara nor Wal were positioned to protect me. The Gousht had prepared well. They had sent these soldiers into an ambush for a chance to spirit me away.

The chaos of a dozen spirits spun within me like phantom blades. I reached into it and The Wind struggled in my grip. The air stirred, but I didn't have the strength to move it with the weight of the other spirits pulling on me.

As the soldier reared back his spear, another spear pierced his horse's chest. Blood spurted from the wound. The animal bucked, whinnied, and collapsed, throwing the soldier to the dirt. The horse's death cry rang out as tortured as any spirit.

Chêta's expression framed her mourning and regret for taking the horse's life, even as she drew her sword from her scabbard. The brush parted as Talise, Adēan, Boda, and Sionia moved into place around the two would-be assassins.

The soldier still seated in her saddle dropped her reins, spreading her arms wide. "We surrender."

Boda broke ranks, strode forward, and thrust his sword deep into the soft of the soldier's back.

As she slipped from her saddle, her head struck the ground first, then the rest of her body crumbled around her.

The final soldier scurried away on all fours like a coward. Talise closed the distance, grabbed the thick of his hair, and opened his throat with the blade of her axe.

Survivors told tales. We didn't have prisons for captives. Death was all we had to offer the Gousht.

Down in the valley, flames from the wagon licked high into the air. Twenty-two bodies lay in various states of burned, bludgeoned, and pierced, while all ten of us breathed the fresh autumn air.

Much could be said of Zusa's tactics, but he had molded us well.

Wal moaned as Adēan pulled him off of me. The spear's edge had sliced deep into his left calf. He would need a poultice and rest, but it should heal fine, not that it wouldn't hurt something wretched.

"It seems like someone's reputation is growing," Wal said, the pain in his voice contradicting his sarcasm.

"It's nice to get some recognition," I said, then I lowered my voice and met his eyes. "Thank you."

"Yeah, yeah," he said. "I'm a hero. We all get it."

Adēan playfully cuffed Wal on the back of the head. "Cha see cha leg bleedin. Don't do tha again, mister hero." Then, he wrapped his thick arms around Wal's chest from the back and pulled him tight, as Wal gave to the embrace.

"What do we do about them?" Sionia pointed to the Sonacoans in Gousht tunics, cowering on the other side of the still-blazing wagon. Tomi had her bow drawn back and trained on them from her perch in the trees.

Relief washed over me like rain on a hot summer day as I let go of the spirits in my belly. "We take them back to Zusa. He'll have questions," I said. "Wal, before you bleed out, would you mind dousing the fire?"

As they knelt in front of Zusa with their hands bound, the Sonacoans pleaded with everything but their words. Their expressions—their posture—it all begged mercy.

Zusa paced back and forth, the campfire flickering over his shoulder. "You shouldn't have brought them here."

"I figured you would have questions," I said.

"They're slaves from the Anilace mines. What should we have done with them?" Liara asked in a tone that negated the question.

"Of course, that's what they told you, but there's no way to trust anything they say." Zusa placed his hand on the hilt of his sword.

"It's true. We swear it on The Mother. Please believe us," one captive said.

"We could make them tell us the truth," Boda said from over Zusa's shoulder. The boy was on his way to becoming as cold and pragmatic as his commander.

"Torture is a good way to hear convenient lies." Zusa pulled his blade from its scabbard.

"Stop. What are you doing?" Liara yelled.

Zusa's blade swiped through the first captive's throat too quickly for anyone to react, least of all the dead man. The second captive scrambled to her feet, but Zusa thrust his sword into her belly before she took a step.

As he eased her down to the ground, he pulled his sword from her gut. She coughed twice before she stopped moving. Zusa wiped his blade on the green tunic. "Be free," he whispered.

"Why?! How could you do that?!" Liara rushed forward, and I threw my arm around her before she could get too far.

"I did what you should have done. If you care so much, bury them well." He stood and walked into his tent.

"Could have told you that would happen," Boda said and turned towards the fire.

Liara rushed to the Sonacoan woman's side, wiping a streak of red from her cheek before lowering her eyelids. "What are we doing if we aren't trying to save our people?"

The cold survivalist in me understood what Zusa had done. The moment the Sonacoans sat on the wagon to drive north, they had died. Nothing they said would have proven their innocence. They represented a risk we couldn't carry.

But I couldn't say any of that to Liara. Instead, I placed my hand on her shoulder and said nothing.

Liara, Tomi, Chēta, and I dug graves, while the others went to their tasks. Adēan tended to Wal's wound, Boda and Mahli made dinner, and Talise and Sionia unloaded the supplies we had raided from the dead Gousht.

As Chēta and I lowered the Sonacoan man's body into a grave, it occurred to me that he had a name. He had family and a home. This man had a story that I would never know.

His weight pulled on my shoulders, but I refused to drop him. I lowered him by the arms until his back settled at the bottom of the hole. Another person who had died so that I could live.

"The Sixth—The Seed, whatever these people have done, forgive them. And forgive those of us who outlive them." I placed my dirt-covered fingers to my lips, then back to the earth before I began filling in the grave.

"Zusa is the one who needs forgiveness," Liara hissed.

Survivors always need the most forgiveness, I thought.

The blanket of melancholy draped over our camp didn't dissipate with the falling of the first Daughter. We ate and tended to our chores, but no one spoke much. I had never killed an Ennean. Too many had died because of my choices, but I had never wielded the blade.

The camp emptied as people settled in for the night. Adéan reapplied the poultice to Wal's injury as they spoke in hushed tones.

In the aftermath of violence, they took joy in each other. Liara and I had only ever weathered the pain together, and that happened more and more infrequently. Even now, instead of seeking solace in the living, Liara stayed beyond to sit vigil over the graves we had dug.

The dead have The Mist, I thought. *We still have to deal with The Waking.*

As I pulled back the furs covering Zusa's tent entrance, they felt heavier. He sat with his back towards me, hunched over a map next to the brazier. The light shined off his freshly shaven scalp.

"I figured I would receive a visitor tonight," he said. "I didn't expect it would be you."

As I settled on the ground and crossed my legs over one another, my thighs embraced the cold of the autumn-chilled earth.

"They fought well today." I cleared my throat. "The Gousht thought to trap us, but they underestimated our strength. They won't do that again."

Zusa folded his map and turned to face me. "Wal told me you asked him to set the wagon on fire before they sprung their trap. You made the right call, and that's the reason they survived to mourn the lives of two strangers."

"I didn't do anything. While the others fought, I hunched over on my hands and knees, as useful as a sparrow fart. Wal has a hole in his leg because of me. I need to be stronger."

"If I was told correctly, The Gousht sent over twenty soldiers, including two riders who specifically tried to assassinate you. Now all of them lie dead, and I didn't draw my sword." He raised an eyebrow. "By your logic, I didn't do anything either."

"You set the plan. You discovered their route. You trained us."

"And you kept the couta from using our spirits against your

compatriots. Other regiments would have died. This group survived because of you," he said.

"There are other spirit thieves."

"Maybe."

"Ones that can withstand the pain better."

"Maybe."

"If I trained harder, Wal wouldn't be wounded."

"Maybe."

"Is that all you are going to say?" My words sharpened as they left my mouth.

Zusa smiled. "There is a reason those riders targeted you. And there is a reason Wal protected you. Kaylo, one day, you will realize your value."

The darkness coalesced into the flowing shape of The Thief's cloak. The black of her cloak appeared richer, fuller, deeper against the black of the world that surrounded us.

Why, given all she could create, did she craft The Mist into this void?

"What new accusations have you brought to me? How have I wronged you this time?" Her voice hummed low and tired. "I do appreciate our visits so, but they are becoming predictable."

I lowered myself to the ground. "Care for a game?"

"You didn't come here to play with wooden markers."

"I didn't come here to fight either."

Her onyx hands emerged from the shadows, another deeper layer of black which stood separate from those that surrounded it. They clutched at her veil and drew it back. The eyebrows over her perfectly proportioned face arched. "What trick have you come to play?"

"No trick," I said. "You have the power here."

Her cheeks swelled in a sly, mouthless grin. "So, you wish to play a game while playing your game. Interesting." She drew two bags from the darkness of her cloak and tossed one of them to me.

One by one we placed runes over the crosspoints. No quick decisions. No lengthy pauses.

"The first time I spoke with The Seed, he reminded me about purpose." I challenged one of her markers with The River.

She revealed The Wind and placed it face up on the crosspoint. "My brother likes to pontificate. Forgiveness is power. Forgiveness is grace. Forgiveness is healing." She laughed softly. "Forgiveness can also be a defeat."

A white-stained ironoak pebble flipped between her fingers, then she placed it down as a challenge. The Mountain defeated The Flame.

"That is what I thought, but he wasn't talking about his purpose. He was talking about yours."

Her shadow cloak continued to billow in the windless black, but she froze. "My purpose?"

I refused to smile. "Your purpose and your true name."

"It's not a secret, boy."

"You were meant to be The Balance. You were meant to prevent power from pooling too deep in any one body."

Her stark white eyes widened. "What is your game, little thief?"

"I've thought about that conversation for almost a turn," I said. "If I close off my emotions and twist my mind in knots, there is almost a strange balance to spirit crystals. Anyone can wield the power of the spirits, regardless of their mark."

When she did not interject, I continued. "The orphan, the first person you gave part of your spirit to, she prayed for Ennea to give her a way to bring balance. Dancers lorded their gifts over the spirit-bound. Everything was uneven."

"I assume you have a point." She enunciated each consonant like a freshly sharpened blade.

"The Gousht claim our land, chain our people, and spill our blood with your crystals. Does this sound like balance to you?" Regardless of how I fought it, a thin layer of anger coated my words, lengthening the space between them.

"This is what my brother said? Twist my name against me? I am The Balance. I am the line power cannot cross. If your people cannot handle a fair fight…"

"Fair! The Gousht are evil. They send armies and slaughter families. They imprison us and our spirits. WE NEVER ASKED FOR A FIGHT!" I screamed. "You're not The Balance. You're a jailor, locking your kin away in a keyless prison."

"You know so little, even for your age," she said. "You are the key, you selfish twit. You and my other descendants. If you want to free spirits that badly, there's nothing holding you back."

"What are you talking about?"

"Every crystal carries a piece of me. My gift imbues the crystals with the power to trap spirits. Without it, the crystal would crumble to nothing."

"You're lying. No one has ever destroyed a crystal before."

"My descendants are few. Hiding from their own people. Hiding from the Gousht. But each of you has the power to free the spirits from their crystals," she said. "Balance is not about equality; it is about opportunity.

"If Enneans cared for my descendants, they would find powerful allies," she said. "The games are unnecessary, little one." Her onyx fingers curled around wisps of shadow flowing past her neck and pulled her hood back over her head.

The blue crystal glowed softly through the worn thread of my robe as I brought it back to my tent. Its echo sputtered like intermittent rain.

"What are you doing with that?" Liara said from outside the circle of the firelight. The dim light painted her skin with shades of bronze as her ears peaked through her budding red locs.

"You on watch?" I looked around to find us alone in the cold dark.

"Kaylo, why do you have a spirit crystal tucked away in your robe?"

"I don't need another one of your lectures."

Her chest swelled before she released a heavy breath. "I don't want to lecture you," she said. "I'm worried about you. Blessed Mother, the Empire sent assassins after you. What happens next time?"

My lips turned with a smile. As annoying as her lectures were, it felt good to be worried over—especially by her. I waved her over to the firepit.

The flames drove away the cold. Liara held me in her eyes as I searched for the right words. Firelight caught the green flecks in her brown irises, and all my thoughts fell to the ground like autumn leaves.

"Were you going to tell me something?" Her mouth teased out a smile, and it pushed her cheeks up, high and tight.

"I spoke with The Thief."

"Kaylo, we talked about this. It's dangerous to go mistwalking. What would happen if..."

"No lectures, remember?"

She took another deep breath to swallow her words. "Okay, no lectures."

As I pulled out the crystal, the light blue gem glowed in the night. "There is a second spirit trapped in the crystal. It's softer. The River's rage drowns it out."

"What are you talking about?"

Under the sputtered chaos of the jailed spirit, a hum without a breath vibrated through the stone. Its consistency blended into and hid behind the noise of the world.

All this time—how could I have missed it? It lay there, within every crystal, hidden tones underneath the screaming echo.

Its tether to the world flittered about. The more I focused on the second sound, the more the thread in the air solidified.

How many times have I been this close to it and never seen it? I tentatively reached forward, placed my hand around the faint thread tied around the fragment of The Thief, and pulled.

A fissure tore through the stone, then another before the stone fractured into countless granules collapsing inward. As the streaming debris poured through my fingers, it glided over my skin like sand. The particles rustled the leaves on the ground louder than our held-breath silence could bear.

An almost imperceptible puff of blue smoke rose into the air and vanished as soon as I thought I could see it.

"What did you do?" Liara's question was full of breath, barely louder than the crackling fire.

A strange spirit twisted within my gut. Unlike the crystal spirits, it didn't rage against me. Nor did it call me to dance like when I stole a dancer's spirit. Liara's echo split in two, one slightly delayed behind the other.

"I think I stole The Thief," I whispered.

"What?" Her voice filled out with confusion and need. "Can you do this with any crystal? What happened to the spirit inside?"

The foreign spirit within me pulled away, almost imperceptibly. It didn't belong to me. Like all the spirits before, it had a place to return to, and I relented to its pull.

"I think it went back to where it belonged," I said. "I think."

"The Thief didn't tell you?"

"We don't need to collect the crystals anymore. We can destroy them." My blood raced with the possibilities. "I can give spirits back to the dancers and The Mist."

Liara hung her head, staring into the fire. "He won't let you."

"What are you talking about?"

"The crystals are too important to Zusa. He would never let you destroy them," she said.

"I get that you don't like him, and sure, he can be a hard man, but what's the point if we don't set things right?"

She looked at me with eyes like prayers. They held an apology and pity, anger and resentment, and, most of all, flickering in the fire's light, they contained certainty.

Her hate stood in the way of her judgement.

I pushed myself to my feet and rushed to Zusa's tent. She didn't try to stop me.

The furs covering the tent entrance flapped noisily as I pushed them aside. Zusa snapped up from his bedroll with a knife in his hand. A bronze key hung from his neck, lying against his naked torso and his collection of scars.

"What's wrong?" He flung the blanket off and reached for his sword.

"No, nothing's wrong."

"Then why the fuck are you waking me up in the middle of the night?" His chest heaved with each hurried breath.

"I have something I need to show you."

He dropped his knife beside me, but his glare grew sharper for it. "You have something to show me?" Each syllable came out in a staccato beat. "Get out."

I walked over to his trunk and held my hand out for the key. "You need to see this."

"This better be worth it, Kaylo. I get far too few hours of sleep as is." He slipped the key from his neck and handed it to me.

The imprisoned spirits filled the trunk nearly to the brim. I could free them all.

As the brazier came to life behind me, I picked the first crystal that caught my eye. The Mountain.

The second echo hummed below The Mountain. I held the stone at the center of my chest, giving Zusa an easy view. The second spirit slipped from the crystal prison, easy as plucking a leaf from a tree. The remnants of the crystal fell through my fingers and littered the ground with dust.

Zusa's eyes gaped.

"We can free them all," I said. "We can give the spirits back to the people."

"No, Kaylo. No, we can't. We need those spirits. How else can we fight the Gousht?"

"What are you talking about? If dancers regain their spirits, we could destroy the Empire. The people would rise up."

He shook his head. "The people had their chance. We need to be more strategic."

"What are you doing with these crystals?" I asked as Liara's doubts became mine. "We have taken crates of them from the Gousht, and every time mysterious riders come and take them away. You said the Missing don't have the numbers to make war with the Gousht, so where are the crystals going?"

Zusa gently nodded his head. "Sit down, Kaylo," he said. "It's time you knew the whole truth."

Chapter Twenty-Six
Current Day Ennea

Kaylo took a deep breath and laid his palms flat against the table, imperfections in the grain rising and falling as he ran his fingers over the wood. Tayen sat a few paces away at the edge of his bed.

Slight as Tayen may have been, her gaze weighed heavy as the mountain hallow itself.

In many ways, his story had led to this moment. Maybe now she could understand why he could never trust the Lost Nation.

"What did he say?" she asked. "What was the truth?"

"There are reasons I never told you this before," he said. "You needed to see reality for yourself."

"What did Zusa say?"

"The Missing was a lie. Sure, there was a small network of runaways—far too small to challenge the Gousht. But that wasn't our purpose." He took a breath. "The crystals we stole weren't going to militia warriors ready to take back their land. They went to supplying the Lost Army."

As she registered what she heard, Tayen's brows furrowed, and her head tilted like her brain was struggling to make room for this new information.

"The Missing were a rumor because they never truly liberated anyone." Old emotions—Zusa's confession as they sat in his tent—took hold of him again. "The Lost Nation created the Missing to distract the Empire while they built their army, funneling resources into their armory and conscripting people to fill their ranks."

"That's ridiculous. If that was true, you would have told me in the first place."

He angled his chair to face her. "You weren't ready to hear the truth. Justified or not, you were angry with me for holding you back. The army promised you your vengeance. Would you have believed me?"

"You're as bad as they are. You hide the truth to get what you want."

"You're still young."

"I'm old enough!" Tayen yelled.

"You see the world as ground or sky, Mist or Waking. Life isn't that simple, and wrongs aren't equivalent," he said. "I should have told you sooner. But that doesn't make me the same as an army that drugs and mutilates its people.

"I told you from day one that you couldn't trust them, that King Shonar wants to conquer the continent, not free the people, and you told me you didn't care." His voice sharpened the more he spoke. If he continued, he would start yelling, which would only push her further away.

Tayen stood up. "You never told me how you knew. You expected me to trust you after you got us captured." She walked towards the door and stopped when she placed her hand on the handle. "Is there anything else you're hiding?"

"I'm not trying to hide anything," Kaylo said. "I am trying to protect you."

"You're doing a great job." She glared at him for a breath before walking out the door.

Kaylo arrived late to train the spirit dancers after a long night of fighting with his dreams. As soon as he closed his eyes, his regrets greeted him in vivid detail. One after another, he had watched his life's mistakes play out, then woken up breathing heavy, covered in sweat, only to fall into another mistake.

When he stepped into the training tent, the three dancers knelt in their ranks, youngest to oldest.

"Kana, I have something I need to talk to you about," Pana said.

"How many times do I have to tell you? Don't call me that." Kaylo held his hand out and waited for his guard, Juniper, to hand him the bag of spirit crystals. The gems clinked together in the bag. "Today, we are going to test your resilience."

"I really have to speak with you," Pana leaned forward as he spoke. The little golden-skinned child nearly fell forward.

"If you insist on calling me kana, then at least listen. No more interruptions."

"But..."

"After training." He stared down at the young boy until Pana lowered his eyes to the ground.

"As I was saying, I have received a dispensation for you to carry the spirits from the tent. As you go through your drills, your studies, the line in the mess hall, when you lie down to sleep, you will hold on to a spirit."

"Why would we eva wanta do that?" Rūnka asked.

If Kaylo had any patience left in his bones, it was gone. Between Tayen, Wal, Nix, these disrespectful trainees, the guards, and the whole damn city, he'd had enough. "Because I told you to," he said.

"You all seem to be unaware of your surroundings. See those guards? How about the army barracks all around the city? How about the uncrossable forest beyond that? You are trapped here. If you do what you're told, they'll march you into war. If you don't, I doubt they would keep a thief who doesn't know their place."

Kaylo's heart bounced against his ribcage. A vein throbbed above his temple. "Once you are in the middle of a battlefield, dozens—maybe hundreds—of echoes will be flying through the air. Each one you take will make you suffer more than the last. If you can't handle the pain, you will die. If you can't control the spirits, you will die. If you get distracted for one moment, you will die."

As he took a deep breath, he reined in the volume of his voice. "This time, right now, is your chance to prepare before your life is at stake. Take it or don't."

The gems shifted around in the burlap sack as he pulled out one crystal at a time and handed them out to the dancers. "For the rest of our time here, practice dancing with the spirit. When you leave, you will take the spirit with you. Tomorrow morning, we will see who managed to hold on to their spirit," he said. "Commander Wal asked me to remind you, if you use these spirits outside of this tent, the soldiers will not hesitate to put you down."

Pana's hands shook as he held the soft muddy-purple crystal. Kaylo had gone too far. These three weren't the problem. They suffered under the same heavy hands that he did.

Three echoes surged forth as the dancers went through their drills. No one uttered more than a few words for the remainder of their time together.

As Pana pushed and pulled the shadows about, and Rûnka guided the wind with lackluster purpose, Kaylo worked with Euri. She had taken to The Mountain with remarkable ease. Slowly, the Sonacoan girl eroded a large rock into the rough shape of a knife. Then, little by little, she stripped away pieces of the stone, refining the edge of her blade.

The guards always made sure Euri destroyed the weapon at the end of training. It was a thing of sorrow to see her well-crafted work crumble to the sand.

If Kaylo's plan worked, everyone would look at these three and wonder, had they helped him? They would question if they knew what he was planning. If they could have stopped him.

Hopefully, General Tanis appreciated their potential enough not to punish them for his actions. She valued practicality above all else, but even practical people sometimes bowed to their base emotions.

As training ended, Rúnka and Euri left without sparing a passing glance for Kaylo.

"Can we talk now?" Pana asked.

"I have somewhere I need to be. Tomorrow, I promise." In truth, Kaylo needed to escape to the library and hide, if only for an hour or two.

"It's important."

Kaylo pushed aside the hide covering the entrance. "Tomorrow. We'll talk tomorrow."

While Daak joined the trail of recruits following Commander Sola towards the hills north of the city to run battle formations, Tayen had to wait in the training tent to play with crystals. Apparently, they had thought better than to put Tayen and Daak in the same training group again—the lucky bastard.

"In two span, you will meet your first trial. You will walk into a room with three spirit crystals, and your proctor will ask you to complete one task with each spirit," Chitere said. Over the past two moons, the northerner's hair had grown such that it puffed up into a ball of curls when she pulled it back into a knot.

"You will not know which spirits they will test you with or what they will ask you to do. The test is one of ability and ingenuity," she said. "While you are practicing today, I will come by with a bag of crystals and asking you to perform different tasks."

Tayen followed four recruits to one corner of the training tent. The Sonacoan boy in front of her held their practice stone, a pale green glow emanating from the crystal—The Seed.

In all her training, she had never called The Seed. Something about manipulating a piece of Kaylo's ancestor spirit, one that had been stolen from him, twisted her stomach into knots.

The Sonacoan boy drove one foot into the ground, sweeping the earth with the other. As the green spirit swirled under the crystal's surface, it grew richer and darker, like a thick plot of grass after a rainstorm.

When the boy's hands came together and clawed apart, the sand swept flat by the boy's foot bulged up. A single green tendril pushed through before splitting apart, again and again. As it unraveled, the stem swelled. In a matter of a few breaths, a young pine tree stood in front of him.

Pressure built up behind Tayen's eyes, and she blinked away impending tears. This tree had grown from nothing. Life, where there had been a collection of dirty sand, burst from The Seed.

What it must have been like to feel the pull of The Seed and breathe creation into the world. Not with some crystal, but to truly experience life taking root.

What would it be like to experience that, then have it stolen away? Tayen thought.

As the other members of her small group focused their attention on her, Tayen became aware of a presence over her shoulder.

"Tayen, destroy the tree," Chitere said.

"What? Why?"

The northwoman's flat expression didn't change, but her tone hardened. "Orders are not requests, recruit. Take the crystal and remove the tree from my training sands."

The Sonacoan boy held the crystal out for her to take, which had reverted to its previous pale muted green.

The imperfections in the stone scraped against Tayen's hand as she took it. She turned it about and studied the tiny prison. *It couldn't be Kaylo's spirit, could it?*

When Kaylo spoke about clearing trees, he spoke about it as a sacrifice. Tayen reached her hand through the needles to the young trunk. The bark layered over itself like sheets of uneven paper. Under the bark, rings of growth circled the core of the tree.

"Sorry." Her lips barely formed the whisper of a word, but the spirits were not mind readers. Prayers, even broken apologies, needed to be spoken.

With each inhalation, she imagined pulling life from the pine tree. Her off-hand thumb rubbed back and forth over the crystal as water leeched from the tree. Below her grasp, the wood dried out and grew brittle before it fell apart like loosely clumped sand.

A pile of dust and debris lay where the tree had been. Life given and taken for practice—for a test. The spirits were meant to be more than this.

She swallowed, and her tongue stuck to the roof of her dry mouth.

"Well done, recruit," Chitere said, her voice as flat and even as her placid expression. "Take turns. One pulls a plant from the sand, then another destroys it. The Seed is our shield. Without him, the Lost Forest would be nothing."

A young northgirl reached her hand out for the crystal.

This spirit didn't belong to Tayen, yet giving it away to be used like a tool made her complicit. She tightened her grip on the stone before relenting. The stone passed between the five of them, and the cycle of life and death repeated more times than she cared to count.

When they finished, she stayed behind and offered a proper prayer for The Seed's forgiveness.

———

Wal flipped between the maps covering the table in his quarters. The grease from his fingers smudged the corners of the parchment, but he was beyond caring.

According to scouting reports, the Gousht forces stationed at their northern outpost had nearly doubled since autumn. No matter how many green couta bastards they killed, more ships arrived on the southern coast. The Emperor seemed to have limitless bodies to cast into a war like logs to feed a flame.

He picked off another strip of flesh from the roasted chicken and absently chewed. It had gone cold, but the fat from the skin kept it from going dry.

Depending on the report and the map, Astilean forces secured most of the western land and the northern coastline all the way to Colian. That still left most of Ennea to the invaders.

If his plan worked, the spirit dancers would give Astile an unforeseen advantage. One well-trained spirit dancer in a skirmish could turn the tide of the battle. He had seen it several times. Those pale pricks relied too much on their stolen power. Their armor and their weapons were well-made, but most of their soldiers were young and stupid.

Maybe that's what happens when one inbred family controls everything from the crown to the army to the church, Wal thought.

Their priests didn't have to earn their command, not like he had. His hand went to the tattoos on his left cheek involuntarily.

Knock. Knock. Knock. His door clashed against the frame.

"Enter," Wal called out, letting his maps fall flat on the table.

"Sir, you have a visitor," a warrior whose name he didn't know said.

"And who is it?"

A small northboy stepped out from behind the large warrior. The youngest spirit dancer. Paken. Petrik. Pictan. Something of that nature. "Sir, Commander Wal, um...I need to speak with you, um, if that would be alright, sir."

The boy's clothes were too fine for a normal recruit, though his hair needed shaping. *Ah, that's right,* Wal thought. *The bureaucrat's brat.*

"You understand the way command works, recruit?" Wal asked, returning his gaze to the maps in front of him. "Even spirit dancers need to follow army regulations."

"Sir, I tried to tell kana...I mean Kaylo, but he wouldn't listen." The boy's voice shook like a leaf in a thunderstorm.

"When we are young, we all think that our needs and thoughts are more important than they are. Maybe there is a reason Kaylo wasn't listening."

"I heard a dancer in the city," the boy spat out.

Wal sat back in his chair to assess the boy. "What's your name, kid?"

"Pana, Commander."

"Pana, how do you know it wasn't a spirit crystal you heard?"

"There's a difference in the way it sounds. It's hard to explain, like a clarity in the echo," Pana said. "When I heard it, I followed the echo, and I saw a girl—a recruit—unwrap herself from the shadows."

Impossible. Every dancer amongst the recruits gave their spirits to the cause, whether they wanted to or not. *Unless...no, it couldn't be.*

"Thank you," Wal said to the warrior. "You may leave us."

Wal stood up from his chair and picked it up. He walked over to the brazier and placed the chair down, then placed another chair across from the first.

"Come in and take a seat, young dancer, and tell me what you saw," he said. "I want to hear every detail from the moment you heard this echo until the last time you saw this girl."

CHAPTER TWENTY-SEVEN
CURRENT DAY ENNEA

Kaylo's eyelids shot open with a start. Another thud ricocheted through his quarters. Cold blue light crept in through the slotted window over his bed. The sun had only begun to cast her first light.

The door flung open and cracked against the wall. Kaylo shifted his feet beneath him and pulled his knife from the bedside, keeping it hidden beneath his quilt.

Wal strode into the room with a wide smile and freshly braided hair. "What are you still doing in bed?"

Two servants followed him into the room with fresh water and clothes. After unloading their haul on the table, they took position behind Wal with their heads bowed.

As much as he claimed to take issue with some Lost Nation practices, he didn't show the slightest discomfort using the servants as suited his needs.

"What is this about, Wal?" Kaylo said, phlegm catching in his throat, disrupting his words.

"Your presence has been requested."

"What does the General want?"

"No, no, no, my friend. King Shonar awaits you. It seems there are questions as to whether you have upheld your part of the bargain we struck." Wal shrugged, wearing an odd smile in the crook of his mouth. "Personally, I think you're doing a wonderful job."

"Funny, it sounded like you said bargain instead of extortion."

"You are quick-witted this morning, which of course I appreciate, but the General and the Scion of Shunanlah don't have my keen sense of humor. You may want to look after your tongue." Wal emphasized the King's self-imposed title in a cutting manner. "Wash up. We don't have much time, but you cannot go before the King looking like a poorly groomed bison."

"You want me to get ready? Get out."

"I didn't realize you were shy." Wal waved the servants out of the room. "We will be right outside. Don't take too long." A strange edge cut through his tone.

None of this made any sense. Kaylo had been living below Shonar's throne for over two moons. Why now? Why first thing in the morning? Why hadn't Wal said something before?

As Kaylo unfolded the robes a servant had laid out on the table, the fabric brushed against his skin with a softer touch than any other material he had ever laid hands on—with the possible exception of chani cloth. The richness of the purple dye lent the fabric depth.

What kind of king hoarded such finery as Ennea and her people survived on the scraps the Gousht left behind?

A small voice in the back of Kaylo's head dared him to slow his pace, wash and dress as he had been told, but allow time its leisure.

The basin of water went thick as a dust storm before he finished washing the outdoors from his skin. Two small vials sat between the clothing and the basin. The first smelled of roses and citrus, the second of spring earth. He combed some of the oil from the second vial through his beard, then donned his new robes.

Captured and kept, this was the closest to free he had felt since Dasoon.

Wal burst through the door. "Maybe I forgot to mention it. The King is waiting for you." He stopped. His eyes rolled over Kaylo from floor to ceiling. "You look good, my friend."

Kaylo's newfound feeling of freedom disappeared on the other side of the door. The entire garden awaited him—all seven guards in a line, carrying matching spears.

"Hazel, I must say, you look especially dashing this morning," Kaylo said to the hulking Tomakan woman. She grunted and nudged Kaylo down the hallway towards the center of the Citadel.

Their boots clapped against the stone in almost perfect unison as they traversed the winding walkways of the Citadel towards the throne room at the peak of the mountain.

If the rest of the immense hallow seemed opulent, it was only because Kaylo had never seen the throne room. Two stormwood doors, each five paces wide and tall as three people, secured the entrance. Sweeping filagree ran the border of the doors and fine-detailed carving made a story of the wood in between. With a day, one might be able to appreciate the artistry of a single panel of one door.

They swung open to a long room decorated with purple rugs and gaudy tapestries. Dozens of sconces cast light into the highest reaches of the mountaintop. Ten stormwood statues lined the left side of the hall and nine lined the right—each carved with such fine detail the individual strands of their hair stood apart several paces away.

At the end of the hall, a throne of stone grew from the floor, the back continuing all the way to the ceiling.

In a room such as this, one might expect The Mother herself to occupy the throne. Instead, amongst the craft of stone and wood carving, fine rugs and intricate thread-work, a small man draped in heavy layers of purple sat upon the seat of power.

General Tanis waited on the right side of the King, as unmoving as the statues lining the hall.

The warriors' footsteps reverberated through the open cavern, a heavy drumbeat towards Kaylo's fate, while the diminutive king tapped his foot in an opposing rhythm. Then the procession stopped.

"I'm glad to see you were able to make it, Commander. We wondered if you had lost your way," King Shonar said, his voice lingering on each word before moving onto the next.

"My apologies, Scion," Wal said, lowering his chin to his chest.

The King stood up and walked slowly towards Kaylo, each step cutting into the quiet. His skin was pale and sun-starved, wrinkled with mid-age. The layers of fine furs dyed purple built his shoulders high despite his true stature, as a jeweled belt held the fabric in place. "And this must be the fabled hero, Ennea's Thief. Quite skinny—and hairy. Surely, there's a man under there who wishes to swear his allegiances."

"I am here, as requested, Shonar" Kaylo said, refusing to lower his eyes before this would-be ruler. The Shadow's trapped echo radiated from beneath the man's thick attire.

"You will address Shunanlah's Scion as King or Scion," General Tanis said sharply. "Did you not train your pet better, Commander?"

"No, no, General, I rather enjoy this. Let the dog bark. We've already stripped him of his teeth." Shonar's lips parted in a sneered grin, showing his perfectly white smile. As he moved, his cloak parted, revealing the spirit crystal hanging from his neck.

Two moons. If Kaylo could just survive a third, but this pale man-child who proclaimed himself Scion of Shunanlah while wearing a stolen spirit could have prevented the occupation. With one word, he could have sent his forces through the Lost Forest and joined the Invasion War. Instead, he watched and emulated the Gousht, ready to claim himself King of the continent.

The best Kaylo could do was bite his tongue to keep himself from speaking.

"You may wonder why it is that we brought you here. It certainly wasn't for pleasantries." Shonar said. "We entrusted three special recruits to your care at the suggestion of your old friend. I need to know, were we right to trust your friend?"

Wal eyed me with a sideways glance. He had placed his future in my hands the day he suggested our current arrangement to the King. With a few twisted words, his life would be forfeit. Of course, the self-sacrifice that required was hardly worth it.

Though that didn't keep Kaylo from enjoying the power that a few breaths of silence gave him.

"One spirit dancer supporting a regiment is worth a dozen swords," Kaylo said. "By the end of the moon, my students will be capable of protecting your warriors from the imprisoned spirits the enemy wields."

Shonar's hand rose to his chest, where his spirit crystal resided.

"Give them another season, and they could wield those spirits better than any warrior with a crystal," Kaylo said.

"We need a shield, not a spear. Our warriors know their way with the spirits," Shonar said. His slow-paced speech hastened. "Besides, you don't have another season."

"My Scion..." General Tanis interjected.

"Hush, General. The Hero of Anilace has a right to know. We will finish what he started. The invaders will be cast from our shores, and Ennea will finally be united." Shonar walked back to his throne and sat on the cold stone. "We will accomplish what our ancestors never could in one hundred turns of warring."

Only people who had never fought in a war could so callously and smugly speak of the bloodshed victory required. This man knew nothing that hadn't been recited to him in pretty words. And yet, the fate of Ennea rested in his unblemished hands.

As the seasons passed, their campaign had run over the land. What survived the blood had been forever altered. And, in the course of the next turn, one flag would fly over the whole of Ennea—green and yellow, or purple and white.

Kaylo swallowed his voice. Words couldn't change a person as sure of their own greatness as this man.

"You hear that, thief hero? We are going to free the people." Shonar smiled like a boy atop his throne. "You could be a part of that. You could lead your little thieves into battle."

And that was it, the reason for his trip to the top of the mountain hallow.

The wrong words might make his escape impossible. Tayen would either die in battle or live long enough to see an Ennea ruled by one pale fool on a throne.

Kaylo lowered his chin. "I'm afraid my knee would make me a liability for the others."

The King's eyes narrowed, and the hall hushed.

"It's true, Scion," Wal said. "Kaylo is not the warrior he once was."

"Pity," Shonar said. "At least you will give me three thieves to take your place. Make sure they are ready for the spring," He waved his hand to dismiss them.

The guards turned in unison, and Wal tilted his head to indicate that Kaylo should turn around.

"Wait." Shonar's voice thinned, losing the air of over-confidence. "Wait. I hear you have been keeping company with Lanigan, the poet." He leaned forward. "Are they well?"

And the warden asks after the well-being of his oldest friend and prisoner.

Kaylo took a deep breath before the truth came out, managing to restrain himself. "I doubt they would mind the company of an old friend."

Kaylo turned and began the long walk back to his quarters.

———

Every step Tayen took, Nix mirrored. They twisted about each other in an oblong path, the older warrior smiling all the while. Their sporadic training sessions always went the same way. Whatever strategy Tayen employed; Nix countered it.

There wasn't a recruit amongst Tayen's regiment she couldn't knock flat, but they were children playing at war.

"Are you planning to pace around the tent like this all day?" Nix said, the firelight casting half her face in shadow.

If only Tayen could call on The Shadow, she might have had a chance, but Kaylo had forbidden it. The paranoid old bastard. She loosened and adjusted her grip on her practice spear—a thin staff of ashburn without a tip. The soft wood brushed over her callused hands.

The gap closed between them, and Tayen feigned an attack at Nix's head, then swept for her legs. Nix drove her weapon longways into the sand to block the attack.

That's it.

Tayen perched her weight on her right leg and rounded her off-foot into her opponent's exposed ribs. The force of the contact crawled up her leg. Then Nix wrapped her arm around the offending appendage.

The older warrior grinned, then twisted her upper body.

Tayen's face crashed into the cold sand a moment before Nix dropped her full weight on Tayen's back, wrenching the leg still caught in her grip.

Tendons in Tayen's hip stretched to their limit. Shocks of lightning popped from her hip joint down her leg and into her spine.

Tayen extended four fingers, folded her thumb into her palm, and raised it into the air. "Yield!" she said. "I yield."

The relief was instant. Her leg still fit into her hip. She rolled onto her back and stared into the canopy of the tent.

"What did you learn?" Nix asked.

"You're a mean bitch who likes to beat up on kids."

"If you didn't know that before today, you're oblivious," Nix said dryly. "What useful information did you learn?"

"Pull my leg back quicker."

"If you are going to use your body to attack, you have to be quick, but you also need to hit harder," Nix said. "If you crack your opponent's ribs, they aren't going to catch your leg."

"You wanted me to crack your ribs?"

"It's cute that you think you could, but yes. By spring, you will be outside of the forest, one way or another. Never fight with anything less than your full force." Nix sat up, brushing the sand from her shoulders.

"Kaylo told me what you saw the other night." The warrior's voice went softer. "Do you need to talk?"

"He should have told me sooner."

"About the Missing or about the servants?" Nix asked.

"Both! I'm not a kid anymore. Why does everyone keep hiding things from me?"

"You and he have a lot in common." The ashburn staves clinked together as Nix gathered them from the ground. "You both blame him for everything. He didn't invade Ennea, he didn't kill your parents, and he didn't trade you to the army for some grain."

"He promised to protect me," Tayen said. The whine of her own voice grated on her nerves. It made her sound like the child she no longer was.

"I don't think you're angry with him. You're angry at the people who aren't here anymore."

If Tayen had her weapon, she wouldn't have held back. "You don't know what you're talking about."

"Put your claws away, little one. Even if you could hurt me, it wouldn't make you feel better," Nix said. "When you torture that Sonacoan boy from Dasoon, does your pain subside? Are you happier?"

"You know what he did!" Tayen clenched her fists and her uneven fingernails cut into the skin on her palm.

Nix nodded. "Yes, I do. I also know that no matter how much you make someone else hurt, it won't stop your pain." She returned the practice weapons to the rack, leaving Tayen lying on the sand in the middle of the training tent.

A chill ran through Tayen's robes and along her back. Chitere had told her that she would have to choose between righteous anger and selfish anger, but what difference did it make if she aimed it in the right direction?

As Tayen stepped out of the training tent, she looked over to the

Honored Fields. Somewhere amongst the dirt and lush clover, Vāhn lay within Ennea's grasp. Tayen hadn't visited the fields since the day they had buried Vāhn. Her friend's spirit had already taken its leave of this plane.

Of everyone Tayen had lost, Vāhn was the only one with a grave.

Whatever fear had held her back before couldn't stand. Tayen had too many battles before her to allow fear any time to linger.

Sand turned to dirt beneath her feet, then the dirt softened the farther she walked. The dead had given themselves back to The Mother, and she flourished for their sacrifice.

From a distance, the Honored Fields appeared smaller. The dense cover of clovers blended into the surrounding land, but standing on the sacred grounds, their size stretched to encompass too many lives.

Tayen knelt, and as she did so, her sister's whistle rubbed against her skin. The hollow piece of wood had survived so much. She held it in her hands.

Nita deserved a hero's mourning as much as any Ennean.

Tears rolled down Tayen's cheeks as she ripped chunks of the earth loose. The tears had many names and many reasons.

Soil gave way to her hands as if The Mother approved. Tayen dug until her elbows sank into the loose dirt. Then she eased the whistle and twine from her neck and placed the last piece of her sister amongst honored warriors.

"Goodbye." She touched three fingers to her lips, then placed them on the ground beside the fresh grave. "I'm sorry."

The heat of the room set Nix on edge. She had grown used to the frigid temperatures of the barracks, the training grounds, and everything between. But the brazier in Wal's quarters filled the air with the scent of ironoak coals—not the most pleasant wood to burn, slightly acrid like vinegar.

"Sit down," Wal said, facing the wall opposite the door.

She pulled a chair from the table, sitting as instructed.

As warm as it was, the hairs on her arms tingled. She became more aware of her breathing. Wal's voice lacked its playfulness. There wasn't food on the table waiting for her like there had been for previous meetings.

Two guards remained on this side of the door as it closed.

Every other time they met, they did so in private. Wal usually liked to charm and smile as he made threats and promises.

"Why didn't you tell me?" Wal said in the lower register of his voice.

"Tell you what?"

Muffled noises, a moan, and boots scuffing against stone came from the other side of the door. Someone fell hard against the stone, but the wall and wood muffled the sound.

"We don't have time for games." His lips formed a straight line. "I need to know exactly what they are planning, and you are going to tell me."

"I told you before. Kaylo is planning to escape, but if he knows when or how, he hasn't told me."

"As I said, we are short on time." He looked to the guards waiting next to the door and nodded.

One of them stepped aside to pull the door open. Another guard in the hallway shoved someone through the door, and the body tumbled to the stone floor in a mess of washed-out, ragged robes.

Nix stood in a rush, knocking down the vase on the table, spilling water and flowers on the stone floor. Two of the guards drew their swords, and the third aimed the point of her spear at Sosun's exposed neck.

"THIS WASN'T OUR DEAL, YOU MISERABLE RAKAT!"

"No, it wasn't." Wal spoke through barred teeth. "Our deal was that you would tell me everything you knew about Kaylo and the girl. In turn, I protected your little plaything." He drew his belt knife and walked four steps towards Sosun, each ringing loudly against the stone floor.

"Now, uphold your end," he said.

Sosun wore a bloody lip and a black eye. Her face was wet. *"Don't tell,"* she signed, quickly. Then Wal's knife settled against her throat, making her skin divot where the blade rested against her flesh.

"The trials!" Nix said. "I'm sure it's going to happen before the trials."

"What is going to happen?" Wal asked. "I need specifics."

"He doesn't tell me details, but he wouldn't let Tayen take part in the trials. I'm sure of it."

"Tell me about the girl," he said.

"What about her? She's angry at the world, and trains like she'll have to fight everyone and everything. That's it."

Wal grasped Sosun's short red curls roughly, arching her neck towards the ceiling. "The spirits! Is the girl a thief? A dancer? What is she?"

"She's nothing. I swear." Nix's voice shuddered behind her words. "I swear, please don't hurt Sosun."

Wal released Sosun, and the girl collapsed back to the floor, sobbing. He smiled, but his eyes still cut like knives. "It seems our friend has kept things from both of us. If you want…" He looked down at Sosun. "This thing to survive another span, you will hold up your end of our deal.

"Find out his plan. Find out about the girl," he said before nodding to a guard.

The guard opened the door, but Nix didn't move. She waited, looking down at the young woman she had put through so much. Before Nix, Sosun had been a happy child trying to hold on to life with a mother she adored.

"The door was a subtle invitation for you to leave," Wal said. "Your friend will be staying a while longer."

Two guards grabbed Nix by each arm before thrusting her from the room.

CHAPTER TWENTY-EIGHT

KAYLO'S STORY

Not much can be said regarding the Lost Nation of Astile in the turns following the invasion. For that matter, not much can be said regarding Astile over the past two centuries. Once they crafted the forest that earned them their moniker, information about Astile became limited. The one unquestionable truth is, the Lost Nation didn't answer the calls of the other nations. They remained safely behind the impenetrable forest of stormwoods.

Maybe they made the right decision. Maybe they have the means to survive this occupation. However, if the other nations survive, history will cast Astile as cowards. The stories will not be kind.

This single passage captured the extent of my mother's thoughts about the Lost Nation apart from the long-told stories from within the guarded nation.

And I had searched.

If only something within her pages could have justified the path they had taken, I could come to terms with my role in the Missing.

"History will cast Astile as cowards." I read over the passage several times and read the last two lines several more. "The stories will not be kind."

But my mother was wrong. Stories always chose a side—the side of whoever claimed victory. If any genuine history remained of our people, it would be because the Lost Nation swooped in like saviors with the army they built on the backs of children and runaways. After that, they would write their own stories.

If the Gousht won, their telling of history would care little about the nation that lingered.

I pushed my mother's book to the side more roughly than I should have.

The resentment percolating in my chest threatened to scream its way into the world. If the Lost Nation had met the call during the Invasion War, everything might have been different. My parents might have lived. The Gousht might have become a story Enneans told their children. And, despite that undeniable truth, Zusa had asked me to keep his lie for him.

For some reason, so far, I had.

While everyone else slept in their respective tents, I pulled my father's knife from my belt and shaved away at a piece of loose wood by the fire. The nights grew colder the deeper we trudged into autumn. The cold bit into my flesh. Tangible pain felt like a welcome departure from the invisible barbs.

By now, I had skimmed through every page of the notes my mother had collected. She had scribbled down as many questions as she had stories. And for every story, a contradicting tale surfaced beside it—a version that fell between the floorboards of history. The things I knew to be true wobbled on their shaky foundation.

She had found at least twenty different versions of how the Hundred Turn War started and couldn't definitively say if any of them were true.

With what I had recently learned about the Missing, I doubted that truth actually existed. If I told the others, nothing could keep us together—and that was what I hated most about what Zusa had done.

Liara and all of her worries would be justified. Adéan might not care, as long as the Missing gave him the opportunity to fight. Boda...he hadn't known much life outside of the Missing, but Niven had died for a lie, probably along with countless others.

Zusa had made me promise to hold on to the truth until he could find the right words. And I believed him at first, figuring he had earned that much, then two days passed without a word on the matter.

The more I sat with the lie, the more I hated him for it.

The furs of the tent behind me fluttered open before slapping back in place. Liara's echo preceded her footsteps. The River sang soft but full, like a looming wave.

"Couldn't sleep?" I asked, still facing the fire.

"You've been avoiding me."

"No, I haven't," I said, regardless of the truth.

Over the past two turns, I had kept one secret or another from those closest to me, but withholding the truth was one thing; avoiding a direct question required something completely different. It came as naturally to me as flight.

She sat down on a large stone next to me. "Have you told Zusa about what you can do?"

"I showed him, and you were right. He doesn't want me to destroy the other crystals," I said. "They're too important for the cause."

"Your knee is bouncing," she said. "You're lying."

Her glare burned into the side of my face like the fury of a thousand summer suns, but I refused to face her. "What would I be lying about?" I forced my knee not to move.

"It's been three seasons, and we haven't done anything besides steal spirit crystals and give them away. Where are they even going? Why aren't we doing anything to help Enneans?"

"How should I know where they're going? I don't get to decide what the Missing do?"

"Look at me." Her voice drifted into her lower register. "Kaylo, look at me."

She leaned towards me, her eyes open and wide, firelight caressing her smooth black skin. "I told him I would give him a few days to tell everyone what he told me," I said. "I promised."

"What about the promises you made me and Tomi, Sionia, Wal, and Adēan? What about us?"

"Don't put me in the position where I have to break one promise or another."

Her shoulders rose and fell with a sigh. "You put yourself in that position, Kaylo. You have since the moment we settled into camp with them. And every time you pick Zusa, why?"

"That's not true."

"No? Then tell me, what is true?"

Every minute sensation, every movement, every tingle, each pulse, the brush of the chilled night air through the hairs on my arms and the gentle heat radiating from the fire felt amplified. This moment held too much weight.

If I told her the truth, it could spin my world out of control. If I lied, she would never trust me again. Not fully, like she had once.

Why am I protecting Zusa's lie? I thought. *She deserves the truth. They all do.*

I took a deep breath. This conversation could run several paths, every one of them some version of ugly.

"I'll tell you, but I need you to promise to listen before you react."

She leaned back. "Fair."

"The Missing is a lie."

"What does that mean?"

"You promised to listen. Let me get through this." I said, and she held her tongue.

"After the Invasion War, the Lost Nation needed to gather information and resources from beyond their borders. They didn't have the military

infrastructure to defeat the Gousht, but the Lost Forest gave them
time. They sent several warriors out into occupied territories to collect
weapons and conscript recruits for their war efforts."

Her eyes widened as she affixed the pieces together.

"I don't know if they called themselves the Missing or if the rumors
created the name on their behalf. But the stories spread until every
corner of occupied Ennea had heard of their small rebellion. The Missing
became a network to supply the Lost Army with warriors and weapons,"
I said. "That's where the crystals go. The Lost Nation is using us."

"That scum-sucking, lying bastard." Liara started to stand, but I placed
my hand on her arm.

"You were right," I said. "From the beginning, you knew better than to
trust Zusa. But maybe he's right too. That's the part I hate. Maybe a small
rebellion can't win back Ennea. Maybe we need an army."

She opened her mouth, then stopped and squinted at me. "Do you
believe that? Do you think that a lie that big can be justified? No, no one
hides a truth like this without reason. I don't know what Zusa's game is,
but I don't intend to stay and find out."

"You can't leave."

"Oh, because Commander Zusa of the Lost Army won't let me?"

"No, because the moment you tell the others, our group will fracture
into pieces," I said. "Don't you get it? I can't lose you."

Liara's anger paused for a moment.

"I mean...I can't lose another family," I said.

Even as she sat there, caught up in her anger and confusion, she
captivated me. Her locs had grown out to frame her face, a face that I
had memorized to the slightest imperfection. The way her cheeks moved
communicated more about her emotions than they had any right to.

"No, you asked me to stop lying, and you're right," I said. "Liara, I can't
lose you because I love you. And I'm sorry if that makes things between
us confusing, but..."

Her lips found mine before I could fumble my way through any more words. The heat rolling off her drove away the autumn breeze, and as I reached for the nape of her neck, her skin teased the pads of my fingers.

Just as my hand found its purchase on the smooth curve of her neck, she pulled back. "If you love me, stop holding me apart."

I answered her in the only way I knew and pulled her into me.

The unspoken and embattled emotions that tied us together became simple as I held her. Our disagreements and my stubborn need to carry the burden of my wounds shrank beneath the freedom I found in her.

I never should have waited so long.

A sharp noise like stone grinding against stone pierced the moment, and I pulled away.

The echo sang at a whisper, but it was there, a single caged spirit to the east. I brought my finger to my lips and drew my knife, then I tapped my ear and nodded out towards the sound. Her attention darted in that direction.

"If all of this is your way of keeping me from telling the others..."

"You're too smart for that, and I'm not stupid enough to think I could distract you." I drew my thumb over her cheek. "Something is out there, and we have to check it out. After that, you can tell the others whatever you need to. Get your sword. I'll wake up Wal."

"Fine, but this isn't finished."

"Which part?" I asked with a smile as I crept into the tent to get Wal.

It took several progressively harder shakes to wake him, but eventually, I managed it. Moments later, Wal stumbled out of the tent, slurring his words. "It's alright, no need to apologize, not like I need sleep." He pulled his blanket over his shoulders. "It was a nice dream too—the type where Adēan doesn't wear clothes."

"It might be nothing, but you need to keep watch," I said. "Sound the whistle if you hear anything and keep that crystal close."

He wrapped his hand around the red crystal hanging from his neck by a bit of old rope. "Get going. Then come back, so I can return to my dream."

As Liara tied her scabbard to her waist, she nodded to me. Somehow, she appeared threatening and enticing with a single look.

"We'll be back," I said, then turned towards the echo from the east.

The Song gave me a clear view of the forest, dark or no. I cut through the trees with Liara at my heels. As we settled into our pace, the forest blurred, and the trees became moonlit outlines.

The echo grew the farther we ran, but remained a solitary call.

No one carried spirit crystals, except the Gousht and the Missing. If the spirits had mercy, it would be the latter.

Isolated in the thick of the forest, I couldn't imagine it would be anything other than a Gousht scout. And a scout meant more soldiers on the way—meant they were searching for something.

After the surprise the Gousht had laid for us during the last ambush, that something was us.

Our feet crunched fallen leaves. Nocturnal animals scurried about. An owl screeched. The sound of the forest drowned out the silence between Liara and I.

As much as I hated Zusa for his lie, I didn't want anything to change. Not now. That lie kept us together, and the truth would destroy everything built atop his deceptions.

The grinding echo grew closer and louder.

As I slowed my pace, I lifted my hand to signal for Liara to do the same.

The light from Ennea's Daughters caught her eyes. Her pupils had shrunk to dots in the ocean of her brown irises.

If we continued through the next cluster of trees, we would find another unpleasant truth. Whatever tension existed between Liara and me, it ran in parallel with our connection. In that moment, I wanted nothing more than to turn around, get our people, and run from the echoes.

A small orange glow highlighted the trees behind her. I tilted my head, and she followed my motion. We had come too far to stop now.

As we shuffled closer to the trees on the edge of the fire's light, a single pale man in the Emperor's green and yellow hunched over a small fire. No helm. Only a small pack of supplies. *A scout.*

No more echoes fluttered out of the silence. No heavy footfalls of marching soldiers or torches lighting up the forest, only one solitary man. We could end him quick, but if we took our time we could leave with answers.

"Steal his eyes," I whispered.

"You sure?" Her brows furrowed, then she shrugged. The River sang through her and dipped down to the ground. She spread her arms wide as her fingers drifted like a wave running back and forth. As she rose from her squatting position, a soft fog rose from the ground with her, then thickened into a heavy gray cloud.

"Who's out there?" An orange glow from the fire radiated out, and the scout stood, a silhouette caught in the fog and fire.

His sword softly brushed over his leather scabbard as he withdrew it. A second glow, smaller than the first, washed over the gray fog, and a fragment of The Mountain sang a grating chorus. The ground shook beneath our feet, then I settled it.

I had what I wanted.

At my signal, Liara let the fog dissipate.

The scout rounded on us, with knees bent and sword drawn. *"No matter your tricks, The One watches over me."*

He charged forward; teeth bared like a wild thing.

As the echo pushed and pulled around me, I collected the pain of The Mountain trapped within me and reached for the earth below the scout's feet. The moment I ripped my interlaced fingers apart and moved them to the echo's rhythm, a fissure opened beneath the scout.

As the bastard song pitched two discordant tones running away from each other, the clay deep beneath the soil shifted, cutting a gash in the ground like a mouth opening. The soldier's foot caught the fissure's lip, and he crashed to the ground, his sword skidding away.

"It seems The One is looking somewhere else at the moment," I said.

Both Liara and I aimed the points of our swords at his exposed neck and face. "What now?" she asked.

"What are you doing out here?" I asked. *"What are you looking for?"*

The scout pushed himself to his knees, his face covered in dirt, and spat at our feet. *"He said you would be hiding in this forest."*

"Who said!"

The scout smiled. *"Kill me. I long to meet The One."*

I had only cracked the ground enough to take away the scout's footing—far from a proper fissure—but as my rage grew, the echo grew louder in my gut, connecting me to all the dirt, rock, and clay beneath our feet.

If he wanted to die so badly, I wouldn't stand in his way.

After a deep breath, I exhaled slowly, making fists of flexed fingers over and over. Each granule of dirt whispered its part of The Song, then shifted as it hardened. My knuckles popped as pockets of dirt below the scout condensed. Stone formed with the pressure along a very specific path, creating a gap beneath the couta bastard as the mouth widened.

He fell just far enough that he had to strain his neck to peer above the dirt.

"Will The One be able to find you when you're trapped in the soil of The Mother?" I asked.

His eyes went wide, and he tried to scramble up the tight walls of dirt around him.

As I continued the ritual, he slipped deeper into the earth until he clung to the edge of the fissure with his fingertips.

"Who said I would be hiding in this forest?" I asked, enunciating every hard consonant of their ugly tongue.

The dirt shifted below his hands. His eyes shined with hatred in the glow of Ennea's Daughters above. *"A priest."* His voice cracked. *"He said he knew a thief once. A boy."*

"How many others?" Liara asked. *"Scouts or soldiers?"*

"Twenty or so," the scout said. His left hand slipped, and he scrambled for another purchase. *"Please, I can help you."*

"You already have," I said. Then the ground moved with me and fell from beneath his feet. The dirt below his white-knuckle grip crumbled, and he fell into the earth.

His scream didn't last long as the mouth closed above him.

The expression on Liara's face straddled anger and apprehension towards my cruelty.

"We need to get back to the others." As I picked up the crystal, the dull brown hue swirled in its prison once again. Then I tugged at the spirit beside it, the quiet one, until the crystal dissolved in my hands.

CHAPTER TWENTY-NINE
KAYLO'S STORY

SOUND WAS THE FIRST thing to abandon me as I raced towards our camp. The small noises of the forest, the leaves crunching under Liara's feet, and my hurried breaths clamoring to keep up with my heartbeat fell silent. Not even The Song pierced my panic.

I had prayed for this in a way. Every time I knelt to offer words to the spirits, I begged for them to guide me to The Priest. Not this way. Not in the middle of the night, as yet another family lay vulnerable beneath the watch of the younger Daughters.

Trees brushed against me as I cut through gaps in the forest, yet the sensation hushed. The ground ceased to push back against my footfalls, and the hammering need in my chest dulled.

Every single male descendent of the Emperor's bloodline claimed priesthood, and the power that came with it. The priest who led his scouts and soldiers in a hunt for my family could have been any of them. But it wasn't. Many things that could have been, simply were not. Tonight, The Priest—my Priest—had come back for my blood.

One rolling ridge of trees traded places with another until Kenke Forest began to vanish as well, and the earth lay flat. Large tents replaced the trees. Smoke billowed through breaks in the leather canopies and gave way to flames.

The Fallen Rock Clan burned anew, but this time, the tent city stood deserted, save a solitary figure. Dressed in red robes with a heavy pendant hanging from his neck, The Priest waited at the other end of the encampment.

My dreams had brought me back to this night too many times to count, but I wasn't dreaming. Almost a full turn of moons had passed since the massacre. It wouldn't happen again. I wouldn't let it. Before the rise of the First Daughter, either The Priest or I would cross over.

A surge of echoes cracked the false vision in twain. One thrumming note after another rose up until they sang a threatening chorus of dissonant tones.

I had trained for this.

The bitter scent of charred wood drifted through the air. Flashes of orange and yellow flames peaked through the trees.

"Not again," I said. "Not this time."

Flames crawled over our stitched-leather tents and reached into the air like tree limbs. A handful of bodies littered the ground, surrounded by a scattering of burning coals from what had been our firepit.

A small hand grasping a charred wooden rabbit flashed in front of me, and I gripped the hilt of my sword until the calluses on my hand screamed their anger.

The couta would pay for every transgression a thousandfold. Their blood would feed the forest for a generation.

The body nearest me, a Gousht soldier, lay face down in the dirt at my feet, her quilted green armor torn and stained. If she had suffered, it hadn't been enough.

Liara rushed past me and lifted the shoulder of a body too burned to identify from afar.

Despite the charred flesh, the patches of unburned skin and fabric confirmed them as another Gousht. She dropped the shoulder, letting the dead soldier slunk back into the dirt before moving on to the next body.

Beneath our tent, flames consumed what few possessions we had in this world—the last of my mother's words.

My fingers had touched every page, traced every word she had scrawled out in ink. I couldn't let her die a second time. The folded notes between the pages and her crossed out passages meant more to me than anything I could lay claim to this side of The Mist.

As I made my way towards the flames, Liara grunted, heaving another face-down body onto its back. She needed me more than my mother did. The ink-stained pages could burn to ash, but the lessons she had left me would not.

I joined Liara, checking bodies one at a time, making sure each pale, padded-armor bastard was dead.

Near the middle of camp, one petite body stood apart from the others. Liara got to her before I could and rolled her onto her back. Burns and blood discolored Mahli's warm brown skin. She had been a child. Now her empty brown eyes stared up at us, unmoving.

I hadn't been quick enough.

A wet cough disrupted the silence, and we both brandished our weapons.

Beyond the light from the burning campsite, Chêta sat propped up against a tree, her arms hanging loose to her sides. Three arrows jutted out from her chest, blood seeping from her wounds and muddying her robe.

"Thought cha were dead." She coughed again, and her lips turned crimson.

Liara walked over to our dying friend and knelt beside her. "Where are the others?"

"Scattered. Wal screamed when ta scout came tru. Ta bastard was a crisp bit a fire when we came out to see wha was wrong." Chêta smiled, then choked on a cough. "Ten a priest and 'is men came...I tried ta save Mahli, but tere were too many."

"You did good," Liara said. "You fought well."

"Go get cha sister," she said. "And kill tose fuckin couta."

My jaw ached with the pressure as I bit down my rage. "I promise you that." I reached down and drew my finger through the blood leaking from a wound in her chest, then dragged the blood across my cheek in an old custom—our blood spilled as one.

The moment stretched. Wet breaths lifted and fell with her chest. She would die either way, but if we left her, she would die in a field of dead Gousht, alone.

"Go. Now," she said.

It seemed a cruel thing, but the others needed our help, and I needed to find The Priest. Whoever survived could mourn her.

"Mist take you. Mother embrace you." I kissed three fingers and placed them on the ground.

The echoes grew thicker as we traveled north, then split in opposite directions. To the west, bells thudded within a low sustained moaning call, a eulogy of sorts. To the east, the spirits screamed, twisting The Song into a melody fighting itself.

"Which way?" Liara asked. Her voice fought the need to make the question a demand.

"There's a dancer to the west."

Liara ran several paces to the west before realizing I hadn't followed. "Come on. We have to find Tomi," she yelled.

"I'm sorry. I can't."

"Kaylo, I need you." She had never looked as vulnerable, not even when I had huddled over her sickbed for several moons.

Earlier tonight, I would have done anything to protect her.

"This can't happen again." I spun away from her, running as she called after me again and again until her voice dwindled to nothing.

She could never understand, but if I allowed The Priest to escape, then all the blood he spilled would belong to me.

The forest became a graveyard littered with the bodies of the Jani. I ran through the bludgeoned and broken remains of the people who had taken me in when I had nothing. Blood stained their sandy robes. Their chani headwraps lay unraveled in the dirt.

Phantom images of those I had failed traveled with me until a cluster
of spirits screamed louder than my guilt. I reached for my sword and
knife from either side of my belt. The next moments would bring about
one sort of ending or another.

"Never again."

Firelight crawled over the dirt, marking the edge of a battlefield. The
soldiers were engaged with someone, but the trees disrupted my view of
the fight.

It took every lingering thread of discipline in my spirit to wait and
evaluate. When I had rushed into a battle too quickly, it had cost Shay
her life.

A torrent of wind wove in and out of the trees like a sewing needle,
its pitch whistling, then dropping to a rumble as it passed. Zusa darted
in between several soldiers holding a smoke-gray crystal as the torrent
whipped around him and kept his pursuers at bay. He rounded an ironoak
and lashed out with his long, thin blade.

He moved with the grace of a dancer, flashes of steel cut through the
air all around him, the trees catching the strikes he could not.

For all his hidden truths and manipulations, in this moment, he
became the warrior I had always needed him to be.

Out of nowhere, Boda leaped from the darkness and crashed into one
of the soldiers pursuing Zusa. Boda picked himself off the ground, but the
soldier remained still with a sword sticking out of his back.

The young Sonacoan hesitated a moment too long, and another
soldier peeled off to engage him.

The two altercations moved quicker than my indecision.

An echo leaped into the air, and the night pulsed as flames ran over
the forest floor, pinning Zusa in.

He needed my help.

The four soldiers spread their formation wide. They lashed out with
their weapons, pushing him closer to the rising flames.

The Priest was nowhere to be found. Maybe he hadn't come at all, but Zusa and Boda were family.

The Flame's echo drummed beneath the earth's surface, a steady syncopated rhythm, a coordinated stampede. The translucent thread anchoring the spirit to their prison dangled in front of me, and just like that, the fire vanished as quickly as it came.

A young soldier turned to face me just in time to see the air shimmer around her as it heated to a boil, then exploded in a burst of fire. She fell to the ground, clutching her blackened flesh.

Two more soldiers abandoned their pursuit of Zusa to attack me, leaving Zusa and Boda to their own sparring matches.

"Where is The Priest?" I yelled out in Gousht as I strode to meet my attackers.

The first swung his axe wildly. If I hadn't twisted to the side, he would have lopped my head clear from my shoulders. Instead, he over-swung, stumbling past me.

I matched swords with my second attacker. *"The one who answers me can leave,"* I said, but instead of answering, he parried my attack.

These soldiers were puppets. The damage they wrought was only an extension of The Priest. In that way, they had earned whatever pain I had to offer them.

The Flame wanted to consume, and I hadn't the patience to stand in their way. The fabric of the sword-fighter's pant hem heated to a spark as I rolled my fingers to beckon the spirit. He screamed as fire swallowed his leg.

"Answer me!"

Instead of dropping to the dirt to quiet the fire, he slashed at me. Our swords tangled, and I thrust my father's knife into his neck with my off-hand. If he wouldn't bend for The Flame, he wouldn't have answered my questions.

But there were others.

The soldier wielding an axe shuffled towards me in a series of half-steps. *"Where is The Priest?"*

He opened his mouth, then fell to his knees before collapsing. Zusa stood behind him with a bloody sword. "This is no time to play around."

"I told you what I was after the first time we met. The Priest is here."

Five soldiers lay in different states of death and dying around us, leaving Boda fighting off the last remaining threat. I stepped forward to help him, but Zusa blocked my path. "He needs to do this himself."

"I thought you said no playing around?" I moved to help again, but Zusa grabbed my wrist.

"Don't underestimate him."

The green bastard had height, age, muscle, and likely experience on his side, but Boda didn't back down. He blocked and parried. His speed could keep him on the safe side of the soldier's blade as long as he could maintain it.

Zusa watched on with a slight smile, like the proud, abusive father figure he was.

The soldier thrust forward, and Boda sidestepped, drawing his blade along the soldier's wrist. When his opponent's sword fell to the ground, Boda threw himself forward, burying the hilt of his sword in the couta's chest as they fell together.

"See," Zusa said. "Now, let's get out of here. Where are the others?"

"I'm not leaving before I kill The Priest."

"Don't be stupid. There is no knowing how many more soldiers are out there, combing through the forest. They are looking for a thief. How many do you think you can kill before they kill you?"

"Kaylo's right, we can take them," Boda said as he yanked his blade from the dead soldier.

"The Mother and the seven fucking spirits. This isn't up for discussion. We are leaving." Zusa said.

"You're the one who said we don't run," I said.

"When there is a fight that can be won..."

"There you are." The voice from my dreams rang out behind me.

"When I first heard about a spirit thief ambushing my caravans, I hoped it was you."

The Priest stood seven paces away accompanied by four soldiers armed with crystals and steel. His shoulders and stature cut an imposing silhouette against the night. The five crystals hanging from his neck bundled around the large broken-circle pendant at the center of his chest.

After all this time, after the prayers and the dreams, he stood in front of me. *It could all end tonight,* I thought.

"Come with me, and I'll spare your friends," he said.

"Liar!" I rushed towards him, but a top-heavy soldier with a thick white beard intervened. We clashed swords, then a second and third moved to flank me. Zusa intercepted one, but the second forced me back.

The two soldiers moved towards me in a synchronized fashion. The rat-faced woman with a spear used her reach to keep me on my heels, and the large man rounded towards my weak side. Every time I considered using The Flame, they launched a series of attacks with the practiced efficiency of hardened warriors. Neither of them bothered to call the spirits hanging around their necks.

The Priest must have warned them.

Zusa and Boda had engaged the other two soldiers as The Priest waited back like a voyeur.

"Young thief, I have no desire to waste blood tonight. You can save lives by putting down your blades." The Priest spoke in his stilted cadence, unhurried by the fighting before him.

How many times had I heard Zusa lecture me before? If I had any chance at all, I had to find a way to step into the spearwoman's guard. She wouldn't be able to wield her weapon as easily, and the swordsman would have difficulty finding an opening without risking his comrade.

Ratface thrust at my side, and I deflected the attack towards my weak hand, stepped in, and thrust my sword into her belly. The heavy fabric resisted my blade, then gave way. As the sword scraped her ribs, the metal vibrated, and I pushed harder.

Then pain tore through my anger as a blade sliced from my shoulder to my elbow, forcing me to drop my knife and leave my sword buried in the dying Gousht woman. I rolled away and came up clutching my wound.

I pulled on The Flame, and the foliage on the forest floor burst into fire, rushing towards the swordsman.

"Enough!" The Priest yelled as he reached for his red crystal and called The Flame. One after another, he called The River and The Mountain and The Shadow.

I took each spirit from the air as he called them. The spirits raised a rebellion within me that forced me to buckle in two, and the fires I had set burned out of my control.

One more echo surged forward.

As he called The Wind, a gust ripped through the trees, crashing into Boda.

The boy fell backwards, and his attacker took advantage. She aimed her sword at his chest, but Zusa deflected the blade in time to save the boy's life.

Then a wet crunching sound broke through all my debilitating pain as the fourth soldier brought his axe down on Zusa's exposed back. The blade tore through Zusa's leather guard as if it were made of paper.

Zusa collapsed face down in the dirt with the axe embedded in his back. His leg trembled, then spasmed, then stopped moving.

"No!" Boda screamed until his voice cracked.

The fury of all five spirits within me aligned with my own.

The axe of a dead soldier lay only paces away. Zusa's old words filled my head. "When you have a choice, I want you to know what weapon fits you best. When you don't, I want you to be able to use what is available."

With my good arm, I hefted the axe off the ground as I dashed towards The Priest. My rage washed away the pain of my wound.

Beneath his veiled robes, The Priest was a man, flesh and blood. All I had to do was connect with one solid swing of this fucking axe to open him up to the world.

Simply because I had decided to stop caring about the other soldiers didn't mean they had made the same decision. The heavy swordsman I had been fighting charged after me and slammed his sword hilt into my head.

The world popped with an intense white light, then dissolved to nothingness.

Chapter Thirty
Kaylo's Story

THE SEED'S ANGULAR FACE loomed above me as I lay on the ground. "Oh Seedling, this is no place to hide."

Beyond him, the strange collection of trees in his forest reached towards the perpetual sun in the cloudless sky, light streaming through the canopy of needles and leaves. As I ran my fingers through the black-as-night soil, tiny granules brushed over my skin.

"Hide?" I asked. The phantom image of Zusa's body lay only a few paces away, the axe handle angling out from the wound in his back. "I'm not dead?"

"Spirit of forgiveness or not, answering the same questions over and over does get a little boring."

As I lifted myself from the forest floor, my muscles didn't fight the push and pull of movement. The small pains I had carried with me every day since Nomar, the cuts and bruises, were conspicuously absent. This wasn't my body. Somewhere in The Waking, my body breathed and continued living, even as my spirit roamed The Mist. The pains would greet me when I returned.

Colorful flowers scattered amongst the forest of misfit trees, making the shades of green and brown all the more wonderful. A cherry blossom nestled between a poplar and a sycamore tree, its white petals blooming like a cloud missing from the perfect blue sky.

In a field of perfection, one flower had yet to blossom. The tiny bud, still a light green hue, waited in a field of red-speckled, white flowers.

As I reached out towards the singular bud and ran my thumb over the sheltered flower, the green petals peeled away. The white petals within spread and opened, revealing the red sweeping from the center of the ovary.

"When you were young—maybe too young to remember—you loved to call flowers from the earth. You would slow them down as they bloomed, so you could watch them unfurl." The Seed's low voice hummed in the air.

"It seems like another life."

"Oh, maybe to you, but to me, only a handful of days have passed," he said.

He walked through the forest—each step deliberate. His body blended in with the trees. The rings that tattooed his oaken skin, the flowers that grew asymmetrically over his body, the natural lines and smooth curves of his form fit perfectly within this world he projected. "Life is always changing, seedling. It grows and fades. Time colors the edges. Change is conflict because what once was, isn't anymore."

"If we're in The Mist, why didn't that flower bloom before I touched it?"

"Conflict is a part of life, as is loss—just another type of change," he continued, as if I hadn't spoken. "You can either fight the change or adapt to it. And how I wish you would learn to forgive the present for not being the past."

The Seed moved further into the forest. His movement shifted between the trees, but I struggled to track him. I pushed into the forest after his voice.

"You can never undo change, no matter how you fight. What has happened cannot be undone. But if you adapt, you can be a part of change. You can move with it. You can dance with time."

His voice carried through the forest clear as ever, but I only caught glimpses of movement through the fullness of the forest.

"Seedling, your anger is you fighting change. You think it makes you strong, but it doesn't. It distracts you from moving forward and moving the world with you."

"What are you talking about? Where are you going?"

A fog rolled over the forest floor, growing thicker and thicker as I pushed through the trees, searching for The Seed.

"Forgiveness is not compliance. It is the acceptance of change and freedom from the constraints of the past." His low, rumbling voice faded. "Fight alongside forgiveness."

The fog rose, and the forest vanished behind it until the fog was all that remained.

The Waking came alive in a series of blinks. An overcast sky peeked through the forest canopy. A bird fluttering from one branch to another. The last leaves of autumn clung to the branches above me.

Then pain cut through it all.

The ground shook beneath me as my head bounced against a flat surface. I went to clutch my shoulder wound, but the binding around my wrists kept my hands locked in place. The rope that cinched my wrists together ran down to another rope binding my ankles.

I started breathing in quick, panting breaths. *What is happening?*

A beat clomped against the ground in a steady pattern. Wood squeaked and jostled below me, then a horse snorted.

Countless thoughts swam slowly through my head, like a dream had caught me and wouldn't let go. Finding a memory was like digging in the earth for the right stone. The more I pushed through the dirt, the more stones I found, just not the right ones.

Jonac whittled at a bit of cedar next to the fire in our tent. I tried to show him how to run the blade with the grain and make wood take shape like my father had taught me, but he never got it. He always ended up with a pointy stick and a few shallow cuts along his fingers.

Shay danced in Auntie Munnie's hallow. Flames ran along the walls before smoldering to smoke all around her. Her shoulders bounced with each heavy breath as the smoke dissipated. Sweat beaded down her ochre skin. She smiled at me.

Zusa held another crystal in the air. I couldn't imagine pulling another spirit into me. The Mother hadn't made us to carry so many. He smiled, and the purple hue in the crystal spun beneath the glassy surface. I cursed under my breath as I reached for The Shadow.

Zusa. For some reason, my mind continued to come back to him, but I couldn't hold on to any thought for long.

Then his body lay on the forest floor. Blood streamed from the axe wound in his back. His body twitched. His leg kicked. Then he settled into the dirt.

Tears ran over the edge of my face. He had been a liar, a rude asshole with a penchant for harsh words and quick hands, but he also believed in me when I hadn't. Maybe that had been his greatest flaw.

Liara! I thought. *Where is she?*

Her echo didn't course through the air. After all our moons together, I had taken the sound of her for granted. But just because she wasn't there didn't mean she had died. Maybe she had escaped. Maybe all the others escaped.

The cart jerked below me, then The Priest's veiled hood loomed over me as he rode atop a brown mustang.

"Don't worry, little thief," The Priest said, his Gousht accent twisting our words. "We're almost there."

I lashed out at him, but my bindings pulled me back into position and my wounds flared white hot for the effort.

"Now, now. None of that." The bastard's tone carried a pleasant timbre. "You see that wagon?"

I followed his point to a covered wagon drawn by a cream-colored colt.

"Your little friend with the rude tongue is in there with one of my soldiers. Unfortunately, my man can be over-zealous in his duties, but for now my orders are that he keep the boy alive," The Priest said. "Don't make me change my orders."

"Why are you doing this? What do you want?"

"Those are good questions, my boy." He adjusted himself on his saddle. "Well, why does anyone ever do anything? Power.

"Power can come from a great many places." He angled his chest to display the five spirit crystals hanging from linked chains around his neck. "In this case, I am interested in the power that comes from knowledge."

"I won't answer any of your questions!" I yelled.

"*Sir.*" The soldier who wounded me walked up to The Priest. He grinned down at me through his thick beard, and patted his hip where my father's knife dangled from his belt. *"A rider has come with a message."*

"The price of power is that you are always needed somewhere," The Priest said. "We will have all the time necess—"

CHAPTER THIRTY-ONE
CURRENT DAY ENNEA

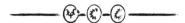

The first two thuds interrupted Kaylo's story. A moment of silence hung in the air as he and Tayen exchanged glances. The second pair of thuds against the door to Kaylo's quarters moved with the same rhythm but grew in urgency and volume.

He handed Tayen his knife, motioning her into the corner. If something were to happen, she needed to be out of view when it did. Between her shadows and the blade, she would have a chance.

She took her place, grasping the knife against her chest, and he went to open the door.

Two more thuds shook the stormwood. The moment he pulled the handle, the door thrust forward, and Nix burst into the room.

"Blessed fucking Mother, what..." Kaylo jumped back from the door.

"Why didn't you tell me?" she demanded.

Thistle looked in past the open doorframe as Nix slammed the door shut in her face.

"What are you talking about?"

"The girl." She about-faced. "You, you little shit. Why didn't you tell me?"

"Tell you what?" Tayen stepped forward cautiously, lowering the knife to her side.

"What are you? You a thief—spirit dancer, whatever the fuck you want to be called? Is that it?"

"No, I'm not a spirit dancer. I'm..." Tayen started.

"Stop," Kaylo said. "This is not the time." He gestured towards the door.

"How many secrets are you keeping from me? Do you have another name I don't know about?" Her eyes widened and her nostrils flared. "And it doesn't matter what the guard hears. One of your little pets told Wal everything."

"What are you talking about?"

"The little thief. The pale kid that looks like he's got soft hands and ain't seen fear before—he saw Tayen playing with spirits." Nix stepped closer to Kaylo. "And now Wal has Sosun. So, now would be a good time to tell me the truth."

All the defensive energy building in his chest deflated when she said Sosun's name. Her anger wasn't born of wounded pride or impatience. That servant girl had already lost too much, and now Wal had his hand wrapped around her like another rune in his game. Asshole.

"I'm sorry, Nix. I know how much you care about her." He gestured to the table. "Can we sit?"

With her hands locked in fists and her lips pursed into an expression that indicated she would rather kill him than sit beside him, she stepped forward to close the gap between her and Kaylo. Then she looked over at Tayen, and her shoulders settled slightly.

Once at the table, Kaylo nodded to Tayen.

"I'm a shadow dancer," she said. "Kaylo thought it best if no one knew. He said that secrets are the only weapons we have."

"What else? What other weapons are you hiding?"

"I have a plan to get through the Lost Forest, but I need more time," Kaylo said.

"No." Nix slammed her palm against the table. "No more time. If you want my help, we leave tomorrow, and we leave with Sosun."

"How can I trust you when Wal has Sosun?" Even as Nix's dark brown eyes bore into Kaylo, he didn't flinch away. "We both have something to lose." He tilted his head in Tayen's direction and Nix's gaze followed.

"I've already made one deal with these purple-robed bastards that I'll never stop regretting. Don't make me make another. Sosun comes first for me."

"If we do this tomorrow, everything will have to go perfectly."

Kaylo knelt in the stiff sand. Only two echoes sang between the three students kneeling in front of him. Of course, Rúnka had lost her grip on the spirit.

Pana sat, shoulders straight and chest out. Given time, he would become a master spirit dancer. Even if his instincts lacked something, he worked twice as hard as the others. His rearing wrapped around his every movement, a Citadel kid with a need for approval that would drive him to great things. Not necessarily good things.

Euri hunched beside him, skin sallow and eyes red as her hair.

"When I was learning how to control The Balance, my kana would force me to hold on to a spirit for several span. Every moment of every day, a small part of me wrestled with the angry spirit trapped within me. I had to learn to separate myself. While the pain seared my flesh, my spirit pulled away and carried on living."

"What was the longest you held on to a spirit for?" Pana asked, like he wanted to know the measure he needed to surpass.

"Two turns," Kaylo said, and the slight smirk disappeared from Pana's face. "I nearly lost sense of The Waking. Seven hundred twenty-eight days of being divided between myself—a part of me always fighting, even in sleep. The day I let go of that spirit...color came back to the world."

"Why did you hold on to a spirit for that long?" Euri asked.

Kaylo smiled with a melancholy memory. "You can let go of your spirits for now."

Euri released her spirit immediately. Pana waited several moments, looking around to make sure that the other dancers noticed before he did.

"For the remainder of our time together, you will be dancing with a different spirit. Focus on the feeling, emotion, sensory memory that you need to reach for in order to call the spirit forward. Every way you pull, the spirit is pulling on you at the same time. If you are calling the wind, reach for the way the wind feels brushing against your skin. A harsh gust feels completely different from a light breeze. To master both, you need to master your own senses."

Kaylo held the sack of gems aloft, and they each picked one. Pana waited behind as the others walked to their respective corners of the tent.

"Can I pick another?" The light green crystal shined in his palm and sang a soft, twisted version of The Seed's melody.

"The Seed protects the whole of Astile. When the crops fail to provide, The Seed provides. Why wouldn't you want to dance with The Seed?"

"We are going to war, not to harvest."

"You are young enough to think there is a difference," Kaylo said.

"What does that mean?"

"The invasion, the occupation, the war—what were they if not a harvest?" Kaylo wrapped the string around the top of the canvas bag and walked away to help Rúnka with her fire dancing before she burned the tent to the ground.

For the most part, the spirit dancers studied the spirits on their own. Kaylo watched as they moved and noted their missteps. Euri's dancing required more finesse. The air either moved with the lightest of breezes or toppled over everything in its path.

Rúnka lacked a similar subtlety. The fires she called forth sprang to life in a flash, growing until she had to smother them. Her barriers to The Song acted like a levee. Open, water rushed through and flooded over the land; locked, the land dried under the hot sun. No in-between.

By the end of their session, a wild garden grew from the sand all around Pana. The boy was barely visible above the stalks of corn and cherry blossoms.

"Form ranks," Kaylo said.

Each of the three returned their surroundings to equilibrium. A few flashes of fire erupted around Rúnka, followed by a series of curses.

When they returned to kneeling, Kaylo knelt as well. "Our next goal is two days. The more you push your body and your natural inclination to let go of these spirits, the more your body will adjust. The pain won't stop. It never stops. But eventually, your body acclimates to the pain."

"Motha, tha sounds horrible," Rúnka said.

"Pana, switch with Rúnka," Kaylo said.

"Why? You said it was important for me to learn The Seed." Pana leaned forward and pouted his lower lip.

"It's also important that Rúnka not burn down the mess." Kaylo gestured back and forth between them, hurrying the trade.

They exchanged crystals, then the three dancers called the spirits forth, pulling the echoes into themselves.

None of them were ready for war. Pana least of all. He had the determination of youth and the unearned confidence to go along with it. When Kaylo left, they would be on their own. Three more spirits to add to his tally.

Tayen's last opportunity walked out the tent with the rest of the regiment. Daak was probably off to see his new friends. Maybe they had midday plans of beating another old servant or torturing a helpless animal. Something fun like that.

Sokan blazed in the sky. The ground softened with the melting snow. An air of change moved with the meandering group of recruits as they filed towards the mess hall—fear, excitement, anxiety, all the promises or threats of a new tomorrow. They would be facing the trials in less than a span, and she wouldn't be there.

She would have shown them all what she was capable of.

As the regiment settled into line awaiting another serving of the same bland slop, Daak cut off from the group.

As if instinct took her, she broke from the line as well, then stopped. She needed to eat. No telling when she would have the opportunity again—either opportunity.

He walked between a cluster of buildings. His hand brushed over the clay brick of a small storehouse he passed. Then he disappeared into an alley.

It was a trap. It had to be.

The line into the mess hung out the side of the tent. Hunger twisted her gut, but Daak's footprints in the slushy remains of winter created the perfect trail. A child could follow him.

As The Song battered against her barriers, the bland smell of cooked oats drifted through the opening of the tent.

A hundred or more mumbling voices buzzed under the canopy, all talking about the same thing they had been speaking about for weeks. The Trials. She had stood in the mess for weeks as one whiny recruit after another asked how many of them would earn their purples.

Slush squished beneath her ragged boots and clung with each step, like mud. Following Daak was incredibly foolish, especially given what the day would bring, but she had to.

Tayen ran her hand along the same building Daak had, his footprints marking a clear path through the outer city. Each step and each turn carried her further from the Citadel and from the mess. Wherever he meant to go, there wouldn't be many people.

It was definitely a trap.

A waterlogged stick and a pile of stones rested against the corner of a building. The stick would break too easily, so she added a couple of the larger stones to her pocket and clutched the largest one in her hand.

If this was a trap, she wouldn't be easy prey.

The footprints ended at the doorway of a partially burned-down ironoak building at the edge of the city. Ironically, the collapsed structure blocked off the doorway, only to create several other entry points through the remaining walls.

Only one set of footprints marred the layer of half-melted snow. If Daak's friends waited for her, they had done a good job covering their tracks.

The weight of the stone in her hand reassured her. She would have plenty of opportunities to die today. Kaylo's plan had more holes than her ragged robes. At least if she died here, she could take Daak into The Mist with her.

She ducked below a charred beam to sneak into the structure. The melting snow made the wood slick. Pieces of wood clinked together as they shifted beneath her feet.

Beyond a collapsed beam and several broken planks sticking up at odd angles, a small space opened up in the middle of the rubble. Daak sat hunched over on a pile of wet wood, his red curls draped over his face.

If this were a trap, it was either too clever or too stupid for her to figure out.

"I thought you might come," he said, head bowed towards the ground.

"Where are your friends?"

"This building burned down one of our first nights here. A recruit with a spirit crystal couldn't handle the pressure and turned this place into an inferno. Of course, they stopped the fire and took him away. Do you think they made him a nameless or did they just kill him?"

"What the fuck do you care?" Tayen gripped the stone in her hand tighter.

"I come here sometimes. At first, because I could be alone. I missed being alone," he said. "Then, after...you know—I did what I did—being around people got that much harder. Anyone who didn't hate me was scared of me."

"Shut up! You don't get pity. You miss being alone? All I am is alone since you killed Vāhn." Her throat swelled like she might cry.

"I didn't mean to..."

"No? And you didn't mean to torture the old man in the Citadel!" She hadn't meant to scream.

"How did you know?" He looked up, his face wet with tears.

"Get up!" she yelled, and strangely, he did.

Daak stood in front of her. His shoulders slumped. Fresh tears blanketed his brown eyes. "Do what you have to."

"Fight me, you asshole!"

"Why? I deserve whatever you're going to do."

Halfway through her swing, the rock's momentum took hold of her arm. A loud pop broke through the air when the rock hit his jaw, and he fell to the wet ground below.

Blood leaked from a cut on his cheek. The fucking rakat wouldn't even fight. If he thought he could save himself by giving up, he was wrong.

"Murderer!" The next blow caught him in the shoulder, and he yelped as he reflexively covered his head.

Each time she brought down the rock or her fist, Daak cried out, but he didn't struggle.

"Fight me!"

Her boot dug into the soft flesh below his ribs.

"Coward!"

The rock clunked against his forearm.

When her arms became too heavy to lift, she stopped. Daak lay on the ground beneath her, a swollen mound of discolored flesh and blood. Her stomach churned bile, and she swallowed it back down.

"Why won't you fight me?" Tears freely streamed down her face.

"Do it. Kill me." His words came out wet and heavy with breath.

She raised the stone above her head, blood trailing down and tracing the long vein in her forearm.

He lay there like some pathetic wounded animal. He wanted this escape.

"No," she said. "If you want to die, do it yourself."

The rock rolled from her hand and fell into a half-melted pile of snow.

The door opened and Nix found Wal sitting at his table with that young spirit dancer. Wal looked up with his classic bullshit smile, and the dancer's eyes went wide.

Her rage settled into the corner of her mind when she saw Sosun asleep on the bed with her hands and feet bound. The girl still had breath in her lungs.

If Nix moved quickly and had a bit of luck, she could kill Wal and the boy before the guard outside noticed. Of course, she wouldn't make it five steps out the door carrying Sosun over her shoulder.

"Did you come here to check on the girl?" Wal asked. "We have been nothing but the most gracious of hosts, haven't we, Pana?"

The boy nodded his head too quickly and too many times. Not fully onboard, she thought. Useful.

"I'm not here to banter with you," Nix said. "I did what you asked. Tayen is a shadow dancer, plain and simple, and Kaylo plans on making his move today."

"How? When?" The chair squeaked against the floor as Wal angled to face her.

"The girl and I are supposed to meet him in the training tents after mess."

"How does he plan to get past the Lost Forest?" Wal's smile decreased and he spoke slower. "I need you to tell me every detail. So does the servant girl."

"Kaylo has been through too much. He's cautious. He won't tell me."

"I thought you wanted your little nameless friend to live," Wal said.

Nix stepped forward, and Wal stood up. As squirrelly and twisted as he was, Wal had the standing of a warrior in his shoulders. Even as she measured him, his steady breath blew across the exposed skin on her shoulder in even exhalations.

"Before this is over, you will learn your—" Wal started.

Pana bent over in a fit of coughing, clutching his stomach. One cough rolled into the next as the boy tried to gulp down air.

"What's wrong with your pet?" Nix tilted one side of her mouth up in a crooked smile.

A small chuckle came from the back of Wal's throat. He knelt down next to the boy. "You're holding onto a spirit, aren't you?"

Between a dry cough and a hurried sniffle, the boy nodded.

Wal leaned down close to the boy, gently patting his back. "Now tell me, can spirit dancers take a spirit from another spirit dancer?"

The coughing subsided, and Pana took a couple of breaths before nodding again.

The corners of Wal's mouth crept up and broke his false face.

Whether he wanted to beat or kill Kaylo, he wanted it with a greater desire than even he knew. No matter how many self-indulgent quips he made, this man was dangerous. Beating a servant girl meant nothing. Betraying his friend meant nothing. If Nix stood in his way, he wouldn't hesitate to bury her and walk over the loose dirt.

Of course, she wouldn't make it easy.

He stood up and walked to the door slowly, as if all the time left in the world belonged to him. On the other side of the door, a guard stood at attention. "Gather the rest of my guard and tell them to leave their spirit crystals behind."

Then he turned back to Pana. "Are you able to find the girl?"

"I think. I know what to listen for now." Pana said, forcing himself to a kneeling position.

"Good, King Shonar is always looking for another shadow to add to his collection," Wal said, then pointed to Nix. "You, come with me."

CHAPTER THIRTY-TWO

CURRENT DAY ENNEA

Kaylo's steps reverberated off the chamber walls, causing each additional step to clatter into the previous. Lanigan wore the same pleasant smile they offered most mornings, but it soured on their face when Kaylo turned the corner.

"What is it, my friend?" they asked. "Did something happen?"

"Everything and all at once." Kaylo pulled out a chair, with no care for how the wood scraping the floor would fill the library with a grating noise layering over itself several times as it bounced off the walls. No one else ever visited the stacks anyway.

He leaned over the table and lowered his voice. "Hypothetically, if I were to escape this place, would you come with me?"

"You know what Akena said about hypotheticals?" Lanigan cleared their throat.

> *To dream with words,*
> *To live a life yet to be,*
> *In search of answers*
> *No one will see.*
> *As deep as a dream may go,*
> *The world is too full*

And people too complex
To be lived in words and the hypothetical.

"I never cared for the poem. Too many rhymes, turns it into a riddle more than a poem, but I believe Akena had a point." Lanigan shrugged. "But who am I to criticize? My life is lived in words."

"It doesn't have to be," Kaylo whispered. "I'm leaving. Today."

"Then I shall miss you, my Anhil. For but a season it has been, you will remain with me for a lifetime."

"I'm serious. This isn't some poem or literary debate. This is your chance to escape." The last word left his lips with too much fervor and filled the room.

Lanigan smiled, shaking their head. "You think I haven't had chances to leave? I told you Shonar offers me freedom once a turn. A single word and he would escort me to the other side of the forest without question."

"Why?"

"Guilt, I'm assuming."

"No! Why do you stay?!" All pretense of a whisper left his voice.

"I may be a prisoner, but my chains rattle." Lanigan sat, staring at Kaylo like they answered the question without room for misinterpretation. The silence between them indicated otherwise.

"Fine, no poetry, no clever turns of phrase. Shonar needs a reminder of his guilt. He needs to see the consequences of his decisions, but the servants are invisible to him, and he spends his days far from the war he is waging. So, once a turn, I remind him. I tell him what his advisors won't."

"It hasn't worked."

"Maybe not, but I see the doubt in his eyes," they said. "When we were young, before he wore a crown and commanded armies, we would sneak around the city. He wanted to know how people lived.

"He stole a necklace once, from an old vendor who didn't have the legs to chase a young boy. It was a gift for me, but when I found out where he got it, I looked at him. That's all it took. One disappointed look. He took it back to the old woman and apologized. He lowered himself to his knees, begging for forgiveness." Lanigan sighed. "His father beat him bloody for it too."

"He's not that boy anymore," Kaylo said. "You've seen what he's done to the servants. You've heard his plans directly from his mouth. Your friend is beyond saving."

"Especially if I don't try."

"I can't leave you behind." Kaylo swallowed, but his throat still scratched. "I've left too many people behind."

A soft smile curved through Lanigan's lips. They reached their hands out and waited for Kaylo to take them. "Then don't leave me behind. Take my words.

"My Anhil, you have been many things—to yourself and others. A friend, a son, a thief, a hero, a deserter, a surrogate father. Be something you haven't been. Be a peacemaker." They squeezed Kaylo's hands.

"I don't know if I can."

"In an old Astilean story, a young man named Anhil lost his family to disease. Instead of accepting his loss, he crossed into The Mist and stole their spirits back. He found a way through the unbreakable barrier, outsmarted the Great Spirits, and gave his family another chance at life. I knew from the first time we met that you wouldn't be here long."

Kaylo indulged in the warmth of his friend's hands in his for a moment, then stood up and walked towards the doors.

"Remember, peace doesn't require war," Lanigan said. "It requires opportunity."

———

Despite the sun in the sky, the servant tunnels grew dark within the first few steps. The scent of susu root grew more potent the farther Tayen crept into the tunnels. As her eyes adjusted, she ran her hand along the rough wall to guide her.

Someone brushed by her, grazing her shoulder. She reached for one of the rocks in her pockets, but it was a servant going about her duties.

Several servants moved around, hefting supplies and tools. One young boy, no more than twelve, hurried deeper into the tunnels with a pack of grain strapped to his back. His dark skin had gone sallow. How long had it been since he'd basked in the sunlight? Or bathed?

The stench of susu root and body odor clung to the stale air. The sooner Tayen could find her way through the tunnels, the better.

She needed help.

An elderly Tomakan woman stood in a storage room. Tayen's grandmother had passed into The Mist before she was born, and this woman wasn't her direct kin, but she could have been. The curve of her face, her soft chin, and her loose braids dangling over each shoulder favored Tayen's mother, given the turns she never had.

The woman smiled a gap-toothed smile to every servant who came in, then shuffled about to find them a place for their load or locate what they needed. If anyone would know how to navigate the tunnels, she would.

A Sonacoan man who had reached the middle of his turns moved from shelf to shelf with the older woman, gathering supplies in a worn basket. Despite the time it took her to move from one corner of the storage room to the other, he didn't rush her. He smiled, offering her an arm. Then, his basket finally full, he clasped her hand between his and bowed the crown of his head to her before leaving.

Even in the most broken of circumstances, people found a way to be who The Mother made them to be. Tayen hadn't met the like of the pain these servants suffered, yet she wore the blood of another Ennean speckled on her robes. This couldn't be what The Mother made her to be.

When the elder saw Tayen approach, her lips pulled back into the same grin she offered to the others. As she smiled, her wrinkles deepened, mapping her face like a story.

"Auntie, I need your help," Tayen said.

The old woman's smile vanished. She waved her hands back and forth before lowering her eyes to the ground.

"I'm not here to hurt anyone," Tayen said, but the old woman cowered in front of her. "I'm sorry, Auntie. I'm sorry for so much."

Tayen backed into the main tunnel in search of another guide. Every person she stopped reacted similarly, bowing and backing away. One young girl ran, dropping her load behind her.

The tunnel opened up into the storage cavern where Tayen had found Daak and his friends the last time. Several servants gathered towards the back wall, partially obscured by the crates and large sacks of food and supplies. Three of the healthier servants stood in front of the others like a wall of protection. Even their robes hung loose around their starved frames.

"Please, I mean no harm. A friend is in danger and needs help. I need to find my way through the tunnels."

The largest woman stepped forward. Maybe a newer addition. Her fat and muscle hadn't withered away, and her eyes leveled with Tayen's. The northwoman clenched her fists.

Tayen wrapped her fingers around a rock in her pocket, but she couldn't bring herself to tighten her grip. This woman was defending her people. She would do the same had the roles been reversed. At least, she hoped she would.

The northwoman bared her yellowed teeth, then a hand clamped down on her shoulder. She tried to yank free, but the hand pulled more insistently. The old Tomakan man who Daak had tortured stepped forward. The bruises on his face had nearly vanished, but his nose still bent to the left.

He pulled a northman out from the pack with him, their fingers interlocked. Age hadn't worn down on the second man nearly as much as the one Tayen had saved, but his hairline had crept further from the lines of his forehead. They shared a look, then the man Tayen had saved contorted his hands and fingers in a series of gestures. He touched his eye and his chest, then dragged his fist down his forearm.

The balding northman looked from Tayen back to the older man's intense gaze, then the tension eased from his shoulders. A melancholy smile filled his lips, then he lifted his fist to his face, dragging the back of his thumb down his nose to his lips.

Eight sets of eyes lifted from the ground and focused on Tayen, each holding a question, but the northman pulled out a writing slate, scratching down a message. As he handed it to Tayen, he reached back to find the hand of the man Tayen had saved.

When you saved Einol's life, you saved mine.

The look they shared as Tayen lifted her head from the writing slate spoke of a bond that meant more than any hardship. Somehow, they had made a life, found love, despite their tragedies, when Tayen had only found anger through hers.

"I'm glad to see you well, Uncle," she said.

Wearing his crooked and wide smile, Einol stepped forward and patted her cheek.

"Family knows," she said. Nothing else seemed to carry enough weight in the moment except for this simple acknowledgement of ties that could not be broken.

"I need your help. Commander Wal took a friend and locked her away in his quarters—a servant named Sosun. I need to find her."

Einol turned around, and his hands danced over each other again. A young Sonacoan boy stepped through the small crowd, up to the two older men. He was probably Tayen's age, maybe older, but the thinness of his face obscured the turns.

After exchanging several rapid gestures with Einol, the boy walked over to one of the three tunnels leading away from the cavern and waved for Tayen to follow.

"Thank you, Uncles," Tayen said. Though she smiled, tears threatened to break over her lids. Even if she freed Sosun and escaped, the servants would still be here, trying to survive another day.

The two men's tightly clasped hands gave her a small hope.

She turned away and followed the boy deeper into the mountain tunnel.

Oil lanterns grew farther apart the deeper they traveled into the tunnels. The boy disappeared into the darkness several times, only for Tayen to find him around another sharp corner. They wove around the tunnels like a maze, the floor sloping upward only to level out as they reached a new set of tunnels.

Once in a while, they passed another servant. The boy's hands danced in front of him like the old man's had, but he never stopped.

Several caverns, as full or fuller than the cavern they had come from, were scattered throughout the tunnels. The Citadel could survive on the wealth of supplies in this mountain for decades. But, without the servants, they wouldn't be able to find any of it.

The rough floor of the mountain tunnels bore into Tayen's worn boots, and her feet rebelled against the jabbing aches. Yet, somehow, her guide bore the journey with bare feet.

Whatever the Lost Army failed to see in these servants only spoke of their lack of vision.

As the tunnel narrowed, the corridor that had been large enough for several people shoulder to shoulder shrunk to the size of a single person. Had Tayen been larger, she would have had to shuffle sideways.

The walls grew smoother until they became the same flat consistency as the Citadel hallways. And finally, their journey had come to an end.

Tayen clutched one of the rocks in her pockets as they approached a door.

Her guide flattened against the wall of the tunnel, waving Tayen through.

"I don't know which room is his."

Even in the dark of the tunnels his narrowed eyes, tilted chin, and heavy exhalation spoke volumes.

The servant squared up in front of her and placed a finger to his lips. Then he reached forward, grabbed her by the sides of her head, and lowered her chin to her chest.

The door creaked as it opened, light pouring in from the hallway. Tayen had to blink several times before her eyes adjusted. She followed her guide's lead and kept her eyes locked on the floor as if she were any other servant.

Another set of footsteps approached from around the curved hallway, growing heavier and louder. The Shadow thumped against her barriers in time with her rapid heartbeat. Her fingers tightened around the rock in her pocket, and an edge poked into the flesh of her palm. Still, she gripped it tighter.

A shadow crept into her limited field of view. Then boots. Nice, polished leather. The gentle clap of a sheath against a leg.

If she had to fight, she couldn't let him pull the blade. A stone could crack a skull, but only given the opportunity. Swords tended to serve as better weapons.

The footsteps were upon them and then continued past without acknowledgement.

The air rushed from her lungs once they were alone again. In these halls, the servants were more invisible than any shadow cloak could make her.

The servant boy stopped at a stormwood door like all the others.

"Thank you," she whispered.

He didn't raise his head or gesture with his hands like he had with the other servants. He simply turned back towards the tunnels and walked away, his footsteps echoing off the walls.

All she had to do was slip in and free Sosun.

The Mother must have loved Kaylo something fierce because his plans broke apart easier than a clay pot, yet he had survived so much.

The door gave way with little effort and opened to a room much
like Kaylo's, only less bare. A purple rug with a woven pattern of white
covered the floor. A large map of Ennea hung on the wall next to Wal's
table. Matching cedar chests lined up along the opposite wall. And a
Sonacoan servant with long matted hair covering her battered face stood
in the corner, shaking.

"Sosun?"

The woman tucked herself further into the corner.

"Nix sent me to find you," Tayen said. "She told me to tell you..." She
placed her palm over her heart, moved it perpendicular to her chest, slid
two fingers down the back side of her left hand, then placed the tips
of her fingers on her bottom lip and tapped several times like Nix had
shown her.

Sosun peered through her hair, eyeing Tayen with confusion before a
laugh burst from her lips and shattered the servant's guarded expression.

Tayen repeated the gesture. She had done something wrong because
Sosun continued to chuckle to herself. Then the servant stepped out
from her corner and walked over to a stack of papers on the table. She
scrawled something on a bit of paper and waved Tayen over.

You said, "I am dirty and annoying."

"Well, Nix is a fucking bitch. I did exactly what she said."

Sosun smiled, offering her hands. The two clasped each other's right
hands in greeting. "I'm Tayen, and I'm not annoying."

The stormwood door behind them crashed into the stone wall.

Sosun yelped and withdrew into herself once again.

A scrawny little northboy and a heavyset Tomakan warrior dressed in
the King's purple and leather sannil stood in the room's entrance. The tip
of her spear caught the light like a warning.

"When the Commander told me to find you, I didn't know I could've
waited for you here," the northboy said.

As Tayen removed the dam, The Song rushed forward like a tidal wave. She moved effortlessly. Her fingers reached towards the center of the room, then one by one curled into her palm. Shadows engorged themselves as they swallowed every bit of light. When the dark reached its apex, she swept her hands away from her body, and all the shadows vanished from the room in an instant.

The resulting flash of light burst into all four corners of the room, leaving everyone but Tayen, who had closed her eyes, pawing at their faces and moaning.

The effect wouldn't last long. She dashed towards the Tomakan warrior, bashing her across the face with a heavy stone. Blood broke open from the wound and spattered in all directions before the warrior crashed to the ground. Gore leaked from the gash in her scalp and traced the gaps between her braids.

She would live—probably—but Tayen didn't have time for such concerns.

She swiped the warrior's spear up from the stone floor, rounding on the kneeling boy, who was still blinking away the light. "Who are you? Why would Wal send a little boy after me?"

"Kaylo hasn't told you?" The boy reached out a hand, grabbing for something in the air that wasn't there, then The Song went silent. "You and I share a kana." His hands swirled, the shadows swelled once again.

A fucking spirit dancer?!

Boots shuffled over the floor in the darkness. Tayen tightened her grip on the spear and angled it across her chest. A chair fell to the floor, and Sosun shrieked as The Song's absence bellowed within Tayen.

"What are you doing?!" Tayen yelled.

The darkness wavered.

Shadows naturally wanted to move with the light, not against it, always pulling themselves back into their original form and place. Manipulating the darkness required a continuous pull, a balance of tensions.

A single stream of light from the window broke through the dark, diluting the shadows. The blackness shrunk from the growing light until the shadows became nothing more than a heavy fog of gray.

A single silhouette moved, obscured by the haze.

"Can't hold on to the shadows, can you?" Tayen said.

The seams of the collected patchwork of darkness weakened and stretched, creating gaps in the massive cloud. Light tore the laboring strains of shadow apart, severing the collection into its many parts. They fell to the ground, found their form, and rushed back to their resting places.

Pana stood behind Sosun with a dagger pointed at her gut and his forearm wrapped around her neck. "The Commander ordered me to take you in alive, but he said nothing about the nameless."

The knife shivered in the prick's soft hands—a boy playing war, having known nothing of it.

"You've never killed someone before, have you?" Tayen asked. "Probably never seen someone die."

"So what?!"

Sosun stood motionless, her arms at her side. What might have been mistaken for fear, her wide eyes and her slightly parted lips, was something altogether different. The scabbed-over cut on her lip and the dark bruise across her cheek helped hide the subtle look of rage settling on her face.

Rage had the capacity to be gentle when called for. It knew how to feign quiet before the kill—that was how it sustained itself. Pana couldn't know that kind of rage because rage like that required true loss.

"You were born in the Citadel, weren't you? Raised calling your servants 'nameless'? They have names, you know," Tayen said. "One of the first lessons Kaylo taught me was to learn my weaknesses."

"I'm not weak!" The blade shook more violently, and his grip on Sosun tightened.

"Everyone has weaknesses, even the things they think make them stronger." Tayen took a step forward and twisted the spear shaft in her grip. "For instance, you think having power makes you invulnerable. Your parents probably have important names. You're a spirit dancer. The things that gave you power made you naïve."

"Stop! Stop right there. I'll kill her. I will!"

Sosun grabbed Pana's knife arm with both of her hands, stomped her boot on his toes, and spun out of his grip.

Throughout autumn, Tayen had run practice drills, driving the tip of a spear into a practice dummy. Her left arm drove forward as her right guided the weapon to its target. Her practice sessions hadn't prepared her for the way flesh would welcome her blade. The metal slipped through the boy into his soft parts without resistance. Bone deflected the angle, then his body hugged the spear.

As his knife clang against the stone floor, a high-pitched wet breath escaped his lips. Then the northboy fell beside his blade, his body still clinging to the spear.

His eyes remained open, dark brown with hints of hazel.

Blood streamed from his wound and spread across the ground like a second rug.

Someone grabbed Tayen's shoulder, but she couldn't look away from Pana. The first time she had killed, the Gousht Commander didn't have a name. Pana had a name. He was Ennean like her. A boy her age.

Sosun grabbed Tayen's face and forced her to look away.

Even as the room teetered back and forth, Sosun grabbed her, and Tayen's feet followed the pull.

One footfall clacked against the stone after the other. But Pana still lingered in front of her. Wide brown eyes. Soft bloody lips.

A thick haze formed on the edges of her vision. The door to the servant tunnels opened, and Sosun pulled her through as the haze swallowed the world.

Tayen's family hut stood in front of her. Stones piled and patched together with mud and clay, smoke rising from the thatched roof. As she stepped inside, the fire burned with a heavy black smoke that contorted around the bodies of her family—stacked like meat in a smokehouse.

Flames claimed her family's flesh like hungry hands forever taking more, all while she stood by unable to save them.

How many times had she seen them burn? Smelled their flesh?

A hand fell on her shoulder, turning her away from the gruesome sight.

A slow white fog swept around her, consuming her surroundings, the light growing bright, like she was standing in the middle of a cloud on a sunny day. Then the fog parted and a long, impossibly thin woman stepped in front of her. With every step, the woman's body bent and twisted. Her purple-black skin solidified whenever she stood still, then broke into a cloud with every movement.

For a moment, she stopped directly in front of Tayen, which forced Tayen to tilt her chin up to meet her charcoal-gray eyes. Her smooth skin shifted between purple and black, as if it were in constant motion— smoke trapped in a jar. The curves of her long body moved gently, despite her standing still.

"Welcome, my child," she said. Despite missing a mouth, her voice flowed as smooth as chani cloth.

"Are you The Shadow?" Tayen asked. "Am I dead?"

"You, my child, are merely walking in The Mist with me. Your spirit needed to piece itself together, and I guided you here."

Pana lying on a rug of his own blood flashed before her.

"Why should I care about him? He held a knife to Sosun. He would have ruined our plan. I need to escape Astile. We need to escape." Tayen's voice was thin as the fog that surrounded her, one sentence bumbling into the next.

"It is not a bad thing to mourn the lives you take. That boy was many things to many people. You did what you had to, but that doesn't mean he lacked value," The Shadow said.

Tayen took a deep breath—at least she tried, but nothing filled her lungs.

If I'm in The Mist, I could see my family. The thought shook her not-body to the core.

"You could," The Shadow said. "You could stay here with your family if you choose."

"No, I can't. I haven't done what they asked me to do. They deserve revenge."

The Shadow's skin broke into a smoke before reforming as she sat on the solid white smoke below them. "My child, when you dream that isn't your family. Blood? If your mother had one word to say to you, would she choose blood?"

"The Gousht murdered them. The bastards took them from me. And I survived. Of course she'd want vengeance."

"You have carried a part of me with you since the day your mother carried you into The Waking," The Shadow said. "Your mother wanted a peaceful life for you and your sister. That's why she and your father took you from the village you were born in."

"And she died anyway. All of them did, lying on top of each other, burning away to char and ash. A peaceful life can't exist with the Gousht!"

"Maybe not, but what would your mother tell you if she had the chance? Would she ask you for more blood?" The Shadow reached forward, and her hand solidified the moment before she touched Tayen's cheek.

Light as her touch may have been, it contained a solidity, as if she touched more than Tayen's face—her spirit. "You need to go now."

"No, I'm not ready," Tayen said.

The white fog stirred around them. "You have all the answers you need, child."

CHAPTER THIRTY-THREE
CURRENT DAY ENNEA

All that remained was the waiting. Winter had begun to break, but without the heat of a fire, the cold weighed down the air like a new snowfall. A dusting of Kaylo's dry skin flaked into the sand at his feet as he rubbed his hands together, trying to warm himself.

Maybe the plan had too many faulty edges.

Everything changed when Wal discovered Tayen's connection to the spirits. They had to rush, and rushed plans worked as well as blunt axes. They could be effective, but they had a tendency to rebound.

The flap covering the entrance to the tent flickered in the wind. "Trust," he whispered to himself. "Seed and Balance. They'll be here"

Leaving in the night would've been better, but pulling Sosun from Wal's chamber at night would've been impossible. And Nix refused to leave without the girl, which set their escape plan an hour after midday. The stupidity of it might have worked in their favor.

Nix pushed her way into the tent and, as she did, she refused to meet Kaylo's eyes. The tension fell from his shoulders. A plan with far too many faulty edges, he thought as Wal stepped into the tent after Nix.

His smug grin grew wider as he ushered in his warriors. Six of the seven flower guards, who had overseen his every move for the past three moons, walked in, clad in their purple robes and leather sannil.

Where was Hazel? Kaylo thought as the guards spread across the sand.

In the array of swords and spears, Calla Lily stood apart. The larger Sonacoan warrior carried an axe, which rested on her shoulder. The edge of the crescent blade caught the subtle light under the tent, but the spike jolting out from the other side of the axe head carried a harsher warning.

Had he known that events would lead here, Kaylo may have given the warriors more threatening names. Being killed by a daffodil seemed a poor way to pass into The Mist.

"I trusted you, Nix," he said. "You asked for my help, and I offered it. What about Tayen?"

Nix didn't answer or look up as she stood near the entrance, staring at the sand.

"She did what she had to," Wal said. "Self-preservation, self-interest—it is the rule of the world. You taught me that, old friend."

Kaylo clutched his knife as the leather wrap dug into his palm. Today, tomorrow, thirty turns from now, he planned to die with this knife in his hand. "And Tayen? What did you do with her?"

"Don't worry," Wal said. "I sent one of my personal guards, and your spirit dancer, Pana, to fetch your sweet toka. A piece of The Shadow would be a terrible gift to waste. After all, our dear scion likes to collect them."

"We don't have to do this. The enemy is on the other side of the forest."

"I'm glad you agree." Wal walked between two of the warriors, stopping a few paces from Kaylo. "You haven't done anything that can't be undone, not yet. But as soon as the General hears you tried to escape, I won't be able to protect you anymore. She'll separate your head from your shoulders herself."

"Protect me? Look at yourself, Wal. What would *he* think of the man you've become?"

"Shut it! Not another word." A darkness that had nothing to do with shadows fell over Wal's face. "You don't get to do that."

"All this for revenge? When does it stop?"

"The Gousht owe blood! You know they do." Wal's knuckles went pale as he gripped the hilt of his sword, still waiting in its scabbard.

"And you would betray your people to the ambitions of an inept king? Please, Wal, don't do this." A prayer wove between Kaylo's words. The man in front of him, no matter his transgressions and flaws, had been his friend.

"For him, I would burn Ennea to ash and soil to snuff the last heartbeat of the last Gousht child from the face of The Waking." The leather scabbard scraped against Wal's sword as he drew it. "You have one last chance. Drop the blade, and I will spare your life."

"You always assumed you were cleverer than everyone else. You don't have all the pieces."

"Don't I? You stole The Seed from that spirit dancer who can't control spirits—can't say she'll be missed," Wal said. "Tell me, Kaylo. Does it hurt to hear The Seed like that? An echo that should be The Song?"

The distorted call of The Seed wove between the grains of sand beneath their feet, pricking at old memories.

"I expected you'd figure that out," Kaylo said.

Wal's eyes widened, and at the same moment, Nix pulled a gray crystal from her robe pocket, holding it aloft. The echo screamed out from its prison a moment before Kaylo snatched the translucent thread waving in front of him.

The Wind howled alongside The Seed in Kaylo's gut—a forgery of The Song's true call, but it would do.

As Wal lunged forward, his outstretched blade aimed towards Kaylo's heart, the sand depressed below his feet.

A moment quicker, a better foothold on solid ground, and Wal would have sent Kaylo into The Mother's embrace. Their friendship that had been wouldn't stop Wal from killing him, but Kaylo had promises to keep as well.

A rush of wind skirted the perimeter of the tent before careening over Kaylo's shoulders and crashing into Wal. His stern brow unfurrowed as the wind carried him off his feet, twisting and turning him like a rag doll before tossing his body into the two warriors behind him.

Nix cut down Daffodil before he had the chance to defend himself, and had locked blades with Juniper by the time the first warrior reached Kaylo.

Of course, it had to be Calla with her fucking axe.

The spike breezed by Kaylo's cheek as he dodged. Every step he took backwards gained him a second before he had to dodge another skull-cracking blow.

Dancing didn't take much time, but it took time he didn't have.

The other warriors regained their footing.

Kaylo stepped back, reached his fist to the ground before wrenching it up.

In a matter of seconds, a small seedling rose from the sand and unfurled into a stout thicket of thorns. Calla tried to pull back, but her momentum carried her forward, tumbling over the thicket and landing on the spike of her axe. It pierced through the sannil, flesh, viscera, and whatever else stood in its way until it rose from her back.

Kaylo couldn't call her a friend, but she had been by his side for a season. A warrior deserved a better death, but under these circumstances, he had to fight with whatever means he had at his disposal.

Blood flooded over the sand as her body spasmed before going still.

Thistle and Chrysanthemum lunged at Kaylo with their spears over the body of their fallen compatriot. No time to mourn a life taken. No time to make peace.

The Wind rattled and then a piercing noise cut through the chaos as he guided a gale into the attacking warriors. They collided and crashed to the ground.

Kaylo drew his knife back to finish Thistle quickly, but Wal and Hibiscus rounded on him before he could finish the kill.

———

When Nix ripped her sword from the giant northman's thigh and ran the edge of the blade across his neck, the big fuck collapsed, lifeless in the sand.

There was no pleasure in the things that needed doing, but that didn't change the necessity of them.

On the other side of the tent, Wal and another warrior backed Kaylo against the canopy as the last two warriors angled to join the attack.

As little as she cared for the man, she needed him. Without him, she and Sosun would be stuck in this backwards, Gousht-inspired nation.

She reached for the empty spirit crystal and threw it at a warrior. The worthless bit of stone actually hit the stocky Tomakan in the cheek. "Fuck your king!" she yelled, bending down to pick the sword from the dead body at her feet.

It certainly seemed to work. The Tomakan and the northwoman about-faced and charged at Nix with their spears.

"If I die before the asshole, I'll pull his spirit into The Mist with me," she said to herself as she moved in to meet the warriors.

———

The northman and Wal moved in one harmonious barrage. When one attack finished, the other was already under way.

Kaylo dodged a slashing sword and deflected the thrust that followed with his father's knife.

Sweat beaded down his forehead, stinging his eyes. The chill air vanished. Each breath grew more difficult as the damn spirits in his gut tore at him from the inside. He had run out of room to back up.

The tip of Wal's sword caught the edge of Kaylo's shoulder, sending searing pain spreading along the cut and a brilliant red blooming through his ragged robes over the wound.

The tormented spirits cried out in rage, feeding Kaylo's own anger. If he didn't survive, neither would Tayen.

He stepped back to the edge of the tent with his right foot, then kicked his left into a quick spin. As wind twisted through the sand at his feet, the grains clouded the air.

Unable to see, his attackers broke their rhythm and swung chaotically into the sand cloud.

The Wind twittered through the air as an underlying thrumming noise moved through it. Kaylo pushed the air with all his might through the cloud.

Sand pelted him as the gust rushed over him into his attackers. He sprang forward with the wind and drove his knife into Hibiscus' chest, landing on top of the man as the sand settled around them.

Kaylo looked the northman in the eyes as he pushed himself up. Hibiscus still clung to life, but he wouldn't last. His reddened cheeks, the basis for the name Kaylo had gifted him, turned pale. He tried to hold on to his sword as Kaylo pried it from his grasp, but he didn't have the fight left.

Nix ducked to the side as a spear jabbed over her shoulder.

Two swords or not, their spears kept her out of reach. They pushed her on her heels as she looked for a way to survive this shit. Her superior footwork was all that kept her from being run through like a rabbit on a spit-roast.

The Tomakan lunged at Nix's left shoulder, forcing her to angle to her right. She thrust forward at an awkward angle, but the sannil deflected the blow.

The northwoman took advantage, jabbing at Nix's ill-placed leg. A cold streak moved through her thigh, then erupted into a burning pain.

She deflected the attacks that followed and limped back to give herself some distance.

They didn't press her. Instead, the Tomakan bastard with the cut on his cheek smiled.

Nix was dead. They just hadn't finished her off yet. All three of them knew it. And once they finished with her, they would help Wal kill or disarm Kaylo, whichever came first.

And that would be alright. Kaylo could die. The bitter asshole had survived more than most and still he moped around like the world had wronged him.

But if he died, Sosun and Tayen wouldn't last much longer. Neither of them deserved what life had given them. Sosun hadn't reached Tayen's age by the time Nix allowed the Lost Nation to steal her away and torture her.

"Alright, you Lost Nation pricks, I am done playing your little war games. You may be warriors with your fucked up tattoos and fancy leather sannil, but I am a survivor."

The Tomakan warrior's smile deepened. But his smile evaporated as Nix threw one of her swords at him.

The blade twisted and spun in the air. Both warriors watched in horror. The Tomakan tried to move, but the blade moved faster than his legs.

Then the hilt crashed into his sannil.

He smiled momentary relief before Nix slammed into him with her shoulder. She tumbled over him and came up in fighting position.

The northwoman lunged, but her attack lacked focus. Nix deflected the spear, closed the distance between them, and shoved her sword through the leather vest with all her strength.

By the time the Tomakan scrambled to his feet, Nix already had the dead warrior's spear leveled at his throat. She didn't wait for his surrender. She simply thrust the spear forward.

As the sand settled around Kaylo and his old friend, Wal looked down at his warriors and the blood-stained sand before meeting Kaylo's eyes.

"So, this is it?" Wal brushed the sand from his robes. "The thief kills his old friend with stolen spirits. I guess there are worse ways to die."

"You could lay your weapon down."

"I thought I was supposed to be the funny one." Wal shifted his weight from one foot to the other.

"Come with us, Wal."

"I made the mistake of following you once."

"If it has to be, then it will be a fair fight. No spirits. No tricks," Kaylo said, relief flooding through him as The Wind left him—though The Seed he kept. They still had their plans.

Wal charged. However, he didn't move like the reckless boy Kaylo once knew. When he thrust his sword forward, he maintained his balance and pulled back to defensive position. He turned Kaylo's slash easily.

They caught each other's attacks, angling for position. Sparks flew from the clashing blades in the relative darkness of the tent.

The mounds of sand shifted under Kaylo's feet as they had the last two moons. Each pivot shifted the grains beneath him.

For all Wal's prowess with a sword, his feet slid slightly with each attack.

Kaylo feigned to deflect Wal's blow, letting the weight of Wal's attack pull him off balance. The first cut sliced through the flesh on the outside of Wal's thigh, below his leather guard.

Each slip in the sand cost Wal another shallow cut. His thrust lacked the power he once had as Kaylo ran his blade along the back of Wal's forearm.

Regardless of the turns of practice Wal had dedicated to the blade, he hadn't spent the past season on these sands. He fell to his hands and knees beside his blade—one too many wounds, one drop of lost blood more than he could bear.

Nix sat in the corner surrounded by four bodies. Too much blood soaked into the sand—Ennean blood. Kaylo kissed his three fingers before pressing them to the sand. "Please take them and give them rest."

Despite the sheer number of bodies surrounding her, Nix only had a single gash running along her thigh and a bloody nose—nothing else. If Kaylo had been forced to fight her, The Mother would have been welcoming him through the veil instead of the guards.

"Stop drawing it out." Wal turned himself face-up. "You were always better with a sword."

His purple robes had turned maroon. Blood darkened patches of the surrounding sand.

"I've seen my old friend. You hide him, but he still exists." Kaylo knelt next to Wal and collected the sword from the bloody sand.

"Spare me the speech and kill me already."

"I'm not going to kill you, Wal."

"Fuck you. I don't want your pity. Kill me or the General will." Tears filled Wal's eyes as he exhaled sharp breaths.

"It's not pity. It's the love I had for a friend I let down long ago. Family knows." Kaylo stood and walked towards the entrance where Nix waited, covered in gore.

"We aren't family!" His words came out breathy and tired.

"If you don't kill him, I will," Nix said, attaching a second sword and scabbard to her belt.

"Not if you want to get through the Lost Forest," he said. "Let's go."

Nix looked down with scorn at Wal, then leveled her glare at Kaylo before turning her back on the two of them.

They left Wal bleeding on the cold sand, in a garden of fallen warriors.

———

Tayen jerked awake as cool water lapped against her skin and dripped down her face. The sweet smell of susu root greeted her immediately. Sosun stood in front of her, holding a bucket and a rag, wearing concern plain on her face. Beyond her, several servants filled the tight cavern, their faces glowing in the candlelight.

"No, no, no. We were supposed to meet Kaylo and Nix." Tayen pushed herself from the cold floor. "Has Sokan fallen?"

Sosun shook her head.

They still had time. As long as Kaylo and Nix did their part, they would be free by the next morning light. No more sleeping in the barracks with ninety-odd unwashed children. No more porridge. No more assholes in uniforms consumed with power.

"We need to go." As Tayen pushed herself up, her vision flashed. The ground stirred and the cavern walls bent out of shape. Several servants reached out to steady her, but she waved them away. "They'll be waiting for us."

Einol, the man she had saved, stepped towards Tayen, his forehead wrinkled with worry like a concerned grandfather, his partner by his side.

No extras. Kaylo had been very clear on that point. Too many people would make it impossible to escape, and anyone caught would hang as an example.

The walls loomed over Tayen, tightening the cavern. This small chamber, filled with boxes, burlap sacks, and too many people, didn't have enough air to support them all. She needed to leave.

If the army found out the servants had helped them, they would die a painful death.

Most of the servants hovering about were older, their varied skin tones softened with age and hair faded into different shades of white. Only one boy, who couldn't have been older than twelve, stood apart— his dark-brown skin warmed yellow in the candlelight. He had a life to live. Surely one more wouldn't matter.

A sharp metallic clang rolled through the tunnels. Again and again the bell sang its piercing tune.

Each strike stopped Tayen's heart for a beat. She shouldn't have left the guard breathing. For all her posturing, her weakness had doomed their plans and forfeited their lives.

Sosun's hand broke into a series of gestures, as all the servants looked to her for answers. Her chest moved in and out like she was struggling for breath.

"We need to go," Tayen said. "The further we get from the Citadel, the safer we are."

Sosun gestured at one of the other servants, and the older Sonacoan woman handed her a slate and chalk. The chalk scrapped against the slate furiously.

We can't go. They'll find us.

"They'll find us either way, but if we stay here, they'll blame more than the two of us." Tayen waved her hand over the others.

Sosun's brow furrowed as she marked the slate again.

I should have never agreed to this.

Of course, Sosun was right, but no amount of wishing could make the day anew. They had one option now: forward.

"You agreed because you wanted something different," Tayen said. "None of us can promise you another day in The Waking, but I promise you won't have another chance to escape."

Sosun tapped the slate again, pointing to her previous message.

I should have never agreed to this.

A hand clamped down around Tayen's wrist. Einol's partner. His lips turned in a worried smile as he turned Tayen's wrist and placed a small burlap sack in her hand.

"No, I couldn't..."

The northman lightly touched Tayen's cheek to stop her before gesturing around at all the supplies that surrounded them.

"Thank you, Uncle. Take care of him."

The worry shed from his expression as he nodded with a smile.

A moment later, Sosun's and Tayen's footsteps bounced off the tunnel walls and they hurried towards the exit. Sosun turned this way and that. If Tayen took a full turn, there wouldn't have been time to map the structure of tunnels running through the mountain. Yet the servants memorized it all—they didn't have a choice.

Every few minutes, the alert bells rang a series of three strikes. Whether they were searching for Nix and Kaylo, or Sosun and Tayen, they hadn't found their target. The bells rang out clearer and clearer the farther they ran, as if their pursuers were closing in.

Light crept through the tunnel, but as much as her body ached for Sokan's light, the grounds also promised more violence.

As Pana's bloody body flashed in her mind, a quake ran through her.

They stopped at the jagged tunnel entrance. A strange quiet settled over the city in between the bell strikes. The recruits would all be locked away in their respective barracks while the warriors combed through the city.

Sokan had begun descending, lending a soft orange glow to the world.

Forty paces separated them from the surrounding city, with all the nooks and alleys it offered, but a great many things could happen in forty paces.

A shadow cloak would only call attention to them, a black cloud in the orange glow. But The Shadow existed in the push and pull of light and dark, not only at their most extremes.

The visage of The Shadow's elongated body danced in and out of solid form on the horizon, while The Song hummed through the air like a chorus of crickets. The low vibration occasionally jumped, then settled back into the subtle thrumming.

Shadows of all sizes and opacities covered the grounds of the city. They rested between buildings and under trees, walked with the warriors and moved with their firelight. The Song connected Tayen to every shade of darkness.

She reached her arms out and slowly turned the piece of her which touched the shadows of the city. Her back arched as she breathed into them, slowly. The bits of shade thickened. They spread and inflated with the breath from her lungs. She bent forward and placed her palms on her chest, then arched her back and filled the shadows more.

No one could move the sun, but Tayen could dim its light for a time.

Sosun looked out into the new dusk and back to Tayen. The light shifted gradually and softly, such that the transition had barely been noticeable. The orange light over the city turned amber. Sunlight passed through a haze of shadows before its dimmed light fell over Myanack.

Three more clangs of the bell pulled Tayen back from her meditation with The Song. She couldn't hold the shade forever, but they didn't need forever.

"We need to move, and we need to move fast," Tayen said.

She didn't wait for Sosun to nod. She simply ran into the gap between them and the first bit of shelter, an old wooden hut at the beginning of the outer city.

In the dimmed light, they stalked through the pathways and alleyways. Before every corner, Tayen paused, but as soon as she moved, she didn't dare question the decision.

Everything about this plan had been foolhardy. Only momentum could carry her through to the end.

At the next corner, Tayen waited. Two buildings to the south and one to the west, an old wood shop sat at the edge of town. If all went to plan, Nix and Kaylo would be waiting there.

Several footsteps and the flickering light of a torch crept through the next alley.

"Back up and head to the next building." Tayen pointed in the direction they had come from.

The constant pull of the shadows, the stress of mistwalking, and the weight of her second kill compounded each other, building unbearable pressure at the crown of her skull.

The light moved closer. Tayen reached for the last stone weighing down her robes.

The torch turned the corner, and Tayen threw the rock with all her strength. A hollow thud sang back to them as it collided with the building behind the light.

"A rock?" Nix's voice came from the other side of the flame. "Your plan was to throw a rock?"

The brightness of the torch softened. Kaylo and Nix stood there in purple robes and sannil guards with weapons hanging from their hips.

"Are you alright?" Kaylo stepped forward. "Did you do this?"

"I know you didn't want me to call The Shadow, but..."

"This is amazing, little shade." He swiveled back and forth. "Really, this—you did good. Are you both okay?"

Tayen slammed into Kaylo, wrapping her arms around him with all the strength she had left to her name.

CHAPTER THIRTY-FOUR
CURRENT DAY ENNEA

Each strike of the alarm bell grew dimmer than the last as Myanack fell from sight until the ringing became a phantom, following Kaylo and the others south.

Kana and Toka had taken over the sky as the four of them trudged towards the Lost Forest. Their pace aggravated Kaylo's bad knee, and he had barely had time to apply a clean-enough bit of fabric to the gash in his shoulder, but he couldn't stop. There was no safety to be had this side of the border.

Six Astilean warriors lay dead beside their severely injured commander. The army would never stop searching.

Even if the twisting in his gut promised escape, it offered little comfort. The stolen fragment of The Seed had forgotten its commitment to forgiveness long ago. After this many turns, Kaylo had grown accustomed to the pain, but this spirit sang The Seed's melody, even if slightly off key. And the sound of it ripped open old wounds.

By now, Kaylo had lived longer without The Song than he had with it.

The countryside rolled up and down in a series of subtle hills covered in waterlogged grass from the melting snow. The ground clung to their boots, filling the air with slapping leather and squishing mud.

It was a fine enough way to stave off the silence. After everything the day had brought him, talking seemed too burdensome—not that Tayen had much to say either.

Splashes of blood covered her robes. Blood, she insisted with the few words she had offered, didn't belong to her.

Three seasons, he thought.

In only three seasons, that girl had experienced a lifetime of troubles. And she had survived...with blood on her robes.

Pride, guilt, rage, sorrow—what was he supposed to feel?

Somehow, she had come to mean everything to him, and still, he couldn't shield her from the world. But he could get her to the other side of the forest. That much he could do.

Someone tugged on his robes, and he reached for the sword at his belt before easing his grip. "Sorry. I'm a bit jumpy."

"Just know, if you pulled that thing from its scabbard, I would have taken your arm." Nix smiled, but her grip remained on the hilt of her sword a moment longer than necessary.

"What do you want?"

"You need to talk to the girl," she said.

"I'm the last person she wants to speak with. If you haven't noticed, she blames me for all of this."

"You are even denser than she is. And you're too old to blame it on your age," Nix said. "Tayen loves you. That's the reason she blames you and gets angry with you. You're all she has, and that pisses her off. Can't say I blame her."

"What are you talking about?"

"Can you really be this naïve? On top of the fact that you saved her life, you're an infamous hero. You cared for her when she had no one. And for the last three moons, she tried to push you away while you stood by her. She's afraid to lose you, shit for brains."

Tayen's echo sung out like a beacon, even though her slight silhouette blended into the night.

"What if I let her down again?" he asked.

"I said my piece," Nix said. "Talk to her or keep walking up front, wearing your ass as a headscarf. It's up to you."

"People don't give you enough credit for your tenderness."

Nix slowed her pace without another word, rejoining Sosun.

In the distance, the Lost Forest rose from the ground like a massive black nothingness, outlined by a deep blue sky full of stars.

Between his three kanas, Kaylo had learned how to forest dance, spirit dance, wield a sword, and plan an attack. No one had taught him how to take care of a fifteen-turn-old. And he had done a remarkably shitty job thus far.

He slowed down, waiting for Tayen to catch up with him. Even as he settled in beside her, she kept her eyes aimed towards their destination. The pain of his knee grew sharper the longer he allowed the silence to sink in. At least, his awareness of it did.

"Tayen." He took a deep breath. "I owe you an apology. I promised to protect you, and I failed—several times. You have been through so much, and you deserve better."

Moonlight glinted off the tears covering her cheeks. She sniffed and shook her head. "No, you wouldn't say that if you knew what I did."

"You survived. You did what you had to."

"I killed him." She sniffled as the tears came harder. "I killed Pana."

The soft hum of the night sharpened into a screeching noise, though no one else heard it.

Pana had been a know-it-all, privileged little shit from the moment Kaylo had met him, but all the kid had wanted was to make his parents proud. The Lost Nation had taken that soft-hearted boy and convinced him to follow a violent path. And they had used Kaylo to do it.

"I didn't want to, but he found me in Wal's quarters, freeing Sosun, and he stole The Shadow, and then..."

"Stop," Kaylo said.

"But I didn't have a choice. I had to..."

He placed a hand on her shoulder. "Stop. I don't need to hear the story to know that you did what you had to. No matter how much you talk about vengeance, you have a caring spirit. The kind of spirit that could see a man in ragged robes and look beyond his faults," he said. "You don't have to explain yourself to me because I already know who you are."

She crashed into his arms, forcing him to anchor himself with his back foot lest they both tumble to the muddy ground. It didn't matter if his knee throbbed. He wrapped her in his arms and held onto her as if she were the only other person in the world.

"I'm sorry. I'm so sorry." She sobbed into his shoulder.

"This pain will fade. You will outlast it, and I will be there for all of it. No matter what."

Nothing apart from the downward slope of a hill and another hundred paces stood between Kaylo and escape into the Lost Forest. And yet, that too had to be a challenge to overcome.

A roaring flame burned away the impending twilight from atop the outpost. It may as well have been a mirror image of the two others before it, a pair of warriors standing watch beside the signal flame, bows at the ready.

"Told you." Nix lay on her stomach next to Kaylo on the crest of the hill.

Just once, it would have been nice to be the stronger force.

The Astilean countryside spread out in a series of long, cresting hills. For two days, they had avoided the horseback patrols, always with an eye searching the horizon, but the longer they lingered, the thinner their luck would run.

If the spirits allowed them to crawl out from under the weight of this sick kingdom, Kaylo would have to adjust his prayers—maybe pull back on the curses.

"I never said you were wrong," Kaylo said.

"No, but you insisted we check another outpost. Again." Nix turned over and sat up to massage the muscle around her wound. "What don't you get about the fact that I have a busted leg?"

"Do you need another poultice?"

"No, I need you to stop running us all over the fucking countryside," she said. "There isn't an easier path."

"You're such a pleasant travel companion."

Nix stopped tending to her thigh and held Kaylo's gaze for a moment before speaking. "If you get that girl killed because of your indecisive bullshit, you will see how unpleasant I can be."

"Keep your threats to yourself. What are you going to do, limp after me?"

"Really? I've seen how you avoid your left knee. Don't try to be cute." She lay back down against the curve of the land. "When the girls get back, we are moving."

If all went well, Tayen and Sosun would return from scouting when the twilight fell to true night. Until then, Kaylo studied the two bastards flanking the signal fire.

No more blood needed to spill. They could pass like a shadow in the dark.

One guard settled on the edge of the roof, dangling her feet below her as her bow rested beside her. Whether this woman had joined the war effort of her own volition or been dragged into it like so many others, she didn't deserve to die for a greedy king. Countless Enneans already had.

Beyond the outpost, bare stormwoods created a wall of black against the purple sky. Three moons had passed as Kaylo searched for a path to freedom, and here they stood on the precipice overlooking their final hurdle. He never took the time to consider what would follow.

She might leave, he thought.

Without an army and an impenetrable wall of trees to block her path, Tayen might charge into the world, searching for the blood she thought she owed. And he no longer had the power to stop her—if he had ever had it.

An echo stabbed at the silence in a string of harsh whistles, announcing Tayen's return.

She was early. Purple hues still clung to the sky.

The staccato notes grew stronger, cutting through the air at odd angles.

"Something's wrong." Kaylo rolled over towards the sound.

Nix and Kaylo searched the hills for the girls, but the darkening sky offered little help. Shades of dark purple slipped into deeper shades of black. If not for the echo and the last slivers of daylight, the patch of thick darkness running through the field would have blended into its surroundings.

"There." Kaylo pointed out the aberration.

"Do you see any purple uniforms?"

Nothing apart from Tayen's echo challenged the silence. No one else broke the sea of near-darkness. For all appearances, the land had settled in preparation for the night.

"Keep an eye to the west," Kaylo said as he looked over the eastern landscape.

The waiting stretched, as did all moments in anticipation of bad news. For now, they were safe, but in a handful of breaths, when Tayen returned with whatever warning had chased them from their post, their lives would be all the more fragile.

The compact fog rolled up the hill against its nature, its blackness absolute.

Less than a turn past, Tayen hadn't been able to sow the shadows together as she stood flat on her feet in the safety of the hallow. Whatever lay in wait for them on the other side of the Lost Forest, she had become a true shadow dancer.

Of everything he had done with his calamity of a life, the small hand he'd had in guiding Tayen would mark the best of his legacy.

Shadows broke away from the rear of the thick fog first. They peeled off and clambered back to their rightful place in the world, slowly revealing Tayen and Sosun beneath. The young dancer's arms folded in and out in sync with the rhythm of the echo, releasing each fragment of darkness from its duty.

"Well done, little shade," Kaylo said.

Even in the worst of moments, some things need to be spoken.

Confusion broke through Tayen's worry, followed by suspicion, only to settle in a small upward turn of her lips. "Thank you, but we don't have time," she said. "There is a patrol breaking west from the ocean headed this way. They'll be here before the sky goes black."

"We never should have listened to you," Nix said, as her hands danced through a series of gestures. "Always searching for a clearer path. This is it." She pointed towards the outpost below.

"Call The Shadow again," Kaylo said.

"Why? Are you going to take her from me?"

"We don't have time for this." Kaylo searched the western hills, and for now they remained empty.

"You saw what I can do," Tayen said. "If we need the shadows, I will guide them. Now tell me what your plan is."

"Less of a plan and more of a bad idea." He grabbed her by the wrist and pulled her to the crest of the hill. "I need you to spread the shadows thin like you did in Myanack. Drape them over us like a cloak, but just enough to obscure us."

"Why, when we could shut out the light completely?"

The signal fire burned tall and bright, stretching out into the night. "Pitch black clouds don't usually move against the firelight, especially before Sokan has fully left the sky. We just need to blend into the dusk as best as we can," he said. "A hundred paces, that's all we need."

Her echo stirred, a thrumming sound that oscillated between soft and jagged. Tayen spread her stance and beckoned the shadows. They swirled and stretched thin until their deep blacks faded and became a gentle fog encompassing all of them.

"You really have grown, you know that," Kaylo said.

Tayen rolled her eyes and looked away, but her cheeks rounded upward as she did so.

As they stalked down the sloping hill towards the forest no one could cross, the soft ground clung to their leather boots. Each break in the silence thumped in Kaylo's chest.

The guards atop the roof meandered about, looking over the hills in a general indifference. One warrior turned towards their thin cloud and continued his roaming search.

"Seed and Balance. This might work," Kaylo whispered to himself, but as the breath left his lungs, Sosun slipped in the mud, landing with a slap against the ground.

Everything stopped.

Tayen gently thickened the shadows, but not enough to clash with the surroundings.

Arrows notched and ready, the warriors' scanned their general vicinity for a target. The slightest movement would be enough to provoke them.

A few hurried dashes away, the forest waited for them. They could make it, but Sosun still lay on the ground to avoid making another sound.

As Nix's hand wrapped around her blade, Kaylo followed suit.

Blood still clashed with the gray of Tayen's robes. She didn't need more weight to burden her spirit.

"When the fighting starts, you and Sosun make your way to the edge of the forest," Kaylo whispered without taking his eyes off the warriors. "Don't go in."

"No, I'm going to fight with you."

"Just remember, don't go into the forest." Kaylo pulled both his purloined sword and his father's knife as quietly as he could.

The ground rumbled beneath them. The pattern solidified and grew louder as the first rider crested over the hill. One after another, warriors on horseback tore down the slope towards the outpost.

The archers shifted their sights towards the converging herd.

"Pick her up and move," Kaylo hissed.

Nix yanked Sosun to her feet, and they pushed as quickly as quiet would allow from one danger to the next as they stepped past the first stormwood giants of the Lost Forest.

With The Song—the true Song—Kaylo would have been able to map out their path through the forest without a whisper of hesitation. But the bastardized melody distorted his view like a flickering torch in a field of pure darkness.

Ideally, they would follow the maze as deep as the forest would allow, only removing their obstacles when absolutely necessary. Each collapsing tree dropped pieces of itself before crumbling into a cloud of dust and debris. In a forest with hidden archers, quieter was better.

Yet nothing about this escape had been ideal.

For the dozenth time, they approached a walled-off path. Whoever had come up with this sick and twisted idea—creating an impossible maze to defend the border—deserved to die as lost and afraid as irony would allow. At some point, a straight line through the forest had to be better than this roundabout path, even if it meant making more noise along the way.

Kaylo pressed his palm against another sacrificial tree.

The rings of its flesh told stories of changing seasons, harsh snowfalls, and droughts. Some of his previously felled victims lacked the abnormalities trees naturally developed with time, a sign they had been called forth by The Seed. This stormwood, however, had been here longer than Kaylo's brief life.

"I'm sorry, brethren." Kaylo pulled at The Song trapped in its core, and like the others before it, the stormwood aged, died, then collapsed into a pile of ash.

Everything about this was wrong.

They filed through the opening, and, as had become habit, Kaylo dropped to his knee to fill the gap with another stormwood.

"You could leave the openings," Nix said.

"And leave the Gousht a way through?"

Sosun's hands fluttered over her chest, but it was difficult to make out in the darkness.

"She either said, 'Fuck the Lost Nation,' or she's hungry," Nix said. "It's remarkable how similar those two are."

Kaylo rounded on Nix. "Would you shut up? There could be..."

Tayen screamed and fell to the ground.

An arrow sank into the dirt at Kaylo's feet.

"Move!" Nix yelled as she tackled Sosun to the ground, covering the young woman with her body.

The blood and darkness made it difficult to discern if the arrow had pierced Tayen in the chest or shoulder. She squirmed on the ground in shock, looking in every direction, yet focusing on very little.

After everything, it couldn't end this way.

Kaylo grabbed a fistful of Tayen's robes before dragging her into the shelter of two adjoining stormwoods. She whimpered, but held back her tears as he leaned her against the rough bark.

"You're going to be okay," Kaylo said.

"It hurts. Get it out. Please, I don't want to die."

"What now?" Nix said from not far off in the forest.

"Don't move. You're not going to die," Kaylo said, keeping the anger and fear from his voice as best as he could. "Nix, you take care of them."

As soon as he swung around the trees sheltering them, an arrow struck the stormwood to his left, forcing him to the ground. These bastards spent days in the dark prison of this forest. They obviously understood how to find less than visible targets.

Movement, he thought. *They'll follow movement.*

Several more arrows struck trees and dirt all around him as he ran. Some lodged into the dense wood, others fell to the ground.

The echo lent him a hazy understanding of his surroundings. Without it, he would have crashed into a tree or an arrow by now. He circled around and kept the unassailable giants between the archers and himself.

"Seed and Balance," he muttered.

An arrow sunk into the dirt immediately in front of him. If he had The Song, he would have been able to find the bastards. Instead, the trees cluttered into a cloud of indistinctive noise within the echo.

Ever since Kaylo had met Tayen, he had hesitated to take the next necessary step, and each hesitation had nearly killed them. No more hesitating. Tayen couldn't die.

He rolled from his purchase behind the tree, dug the toes of his boots into the dirt, and sprinted forward. Arrows pierced the air, crashing into the ground one after another. A bolt cut through his borrowed sannil armor before grazing his right shoulder. Another tore through the top of his left ear.

"Blessed Mother, let me save her."

The archers were stocked to hold back armies. They wouldn't run out of arrows soon.

Blood ran down the side of Kaylo's face.

The angle of the arrows sharpened, and there in the tree, an archer's perch wrapped around the trunk.

All Kaylo's usual empathy for the warriors of the Lost Nation had vanished with the sight of Tayen's blood. The caged spirit fed on his rage, and the broken Seed screamed. Bark dried with age. Dense wood turned brittle.

Dead archers don't loose arrows at young girls, he thought.

A bolt careened straight down and pierced his right hand with a white streak of pain. He toppled backwards with the force of it, and another arrow impaled the ground next to him.

It was only right that they fight for their lives. After all, that was what he aimed to take.

He rolled and crawled to his feet as the arrows fell like rain.

A spark of The Seed formed in the heart of every tree, waiting to rejoin the spirits. Kaylo dug his uninjured hand into the stormwood, and there he sang a matching melody. The echo swelled, then collapsed in on itself.

The first branch that fell shook Kaylo from his footing, sending him scrambling for cover as a series of snaps and cracks sounded in the highest reaches of the tree. Then a trio of competing screams displaced the chaos until the silence returned abruptly.

A cloud of debris and dirt billowed into the air like it had done so often before. However, this time, an odd collection of appendages jutted out from under broken planks and cracked branches, simply too old to hold the weight.

The bolt that pierced Kaylo's hand lingered in the wound, and Tayen lay somewhere bleeding, but he couldn't pull himself away from the sight.

The few identifiable pieces of the warriors entwined with one another. Slats of wooden planks protruded from a battered torso, a leg folded improperly, and parts that shouldn't be outside the body rested amongst the rubble.

The world wobbled a little back and forth. His headache turned harsher, threatening to crack his skull open front to back. A moment ago, he had wanted this bloody mess.

The others remained huddled in a pack of trees, right where he had left them.

"Is she...?"

"She's alive and breathing, but she passed out. The bolt went through her shoulder," Nix said.

Kaylo sat down next to Nix and held his hand aloft, the arrow sticking through his palm. "Do you mind?"

Nix grasped the arrow with one hand and snapped off the tip with the other. Stable grip or not, the arrow shook when it snapped and a wave of pain tore through Kaylo.

"You know how to mix a poultice?"

"If I have the ingredients," Nix said.

Kaylo closed his eyes to search for moonlight hazel and barberry in the echo.

———

Tayen blinked, and pain lit up along with the world, twisting in her shoulder and diffusing into her chest. Light squeezed through the gaps in a collection of dark trees rising and curving into a dome as they crept higher.

It smelled of wet grass and sweat. Her tongue scraped the dry roof of her mouth.

The last time she had walked into The Mist, it hadn't felt like this. There hadn't been pain or discomfort. She hadn't felt anything at all. Maybe death worked differently.

She tried to speak, but the air scratched her throat, and she ended up coughing instead. Then one cough turned into a clattering of coughs, pulling her diaphragm taut with each expulsion of air, which in turn, pulled at the wound in her shoulder.

Kaylo leaned over her; his face brushed in the shadows of the tree, a poultice covering one of his ears.

Did we all die?

She spasmed with another dry cough.

"You're going to be okay," Kaylo whispered as he tipped a waterskin to her mouth.

The gentle touch of the water dribbled over her lips. She wanted more. She could drink the Sanine River and still need more. The droplets of water only teased her sandy throat.

"Slowly," he said, and she acquiesced, allowing the muscles in her neck to loosen as she rested back against the ground.

If they weren't dead, where were they? How long had she slept?

The bark of the surrounding trees was too light to be stormwood.

Ironoak, maybe.

Kaylo removed the waterskin from her lips and then pulled the fabric of her robe past her shoulder. "No infection, but you should keep it still for at least a span. You won't be training with your right arm for at least another moon."

His fingers prodded the flesh around her wound. Each touch sent another jolt of pain through her body. She ground her teeth to keep from crying out. Then the wound cooled as he applied an additional layer of his poultice.

The smell crinkled her nose, but at least the burning sensation subsided.

"Where?" Even the single word slid from her mouth like a dual-edged blade.

"We are about a day south of the Lost Forest." He went to wipe his forehead with his hand, but it was wrapped in a strip of fabric. He dropped it back to his side. "Nix and Sosun are sleeping. They are alright. Although Nix hasn't stopped complaining about her back after carrying you for the last day and a half."

She chuckled, and the burning pain tore through the cooling poultice.

"Sorry, I forget how hilarious I am. It's a curse." Even as he smiled, the concern never left his eyes. "You should get some more rest."

Nothing in her wanted to rest. If not for the pain, she would rather run through the woods and dive into the nearest body of water. She had been asleep for days and it felt like it.

"No," she said. "I'm not tired."

"Your body needs..."

"I've had enough of my dreams. Tell me about Oakheart."

His brows turned in as he shook his head. "Another time. That's not important now."

"We had a deal," she said. "You owe me a story."

He chuckled. "That we did. That we did."

CHAPTER THIRTY-FIVE
KAYLO'S STORY

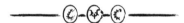

HAD I TURNED WEST instead of east, following Liara instead of the promise of blood, Zusa might have lived. At the very least, I wouldn't have woken up with a crick in my neck and my wrists lashed to a cart.

Hopefully, Liara had been smart enough to find her sister and run far from that place. That hope had to be enough.

Light's first breath spread out into the night sky in shades of orange, casting away the darkness. If I could believe the soldiers, I wouldn't see Sokan rise again.

None of them stayed their tongues around me. They made a game out of trying to make me squirm, and when I didn't give them the satisfaction, they found other ways to make me break. By the fifth day, the edge of one bruise faded as the next began.

By the time the First Daughter fell from the sky, our caravan would arrive at the god caves—the Anilace mines—where The Thief had led the priests to their salvation. Since then, the couta had discovered several other caches of crystals buried in the mountains, but none of those mines carried the same history.

Since I was old enough to understand, nothing had scared me more than being sent to the mines. Serving the Gousht without end. Ceasing to be a person. Becoming a tool.

Now, they would bury me where The Thief had gifted them Ennea.

There had been prettier sunrises, but the way streaks of pink wove through the gradient of orange just over the snow-capped mountains made me smile. The sky looked like a burned offering.

Eventually, The Priest would come to understand I didn't have the information he wanted. When that happened, his curiosity regarding my connection to The Thief wouldn't keep me alive.

I had until that point to find an opportunity. Not to survive. That chance had died with Zusa, but I didn't have to walk into The Mist alone.

People like The Priest assumed their control over the world and forgot they had to sleep next to the rest of us. The first time he dropped his guard, I would be waiting.

"Fuck you, couta prick!" Boda's voice cut through my violent imaginings. Apparently, he needed more time to accept our fate.

Even after five days of traveling with his life dangled in front of me like a threat, I hadn't seen the boy. They kept him stowed away in a covered wagon under constant guard. But I didn't have to see Boda to know he was there. He filled the waking hours with obscenities. If the soldiers understood half the things he said, he would probably be dead, regardless of whatever orders The Priest had given.

Accidents happened.

His morning profanity stirred the camp like the ringing of Gousht prayer bells. Those soldiers who weren't on guard woke and meandered around the circled caravan, seeing to their duties.

They washed their pale faces, set pots to cook over firepits, and tended their horses. Without their green and yellow padded armor, and that stupid seal stitched into the shoulders, they may have resembled something close to human.

Five stolen spirits moved through the camp as one. The Priest might as well have thrown a bell around his neck. As I turned to meet him with a show of defiance, the stitches pulled taut over my shoulder wound, turning my stone glare into a grimace.

He placed a bowl of boiled oats on the cart next to me. "I trust you slept well, young thief."

"I'm going to kill you." As I threatened him, I stared into his red veil. "When I do, you will deserve every last fragment of pain that you experience."

He wrapped his knuckles against the ironoak cart. "Fragment? What is this word?" he asked whenever he found a gap in his vocabulary. "No mind. Your bravado will not see you through this. You will comply. Sooner or later, your threats will become pleas."

I spat on the hem of his robe, and the globule streaked down the fabric.

"I think you would have made a good Gousht. Pride can drive people to great deeds," he said. "Eat up. You'll need your strength."

As he walked away, he barked orders at the soldiers he passed, each of whom moved with a sense of immediacy as soon as he addressed them. Every priest could draw their blood back to the Emperor, but that didn't account for the soldiers' fear. The priest back in Nomar didn't elicit that type of response from his soldiers.

They'll be shocked when they find me covered in his blood, I thought, then scraped my spoon through the oats. He had been right about one thing. I would need my strength.

A doubled wall of ironoaks ran from the base of the mountain to the compound gate, a set of metal doors that must have taken two dozen strong backs to set into place. Lucky for the Gousht, they had as many working hands as they ensnared.

A pair of guard towers rose over the wall, where archers watched the caravan with their bows drawn. They only lowered their weapons after The Priest passed something through an opening in the gate.

The gate's hinges creaked, but the screech of the metal paled beside the screaming cache of echoes within the compound. If my bindings hadn't been pulling me at pace with the cart, I would have crumpled to my knees. As it was, I had to lean on the cart bed to keep myself upright, my head throbbing with the tormented cries of hundreds of stolen spirits.

I set my barriers to The Song and its counterfeit offshoots as steadfastly as I could, but I could just as likely stop the wind with a net.

Hundreds of my people moved about the compound grounds in ragged clothing, surrounded by young, pale-faced soldiers watching their every move. People from every nation filed into several openings at the mountain's base. Their bodies ran thin with hunger and their skin had turned sallow.

A Tomakan girl, no more than fourteen, emerged from the mines covered in soot and debris. Her youth stood out. The work had whittled her arms down to bone and muscle, which made her all the smaller compared to the others. As she pushed a cart filled with pieces of the mountain, the soft echo of The Thief sang from the stones in her cart. She stumbled, but caught herself, and rolled the cart under a leather canopy where older Enneans chipped away the superfluous bits of stone from a pile of rocks.

Her load tumbled out of her upended cart, adding to the collection under the canopy. Once she righted the cart, she stopped to wipe the sweat from her brow.

Blood passing how it did, we could have been family.

A soldier grabbed her cart and shook it as his voice pitched into the air. This far away, his body language spoke in place of his words. His arms flailed towards the hungry mouths at the base of the mountain. Then she met his eyes. And that was enough. The soldier cracked the back of his hand across her cheek, sending her to the dirt.

I lunged towards the scene, but the ropes yanked me back into place.

None of the Enneans surrounding the young girl stopped their work. Few even lifted their heads.

The girl who could have been my kin stumbled twice before she could pick herself up. The soldier waited with his hand on his sword hilt, but she tucked her chin to her chest, put both hands on the cart, and pushed it back towards the mine.

Soldiers in Nomar had used the mines as a threat to keep us in line. The priest there liked to remind us how easy we had it living in the city, being taken care of by him and his soldiers. Their threats had turned my dreams into clashing nightmares of what the mines would truly hold, but no matter what I had imagined, the reality broke my spirit.

The Gousht had stolen more than our land or our connection to The Spirits.

Since the nations came to be and before, Enneans had worked this land, crafted art, created cultures centered on our connection to each and every spirit on either side of The Mist. We failed in our ideals time and time again, but we had much to be proud of. And despite all of that, they had strapped a yoke around our necks and turned us into beasts of burden who didn't look up when one of our own was struck down.

Before today, my anger had been a petty thing, concerned with a long list of personal grievances. As the caravan pulled me towards the stone compound across from the mines, a new anger was born.

This anger understood what I previously could not explain. The Gousht hadn't only taken my past and my future. They had taken away what it meant to be an Ennean. They wanted to erase our existence from The Waking and raise us like livestock. New children bringing the possibility of more spirits to steal, while the rest of us worked the land that used to be our own.

As we reached the stables, the caravan stopped, and the soldiers untethered the horses, passing them to a trio of northmen with their eyes lowered to the ground.

"Prick!" Boda's voice came from the wagon ahead, then he fell through the fabric covering the wagon-bed, landing flat on his back.

Life might have been less painful for Boda if he stopped cursing the soldiers, but he had never been one to give up. The right side of his face was swollen, dried blood collected in strains below his right ear, but he stood up like they had left him more or less intact.

Then he faced the mines, and all his fight shrank from him before a soldier pushed him towards the compound.

None of this was right, yet, in a way, it was my legacy. The Thief, my ancestor spirit, had allowed the Gousht to bind us in their service.

The rage of countless spirits washed over me.

A young soldier, with long silver-white hair sweeping over his shoulders, reached a knife forward to cut me loose from the cart. As soon as the binding broke, I wrenched free of his hold and slammed my elbow into his jaw.

I grabbed his knife from where it fell and ran towards the soldier beside Boda. Her eyes went wide as she froze in place, but before I could find a home in her chest for my new knife, a rather large soldier tackled me to the ground.

The soil had gone soft from the constant tread of horses, and it clung to my face. Heavy blows crashed in the back of my head. I tried to protect myself with my still-bound wrists. Dirt and blood lined my mouth and flooded into my lungs with every hurried breath.

Let this be it, I thought.

"That's enough," The Priest said in Gousht. *"I still have use for the boy. Take him and the other one to my study. And make sure their bindings are secure this time."*

Two soldiers grabbed me by either arm, lugging me towards the compound with my feet dragging behind me. The metallic taste of blood coated my tongue, and my heartbeat throbbed in my temples.

"I'll kill you all!" I yelled. *"I will kill you all!"*

———————————

Time lagged and sped up in odd spurts as the guards dragged me through the halls of the compound. Oil-lit sconces lined the stone and mortar walls of the immense building. Each time the soldiers swung around another corner, my head tossed about, and my stomach churned bile.

By the time we reached our destination, my insides were ready to splatter onto the floorboards with my breakfast.

I focused on a singular point in the room—a painting. The colors blurred into one another, either by design or as a consequence of the multiple blows I took to the head. Shades of gray and blue took shape, forming a castle built into a mountain just below the snow. The center spire of the castle had been sculpted out of the mountain itself. Dark shadows accented the colors and collected in a deep black towards the lower right-hand corner of the painting.

Denanla san Terriac. The Center of the World.

One of the first lessons they had taught us in our schooling back in Nomar explained how the twelve sons of the One True God set out to build their new country. They started by taking the fortress that no army had conquered, a castle built into the face of a mountain. The winding path that led to the great gates slowed every army, laying them out as easy targets for the archers on the fortress walls. But the twelve sons didn't raise an army or charge the gates. They took the castle from within its walls with subterfuge and manipulations.

Of course, that wasn't how they taught us the story, but the truth lay in the unspoken words.

Once they liberated the castle, they renamed it '*The Center of the World,*' like the arrogant pricks they were.

Somehow this painting made the Emperor more real, not just a story of a man sitting on a throne on the other side of the ocean. The castle had walls with perches for archers and stone towers jutting into the night.

The soldiers left Boda and me with our feet tied to the legs of our chairs and arms tied behind the chair backs.

"That was stupid," Boda said from his chair on the other side of the room. "Why is it that people think they have to stand up for me? It hasn't done any of you any good."

"You saw the mines, didn't you?" I asked, still staring at the painting. "Those are our people out there being beaten and worked to death, all to dig some stupid crystals from the base of a mountain."

"Why don't they just use The Mountain to mine the crystals?" The anger softened in his voice.

"Something about the crystals isn't natural. Earth dancers can't find them or move them with The Song. Damn sure can't break them. The Mountain can't do much more than clear the stone from crystals once they're pulled from the earth. And it's not like they're going to give slaves that kind of power."

"Are we going to end up like them?" Boda asked. "I would rather die than live like that."

"I'll get you out of here, I swear."

"How?!" Boda's anger returned sharper than it had been. "If you haven't noticed, you're tied to a chair in the middle of a Gousht compound flooded with soldiers."

His shoulders rose and fell with each heavy breath. Fine red hairs had grown from his shaved head after several days without a blade. His cheeks went taught as he bit down his fury. "No. I don't want your help. My brother trusted you, then you went off and got him killed.

"Zusa wanted to run, but you stayed to fight. Now, look where he is. Lost to The Mist too." Tears ran down Boda's face. "He died saving me. Why? Why did he do that? He hit and criticized me every day since I met him.

"I hated him. He knew I hated him. So why did he die for me? Why?!" Boda's head fell forward as he sobbed, unable to wipe away the tears with his bound hands.

"I'm sorry Boda," I said. "I'm sorry for it all."

His stuttered breaths and sniffled cries reverberated in the small chamber.

After almost a year, we had not spoken this much—not this honestly.

I had no words to soothe his pain and, bound to a chair across the room, words were all I had. So, I gave him the space to cry and said nothing.

Hours passed in the windowless chamber while neither Boda nor I said a word. When his tears ran their course, a heavy silence filled the space between us.

As soon as The Priest decided he didn't need the boy to threaten me, the Gousht would either kill him or send him into the mines. For his sake, I hoped they would kill him.

Light from the oil lamp on a table by the door faded, not that it made a difference. I had finished studying every corner of the chamber hours ago. The near-barren room left little to entice the imagination. Apart from the painting of *Denanla san Terriac*, the walls were nothing but stone and mortar.

To Boda's right, a desk fit into the corner, nearly empty itself. A lone, half-burned wax candle waited on a silver tray, a set of Gousht books settled on a shelf above the desktop, and a dried ink stain marred the pretty finish. I tried to read the titles of the books on the shelf, but my comprehension of their written word had always lagged far behind my spoken grasp of their ugly language.

So, when the oil lamp puttered out, I resigned myself to sleeping upright with my hands tied around the other side of the chair back. The position made my shoulder wound ache, but everything ached anyway.

Then, as if he had been waiting for the light to go out on us, The Priest pushed open the door, allowing light to creep in from the hallway.

"Oh no, I didn't wake you, did I?" His voice retained its usual deep timbre, but there was a playfulness in his tone. "I would never want to play a poor host."

"Fuck you!" Boda yelled at The Priest.

"Speak again, and I will remove a finger," The Priest said with a sharpness, then placed a fresh oil lamp next to the other. "Understood?"

he asked, though he didn't wait for an answer.

"This room serves as my study when I need to settle down in one place." His voice settled back into the lighter tone. "After our time in the mission school, I have been dreadfully busy. You see, my soldiers and I serve as problem solvers of a sort. And when I heard of a thief making trouble with our cargo runs, I had to find out if you had something to do with it. Little thief, I am very pleased to see you again."

He left a silence between us as if my turn to speak had come, but I had nothing to say to the vile man, unless it involved me and my father's knife.

"If you wish to remain stoic for tonight, I will not begrudge you this small freedom," He stepped further into the room, letting the door close behind him.

His crystals hung from his neck like shiny temptations. The things I could do with a single spirit and time.

"In the coming days, I will have questions, and you will answer them, or I will hurt you and then you will answer them. Please don't take that as a threat, little thief. I don't threaten. It's crass. But you have information I need, and I will take it from you if you make me."

Boda's nostrils flared, and his eyes narrowed, but he didn't say a word.

The Priest's robes dragged along the wooden floorboards as he walked to his desk and pulled the chair into the middle of the room, sitting between Boda and I. "But tonight, I have a story for you about the nature of power. I assume you know something about the Empire's command structure, yes? You know what these robes mean, don't you?"

He paused again, as if this were any other conversation.

"Well, the short version is that all priests are blood-bound to the Emperor—we are his brothers, uncles, cousins—and we lead his church as well as his armies." He coughed and cleared his throat. "You must also know that the Emperor is the youngest son in a line of youngest sons going back to the children of The One True God, yes?

"I hate to be redundant, so please let me know if you've heard this before."

Despite my dry throat, I gathered what saliva I had and spat on the floorboards at the mention of his god.

"Don't be rude." His tone cut sharply through the air. "I don't care what you believe, but you will listen. Nod to let me know you understand."

I stared at him and held my head as level as I could.

The Priest shifted in his chair, raised his fist in the air, and brought it down on Boda's thigh. Boda moaned and gritted his bared teeth. Then The Priest angled his veiled face back towards me, and I nodded.

"Good, back to it," he said. "The previous emperor, Erdart II, was my father. In fact, I was his youngest son, groomed for the throne since birth. You didn't know that, did you? My whole life I prepared to lead my people, as a direct descendant of The One True God himself."

He stood up and walked towards the painting on the wall.

"I studied warfare and politics, combat and oration. When I came of age, I led campaigns to the south of Gousht." The final consonant ticked off the stone, reverberating through the chamber. "Where we fought, the land of our country expanded."

He turned back to face me, though the veil stood between us. "Then my father's whore conceived a son. After that, everything changed. When your line of succession is based on God's will, there is no question. My baby brother was to become emperor." His voice slowed and turned hollow. "I was sixteen when I learned the true nature of power.

"As long as there is someone with more power than you, your power means nothing. No matter how tightly you grasp it, your power can be taken away."

His robes bunched as he reached into a concealed pocket and drew out an empty spirit crystal. "Let me show you."

My breath caught in my chest, and my scream came out as a murmur. "No."

"Leave him alone!" Boda yelled, but The Priest ignored him and took a step closer.

I yanked against my bindings, and the chair teetered beneath me. As the Song roared from deep within the earth, I welcomed it. Even bound as I was, I pulled on The Seed. The floorboards cracked and folded back as an ironoak sproutling tore into the room, crashing into the ceiling above. Dust and debris snowed down from the heavy impact.

The Priest stepped around the impediment. "Impressive," he said. "As hopeless as your situation is, you still fight. I admire that."

He extended the crystal towards me. "I have been waiting for you to finish my collection."

My stomach turned cold, and the chill crawled outward from there. The Song screamed, oscillating between a blaring noise and nothingness.

"No, please don't."

"The lesson isn't over." The crystal glowed a faint green in his hand.

Something stirred in my gut as he held the tiny prison in front of me. The fragment of The Seed, the spirit that I had walked with as far as my memory went back, took clear form within me.

I had always felt The Seed's presence, but it had never been something separate from me until this moment. The edges of where The Seed's fragment ended and I began tore from each other.

It wasn't painful, only unnerving, as if feeling the organs of my body as something distinct and separate from the whole.

When I reached for The Song, it responded with the dullest edge of a whisper.

The image of The Seed walking through his collection of mismatched flora settled in my vision for an elongated moment before fading to nothingness.

When the last of The Seed leeched from my spirit, my flesh went numb. Tears fell and collected in wet patches on my dirty robes. The echoes remained, but they lacked The Song's foundation.

A deep green shined from the crystal onto my robes and the floorboards beneath my feet.

The Priest tucked my fragment of The Seed into his robes. "Don't worry, little thief. The first lesson is over."

"I'll kill you," I sobbed. "I will kill you."

"You're learning already," he said. "If you want power, you have to take it from someone."

The sound of his steps as he walked away repeated in my mind long after he left Boda and I tied to our chairs in the empty chamber.

CHAPTER THIRTY-SIX

KAYLO'S STORY

THE PRIEST DIDN'T BEAT me himself. He repeated his questions over and over as the portly, balding soldier with oversized hands, whom he called Kellan, did his work for him. The same soldier who had wounded my shoulder and wore my father's knife. It swung from his hip even as he beat me.

At first, Kellan used his fists. He worked around my body in an odd pattern. He slammed his fist down on my thigh like a hammer, punched me in the gut, then slapped his heavy hand over my shoulder wound.

Each unanswered question preceded another blow. When my body tried to fold in on itself, the chair refused me.

At some point, my stitches tore, creating a river of blood running down the sleeve of my robes. The part of my brain that shut off from the pain found it interesting how they had sewn my flesh together, only to rip it apart again.

Eventually, my blood became many rivers, and the questions fell muffled beneath the pain. But it didn't matter whether I heard the questions.

Kellan cracked me in the jaw with his heavy right hand, and the bones crunched when they collided.

Spots of black blinked in and out of my vision.

The bearded, bald bastard clutched his hand and yelled in pain before he threw himself on top of me. We crashed to the ground, even as I remained tied to a chair. He grabbed my braids and slammed my head into the floorboards until the world vanished.

I woke up staring down at a puddle of my blood pooling on the floorboards and seeping through the cracks. The chair had been turned upright and the entirety of my face throbbed like pulsing fire.

My abuser glared down at me like I had crossed a line. He cradled his bandaged hand with his uninjured one.

Kellan showed off his crooked teeth as he broke off a stick from the sproutling growing in the middle of the room—the last thing I had called from The Song.

The questioning continued.

I moaned. I screamed. I cried out. But I never said a word.

Pain tied the days together in a collection of half-memories.

———————

"You have to tell them something." Boda's voice pitched, high and whining. All of his forced bravado had abandoned him.

A weight held my right eyelid shut, no matter how I tried to open it.

The room shifted on an ever-changing axis, but my tree centered me. It hadn't grown properly in my rush to call it forth. Knots and divots covered the winding trunk as it split in two before crashing into the stone above. Kellan had broken off most of the strangling branches that had grown, leaving gaps in the tree.

It deserved a better life than the one I had given it, living only to die in a windowless room.

A series of slight pains screeched through my flesh. When I tried to breathe through my nose, I fell into a coughing fit.

"Please, tell them something."

"It doesn't matter." My voice tore through my dry throat, but the irritation meant nothing amongst the pains scattered throughout my body. "I'm dead already."

"You don't know that," Boda said.

"Your brother was a good man, and he died trying to save me. It would have been better if he survived instead. Don't make the same mistake."

"Don't do that." The earlier shrill in his voice left. "Not now."

"There won't be another time, Boda."

"No, we can find a way out. You're a thief, right? Can't you do something?"

Echoes sang all around me. They rang out through the floorboards and beat against the stone. The mine thrummed with The Thief's hidden echo. And for all of that, I couldn't do a damn thing. The Mother help me, I could only listen as the twisted version of The Song taunted me.

"Even if my hands weren't tied behind me, someone would have to reach for a spirit for me to borrow it. And The Priest is too smart to let that happen."

Talking about The Song made the emptiness in my spirit sing even louder. I would die with part of me trapped in The Waking.

Even when I had blocked out The Song in Nomar, it had cut through my barriers occasionally. Its hesitant sound would reach for me, and I knew if I reached back, I could have danced in the pull of The Song.

This silence was different.

"No, Boda. I'm done," I said. The Gousht had taken three families from me, then they had taken The Song. Whatever scraps remained, they could have.

"That's stupid. You are breathing. My brother isn't. You have to..."

The floorboards creaked on the other side of the door before it swung open. "Just be quiet," I said.

"The guards posted at your door said that they heard voices." The

Priest walked in followed by his shiny-headed enforcer. "That's great. I'm glad you're in a talking mood."

All my fears had found a way to come true, and as The Priest stood, outlined by the light from the hallway, I realized I had failed in my vengeance as well.

"Save us all the time and kill me, Priest. I'm not going to answer your questions."

"Oh, my boy, no. You will die, but only when I say. Until then, you are mine. I thought I had taught you enough about how power works for you to realize you have none. You can't even die without my permission." The Priest walked over to me. The sound of his boots against the wooden floorboards rebounded off the stone walls. He lifted my chin to meet his veiled face. "This time we will try something new."

He tilted my head to the side until my eyes focused on Boda.

"No." My voice came out as a hollow whisper.

"You see, I have plans that don't involve you, but before I can leave, I need you to answer my questions," The Priest said.

The wood creaked beneath Kellan as he walked over to Boda. My father's knife hung from his belt and caught the light. The brute dragged Boda and his chair flat against the opposite wall.

"Fuck you!" Boda screamed at Kellan, and the soldier smacked him with the back of his weighty hand.

"Shut your mouth, insect." Kellan said with a low grunt.

"Tell me what I want to know, and you can die. The boy, he can work in the mines with the rest of your kind," The Priest whispered into my ear.

The bald bastard ran his hands over my tree, searching for the few remaining sticks for something to beat Boda with. Each time he stopped to assess a branch, he looked over at me to show me his jagged smile.

"Tell me everything you know about the Missing. Where are their camps? What are they after? Where did they take my stones?" The Priest asked. "You can save this boy all the pain you suffered."

I tried to turn away, but The Priest's hand held my chin while his other hand grabbed the back of my head.

"I don't know anything."

"We will see." The Priest spoke into my ear.

Kellan reared back with a slender, undergrown ironoak branch and slammed it into Boda's shin like he was chopping down a tree close to the root. Boda screamed in pain.

"You couta son of a whore!" Boda spat at the soldier.

The soldier aimed his instrument higher, and the wood crashed into Boda's shoulder. Then he pulled back and swung the ironoak into Boda's stomach, and the boy buckled as far as his bindings would allow, coughing.

"You have to know something. I don't think this boy can withstand the punishment like you can." The Priest said his words casually.

"The Missing isn't real," I said, my words falling out of me.

"Explain," The Priest said, and when I didn't say more, he waved to the soldier.

Kellan raised the branch over his head. "No!" I screamed.

"*Wait,*" The Priest said. Kellan's lips folded into a frown as he restrained himself. "Explain, little thief."

"The Lost Nation needed to keep an eye on this side of the Lost Forest, so they made up the Missing. All we did was collect information and weapons for the Lost Nation," I said. "They used us."

"You don't think I knew that?" The Priest asked. "I have broken plenty of little whelps like you and your friend over there. What I need to know is, where are the other camps? Where are they hording my crystals before they take them back to the Lost Nation?"

"I don't know."

He started to wave at the soldier.

"I don't know!" I screamed. "You have to believe me."

The Priest patted me on the shoulder. "I do, my boy. I do." Then he waved his hand.

Kellan brought the length of ironoak across Boda's face with all of his might. A loud snap pierced through my screams, and Boda crashed down to the floor, still tied to his chair. Blood gushed from a wound on the side of his face.

"You see, little thief. Everything, every single thing, is about power." His hand still rested on my shoulder as he spoke. "And the only thing you can do to make sure no one takes your power from you is to have more than them.

"What you never understood was, I don't care if you call The One, The Thief. I don't even care if they are the same deity. It doesn't matter. Belief doesn't win wars. Knowing how to use other people's belief does. I thought you were smart enough to understand that."

Kellan tossed his broken branch into the corner before clapping the dirt from his hands.

"When we are done with this land, the truth will be what we say it is." The Priest leaned in. "With enough time, even your people will believe it."

The Priest walked to the door, turning to Kellan. *"If the boy survives the night, give him to the mines. Kill the thief in the morning but make it public. Let the slaves watch him die. Then ride with the supplies after you're finished. I'll have plenty of work for you in the east."*

Kellan smiled like a giddy boy, following his master to the door.

"Goodbye, little thief." The door shut behind them, and The Priest was gone.

"Boda." My tears stung the wounds on my face. "Get up. You have to get up."

I struggled against my bindings, but my legs remained firmly lashed to the chair and my hands behind the chair back. Even if I had all my strength, I couldn't have broken through the ropes, not like this.

"Kid, you can't let them win. You have to fight."

He lay with his face pressed against the ground, still bound to the chair, blood painting his dark skin.

"Guards! Guards! You have to help him!"

Four walls of stone surrounded us. The only thing in the room besides the lamp was my tree—my last connection to The Song and the unwilling participant in my torture.

Kellan had broken off nearly every branch that the adolescent tree had sprouted. The wrapped trunk jutted into branches that broke off in jagged ends.

That coulta fuck left us a chance, I thought.

It took all my will and wit to slide myself over to the tree as slowly as I could, and still the legs of the chair scraped the floorboards with every push.

If the guards discovered me, my chance would be forfeit. I couldn't escape. I couldn't free Boda, but I could try to keep him alive.

The minutes stretched as I moved closer and closer until my chair back hit the tree. My vision wobbled with every small exertion. Too much of my blood had soaked into the floorboards.

Propped on my toes, I pushed my hands back towards the lowest bit of jagged wood.

Every time I pushed myself against the broken branch and let myself fall, the tendons in my ankle threatened to snap. But the past several days had adjusted my tolerance for pain.

"To the first, The Shadow, with all your wisdom, it seems like you could really do something to figure this shit out down here."

As I sawed at the rope, the jagged edge bit into my hand for the dozenth time.

"To the second and third, the twins, The River and The Flame, I think we have been patient enough, don't you? It's about time we saw your strength."

The rope dug deeper into my wrists like it would cut clean through my flesh before the tree cut through it.

"To the fourth, The Mountain, why don't you collapse these fucking mines?" I asked. "To the fifth, The Wind, we could definitely use some fucking guidance."

My breath caught in my throat, and I kept coughing.

"To the sixth, The Seed, I tried." I gritted my teeth. "And to the fucking seventh, The Thief, the cruel malitu that started all of this, fuck you."

Pushing harder against the broken branch, I sawed at the rope faster.

When the last strand of the rope severed, I crashed to the ground—freer than I had been a moment ago, but still trapped in my pain with another boy bleeding onto the floorboards. After I worked my legs from their bindings, I crawled over to Boda.

The pool of blood had turned the wood beneath him into a sticky mess. I placed my hand in front of his mouth, and a soft puff of air brushed over my skin.

"Boda." Tears ran down my face as I untied his bindings. "Hang on, I'm here. It will be okay."

He fell dead weight to the ground. I removed my robe before ripping off the few pieces not covered in blood into bandages. The gash in his face tore through the skin from the corner of his left eye to just below his temple. His blood turned the strips of fabric burgundy before I could even tie them in place, but I cinched them tight all the same.

When I had bandaged what I could, I sat with my naked back against the cold stone and laid his head on my lap. The blood continued to seep into the fabric at an alarming rate as I kept pressure against the wound.

"You're going to survive this," I said. "You're too stubborn not to."

I ran my hand over the new growth on his head and sang softly.

Even when the night is cold
There's always a way home
Stars hidden by the clouds above
There's always a way home
Body is weary and bones are old
There's always a way home
Long days missing those you love
There's always a way home
Just follow the river, follow the river
Follow the river home

CHAPTER THIRTY-SEVEN

KAYLO'S STORY

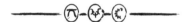

BODA'S CHEST BARELY MOVED, but light exhalations ran over the back of my hand every time I checked if he had spirited on. A film of sweat formed over his forehead as I cradled him in my lap and held the bloody strips of my robe to the wound. The collapsed bone near his eye transformed the shape of his face.

Another victim, I thought. *At least, when they execute me in the morning, I won't be able to hurt anyone else.*

If I had The Seed with me, I could grind together a poultice and clean his wounds properly. As it was, I did all I could to keep his blood in his body.

"I remember when we first met," I said. "Do you?"

Boda puffed out another shallow breath.

"You wore those waves in your hair like a spiral crown." I sniffled to keep my nose from running. "To be honest, it never fit your head right. I mean, I get that you wore those waves for different reasons, but this fits you better."

The new growth tickled my palm as I stroked his scalp. "We have to clean you up a bit. A fresh shave and you'll be back, getting on my nerves and trying to fight the world.

"Oh, Boda. You never had anything to prove. At thirteen, I didn't have

half the skill you do with a blade. Zusa only gave you grief because you
could be great. That asshole didn't know how else to push you."

No sniffling could stop the deluge of tears running down my face.
"Boda, I need you to make it through this. I need you to survive. Too
many of my people have crossed over. And you are my people, as much
as you might deny it."

Cold seeped into my bare back as I leaned against the stone.

In a sea of a thousand echoes, they all stood too far out of my reach.
No one called for a single spirit. The Priest had seen to that. And now he
had left. Off to lord his power over someone else.

And he would carry a piece of me with him as he did.

Here, in this evil place, surrounded by suffering, the echoes knit
themselves together like a patchwork. The bastard songs filled in each
other's gaps and became the nearest reflection to The Song as I had ever
heard. The ground stirred with it. It drifted through the wind and the
fires throughout the compound. Shadows served as a foundation for the
clattering orchestra of tortured spirits.

I closed my eyes, allowing the echoes to wash over me. Either
because of the combination of blood loss and head injuries or the act of
surrender, I fell into a dark, dreamless sleep.

A thud on the door of our makeshift cell jerked me awake. A man
screamed. Metal clanged against stone, then rattled against the wooden
floor.

"Boda!" I shook his shoulder. "Get up. Get up now."

But the boy didn't move. His head lay still on my lap.

The door shook as something struck it from the other side. It shook
again and again. The wood splintered, then the door broke from the
frame and flew inwards, splinters scattering as the door crashed against
the stone wall.

"Subtle," Sionia said from over Talise's shoulder. "We aren't supposed to draw attention."

"Did you see a key?" Talise stepped over a guard's body, which lay draped over the threshold of the room.

"What are you doing here?" I asked.

Talise tilted her head sideways, looking back and forth with her eyebrow cocked in confusion. "I thought that would be pretty obvious."

Sionia rushed past her to my side. "Is he alive?"

"For now." I brushed my hand over Boda's scalp. "Where are the others?"

"We need to get going," Talise said, her axe hanging in one hand as blood dripped from the blade. "As it is, we are already behind schedule."

"What schedule?" I demanded, then a series of explosions thundered in the distance.

"That's the cue," Sionia said. "Can you walk?"

"It already took too long to find you. That sentry gave shit directions. I should have made his death hurt more," Talise said.

This had to be a dream, some sad, wishful part of my mind playing a trick on me. Then Sionia placed her hand on my shoulder. "Can you walk?"

"Help me with him," I said.

My body rebelled against each movement. Cuts peeled open, bruised muscles stretched in pain, and every limb of my body resisted me, but I pushed myself up despite it all. Boda needed me to.

For as small as the boy was, it took all of my grit to lift him off the ground with Sionia. We wrapped his limp arms over our shoulders as we clutched him around the waist. Any one of the jarring movements could have woken him or worsened the injuries, though the latter carried more likelihood.

The tree—my last tangible connection to The Seed—spread out into the room far more than I had realized from my previous vantage points. It had provided the implements for our torture and given me the tools to shed my bindings.

I whispered an apology to the ironoak under my breath, then Sionia and I shuffled over the bloodstained floorboards towards the hall.

A dead soldier blocked our path, but he left his sword for me, so the inconvenience could be forgiven. The weight of his weapon nearly pulled me off balance as I bent to collect it while still propping Boda up. The Gousht had an affinity for ridiculously heavy swords, and in my state, it would only hinder me, but it felt good to have a weapon.

A second boom shook through the air. Wal and his damn firestarter explosions. They didn't have enough firestarter to take out the tree wall, much less the compound. It would take several turns to reduce that much oil.

"What's going on?" I asked.

"Do you want an explanation, or do you want to get out of here?" Talise didn't even turn around to ask her rhetorical question.

The corridor hadn't been built for three people to walk side-by-side, but we managed.

As the stone scraped against one of my shoulders, Boda's weight tore at the other. His feet dragged behind us and filled the hallway with a foreboding scratching noise.

They shouldn't have come for us. I didn't deserve it, and Boda wouldn't likely make it. If any of us had a chance to escape these walls, we needed the spirits walking in lockstep beside us.

As we turned a corner, two more soldiers lay slumped against the stone wall. If not for the puddles of blood and their stained uniforms, they would have appeared peaceful.

After everything they had taken, their bodies deserved to be painted with more pain.

Echoes surged into the air, followed by stone-muffled noises that may have been screams. As the ground shook beneath us, my knees nearly buckled. Whatever plan the others had conjured up, it had gone thoroughly cocked.

Talise looked back with a wide-eyed glare, then started rushing towards the end of the corridor without a word.

"Assuming that's not a part of the plan," I said.

"We need to find a place to keep Boda. Whatever is going on out there, he'll be safer in here." Sionia pulled forward.

"You never should have come."

Sionia paused to look at me. "Not a single one of us questioned it for a second. Now, help me find a safe place for Boda."

More echoes and battle noises traveled down the thin stone walkway. Liara and the others were out there, and time didn't permit me the indulgence of questioning their decisions. We rushed down the hall, Boda's limp body jostling between us.

My seizing muscles warmed with the movement. An hour ago, I knew I was going to die in the morning. Now, I might die tonight, but at least I could take some of the couta fucks with me.

Halfway down the hall, Sionia kicked open a door. It swung into a thin storage closet. Sacks of grain, jars of oil, and other supplies lined the shelves. We laid him down and propped his head up with a burlap sack of beans.

If things go poorly on the other side of these walls, Boda might outlive all of us, I thought.

"If you are too injured to fight, you should stay here too," Sionia said.

"Piss off." I gripped my stolen sword, stalking down the corridor after Talise.

The noises of battle grew stronger and stronger the closer I got to the end of the hallway. When I threw open the door, the tableau of the battlefield lay before me in calamitous beauty.

Fires climbed over the fog-laden grounds. The archer towers had become pyres, lighting the whole of the bloodshed symphony. Freed slaves wearing scraps of clothing, wielding stones and pilfered weapons, clashed with fully armed Gousht soldiers. Bodies lined the earth like stones. Enneans outnumbered the Gousht, but the soldiers had been trained to battle with the weapons they carried.

Another series of explosions from outside the tree wall jolted me from my stupor.

A screaming soldier bore down and charged me with a spear aimed at my heart, as I stood flat-footed and bare-chested in the cold night air. I lifted my sword too late.

Then a blur swept through the fog and collided with the soldier from the side.

A Sonacoan man screamed as he landed atop the soldier, raised a heavy stone above his head, and brought it crashing into the soldier's skull. He hit her until the sound turned wet. Then he ran off into the chaos with her spear in hand.

Arrows launched into the fog from atop the compound. Without their perches, the archers made do.

Silhouettes of bodies fell within the flame-softened fog.

All this death, over me? I thought. *It's too much.*

The Flame screamed alive in the air, and I silenced him. My body was already an amalgamation of various pains. I grabbed for one, then two, three, and four more spirits in quick succession. Their rage made the night's chill vanish. I fell to my knees, reaching for more.

Sionia clashed with a soldier to my right. Their swords locked and disengaged in a series of sharp tings. Then she slipped past his guard and sliced her blade across the bare skin of his throat.

"We need to move," Sionia said from behind me. "To the west wall."

She pulled me to my feet and led the way.

More and more Ennean bodies settled on the dirt the deeper we pushed into the battlefield. A heavily built soldier brought her axe across a Tomakan woman's chest, and I did nothing. I followed Sionia.

A new echo surged into the air, twisting and churning like an undertow at high tide. One thrusting pitch overtook another and spun them into a cycle, each fighting for position.

Liara.

Her echo built like a storm at sea. Then vanished.

"No!" I screamed as I charged towards where her echo had been.

Sionia called out for me, but I threw myself into the thick of the fighting.

Let them all die. The Gousht. The Enneans. But not her. Not for me.

Her echo stuttered to life, but it lacked the same fury as before.

A long-haired, pale-faced soldier moved to intercept me and drew his sword.

The Flame called to me with subtle ticks, like a knife striking flint. I thrust my right leg forward and swept the ground with my hand. Fire crawled along the dirt, growing larger and hotter, until it swallowed the soldier whole. His flailing corpse twisted in the blaze before collapsing.

Liara's echo tore into the sky louder than before. Something was missing. For almost a full turn, the echo of The River had never been without The Wind.

I rushed towards Liara, feeding my fear and anger to the pain.

There, through the fog, Liara crouched over Tomi's motionless body and a second Sonacoan woman as Adéan and two freed Enneans clashed with a squad of soldiers.

Adéan fought like a daemon. His long axe swept back and forth, keeping the soldiers out of striking distance, but the Gousht had the numbers.

I pulled on The Mountain, shaking the earth beneath the soldiers.

Adéan took advantage and drove the spike of his axe through the heart of one man, then dug it from his chest in time to bury the blade in a second soldier's gut.

The Wind lay in wait, a tornado of resentment and fury, ringing out in a series of low blaring noises. I reached for him, then pain tore through my knee, and I collapsed into a pile of injured body parts with an arrow sticking out from either side of the pain.

An archer notched another arrow from atop a shack near the mine entrance, then he turned and leveled his bow at my friends.

The arrow slowed as it soared through the air until the moment froze.

Adēan's axe waited, poised for an attack. A Tomakan man fighting beside
him faltered backwards with a spear embedded in his shoulder. Liara held
her sister in her arms and her gaze, as the person who meant the most
to her lay on the ground next to the caves where The Thief had given
the Gousht her gift.

How could this be balance? I thought.

Time rushed to catch up with itself. Adēan reeled backwards as the
arrow pierced his gut. As his guard dropped, another soldier thrust her
spear into his chest, and the big Renēquan toppled to the ground without
ceremony.

It wasn't possible. Adēan stood too tall and strong to fall like this.

The men fighting beside him rushed to meet the other soldiers, but
were cut down in an instant, leaving nothing standing between the
Gousht and Liara.

I had thought I lost everything when The Priest stole The Seed
from me and ordered my death. The world had turned hollow and
meaningless. But as I crouched on the ground, watching what would be
Liara's last breaths, I still had far too much to lose.

She stood with a sword in her hand to meet the five soldiers.

Of course, she wouldn't fade into The Mist without a fight.

In that moment, all my barriers against the world and the spirits that
dwelled within it broke. No amount of anger or stubbornness would save
her.

Whispers flittered all around me. They captured the night air like
fireflies. The noise layered upon itself until small vibrations formed a mass
large enough to overtake everything. Nothing else existed as thousands of
echoes all sang the same nearly inaudible song.

The Thief.

Her echoes called from deep into the earth, where the mines would
never reach, as well as from every corner of the battlefield.

When all the fragments of her joined together, the melody filled out
and became whole.

I reached into the air above me and grabbed hold of every last whisper. Then I pulled all the disparate pieces of The Thief into me.

As if they were each a piece of me, the countless cracking crystals sent shudders through my flesh. My body convulsed. The world flashed into darkness, then became a series of images.

Fires raged in a circle, encasing Liara, Tomi, and the unfamiliar woman beside them.

The archer notched another arrow.

The wind roared up and cast him to the ground a dozen paces away, his body twisting unnaturally.

The freed Sonacoan woman beside Liara danced with heavy movements.

The earth opened up to swallow a soldier.

Then darkness, and The Thief's raspy voice came.

"We've done it, my boy. We've finally done it."

CHAPTER THIRTY-EIGHT
KAYLO'S STORY

"KAYLO."

A voice without texture called to me in the darkness.

"Kaylo." It repeated my name. And each time, the shape of her voice gathered more of itself until her tone cut through the haze.

"Liara," I said with my eyes still closed.

"Kaylo, yes. Oh, Kaylo, you're back." She touched my cheek, and it stung, but not enough for me to want her to stop.

When I opened my eyes, we were back in the stone prison, only this time, I lay on a cot. Each breath brought another stinging pain, but the worst of it radiated from my knee. I reached down, but she caught my hand.

"You have to let it heal," Liara said.

She sat beside me in a chair. A few scrapes blemished her face, but it was her. I thought I had seen her for the last time.

"What happened?"

Her lips turned in a melancholy smile. She tipped a waterskin to my lips, and the water tasted better than a Shunanlah feast.

"I could ask you the same," she said. "When you did...whatever you did, all the crystals the soldiers carried broke into pieces, and the spirits escaped. Some of those spirits returned to the same Enneans being forced to mine the crystals.

"That turned the battle. With the spirits and the numbers on our side, we were able to take the compound." She reached down for something on the floor and placed my father's knife on the cot beside me. "And we found this on some Gousht bastard's body."

My lips curled on their own. *Kellan deserved a slow and painful death for what he did to...*

"Oh, no!" I yelled, and the strain of it ground at my vocal cords. "Boda. He's..."

She placed a hand on my shoulder, pushing me back into the cot, then moved slightly to the side.

Across the room, patches of Boda's face showed through the bandages wrapped around his head. A green mixture of healing herbs lined the gray cloth layered over his skin. The eye that wasn't covered remained shut and swollen, but his chest continued to move.

"They say he's going to live," she said. "But the healer doesn't know if he'll ever see out of his left eye again."

I couldn't do anything for him from this bed, but he was going to live. That had to mean something. But what had it cost?

Liara leaned over me like I might disappear if she looked away. I met her soft gaze. "Who?" I asked. "How many?"

"Who, what?" Her confusion faded an instant after she spoke her question. "There were a few dozen over two hundred people enslaved here. A hundred eighteen made it through the night. But a few more will die from their wounds."

She paused and looked down at the floor. "Tomi got sliced up pretty badly, but the healer says she'll be okay. Adéan wasn't as lucky. Neither was Sionia."

"What?! No!" I shook my head, and the movement cracked my skull in a throbbing headache. "How? What happened?"

"Talise said she was with you," Liara said. "If you don't know, I don't think anyone can answer that."

The pressure behind my eyes built, and tears poured down the cuts and scratches along my face. The image of Sionia pulling me to the west tree wall, then calling after me as I ran from her, played out in my mind. Her voice faded as she called.

How much longer had she lived after that? I thought. *I left her alone to die.*

"Why did you come?" My words mixed with my breath, quiet and heavy.

"Why did you run away from me in the forest?" Liara asked, still staring at the ground. "We were supposed to stick together. But you had to find your priest."

She pushed herself out of her chair. "You need to get some rest, and I need to check on Tomi."

"Where's Wal?" I asked.

"You're not the only one who blames themselves for last night. Wal came up with the plan. He hasn't left Adēan's side."

"I'm sorry," I said.

"I know, Kaylo." She walked to the door. "But apologizing means that you need to make a change."

The door closed behind her, and the silence she left me with smothered the room.

Over a hundred people died had last night. Sionia. Adēan. Yet, somehow, I survived.

———

When I woke again, a cold bowl of soup sat in the chair beside my cot where Liara had been. I hadn't eaten in days. A spoon rested next to the bowl, but it would have gotten in the way.

The chilled liquid ran over my lips and filled my waiting mouth. Salty, fat broth coated my tongue. There had been days when I hated the thought of soup. Too many days when I craved something to sink my teeth into. But now, as I gulped down my meal, I mourned the drips that escaped down my chin.

I finished, dropping the bowl back onto the chair.

Boda's shallow breaths punctuated the silence, but his eyes hadn't opened.

A pair of slits in the stone wall let daylight pour into the room. As much as this room differed from The Priest's study, the stones were the same stones and, whether or not they had been stained with my blood, these floorboards looked no different from the others.

My whole body wrestled against my movement, but I pushed myself to standing. I tested my knee with a bit of weight and nearly collapsed to the ground for my effort. The fiery pain that had shot through my knee when the arrow pierced it reignited.

I could have waited, lay back down and ignored the stone walls, but it wouldn't have worked. These stones held memories.

Only my stupidity and stubbornness kept me upright. I used the wall and hopped on my somewhat good leg to Boda's bedside. Each hop stirred the pains in my body, but nothing like standing on my left leg.

"We will find a way through this," I said. "You never stopped fighting before. You can't stop now."

His hair had continued to grow, and short red curls found their way through his bandages.

"I won't be gone long," I said before limping to the door, pausing every few paces to catch my breath and my nerves.

The bloodstains in the corridor hadn't gone anywhere.

The last time I had stumbled through these halls, Sionia had walked beside me.

I had seen Adéan fall and the memory of it hurt, but not knowing what had happened to Sionia made it hard to believe she had really crossed into The Mist. Maybe someone had made a mistake.

My breath caught in my chest when I reached the door to the grounds. When I opened it, I knew there wouldn't be flames and clashing blades, but spirits be damned if I could convince my shaking hands.

The wooden door swung outward, and Sokan caught the mountain range in her descent. Echoes filled the grounds. Not tortured spirits, but bonded spirits walking with their dancers. A large firepit roared and people lingered around like these grounds hadn't soaked in the blood of their kin.

"Hey, you," a Sonacoan man jogged over to me. "You shouldn't be out of bed."

A burn swept over his cheek and down his neck. The skin had long-since healed, and his scarred flesh couldn't steal away the kindness of this man's features. His full cheeks and bushy red brows gave him character. Though whether he wore his head shaved or it had been forced on him by his captors, I couldn't have said.

"I can't stay in that cursed building." I hopped to regain my balance.

The Song of The Flame rolled off him easily, wading through the air like ash from a pyre. "Then let me help you."

He stepped closer and sparked a memory. That night, just before I had passed out, he had called The Flame and battled back the soldiers. The anger he had unleashed blazed hotter than the fires he had called.

"The name's Annit."

"Kaylo," I said as I leaned my weight on his shoulder, and the smell of sweet sage rolled off him—susu root. It had likely been forced on the enslaved people here.

He smiled, shaking his head. "We all know who you are."

As he spoke, I looked up and found a sea of eyes returning my gaze, each of whom knew my secret—I was a thief.

"You saved us," he said.

We walked to the fire, the eyes of the people following.

"I never thought I would live another free day in The Waking, much less have my spirit back," Annit said. "You gave that to me."

Liara met us next to the fire, and Annit helped me to sit beside her.

"They have been waiting for you," she said.

"Why me?"

"You are a short-sighted fool, Kaylo. You did something no one has been able to since the Gousht found the first crystal in this mountain. They are free. Some of them have their spirits back."

"I'm not a savior," I whispered at her.

"Are we goin ta join the Missing?" A northwoman shouted from the crowd that continued to gather.

"Can we go home?"

"What if we don't have a home to go to?"

"I can't hear The Song. Why didn't The Wind come back to me?"

"How can we trust a thief?"

The questions quickened and raced around the grounds. My stomach rose into my chest, shoving my heart into my throat.

"Friends!" Annit shouted over the chaos. "I am sure that Kaylo will answer your questions if you allow him the space." He looked down at me with a wink.

Liara shrugged at me. She had no intention of stepping into the fray.

Annit reached his hand down to help me up. Working in the mines had stripped his arms down to compact muscle. As he pulled me upright, I tried to keep the pain from my face.

The people didn't need to see that, not now.

"I am not a savior." Only the wind tested the silence as I searched for the next thing to say. "Unfortunately, neither are the Missing. The Missing was a lie the Lost Nation made up to keep track of our suffering and steal warriors to their cause. But that doesn't mean we are without hope. Last night was not a riot. It wasn't a rebellion either. It was an uprising."

The words came straight from my lungs, bypassing my brain all together.

"Yes, I am a spirit thief, though I prefer to think of it as borrowing." I smiled, but only Annit joined me. "The Thief gives me the ability to destroy the crystals that imprison our spirits. Even if there are no more crystals in this mountain, the Gousht still have plenty spread throughout Ennea. We must return those spirits home.

"You can join us if you choose, or you can go and search for your people. Free people will not have decisions forced upon them. But now is not the time to decide. Tonight, we bury our dead. We return their bodies to The Mother and ask her to guide us along whatever path lies before us."

All the faces staring back at me wore some version of the same mournful anger. When I stopped speaking, our shared silence contained the weight of all those we had lost.

Someone in the crowd chanted, "Thief!" It carried through the crowd until it became a common heartbeat.

They all knew my secret, and instead of shunning me, they embraced me.

The freed people of the Anilace mines constructed two pyres beneath Kana and Toka, and the flames challenged the clouds in the night sky. Beneath the firelight lay one hundred twenty-three graves torn from the grounds. It had taken two earth dancers the entirety of the evening, but they had worked without complaint.

One by one, we placed our dead in their resting places, and those who knew them offered words over their bodies.

After they lowered Adēan's body into his grave, Wal climbed into the hole beside him. He bent down, kissed him on the forehead, and whispered words to the man he loved. Liara helped him out of the dirt as the dancers covered Adēan's body.

For the first time since the battle, Wal walked over to me. His eyes raged behind his tears. "If you are serious about continuing this fight, I am there, but you need to promise me that we will kill them all."

I nodded to him. "Or die trying."

He stalked off into the darkness of the night.

Sionia was one of the last bodies we buried that night. Her skin had lost its glow, but she looked peaceful. She could have been asleep, but she wasn't.

"I have never known a person with more faith in others," I said. "You refused not to see the best in our people. If I can ever become a shadow of the person you thought I could be, it will only be because I had you in my life.

"I'm sorry, Sionia. I failed you."

As the dancers covered her body with dirt, every pain in my body went numb.

CHAPTER THIRTY-NINE
CURRENT DAY ENNEA

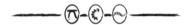

"The next day, the grounds of the compound looked like one large mound of unsettled dirt," Kaylo said. "One hundred twenty-three bodies added to the soil beneath Oakheart Mountain. The Gousht had buried some obscene number of our people in that dirt before, but I doubted they had ever ended that many lives in one night.

"Before we left, I made my way back to the room where The Priest had stolen The Seed from me and knocked a hole in the wall. I had to give the last seedling I pulled from The Song a chance to survive."

Kaylo shifted and repositioned himself against one of the ironoak trees that surrounded them. "In the coming days, another thirteen people died from their wounds. Forty-nine left, searching for whatever remained of their families, most likely never finding the happy ending they hoped for. The other fifty-six decided to join us, either because they had nowhere to go or their anger outweighed everything else."

A bird chirped before taking flight, causing a small branch to shake above them. The way the tree moved still teased him all these turns later.

"The Uprising?" Tayen asked softly.

Kaylo nodded and reached for a waterskin. His mouth had gone dry long ago, and the knot in his throat strained his voice.

"Where is your priest now?" Nix asked. She sat at the far end of their small enclosure with her back pressed against a tree and Sosun's head resting on her shoulder.

"From what I heard, he eventually made it to the Stone City and never left."

"No, that can't be. They don't station multiple priests in each city. And the priest in the Stone City is...wait." Nix's eyebrows rose. "Your priest—The Priest—you can't mean Kyernan Janome? The Emperor's voice on Ennea? Their wartime general overseeing everything this side of the ocean?"

She paused, underscoring the importance of her question. "That's not who we are talking about, right?"

"That wasn't who he was when we met. He's always been The Priest to me. Whatever titles he's given himself since don't matter."

"Oh, no. They matter. Your vendetta is with the most powerful couta on the continent." The timber of her voice sharpened into an accusation.

"I gave that vendetta up when I left the Uprising. Revenge gets people killed—the wrong people." He turned back to Tayen. "You need to rest."

"I'm going to find them," Tayen said. "The Uprising. I'm going to find them."

Kaylo closed his eyes. *After three seasons together she hasn't heard a word I've said,* he thought.

"I know you think I'm too young," she said.

"Haven't you been listening?"

"That's the thing. I have been, and you were right. Vengeance is a waste of my life. I couldn't kill enough soldiers to bring back my family," Tayen said. "They're gone, but that doesn't mean I should hide away for the rest of my life."

"If you fight, you will die," Kaylo said. "The Uprising don't have the numbers to fight the Gousht. Even if they did, the Lost King won't stop until Ennea is his. It's a losing battle."

"It's a battle that has to be fought." In an instant, her youth vanished. Her jaw set. Her eyes held his. "Sionia and Adéan freed one hundred eighteen people before they died."

"And countless more died because of what we did that day!" His grief and anger combined in a growly tone. "It all has consequences."

"So does doing nothing!" Tayen matched his volume, then winced at the pain in her shoulder. "That day you saved me from the soldiers, you made a decision. Now, I have to make a decision. I am going to find the Uprising, and I hope you come along."

A stone cracked against the trees behind Kaylo, and he turned. Sosun stared at him with her dark brown eyes before flashing a series of gestures.

"We're going too," Nix said. "Well, she said she's going, and I am not letting her out of my sight."

"Why is everyone around me always so willing to die?" Kaylo asked.

"Must be the company," Nix said with her closed-mouth grin.

"If you want the chance to change my mind, come with us," Tayen said.

"Seed and Balance," he whispered.

The angry fragment of The Seed rattled within its cage, singing the war cry of a long-forgotten prisoner.

After eighteen turns, the hole inside him where The Seed belonged still waited, but this spirit didn't fit. With a simple breath, he let it slip off into the world, back to the crystal on the other side of the Lost Forest. Maybe one day it would be free.

"We're not moving until you can use your arm," he said. "If we're going to die, you should at least be able to fight back."

EPILOGUE
CURRENT DAY ENNEA

A brazier burned in the corner of the small windowless room. It wasn't Wal's room. Nor the Citadel. Clay brick walls, a thatched roof, and a cot of straw.

Why here? he thought as he recognized the unkempt recruit's infirmary outside of the Citadel.

Something moved near the door. A small nameless boy peaked in through the doorway and ran as soon as their eyes met.

Each breath hurt. Moving hurt worse, not that he could move much. They bandaged him up like a cloth doll, all stitches and fabric. The bitter stench of crushed moonlight hazel and dried mud filled the room.

Kaylo should have finished his work.

Whatever lingering sense of communion Wal had felt for the fucking thief died when Wal should have. First chance he found, he would run his blade through the sanctimonious fuck. Forget the history and broken promises between them, he would stab Kaylo through the heart and mourn what they once had after he buried the bastard in the ground.

I'd like to see him run away then, Wal thought.

A dark figure filled the doorway, tall and lithe. Of course, Tanis had come to gloat over his sickbed, undoubtedly full of accusations and ridicule. She had never liked him. 'The Astilean army should be run by Astileans,' and all that nonsense.

When the King had authorized Wal's idea to train a group of spirit thieves, it had only fed Tanis' hatred. The blowhard only approved of one voice in Sonar's ear—hers.

She had actually cornered Wal once and made all sorts of threats—head on a pike, archers using his body for target practice, something about fire and his good bits. People usually cowered in her presence, so he had smiled at her threats. He had made himself indispensable.

Or so he had thought.

"Your guards died. All of them," she said, without any mourning or sorrow.

"When are their burial rites?"

"Unfortunately, you slept through them. The healers didn't expect you to wake. Pity they were wrong." The general stepped forward, the light of the brazier flickering over the harsh lines of her face.

"Sorry to be an inconvenience."

She knelt next to the straw bed, back perfectly straight. Her lips betrayed the slightest smirk on her otherwise impassive face. "I wish you were—regretful. A small amount of shame might make you tolerable."

"What do you want, Tanis?"

"I want to know where your friend went. You southerners like to make trouble, and I intend to end that trouble."

A shadow shifted outside the doorway, as metal clinked against the brick wall. Tanis hadn't come alone.

"The moment I can move, I'm going to hunt that bastard down myself."

"Interesting. The bastard who left you alive after he killed your guards, that bastard? The bastard you honored with quarters in the Citadel? The bastard you defended to me and the King?"

This would be her move. She would cast doubt on Wal's judgment and loyalty, allowing the embarrassment of Kaylo's escape to pull Wal down from the heights he had climbed.

"Kaylo betrayed me for the last time." His voice cracked with the dryness of his throat.

"When did you first suspect that Ennea's Thief would try to escape?"

"He was a prisoner. What prisoner doesn't want to escape?"

Tanis smiled at that. "Of course they want to. That's why we lock them away in the dungeons instead of honored quarters. When did you know he was planning to escape?"

"The youngest thief, Pana, he came to me and confirmed my suspicions. Ask him and he'll tell you."

Tanis clicked her tongue as she shook her head. "Oh, didn't you know, they killed the boy—nearly killed the guard with him as well," she said. "Did you know that his parents are friends of our dear King?"

Even as she delivered the news of a child's death, all Tanis could think of was the connection Pana's parents had to the King. Fuck Pana's parents and their connections, that kid had a gift. He believed in the cause, and Wal had let him down.

At least Shiena had survived. But in the wake of so much blood, it seemed so little.

"Now, for the last time, where did your gray-haired friend go?" Tanis leaned over him.

"Give me one moon, and I'll find him. I'll bring his body back to burn."

"No." She shook her head. "It's endearing that you think you still have the army's trust. No, you are alive because the King has a soft spot for traitors."

"I'm no traitor!"

Tanis stood and walked over to the brazier, placing a metal rod over the flames. "Maybe not, but you are a liability, and Astile can no longer afford liabilities."

"Give me another chance. Please, I'll do anything. I'll lead the first line into battle. Let me die fighting."

"Interesting. It took all this trouble for you to find your place." The rod started to glow in the flames as she twisted it. "No, no more chances. You'll die in the darkness with only your thoughts for company."

The rod burned with a yellow-orange hue as she plucked it from the brazier and walked towards him. He squirmed despite the pain, but he had nowhere to go. She gripped his braids with her free hand. "Don't move. I wouldn't want to make a mistake."

The rod's overwhelming glow moved closer and closer to his face. The muscles in his neck seized and flared, but her iron grip held him in place.

This would not be Wal's end. His whole life had turned into one barrage after another, and he had survived. He took a deep breath, then his cheek went cold, like he had fallen face first into the snow. The cold flashed over, breaking into searing pain that bore through his entire body.

He fell limp to the straw bed. If it hadn't been for the sizzling sound and the smell of cooking meat, he wouldn't have noticed her scorching away the second set of tattoos along his other cheek.

The Lost Nation had always been a means to an end. If they wanted to stand in his way, they could fall like the rest.

Tanis darkened the room as she leaned over him to whisper something he didn't hear. Her shadow left, then two large soldiers entered the room in her place. They barely fit in the cramped space, but they made do. Each grabbed one of Wal's arms, and they hefted him off the bed.

As he hung between them, limp as a freshly dead body, feet dragging in the dirt behind him, he thought about how close he had come to rejoining those he had lost on the other side of The Mist.

Pressure bubbled under the skin below Wal's eyes, but he forced them open. He hadn't fulfilled his promises yet. If he had any chance, he had to know where they were taking him.

The warriors weren't gentle when they tossed him into his cell beneath the mountain, and the stone greeted Wal's broken body like a bitter enemy. Cold swept through the rough stone floor into his body. It eased the immediacy of pain bearing down on him.

If his stitches survived the warriors' hospitality it was only by The Mother's good will.

NO SAFE HAVEN 439

Wood cracked against wood as they slammed the door to his new quarters without a word.

He would have attempted to inspect his wounds, but the single candle flickering away through the barred window in his door was less than accommodating to the task.

The smell of shit, death, and more shit permeated the air. If his wounds didn't kill him, infection might.

Every time he had relied on Kaylo, he lived to regret it. This time he could only blame himself. At a certain point, he should have known better than to trust the prick.

Pain abused his last remaining faculties to the point of submission, but he pushed himself to his knees regardless to inspect his new quarters. The cell stretched only as wide as his arms spread, and maybe a pace longer in the other direction. Solid stone surrounded him with an ironoak door leading out into the rest of the dungeon.

He ran his fingers along the wall. A series of letters interrupted his inspection. "May The Mist greet you soon," it read.

At least they were kind enough to leave a bucket in the corner, though it hadn't been emptied. *Hence the smell,* he thought.

"What brings you down here, my friend?" A voice called out from the next cell.

"I knew the wrong man." The searing pain from Wal's burned cheeks screamed out as he spoke.

"That is quite a crime." The voice carried a ginger and light tone, like they weren't speaking to each other through adjoining stone cells. "I myself had the wrong opinion, then I knew the wrong man."

"Friendship is a dangerous lie. This is what I get for trying to befriend a fucking thief," Wal said, despite the pain. "Again."

"Was this man perhaps a sullen Tomakan with a knack for putting himself in the trouble he's attempting to avoid?"

"Who are you?" Wal winced.

"A poet. A believer in great change and great deeds."

"Do you always speak like you're about to break into sonnet? Because we are going to be neighbors for a while, and it might get old."

"If our mutual friend's description was close to accurate, you must be Wal," the poet said. "The name is Lanigan."

"Not a friend. From my perspective, after someone stabs you a few times, the friendship ends." Wal lay against the stone and closed his eyes.

"Stories always have more sides than written, but I wonder, why did you capture and hold a man who was supposed to be your friend?"

"Listen poet, I'm not going to justify myself to you."

The ceiling of Wal's cell glowed a gentle yellowish-brown in the candlelight. The light ebbed and flowed like a wave on the stone.

"No. No, you don't have to justify yourself to anyone. Purely a philosophical question, what would make a friend do such a thing?"

"Long ago, Kaylo and I were brothers, but he left. He left, and I became this," Wal said.

> A broken wing
> May bind a bird
> To the earth, steal it
> From its flock, turn it
> From its path
> And yet a bird it is

"What is that supposed to mean?" Wal asked.

"Life will put us through untold challenges, but we still are who we are at our core, despite what has happened to us."

In some small way the poet was right. When Wal closed his eyes, Adēan's face hadn't aged. His soft brown skin, full lips, and tender eyes never changed. Neither did the dreams in which Wal held the young man's battered body.

Adēan's beautiful, broken face had been resting in Wal's lap when he had made his promise. Wal had brushed the blood and dirt from Adēan's lips and kissed them one last time. "I swear," he had said. "I swear that they will feel this pain before I kill them. I swear that I won't stop until the couta are dead and gone."

He touched his blistering cheek where he had marked the steps towards his promise. A lifetime had passed, and he had failed. His meaningless life was the only one he had left to offer.

"I'm sorry," Wal whispered to the stone. "I'm sorry, and I love you still."

The words may have carried beyond the cell, but it didn't matter if others heard them. They were meant for Adēan, and spirits only heard the prayers spoken aloud.

The Great Spirits

The Shadow: The first of the Great Spirits, known for her wisdom. She blesses her descendants with the ability to manipulate shadows.

The River: The second of the Great Spirits, known for their patience, and twin to The Flame. They bless their descendants with the ability to manipulate water.

The Flame: The third of the Great Spirits, known for their strength, and twin to The River. They bless their descendants with the ability to manipulate fire.

The Mountain: The fourth of the Great Spirits, known for her constant support. She blesses her descendants with the ability to manipulate the earth.

THE WIND: The fifth of the Great Spirits, known for his foresight. He blesses his descendants with the ability to manipulate the air.

 THE SEED: The sixth of the Great Spirits, known for his forgiveness. He blesses his descendants with the ability to manipulate plant life.

 THE THIEF/THE BALANCE: The seventh of the Great Spirits, known for her pursuit of power or equity depending on whose story you read. She blesses her descendants with the ability to borrow other dancers' abilities.

GLOSSARY

ANILACE MINES/GOD CAVES: The Gousht's name for Oakheart Mountain, where the first spirit crystals were discovered.

BLOOD BANNER: A derogatory term for Enneans who work with the Gousht as soldiers, spies, informants, and city bureaucrats.

CHANI CLOTH: A light cloth of woven silk. Before the invasion, good chani cloth was worth a goat in trade.

COMMON TONGUE: As the nations developed from tribes and villages, disparate languages and dialects began to merge, resulting in a shared language referred to as common tongue.

CONCLAVE OF SPIRITS: Throughout the Hundred-Turn War, citizens of each nation sought peace from the fighting, taking on a nomadic lifestyle. Eventually, a large group of the nomads representing each nation brought together a meeting of the four nations, where they negotiated an end to the fighting. This was also the origin of the fifth nation, the Jani.

Couta: A curse that means child of incest. It became a popular slur for the Gousht due to their pale complexion, which Enneans took for sickly.

Dancer: An Ennean who was gifted with the ability to hear The Song and wield one, or in rare cases two, of the Great Spirits' powers. Also known as children of Ennea or spirit-marked.

Daemontale: A make-believe story told to pass down lessons to children.

Denanla san Terriac: Gousht for "The Center of the World" and the name of a castle from which the King of Gousht rules. According to the Writ, The One True God's twelve sons wrestled control of the castle to being their conquest in the name of their God and father

Ennea/The Mother: Ennea is the genesis of life. She is the land and mother to the moons and the sun, the spirits, and the people.

Firestarter: A distilled oil that is extremely flammable. Under the right circumstances, it can cause explosions.

Freecity: A formerly occupied city abandoned by the Gousht after the reclamation war broke out, which runaways and refugees have reclaimed.

Gousht Priest: Direct descendants of The One True God who serve as leaders of the church and armed forces.

GREAT SPIRITS: Ennea created seven spirits which gave form to The Waking and later gave pieces of their gifts to people in the form of The Song.

HALLOW: A shelter built using The Song and the Great Spirits.

HONORED FIELDS: The burial grounds for Astilean warriors in Myanack.

HUNDRED TURN WAR: For ninety-two or ninety-three turns, depending on who was counting, the four original nations of Ennea engaged in a series of wars over territory, which often overlapped. Also referred to as the Great War, Ennea's Reckoning, the Century of Mourning.

KAMANI: A being whose spirit is not bound two any single conception of gender.

KANA: Ennea's second daughter, the first moon. This also became a term of respect for a mentor and teacher.

KONKI: A tart, sweet fruit with red flesh and a brown husk. The Gousht turned this into a derogatory term for Tomakan people.

KUNNIT: A Gousht word meaning sour blood, which they used interchangeably for blood infections and people of mixed-race heritage.

LODESTONE: The Jani raised these naturally magnetic stones across Ennea as peaceful meeting places during the Hundred Turns War. Traditionally, Enneas relinquish their weapons to the magnetic pull of the stone while they meet.

LOST FOREST: A forest of stormwoods the Lost Nation grew to cut themselves off from the rest of Ennea after the Hundred-Turn War. It is rumored to be impossible to navigate without a forest dancer.

MALITU: A corrupt spirit or dancer who uses their abilities for selfish gain or ill-intent. Often referring to spirit thieves, however, it can refer to any dancer or spirit.

MISTWALKER: A dancer who is able to send their spirit into The Mist, speak with the spirits, and return to their bodies in The Waking.

MOON: A measurement of time based on the cycles of the moons, approximately thirty days long. When Toka disappears from the sky every third span, it marks a new moon.

NAMELESS: A failed recruit in the Astilean army now forced to serve in the capital city, Myanack.

RAKAT: One of the foulest curses in common tongue. It refers to one who's spirit is too tainted for The Mist and is undeserving of life on either plane of existence.

SCION OF THE SHADOW: A title given to the line of royalty in Astile due to the claim they are the descendants of the first shadow dancer, Shunanlah.

SHUNANLAH: Shunanlah was the first person to be marked by Ennea and gifted The Song and The Shadow. The namesake of the autumnal equinox ceremony.

SKIN SWITCHER: A derogatory term for kamani people, which gained popularity after the regressive values of the Gousht began to spread with colonization.

SPAN: A measurement of time equivalent to ten days.

SPIRIT-BOUND: An Ennean who is unable to hear The Song. Their spirit is bound to their body and to The Waking.

SOKAN: Ennea's first daughter, the giver, and the sun.

SUSU ROOT: When it was first discovered, Ennean healers used susu root as a medicine to dull pain. It's addictive and dulls the brain, making people apathetic. In small amounts, it is a powerful and useful sedative. Long-term use can make people irritable and detached. Severe use can be deadly.

TANONTA: A word that grew from a time before the nations, Tanonta refers to the first new day, the spring equinox. It is the celebration of rebirth as well as a transition of life. At night, when the moons are at their highest, those of age pledge themselves to The Mother.

THE MISSING: A rumored group of Enneans organizing against the Gousht Empire.

THE MIST: The spiritual plane.

THE ONE TRUE GOD/THE ONE: The Gousht god. Religious texts say that The One took human form and sired twelve children, the youngest of whom became the leader of the Gousht church and nation-state.

THE REAPING: After the Stone City fell, Gousht priests destroyed everything deviant or unholy in the eyes of The One True God. Soldiers swept through each village and town, burning books and relics, as well as people. Kamani people suffered greatly during the reaping.

THE SONG: Energy in The Mist seeps through the barrier between planes into The Waking. Dancers have the ability to hear a portion of this energy representing their great spirit ancestor(s). This allows dancers to access the power of their spirit ancestors.

THE STONE CITY: The capital city of Sonacoa and the last city outside of the Lost Nation to fall to the Gousht invasion.

THE WAKING: The physical plane.

THE WRIT: The Gousht holy book. Each crowned Emperor, thought to be direct descendants of The One True God, adds a section to the Writ before they stepdown, documenting the history of the Gousht Empire.

THIEF'S NIGHT: A colloquial term for a night sky in which neither moon is visible. People often act erratically on these nights and blame The Thief for their behavior.

TOKA: Ennea's third daughter, the second moon. This also became a term of respect for a mentee and student.

TURN: A unit of time measurement equivalent to four seasons, twelve moons, or approximately three hundred sixty days.

TWICE-MARKED: A dancer who is gifted with the ability to wield two of the Great Spirits' power.

ZEZE: In a pre-common tongue dialect, zeze meant black, as in the night sky or the darkness of the rich soil. However, when the Gousht arrived, they turned it into a slur for Sonacoans, who typically have darker complexions.

Note from the Author

The Malitu Trilogy is many things, one being the continued exploration of the effects of whiteness/white supremacy, colonialism, and power. My intention is to speak as a white person about the consequences of these violent ideologies and practices. However, I am aware impact can never be defined by one's intentions. Hopefully, I have given the characters in Malitu humanity and personhood in a way that positively adds to this conversation.

My voice is one of many within a much larger conversation that should center BIPOC voices first and foremost. If you have not read authors of color who are creating amazing works in speculative fiction that decenter white narratives, I encourage you to start. There are countless important voices to add to your to-be-read (TBR) list. Below, I have listed some authors I have read and enjoyed.

Tomi Adeyemi, Octavia Butler, C.L. Clark, Tracy Deonn, Justina Ireland, N.K. Jemisin, R.F. Kuang, Fonda Lee, L. Penelope, Tatiana Obey, Nnedi Okorafor, PhD, Kritika H. Rao, Rebecca Roanhorse, Andrea Stewart, Moses Ose Utomi, ML Wang, Evan Winters

In taking on this project, I am not looking to tell anyone else's story for them. While the colonialism depicted in Malitu is not based on any one example from history, it pulls from aspects of real life. Colonialist regimes and those who rise to power within colonized nations across the globe have and continue to create means of manipulating the belief systems of indigenous people, controlling populations through violence, and forcing members of those populations into slavery. Unfortunately, these practices continue all over the world today.

At the end of the day, I believe issues of power and oppression are issues we all need to thoughtfully interrogate. Artists who are privileged within systems of oppression, like myself, must educate ourselves and take care when addressing these subject matters. Even with that said, I have made mistakes along the way. Those I am aware of I have and am attempting to remedy to the best of my ability. I am dedicated to listening, learning, and continuing to improve. I am continuing to grow in my understanding of where I fit into this conversation.

I made a mistake with the cover art I commissioned for No Safe Haven. A community member was gracious enough to bring their concerns to my attention. I have addressed this in a larger format on my blog. In short, the cover art for No Safe Haven depicts the anger of a Black girl in a very raw and visceral way. While this is in keeping with themes within the book, there is a larger context of covers with Black characters and the portrayal of Black anger. The portrayal of Black anger is a loaded subject considering the stereotypes/depictions of Black people's emotions and personhood throughout history. As a white person, it was not my place to deviate from conventions where Black authors and artists are often not permitted to, especially in traditional publishing.

As a result, I worked with my cover artist to make adjustments to the cover. I believe this artwork is a better representation of No Safe Haven and does a better job of fitting into the larger context of covers featuring

Black characters.

I have openly dedicated myself to take accountability for any harm my books cause marginalized communities, and will continue to do my best be a part of this important conversation. That does not negate the harm I have caused, and for that I apologize.

I believe in and love this story, and I am responsible for its content and impact.

Thank you for the opportunity to tell this story.

James Lloyd Dulin

Runes

Runes is played on a grid of two sets of three intersecting lines, creating nine intersecting points called crosspoints, and wooden markers with a spirit rune carved on one side.

At the beginning of the game, each player is given a bag including fourteen markers, two markers representing each of the seven Great Spirits. One set of markers is dyed black and the other white. Players will draw five markers from their respective bags. At all times, players should have five markers in their hands. When a marker is defeated and removed from a crosspoint, it should be returned to the player's bag.

The player with black markers takes the first turn. On each player's turn, they can place a marker rune-side-down on an empty cross point or challenge one of the other player's facedown markers. Turns cannot be skipped.

When a challenge is issued, both markers are turned over, and the winner is determined by the chart below. If matching runes are revealed, the challenger wins the crosspoint. If the challenger wins, they will draw a marker to bring the total in their hand to five runes and place one marker face down on the crosspoint. The challenger can then choose to make another move or end their turn. If the defending player wins, their marker will remain face up on the crosspoint, signifying their claim.

The game is over when a player has claimed five of the nine crosspoints with faceup markers.

	The Shadow	The River	The Flame	The Mountain	The Wind	The Seed	The Thief
The Shadow	The Challenger	The Shadow	The Flame	The Shadow	The Shadow	The Seed	The Thief
The River	The Shadow	The Challenger	The River	The River	The Wind	The Seed	The River
The Flame	The Flame	The River	The Challenger	The Mountain	The Wind	The Flame	The Flame
The Mountain	The Shadow	The River	The Mountain	The Challenger	The Mountain	The Seed	The Mountain
The Wind	The Shadow	The Wind	The Wind	The Mountain	The Challenger	The Wind	The Thief
The Seed	The Seed	The Seed	The Flame	The Seed	The Wind	The Challenger	The Thief
The Thief	The Thief	The River	The Flame	The Mountain	The Thief	The Thief	The Challenger

Acknowledgements

—————

Self-publishing is a misnomer. Neither No Heart for a Thief nor No Safe Haven were independent works. I received help from far too many people to name. Malitu is a collaborative effort, and I am eternally grateful to everyone who helped me along the way by answering questions, editing, reviewing, or simply reading this story.

Not being able to list out everyone won't stop me from thanking some key people.

I need to start my gratitude with those that deserve it the most. My wife, Aneicka, and my sons, Gladson and Dominic, make me the person I am. They have taught me so much about who I am, and I do my best to bring that truth into my writing. It may be fantasy, but it requires humanity, and they are vital to mine.

Whatever grand plans I have had for this story, it would not be what it is without support from my beta readers, sensitivity reader, and editors. My unwavering thanks go out to Taylor Banks, Emeric Davis, Angelicka Morgan, Victoria Gross, and Dominic McDermott. These wonderful people helped me understand the story I was trying to tell and tell it as well as I could.

ACKNOWLEDGEMENTS

There are too many good stories in the world for any one reader to get through them all. People have to be decisive, and one of the first things that draws a reader's attention is the cover. Martin Mottet did an incredible job with the cover art for No Safe Haven, and my brother, Michael Dulin, made the art into a beautifully designed cover.

This cover will help bring readers to Malitu, but if it wasn't for my wonderful ARC (Advanced Reader Copies) team, my story wouldn't have found the readership it has. My ARC team gave my unknown story a chance and shared their reviews. My imperfect story connected with readers who saw something in my words, and I can only hope this second entry continues to connect with those readers and more.

To my ARC readers, whether you joined in with No Safe Haven or were there since No Heart for a Thief, I cannot thank you enough.

Lastly, thank you, the reader, for deciding to read these pages. Without you, these pages are just a collection of words. You made them into a book. If I can ask you to help me take this one step further, please review this book on Amazon, Goodreads, and any other platform you might use. Reviews are the lifeblood for self-published authors. Reviews encourage others to give a book a try, and I want to share this book with as many people as I can.

Kaylo and Tayen will be back with Only a Grave Will Do, Malitu: Book Three.

About the Author

James is a nerd with a head full of stories and limited time to put them on the page.

He grew up in Grand Rapids, MI, spending an excessive amount of time at a local community theater where he developed his affinity for storytelling. This affinity grew into a deep admiration for language and spoken word poetry while studying mathematics and education at the University of Michigan. A few hundred mediocre poems and lackluster performances later, he decided his dream of writing a novel might not be as ridiculous as he once thought. He firmly believes that art—even silly books about magic, or maybe especially silly books about magic—has the ability to tell stories that sink beneath the surface.

Made in United States
Troutdale, OR
07/20/2024

21440616R20289